About the Author

An established writer, recently interviewed by the BBC about one of his nonfiction books. Paul has travelled over five continents, living in London, Amsterdam, Philadelphia and Miami. He spent seventeen years living in South Florida, which inspired him to write this novel. He has climbed Kilimanjaro and cycled from London to Paris and back seventeen times to raise money for Operation Smile. This charity provides reconstructive facial surgery for children born with deformities. He has raised enough money for two hundred ninety children to have the surgery. His work focuses on loss, recovery and building a new life amidst complicated social cultures.

Riders from the Storm

Paul Clutterbuck

Riders from the Storm

Olympia Publishers
London

www.olympiapublishers.com
OLYMPIA PAPERBACK EDITION

Copyright © Paul Clutterbuck 2025

The right of Paul Clutterbuck to be identified as author of
this work has been asserted in accordance with sections 77 and 78 of
the Copyright, Designs and Patents Act 1988.

All Rights Reserved

No reproduction, copy or transmission of this publication
may be made without written permission.
No paragraph of this publication may be reproduced,
copied or transmitted save with the written permission of the publisher,
or in accordance with the provisions
of the Copyright Act 1956 (as amended).

Any person who commits any unauthorised act in relation to
this publication may be liable to criminal
prosecution and civil claims for damage.

A CIP catalogue record for this title is
available from the British Library.

ISBN: 978-1-83543-447-5

This is a work of fiction.
Names, characters, places and incidents originate from the writer's
imagination. Any resemblance to actual persons, living or dead, is
purely coincidental.

First Published in 2025

Olympia Publishers
Tallis House
2 Tallis Street
London
EC4Y 0AB

Printed in Great Britain

Dedication

I dedicate this book to all those facing existential threats, regardless of their identity.

Acknowledgements

A special thank you to Angela. Also, thanks to Cathy Verghese, Norman Gaslowitz, Patrick Hosey, and William Tulskie for their patience, support, and ideas. Sources, Acknowledgements and Inspiration • Totch by Loren G. "Totch" Brown • A Land Remembered by Patrick D. Smith • Everglades, The Story Behind the Scenery by Jack de Golia • Florida, A Short History by Michael Gannon • Gladesmen, Gator Hunters, Moonshiners and Skiffers by Glen Simmons and Laura Ogden • Last Train to Paradise by Les Standiford • Storm of the Century by Willie Drye • The Creek by J.T. Glisson • The Everglades, River of Grass by Marjory Stoneman Douglas • The Florida Keys by Joy Williams • The Story of the Chokoloskee Bay County by Charlton W. Tebeau • The Railroad That Died At Sea by Pat Parks • The Underground Railroad by Colson Whitehead • Voice of the River by Marjory Stoneman Douglas • The History of the Bahamas by Michael Craton • Educating the Seminole Indians of Florida 1879–1970 by Harry A. Kersey, Jr • nationalgeographic.com • fcit.usf.edu • seminolewars.org • reason.org • semtribe.com • Who murdered the Vets? By Ernest Hemingway A first-hand report on Florida's "Labour Day Hurricane", published by the "New Masses" magazine. • Inspiration was taken from a speech, probably made in 1854, by Chief Seattle, Chief of the Suquamish and Duwamish people. He was a leading figure among his people. The city of Seattle, in Washington State, was named after him. His exact words and who was present at the time are disputed. Still, it is commonly held that the speech was directed at Isaac Stevens, the Governor of Washington Territories at the time, and consequently, the then President of the United States (The Great Chief in Washington DC), Franklin Pierce. • Big Cypress National Preserve – National Park Service, US Department of the Interior. • Marjory Stoneman Douglas (1890–1998) for bringing the world's attention to the need to preserve the Everglades as the unique, beautiful and spectacular place that it is. • The Underground Railroad Records (book) by William Still • The University Press of Florida • Pineapple Press

"It is a mistake to look too far ahead. Only one link of the chain of destiny can be handled at a time."

– Winston Churchill

INTRODUCTION

It was August 1935. A scattering of wind-driven thunderstorms tumbled westwards from the West African coastal area and rolled towards the Mid-Atlantic Ridge, a planetary scar dividing Africa from the Americas. Usually, these tropical waves are no more than seedlings that can develop into tropical storms and occasional hurricanes. Mostly, they don't. Those that do need the right conditions. The threat would come if a storm grew in strength and picked up a counter-clockwise circulation, turning into a hungry monster stoking itself by sucking energy from the warm, moist, late summer ocean air.

Stupidly, in July 1935, the US Weather Bureau launched a proud national advertising campaign to assure Americans that it could now detect Atlantic hurricanes before they approached land. They would regret the boast for decades. In 1935, radar was underdeveloped, and weather satellites were unimagined.

By Friday, August 30th, a late summer storm had developed under perfect conditions far from the view of close-to-shore fishing boats. Occasionally, international cargo shipping had reported some weather disruption but saw no cause to alarm anyone – just yet. From their brief reports, the national bureau assumed it was approaching Cuba.

By stealth, it reached the Bahamas, just one hundred and sixty miles from Florida, and surprised the islanders. Most of the island's power was out. No one had detected the storm until then, with the Bahamians preoccupied with protecting themselves.

Whom should they contact anyway? Miami? Havana? Mexico City? Nobody told them a bad storm was coming, not even the comparatively well-funded, well-supported, well-advertised US Weather Bureau.

Detecting a hurricane is one thing, but like a human life, predicting where it will go is another.

PART ONE
Human Nature and Mother Naturel

Chapter One
Isolated

The Florida Keys, Labour Day Weekend, 1935
Kimbo had always thought the world didn't change in front of your eyes; it changed behind your back. At the end of this day, he was wrong.

Walking the narrow beach, his dog alongside, he ignored the sharp shells crunching under his bare feet. He smiled, thinking of Zella, constantly asking him to slow to her pace when together, but his dog loved how deceptively quick he was. Anyone watching him would understand his body's strength just by how he walked. Three hours earlier, Zella had teased him, claiming she would beat him in a fight after he foolishly mentioned that no one had ever landed a blow to his head. A bet was made. She caught him with an open hand on the left side of his face, enough for him to feel it but not enough to leave a mark. What hurt him was the house cleaning he'd had to do for losing.

"See, danger can come from any direction," she joked, kissing him sweetly where her hand had landed.

As he walked, thinking about Zella and their twins, he smiled at the constant rebukes Zella dished out to him and almost anyone she encountered. She wanted people to be better than they were; it was her way. Kimbo only cared about keeping his family safe.

The air changed as a mosaic shadow crossed his path.

Sengo looked up at him, barked softly, and then quietly growled. Kimbo stared at his friend.

"What?" he asked.

Sengo only barked when something threatened. Man and dog knew each other well. Sengo let out a high-pitched yap, his eyes wide now, white with fear. Kimbo Hopper gazed at the sky and sniffed the wind. He saw, high up, a dozen frigatebirds, their wings beating rapidly, their beaks pointed in a westerly direction. It was common to see a frigatebird along southern Florida's coastline. It was odd, strange, for frigatebirds to flap their seven-foot wingspan; they would soar most of the time. It is created perfectly to swoop down and skim the water's surface to catch flying fish or floating squid. But they weren't skimming. They were fleeing.

Kimbo's face wrinkled. A flock of frigatebirds in a hurry to get somewhere else? He had never seen such a thing. And all flying west? That would lead them over open water to the Dry Tortugas, seventy miles away. It made no sense; there was no land before them, and frigatebirds lacked oil to waterproof their feathers. These graceful birds were panicking.

A familiar dread entered Kimbo's life.

"Sengo, home!" Sengo ran, and Kimbo quickened into a jog. He arrived to find Zella singing and cooking his favourite soup. He painted the scene at the beach for her.

"*Well, mudda sick,*" using an old Bahamian expression for "you are kidding". She had often made it clear to him that she didn't like his "thinking in old ways".

"If you doin' that thing you do, you know, sniffin' the wind or whatever it is, then do it where the twins ain't gonna see you. They get kinda spooked when they see their papa sniffin' the wind. You always thinkin' troubles are brewin', ain't ya? Those vets ain't gonna trouble us again after you see off those two drunks snoopin' around last Saturday. Maybe they think you are the trouble."

"It ain't the vets. I just don't know what it is, Zella, but from what I see at the beach, I know we ain't gonna be safe. Seems likely we ain't gonna be safe."

After sighing at his habit of repeating his thoughts, she reminded him, yet again, that America had new ways of telling what would happen with the weather.

"You'd better start trusting them. We can't see the future by lookin' through that old Bahamian past. We gotta have a better life than that." She shrugged.

Zella had a habit of reminding Kimbo about a lot of things. She was a constant voice in his head, helping him make decisions wherever he was. She didn't have to be close by for him to hear her talking to him. She was in his head most of the time, wherever he was. Kimbo couldn't see what could change, but he'd sensed it. He just knew.

Kimbo Hopper was less than an ordinary man if he was assessed by how people treated him. Socially regarded as worthless, he felt worthless. He was illiterate in a world that was slowly but increasingly getting educated, born only months after his parents had arrived in 1910. They hoped for a better, more prosperous life in the Florida Keys.

His and Zella's parents had worked on the same pineapple plantation, on the Queen's Highway, on the Bahama Island of Eleuthera. Several generations had worked and found freedom there. Living in the lower part of the Keys, there was little commercialism. They liked being further away from hostile mainland cultures, as the lower Keys could only be reached by boat or the famous Miami to Key West train. As offspring of formerly enslaved people, it gave them a rare sense of living independently. The Keys had similar weather, with abundant turtles, fish and other seafood – it could not have been more suitable.

As a child, Kimbo worked around the house, where his mother found plenty of chores. He learnt essential, practical skills, especially cooking and protecting a home. Then, when Kimbo was eight, his father announced there was to be a change in his daily life.

"Son, you gonna learn how to live off this land and sea. If you learn this, then you'll never go hungry. You always gonna have food."

His father took him everywhere, and Kimbo was a quick learner. He would heap work and responsibilities on him. He learnt to catch, skin and cook all and any sea life and wildlife they could find, with few exceptions. He mastered the dangerous skill of finding, killing, and skinning snakes, alligators, and crocodiles.

"Son," – he rarely called him Kimbo – "you now gonna work wid me, and you gonna learn how to cut timber, and we gonna learn you wreckin'!"

"Papa, I don't know what is wreckin'. Is that like destroying somethin'?"

His father laughed. "Son, it's picking up stuff from the seabed. Years ago, them Spanish galleons came through these parts and got wrecked in storms or just ran up against the coral rock and barrier reefs. Plenty of gold and silver lay on the seabed. But, son, plenty of bones and skeletons down there too."

Kimbo's eyes grew wide; he soaked up every word.

"So, we gonna get rich if we get there before those settlers comin' down from up north. These stories of gold I'm telling ya are spreading north, and them folks comin' from places called Georgia and the Carolinas or sommat. They bring bad feelings about folks like us. They see us as uneducated black folk, like we got no right to riches or no good life. I'm telling ya, son, we gotta watch out. Keep ourselves private, and we gonna be okay. I ain't gonna let no white folks know where I got my riches, and I ain't gonna let them see me drunk or nothin'. They gonna rob us blind if they can, 'cause they know they gonna get away wid it."

Kimbo crouched behind doors, trees, or mangrove clumps numerous times, trembling as settlers beat his father or, worse, hit his mother and stole whatever they could take from their home. No comebacks. No law enforcement. As a young man, Kimbo quickly learnt to recognise settlers with hostile attitudes and those who didn't. Not every white man was looking to beat them or steal from them.

"Now listen, Kimbo, stop messing wid your food," his mother would say most evenings as the three sat for their end-of-day meal, often retelling the same stories. "Gullahs come from the low country areas – places wid names like Georgia, Florida and the Carolinas an' all. Our old folks moved into the Bahamas after sommat called a Revolutionary War. White folks battlin' each udda. It always made me smile to m'self that them British folks looked down on the white Bahamian folk and called them 'Conchs' cuz all they'd eat was conch shellfish. Not only did those white folk eat it, but they used the shell to make music."

Kimbo's mother would throw her arms in the air every time and laugh uproariously at this story. Kimbo didn't understand why it was so funny.

Many stories were repeated at supper time. Kimbo learnt that hundreds of enslaved people and some Seminole Indians escaped to The Bahamas, giving the islands a mix of Africans and Native Americans. His young life now revolved around his father and learning everything he could teach him. Being taught how to live off the land was to be vital.

As a grown man, he mostly avoided those who threatened

him or his family, but not always. Those few men he liked and sometimes talked to would ask straight questions.

"Hey, Kimbo, you must be troubled by some of the things said to you and your wife. Don't ya get angry?"

Kimbo stared unblinkingly at them, gently smiling and changing the conversation. He knew anger would provoke folks and stop him from finding a purpose for himself and his family beyond starvation, misery, and early death. He also knew hunger, hardship, and the lack of opportunities were common among his kind, black or white. He wanted to break free from that fate.

Growing up, he would always win when forced into a fight. Now, on occasions, he felt a guilty satisfaction when he took on and beat his family's enemies. He beat them so they would no longer try to harm or threaten him or his loved ones again. That gave him physical confidence as well as guilt. Violence was not his preferred way of deterring, but he learnt it was the most effective. He sought and found work – the hard, physical work available to the uneducated. He first toiled on the railroad as a maintenance worker. Now, six feet six inches tall and with the strength of two men, he was helping build the road along the necklace of islands to Key West. When asked, on rare occasions, to sign papers, he stated shyly, "I got no schoolin'. I got no readin', no writin'."

The paperwork of cheats easily tricked him. He lived with low expectations, but although hope and ambition glowed inside him, there were no opportunities to hook onto and give him a way forward. He'd known Zella since childhood, and they knew they were attracted to each other, even as children. After marrying, they set up a home on Upper Matecumbe Key in the middle of the long tail of islands. Zella knew Kimbo as a gentle and kind man, born with a natural recognition of right and wrong. She had seen him appreciate people who brought joy, laughter, and honesty, but these qualities had been a rare experience outside of family life. The world's ways were perilous and rooted in their daily experience.

But now, standing in his home, with Sengo whimpering at his wet feet caked in sand, he faced a sceptical Zella. As always, she had dismissed his thoughts of impending danger, tired of his anxiety.

But what was this uneasiness, this dread? How could he make Zella and his beautiful twins, Myron and Zakari, safe? Safe from what?

What or who do I have to fight this time?

He was exhausted by his life.

Surrounding Kimbo's home, work camps were set up with six hundred and fifty World War I veterans, dubbed the 'bonus army'. These men had marched on Washington a few years before protesting that veteran bonus money promised by Congress had not been delivered. President Hoover had sent armed troops into their Washington DC park camps, using tear gas to disperse their inconvenient presence. Essentially they were evicted. The vets were an obvious and noisy political embarrassment. The protests and eviction became a public relations fiasco for Hoover and his administration. It was considered one of the main reasons why Hoover lost the election in 1932, along with his inability to deal with the Great Depression. When in power and closer to the political truth, Roosevelt had this glaring problem to solve. How to rid Washington of them.

"Well, let's kill two birds with one stone. Why don't we send the vets to build a highway through the Florida Keys to Key

West? This road building will provide the vets with jobs and boost much-needed tourism in this poor area. We can build that road alongside old Henry Flagler's railroad, you know, what do they call it?"

"Sir, it's called 'The Florida East Coast Railroad' – Key West Extension."

"Anybody got a better idea?"

President Roosevelt's idea had been agreed upon without a dissenting voice.

Two days before he walked along the beach, Kimbo Hopper had been working with the veterans sent by Roosevelt from Washington. Veterans with nowhere else to go. These men would constantly forget that Kimbo might be softly spoken but capable of physically defending himself and his family. He was the only non-white worker in Upper Matecumbe Key. His mere build and strength would attract trouble. The workers around him would see him as a daily challenge, someone to take on, to fight when they were drunk. They would have to be drunk or not of sound mind because nobody in their right mind would want to pick a fight with him. After Kimbo had been tested many times in many ways, he was eventually accepted by these men. Now, he was rarely challenged, insulted or set upon, and most had never mixed with, worked with, or lived near black people. He was a novelty. Initially, some vets saw him as someone who could be treated worse than they had been. They saw he was weaker and more vulnerable, which was a novel and valid reason to pick on him. Recently, he was asked to help break up fights between those who used to pick on him. Almost no one tried it on with Kimbo Hopper any more; if they did, it would take unusual provocation for Kimbo to respond. He would hold someone away from him by gripping their shoulders or hugging them so tightly they gave up.

Kimbo's family were his life, so his tolerance evaporated when they came to his home. One blow would typically be enough to halt one, sometimes, two drunks. Initially, men who foolishly wanted to "punch him out" had been drinking enough hard liquor to think they could. Nursing a black eye or broken nose would be enough for them to remember not to try it again.

Isolated from the rest of America, their deep-seated feelings of alienation and mind-numbing boredom were seedlings for their own storm. Drunken brawls were a payday ritual for many as they drank hard liquor to forget their troubles and ease the pain of injuries and disappointments. For these forgotten men, the liquor ignited anger, causing inarticulate, violent eruptions. Initially, the men sent to manage the vets were somewhat sympathetic and easy-going with the men. However, it quickly became a problem when the sober, hard-working locals had their Methodist teachings of tolerance and compassion tested to the limit. As a result, local pressure ensured that a rule was introduced prohibiting whisky in the workers' camps. This led to increased resentment as the vets could only acquire booze through bootleggers, inevitably with increased prices.

Apart from their drunkenness, the residents had a low opinion of the vets for several reasons. The country struggled to come out of the Great Depression, and The Keys' permanent residents were living on the breadline, barely getting by from day to day. They saw the vets were provided jobs and secure, regular pay. Men whom they deemed work-shy and ill-equipped for their work. Some judged them as just lazy, and others considered them "psychos", as they put it. They had little knowledge of the physical ordeals these men had endured during *The Great War*, as it was known then, and no understanding of the psychological damage done by their experience of it.

The perfect contribution to this social disaster was the poor quality of people assigned to manage the road building and lead the veteran workforce. The managers lacked experience in marshalling and organising troubled and rebellious workers. That was more than enough of a toxic cocktail, but it was coupled with little understanding of how to get the job done in a hostile, sub-tropical climate.

The forgotten vets felt dumped out of sight in the remotest part of the country. They lived alongside locals, the vast majority on the breadline themselves, and who thought Washington politicians, the Florida ERA and the highway construction leaders were mollycoddling the vets. However, for their part, the leaders of these organisations were handed an inadequate, inexperienced, psychologically damaged workforce in an inhospitable workplace.

Kimbo understood the vet's depression and sense of hopelessness, but his understanding came from different experiences. They called him 'Conch', 'Kimbo Conch' or 'King Conch', this last one after the 1933 film King Kong. It just depended on the vets' moods or prejudices. Almost no one called him just 'Kimbo'. Calling him a conch was intended as disparagement, but knowing the term's origins, it always made him laugh. The vets were always a little puzzled as to why it amused him. He worked alongside them, but Kimbo struggled to like them. Not only because they treated him and his family callously at times but because they were lazy drunks who didn't even care about themselves or anyone else. They didn't think they had anything much to live for. Kimbo had no experience being "shell-shocked", but he did understand being ill-treated, disregarded and ignored. He understood isolation, loneliness and being an outcast. Black Bahamians were used to their fortunes changing suddenly without their say-so or consent, totally outside their control, with their fate out of their hands. Kimbo was used to being undervalued. Kimbo and Zella were enjoying a day off from their routines on Monday morning. Kimbo deliberately took her to see danger for herself, hoping Zella would notice. They had set out on their three-mile family walk along the shoreline of Upper Matecumbe after an early breakfast traditional treat of crab and okra soup.

West African food was everywhere in their life if they could source it or afford it. Sengo followed Kimbo everywhere when he was not working and stayed with the family when Kimbo was away at work. A faithful and devoted dog, he kept snakes and other unwelcome wildlife away from the family home, built on the side of one of the large outbuildings of a lime-packing shed. One dog bark was enough to send most vets running when they strayed too near the Hopper home. The six work camps had packing and building material supply sheds between the Matecumbe and Windley Keys. It was a good home, Kimbo thought. Although he had spent a few years on the railroad as a maintenance worker, he realised he would never be considered for more responsibilities. He was a rare and skilled offering from the Florida East Coast Railway company to the vets' workers' bureaucrats.

"This man Hopper will be someone who can pass on his know-how and experience in railroad maintenance to help build the highway."

It wasn't difficult to convince the road builders of his value, but getting opportunities to organise and manage the work would never be available. To Kimbo, it didn't matter where he worked; it made no difference. He was an illiterate black man.

A combination of opposing forces, strong and weak, were

about to test each other. A perfect human storm was also developing.

Squalls at the Weather Bureau
That same Friday, the phone rang in the Jacksonville, Florida, offices of the US Weather Bureau. It had been set up to advise on conditions for Florida, Georgia and Carolina residents. In particular, the fishing industry needed highly reliable forecasting, and booming tourism needed to make visitors feel they had made the right decision to spend a little vacation money there during the bleak period of the Great Depression. These two factors were vital to a thriving local economy, and the Bureau had to balance forecasting weather with the pressure not to scare tourists away.

A man called Fred Povey picked up the phone on his desk.

"This is Gus Baldwin from the Federal Emergency Relief Administration responsible for the vets based down here on Matecumbe Key. Can I speak to someone in charge?"

His voice betrayed anxiety.

"Who are you? We normally have a different contact name from FERA, er, normally, er, let me see now, ah yes, Herb Long calls us. We always speak to Herb. Who are you? Where is Herb?"

Fred Povey was a cautious weather bureau man.

"Herb is in Key West on vacation. He's finishing his honeymoon. He's my boss."

"Okay, Gus, did you say? Gus Baldwin?"

"Yes, Gus Baldwin," he said slightly shrill.

"Okay, what's your problem, Gus?"

"It's clear to me we've got a huge storm coming. Have you guys got a handle on where it's going to hit? Are you the boss there in Jacksonville?" Gus demanded.

"Yeah, I'm Fred Povey. Herb and me, we got a good relationship. I've already put out an advisory, but we don't think it's more than a windy rainstorm. You know, the usual windy summer rainstorm."

In the back of Povey's mind, he remembered what Herb had said about Gus Baldwin.

"A very conscientious and highly competent professional kinda guy."

But many people, including Herb, who worked with him in Matecumbe, knew Gus as a nervous, overly cautious man who imagined danger and was obsessed with potential problems.

"Fred, this ain't no regular rainstorm. This is gonna blow real hard. Summa, the locals are getting real jumpy. We need to get a train down here, as promised, if we gonna get a bad one comin' through. When I call the Florida East Coast railroad boys, I need you to back me up." Baldwin pressed hard.

"Look, we forecast and give advisories. If you gotta problem with that, you'd better talk to someone who can do somethin'."

Fred Povey hung up with the arrogance of knowing the strength of a whole organisation would be there for him to hide behind.

The phone rang in Shell Dawkins's office. He was responsible for Florida's part of the Federal Emergency Relief Administration (FERA) and, in effect, was Herb Long and Gus Baldwin's boss. But he was also based in Jacksonville – five hundred miles from Key West. Specifically, Dawkins was responsible for both the welfare of World War I veterans and getting the road to Key West built on time and within budget.

The phone rang five times before he slowly answered it.

"Yep, Dawkins."

It was Herb Long calling from his honeymoon hotel in Key West. Shell Dawkins was responsible for setting up and managing the three cheaply constructed beachfront work camps in The Keys at the direction of the Franklin D Roosevelt Administration. He also knew Herb took the safety and well-being of those men very seriously; maybe he was a bit too serious. Shell had always thought so.

"Shell, it's Herb. I just got a call from one of my guys, Gus Baldwin. Seems we gotta big blow goin' on in the middle keys. It's starting to get rough here in Key West, but it sounds worse where he is, and most likely, we're gonna get hit bad. We need that train to evacuate the vets, just like we said to the FEC railroad guys. So, better send it right away. I'm making my way back to Matecumbe myself pretty soon. I'll be there this evening and arrange to get those unruly and stinkin' drunks ready for the train to ship 'em out. I'll call you first thing."

"Whoa, Herb, hang on. I don't see no tropical storm warning, just an advisory from the weather bureau. Says here it's a rainstorm." Herb had rung off before Shell could make his point.

Damn. Better call Ben Coleman, Shell thought. Well, maybe in the morning. Ben was his contact point for the railroad, based in Miami, one hundred sixty miles from Key West.

I'm gonna keep it simple, he thought. *I'm responsible for the men, and Ben's responsible for the railroad. Things may have blown through by the morning.*

Shell wasn't sure what good he could personally do from there anyway. It was *best to leave it to the men on the scene. I'll wait and see.*

Discussions between all parties responsible had been mainly non-productive. Each considered the others cagey operators. Although the idea of sending a special FEC train from Miami to evacuate the vets if a severe storm appeared was agreed in principle, there had yet to be a commitment.

The railroad hadn't made clear that keeping a train in constant readiness, somehow on a side track, wasn't affordable for the railroad and certainly not for the FERA budget. If the train were sent for no good reason, there would be a significant cost item, which would undoubtedly cause a massive row between the Federal Emergency Relief Administration and the Florida East Coast Railroad. Given the low-level weather advisory, the railroad had to make the decision. It was Gus Baldwin pushing the panic button on Matecumbe. All parties with budgets to protect assessed the situation calmly, thoughts streaming logically, always thinking about the outcome. Will our jobs be threatened if we act?

Shell Dawkins sat comfortably in his FERA Jacksonville office and pondered the situation.

Baldwin was pushing the panic button and had always seemed easily flustered and overly cautious. That was fine and just his way, but Gus wasn't the guy who would be shouted at or blamed if a train was launched for nothing or worse. Someone might get singled out and fired for initiating inappropriate use of funds. My neck would be on the block. Getting fired for reckless use of funds wouldn't look so good to other prospective employers if I had to look for another job.

Shell Dawkins made his decision. On his way home, he left his office for a beer. His wife, Mabel, told him to expect southern shrimp and grits for supper. He was contented with his life in Jacksonville, a proudly modern city. As he walked, he made his next important decision – where to have his beer – Shell Dawkins had a weather advisory of a summer rainstorm covering his rear end.

At this point, all those living in southern Florida were at the mercy of different organisations responsible for entirely different aspects of the situation. With politics thrown into it, both local and national, a storm of its own was brewing. Human nature and Mother Nature were about to be inextricably mixed. Nobody could predict what either of them was going to do next.

The next day, Saturday, August 31st, the phone rang non-stop. Still groggy, Herb Long woke early in his Islamorada hotel, where his veterans' road work programme to Key West was headquartered. The first call was from the local Miami Weather Bureau meteorologist.

"In summary, Herb," he said, "things might get a little rough by Monday."

Herb had cut short his honeymoon for a second time – the first was to sort out the deaths of two men killed in a brawl a month ago. He was getting irritated with people who were paid to know what was happening with the weather. Understandably, his new wife had got angry, which didn't help.

"Okay, the fuck does that mean? A little rough? You telling me that today, Saturday, the storm might get a 'little rough' by Monday? I've got the responsibility of six hundred and fifty men, most drunk when they are not working and some drunk when they are working, and you're telling me it might get a little rough in two days? These vets live in tents, ten to fifteen per tent. If you lived in a fucking tent, what would a little rough mean to you?"

"Whoa, Herb, now hold on. Locally, we think, at worst, it will hit Key West. Our boys are plotting the storm on a map. The direction is looking far ahead of the actual storm. We reckon it will, most likely, strike Havana late Monday. It might get rough for you where you are… er… where is your camp again? Well anyway, about Monday, that sort of time, you might get some heavy rain…at worse…probably."

Straight-line plotting of a tropical storm was always wrong. At this point in the conversation, any of the vets living squalid lives in flimsy tents and makeshift sheds could repeat the old military saying, 'No plan survives the first contact with the enemy'.

Five minutes later, the second call to Herb from Jacksonville's US Weather Bureau toed the same line as the local,

Miami, forecast. No one knew what would happen. Herb Long, a man responsible for the lives of hundreds of vets, could not possibly know that the Weather Bureau forecast was off by miles, many miles.

Cuba

Cuban officials in Havana were not convinced by the US Weather Bureau advisories they had picked up; they were not reassured by any means. Nevertheless, they had their own ideas and methods. An ex-American Navy pilot, Joel Biggs, had been hired by one of the Cuban political heavyweights to train their military pilots and was also tasked to fly into and around storm systems to detect speed, direction, and strength. Joel loved his job and the sense of danger it gave him. He was only employed during the active period of Atlantic hurricanes – June to the end of November each year. It was perfect for him. From December to May, he lived in Miami and Key West, fishing and drinking with his buddies.

Joel got his orders to prepare to fly out early Monday into the Florida Straits, the area between Havana, Miami and The Bahamas. He was ordered to find the storm, assess it, and report on the conditions he found. It was made very clear to Joel that the report was for his employer's eyes only in Havana. Alerting the US Weather Bureau was not part of his job, and he would be punished if he notified them. That was made crystal clear.

Matecumbe Key

Construction of The Keys highway had reached the lower Matecumbe Key. Roosevelt's actions were a little more humane than those of his predecessor, Hoover, in his attempt to provide the vets with purpose and employment. Tragically, the shell-shocked workers were not managed or supervised by local, seasoned residents who knew the challenging conditions manual workers would endure. It would have been better for the FEC overseas railroad engineers to prepare and nurture a workforce dealing with high temperatures and cruel humidity. The FEC employees had accumulated knowledge of working and living conditions from the eight years it had taken to build the railroad and the twenty-three years maintaining it since. Unfortunately, the government ignored the experienced railroad workforce – a workforce on the doorstep of the road construction programme. It didn't fit the politics of the day.

Mosquito-infested tents housed the vets. The wildlife was vicious. It was common for the men to be bitten by snakes, and American crocodiles who liked the brackish waters of the Florida Keys and Florida Bay occasionally attacked them. These men used to the more distinctive seasons of the northern cities, endured unfamiliar, hostile conditions as they undertook the hard, manual work of clearing and road building in swamps. The relentless "skeeters" were the main reason many workers quit and went "back north". The men in charge were only Federal Emergency Relief Administration (FERA) government officials. Tragically, these bureaucrats knew nothing about the Florida Keys climate or the living conditions in this part of America.

On Matecumbe Key that Labour Day weekend, the vets played card games or slept off the night before. A few found a boat to take them south to Key West for the weekend of Labour Day. They were due back sometime Monday, but some had decided to go '*AWOL*' until later in the week and face the consequences.

Chapter Two
Boats, Planes and Trains

No Time to Prepare
It was Monday, September 2nd, and those who didn't read newspapers, visit bars, or congregate in community shops would have no time to prepare, if any. Kimbo Hopper walked along the shoreline holding his three-year-old son Myron's hand. Behind them, Zella Hopper and their daughter Zakari followed. They strolled along the thin sandy stretch of beach between the water, the seagrape and the mangroves. These indigenous trees were bunched and clustered along the shore, bridging land and sea. They were bedded on heavy sand and limestone. In this part of the Keys, red, black and white mangroves grew prolifically, binding the shell mounds – a mixture of animal bone and botanical material. The mangroves were a vital, sustaining part of marine life in The Keys. Kimbo knew all about the land he lived on, but on that day, the Hopper family was not out of place – but in the wrong place. It was Kimbo's only day off from those indigent veterans sent to build the overseas highway. Usually, Kimbo would have a break on Sunday, but as it was a so-called holiday weekend, Kimbo was told to work that Sunday and switch his day off to Monday.

Consequently, that Sunday, his job was to tidy up the usual mess left on a Saturday as the other men couldn't wait to start their leisure activities. They would be doing all day Sunday what they did each evening: drinking and gambling. It was worse when they were paid their wages – almost a ritual.

The family walked, Sengo on one side of Kimbo, Myron on the other, holding his father's hand, Zella and Zakari behind. Sengo stopped suddenly and barked at the black clouds forming on the horizon. He sniffed the air, nuzzled Kimbo's leg and crouched as if to hide. Dog and man again both sensed something was dramatically changing, and Zella stared at her husband. Without a word passing between them, she finally understood something was different.

They looked at the sea and noticed that the pattern of breaking waves on the beach was just two or three a minute. Under normal conditions, the frequency along this coastline would be between twelve and fifteen a minute. It seemed the ocean was drawing itself in and away from the shore, drawing its' skirts higher and higher. They gazed at the black and purple clouds gathering over the ocean's easterly horizon. Gigantic dark lines poured out of the sky as they moved slowly towards the speechless family. Zella noticed the temperature drop and then plummet. She recognised the growing stain of pink and purple and the familiar clouds interspersed with the rain streaks. She could no longer deny what she was seeing or what Kimbo had told her for days.

"Kimbo, let's get home. Storm's coming," Zella said. "I think this is goin' to be a stinker. Let's prepare shelter. Let's get home."

She saw Kimbo's look but returned it with a *don't say anything* stare. He decided not to say anything. His words were written on his face. They picked up a child each. Kimbo held his son, and Zella clutched her daughter as Sengo led the way. The dog already knew he wanted to go home; he knew the way and wanted to run as fast as possible. He was becoming impatient with his human family moving so slowly. He was an anxious dog with frightened eyes.

Now, it seemed that the whole world was turning lead-grey.

The world around them appeared waiting to be sucked up and spat out. The cirrus and cumulus clouds they had seen earlier were replaced by heavy, intense bands of jet-black clouds, reaching across the sky and rapidly coming nearer. The daylight was pinkish. Kimbo realised that there would be no hiding place. They would still be caught even if they were a hundred miles away. Kimbo and Zella started to run after Sengo, with both children jogging up and down in their arms. They both began to cry, sensing their parents' panic. Sengo was halfway home when they all realised there would be no shelter from this storm.

Ernest Worries About the Love of His Life
The Labour Day weekend began for Ernest Hemingway on Saturday, August 31st, when he had completed the day's editing of his brutally honest book, *To Have and Have Not*. After moving to Key West in 1931, he amassed stories and anecdotes about the lives of people smugglers and Cuban murderers. He talked to anyone who would share a drink in his favourite local bars, most notably 'Sloppy Joe's'. Friendships were forged through late-night drinking and deep sea fishing. He was always touchy and difficult during the last phase of his work; he carefully chose each word. He'd worked hard, and at the end of his workday, the tall and strong-minded author walked out of his purposely furnished, second-storey studio in the back of his property. He hurried down the wrought iron staircase across a short path embedded in the patio, entered the main house, and into the kitchen. He poured himself a large whisky and soda, walked out again and sat on his spacious porch with *The Key West Citizen,* the daily paper. He always picked the same spot to start his evening drinking, away from the curious and prying eyes of the tourists.

At this time, Hemingway was one of the few notable

residents of Key West. It irritated him that an official had published a pamphlet to boost tourism on the island and listed him as *Attraction Number 18* – one of the island's top twenty attractions. He didn't see himself as an attraction, and being listed as low as 18 didn't help his temper either. He became more than annoyed when so-called tourists started to stomp around his property, peering in windows and staring at him as he tried to relax on his porch, drawing on a cigar and sipping a drink. He was outraged when one visitor brazenly pulled down on the handle of his front door, strolled into the hallway and proceeded to view his living room, reception room and kitchen as though his house was a museum. He'd had enough. He got permission from the city bureaucrats to build a six-foot-high stone-brick wall around his property on the two sides that bordered roads. Quite quickly, the two roadsides of his property, exposed to what he would call "voyeurs", were walled off. Thick tropical trees and large plants blocked the other two sides. He had hoped the city would take him off the tourist list now that he was secluded.

"Some hope," he muttered every time he thought about it.

Although there was often a sea breeze to cool the heat and humidity in his two-story home on Whitehead Street, the porch's shade added to his relief as he picked up the paper to read. It was six short blocks from the ocean but close enough to benefit from the fresh, salty air.

The banner headline glared at him now that his workday was behind him. Hidden from the public, a drink in hand, the light breeze made his newspaper flutter:

STORM WARNING!

As with all weather predictions, especially in the early days without sophisticated tracking technology, the newspaper story waffled, giving scant details of the storm's direction, strength, and speed. It provided a weather bureau prediction that it was, at worst, a tropical storm. The article said, "It could turn into, possibly, a hurricane." This was a typical, safe statement. It mentioned Cuba and the Florida Straits as the most likely victims.

Ships sailing south towards Cuba had been the first to pick up the tropical disturbance and telegraphed back to Miami. Newspapers did not consider weather reporting a priority, but eventually, reports were building a picture that editors in Miami could not ignore. Their concern, however, was Miami. The editor wasn't thinking about anywhere else. Although the winds kill, flooding does the most damage. Hemingway knew the highest point along the one hundred and ten miles of the Keys' rocky limestone islands and mangrove swamps was only eighteen feet above sea level. What scared him was that, on average, it is only three to four feet above. Highly vulnerable to large sea swells.

Hemingway walked back from the porch, downed the remainder of his whisky, poured another, and searched for his filed-away storm charts detailing every one of the forty hurricanes to hit Florida since 1900. Tracking what had happened was reasonably straightforward; hurricanes had left a clear path of destruction. Nevertheless, he threw them aside, knowing it didn't help with prediction. If the worst happened and it was heading his way, he calculated he had until lunchtime, Monday, September 2nd, to prepare. Most Key West residents knew how to prepare for this possibility. Word spread quickly in Key West, between rich and poor. The perception of a common enemy approaching instilled a rare sense of community.

Hemingway then picked up the phone to talk to Doc Slim, a

friend he had made when he first moved to Key West. The doctor now lived in Homestead, having worn himself out attending to anyone and everyone who needed a doctor, regardless of whether they could pay. It was Doc Slim's humanity that drew Hemingway to him.

"Doc? Yes, it's me, Papa, and yes, I've got a drink in my hand. Have you heard anything about the coming storm?"

"Ernest, when you drink, you get irritable, you can be violent, and you know what I think about that! So, you have got to be your own doctor!"

"Doc, I've told you many times to call me Papa, goddamn it. Look, there is something important I need to tell you. Folk in Key West expect a storm to come through or near here. Maybe Cuba, but that's not the point. You'll be busy if it hits The Keys or anywhere near Homestead. I will help, but the doc who replaced you in Key West is a worse drunk than me. We can't rely on him. Do you think you could come and help in The Keys if we get it bad here?"

Ignoring Hemingway's usual bellicose manner and insistence on being called 'Papa', Doc Slim responded calmly and reassuringly.

"Ernest, of course. If it comes to the Florida Keys, anywhere along the islands, I will organise as much help as I can as soon as I can. When might it hit the area?"

Hemingway told him and thanked the doctor, said goodbye, poured another scotch and soda, and smiled. The best doctor in South Florida would be on the job if needed. His thoughts then turned to what was troubling him.

Hemingway knew he should secure his boat, *The Pilar*. It was the absolute love of his life. He was sometimes heard talking about his boat as if she were a lover. She had been tailor-made for him the year before by a shipyard in New York. A forty-foot, engine-powered fishing yacht, a source of joy and adventure. Securing it was one of his primary concerns. He had to get *The Pilar* away from her current moorings, as most other boats were tied only by flimsy lines. That would mean they would become missiles in a storm.

That day, fame bought Hemingway nothing. As chaos threatened, people wanted some order. Fame or justice didn't count. Hemingway eventually purchased some of the strongest available hawsers and tied his boat up in the safest part of the submarine base. He stared for a few minutes at his loved one and hurried home.

All of Sunday, September 1st, deep into the evening and continuing the following morning, Hemingway was busy. Knowing his boat was as safe as he could make it, he impatiently secured garden furniture, brought in well-loved plants, and herded his many ever-present cats inside the house. He hammered makeshift shutters over the windows and air vents as much as he could, and he could hear hammering echoing across the whole town of Key West that morning as everyone prepared. Then, a few hours later, the city of Key West became still and deathly quiet.

On Monday, with all the preparations he could make now completed, Ernest Hemingway and Pauline Pfeiffer – his wife during that period – stayed inside their house from mid-afternoon. They heard the pounding wind and rain thrashing against their windows and doors during the evening and night. But they were spared.

That evening, around seven p.m., the author opened his door and shone a light on the grounds of his house. He shouted to Pauline above the storm's din.

"Only a tree down across the walkway, and that old Sapodilla tree is down too. Looks like this one missed us. The real storm has gone north of us. Somewhere between us and Miami."

Cuba
Early on Monday morning, there was no rising sun. Those deep, lead-grey clouds the Hopper family had seen hung over Cuba and the Havana airfield as Joel Biggs pulled back the throttle. He flew straight up, heading over the Florida Straits. The fully fuelled, small biplane fighter was older than Joel would have liked, but he knew his way around every inch of it. Around mid-afternoon, Monday, September 2nd, 1935, Joel spotted what he was looking for but couldn't believe what he saw. He was stunned and shaken.

Rising from the sea to 12,000 feet was the most extensive cone-shaped body of clouds he had ever seen. It had an inverted shape sucking upwards from its base at sea level. He knew that the average eye of a hurricane would be somewhere between twenty and forty miles wide. What astonished him was the eye of the storm – by his rough calculation, a width of about five miles. That meant extremely powerful winds around the eye wall, the most devastating part of a hurricane.

"Holy shit! I hope my buddies are somewhere safe…" Joel whispered to his cockpit.

He looked down to see the waves below him run against each other, smashing themselves as if each wave were panicking. What shocked Joel most was that this storm was far from the path he had been given in his brief, a path plotted, predicted, and stolen from the US Weather Bureau. It was further north and headed for the Florida Keys, not Cuba. A fact he knew, sadly, would cost many American, not Cuban, lives. He estimated it had already crossed Andros Island, the largest island in The Bahamas. He'd seen enough and returned to the Havana airfield, bouncing through some of the most turbulent conditions he had ever experienced.

He reported everything he saw and gave a low-level damage assessment for the city of Havana to his Cuban political and military boss. After his debrief, he briskly walked to *La Bodeguita del Medio*, his favourite bar on *Empedrado*, in old Havana, near the docks and ferry port. He drank until the barman closed for the night, helping him off his barstool and putting him out in the street like a stray cat. It was raining hard, but Joel had only two streets to walk before entering his hotel for the night. Ironically, his hotel on Calle Obispo was called '*The Florida*', an old Colonial-style lodging with a free breakfast.

Joel was not religious, but what he saw had put the fear of God into him. He didn't pray but lay awake wide-eyed despite his reeking drunkenness. Joel imagined people in his head, silently screaming. He woke the following day naked, in a pile of sweat-soaked bedding.

Old 447
It was two thirty p.m. that Monday afternoon. Herb Long picked up the phone in the offices next to the flimsy tents and bedroom shacks on Long Key. His boss, Shell Dawkins, was reading the paper, feet on the desk, five hundred miles away in Jacksonville. But Herb wasn't calling Shell; instead, he called his railroad contact, Ben Coleman, in Miami. Finally, Ben was someone he could trust and rely on. Someone who could do something practical – a train to get them all out of there.

"Ben! Ben! It's me, Herb. Herb Long. Can you hear me, ok? We're in trouble. It's blowing in from hell here. This is going to be a giant storm coming through. We need you to get the train down here. Pick us all up and take us all as far north as you can before this thing blows us back to hell!"

"Wait, Herb, hold on. What are you talking about? Nobody's bin telling me there's a storm brewin'."

"Ben, it's not fuckin' brewin'. It's brewed! And what's more, it's 'bout ta spill over all of us. We got an agreement that you'll send a train down here if we got a big one comin' in. I'm pleadin' with you, Ben. We have a serious situation. We don't get time to discuss this. Send that train now!" Herb rang off and started organising the vets to get ready to be evacuated. Most of them did, but a few weren't bothered or were passed out.

Ben knew Herb well. He was a good man and solid in his thinking.

"Shit. It's gonna be more than hell to get that train ready," he said aloud to his empty, silent office.

Two hours later, a locomotive was "steamed up" and assembled with eleven coaches, boxcars and baggage cars as he could find. It was the best he could do. One of the cars had to be repaired, which took extra time. The engine was 'Old 447', made in Schenectady, New York. It was a heavy, 106-ton, 4-8-2 model – a massively powerful locomotive. With the only available crew on board, the train pulled out of its Miami yard at four thirty p.m. Ben Coleman watched as it disappeared along the single track. Had he done the right thing? If he had, was it going to be in time?

It was a holiday weekend, and the boat traffic on the Miami River was heavy.

"The fuck is this!" Jack Root screamed at the open turntable bridge, which allowed the holiday boats to pass through. Jack Root, a man close to God, rarely used curse words, only to release nervous tension. He shouted instructions at the bridge operator, and ten minutes later, he drove over the river and set the train at full speed, travelling south.

Jack was the train engineer and a ten-year Miami to Key West single-track railroad veteran. He'd worked his way up as a sixteen-year-old, learning as he went along, and he loved the life of a train driver. He'd seen his fair share of tropical storms, but this one already looked different. He noticed the green-grey cast of the sky. The sense of foreboding hit the pit of his soul, pointing and shouting at his fireman and train master, both with him in the cab.

"Look at that, for pity's sake!"

On reaching Homestead, Jack shifted the powerful locomotive from the front to the train's rear at this last mainland stop. He reckoned that it would be better to pull out of the storm on the journey back to Miami rather than back out. This switch took another fifteen precious minutes. He cursed but thought this was his best plan despite costing more precious minutes. He was the man on the spot and had to make the decisions – that was his job.

The train master looked at his pocket watch; it was nearly five thirty p.m. The winds were now howling through the trackside guy wires, stays, eaves, power lines, trees and bushes – vibrating, whining, moaning with high-pitch whistling, causing a cacophony. The train crew had all lived through tropical storms of various strengths, but this? This orchestra of unrelenting sound even struck fear and dread into these hardened railroad men.

Jack Root pushed on despite the hard rain blasting his face, stinging like a hundred needles were stuck into it. His open cab was the victim of anything that wanted to enter it. He cut his speed to around twenty miles an hour as the wind swiped sideways against the cars, making them wobble precariously.

Finally, he passed over Jewfish Creek and onto the first island of The Keys – Key Largo. He saw in the dimmed light that the wind had driven the tide hundreds of feet across the relatively rocky but flattened land. It was starting to lap against the track, and he could not clear his head from the heavy thought that hundreds were trapped ahead. They depended on him.

Chapter Three
Like a Beast in the Night

Kimbo Hopper and his family had reached Kimbo's well-built home, meshed and joined at the side of the large packing shed. They had made it their own, styled inside with furniture mostly found or donated by a few residents. Inside the packing shed, the hopeful veterans were shouting about who would come to rescue them. The Hopper family heard the men's words.

One voice shouted, "I ain't gonna get licked by no rainstorm."

Others yelled, "I'm gonna tough this out," and "I ain't gonna let no rainstorm beat me!"

Another roared, "I heard they will send a train…"

Most were mumbling about "…packing what's mine and high-tailing it to the station," and "Well, if there is a train outta here, I'm gonna take it by God!"

Those choosing to leave knew the station would be the only pickup point and their only hope of getting out of The Keys safely. Kimbo had doubts about whether the station would be a safe place. It meant going further south, where the highest point would be the rail track, which was only four feet above normal sea level. This night, there would be no normal sea level. He had picked this high spot for their home, building it against the most robust packing shed on Upper Matecumbe. It offered the best shelter against the regular seasonal, sub-tropical weather. It faced *Bayside* and was the least likely to get directly hit by a storm surge from the ocean. After a short discussion, Kimbo and Zella decided to stay inside their home. Would they be welcome if they joined the locals in collecting their things and going to the station? Then, they heard most of the vets leave the shed. The hopeful passengers headed south towards Islamorada and the train pick-up point.

It was around seven p.m. when the whole packing shed and the Hopper's adjoining home started to throb. Sengo had stopped barking and lay down, whimpering in the dim light, his eyes not leaving Kimbo's movements. Suddenly, the building was pounded by huge, prolonged, heavy gusts, thumping hard like an irregular heartbeat. Kimbo realised it might blow apart the timbered structure at any minute. He leant against the main door as it rattled, vibrated and shook. He knew that the packing shed, and therefore his small house, was built on a platform to assist with loading and unloading building materials. This should be helpful, as it was the highest point in the area.

He felt fear shock his body. He felt something wet surge around his feet and realised it was seawater. The whole island must be underwater. Kimbo looked at Zella and saw the sheer terror in her eyes. He knew she couldn't swim.

"What we gonna do now?" Zella screamed.

Sengo was half swimming, half standing, looking to his master for help. Kimbo bawled above the din.

"We gotta get out! We gotta leave and head north towards Windley Key, or we gonna drown. There is higher ground there. Zella, take Zakari and tie her as tight as possible with these sheet strips. Wrap her head with these blankets, as tight an' firm as you can. Quickly, I'll do the same with Myron. When we leave, I want you to hug Zakari into my back, grab my clothes, and don't let go, no matter what…I'm telling ya, Zella, hold on to her and me no matter what! We gonna walk as one family into this storm, and we going to all survive. I will hug Myron to my chest. Are you ready?"

Kimbo looked at his wife. He kissed her sweet face and wiped her terrified eyes with his thumbs as he held her in his large, strong hands. He smiled, hoping his courage would help Zella. At ground level, Sengo had no one to help him in this chaos. His eyes were wide and unblinking, his instincts in turmoil.

Kimbo opened the door, and they all went out into the dark, howling night.

Old 447 coming down the track
Jack Root strained to see ahead. Visibility was close to zero. The darkness below his cab was ignited by flashes along the tracks and up to wheel height. The wind had lifted millions of tiny sand grains and sent them crashing against one another, creating eerie static charges that electrified the earth like ground lightning. Jack looked at it, trying to make sense of what he saw. He couldn't. It was as if the flashes were millions of shrieking fireflies.

It was seven p.m. when the Old 447 locomotive and its six passenger cars, two baggage cars and three boxcars approached Windley Key, the first significant span of open water. Jack Root had the train headlights on full, which helped a little as any natural light had disappeared, but he could see green lightning high in the cloud-built heavens – ugly forked lightning, searching for something to ignite. The backcloth of clouds was lit by white flashes, making it look like the heavens were a vast cathedral ceiling.

The train reached Snake Creek Bridge, which would take them onto Windley Key, but Jack Root caught sight of people crowding along the track. They were knee-deep in seawater and panicking. He knew he couldn't just ride past. His orders were to rescue the hundreds of vets and local people gathering around Islamorada Train Station, but surely, everyone needed rescuing no matter who they were. He didn't hesitate and braked. The storm's refugees didn't hesitate either; everyone standing there boarded. When he restarted, the train charged slowly towards the waiting vets while Jack calculated the maximum speed at which he dared try. Suddenly, the engine and, consequently, the whole train crashed to a screeching halt. The men in the cab were thrown to the floor. The train master found the problem as Jack Root stared at his crew in disbelief. It didn't make sense to him. Nothing should hold back the mighty thrust of his herculean locomotive engine!

A gravel pit boom cable, brought low by the wind, had sagged into the open cab, missing the tender car but strangling the mobility of the iron steed. Shocked, Jack stared at his engine controls, completely mystified. The fireman pulled him away, bringing him out of his stupor as the train master pointed to the problem. Jack saw it immediately, thankful that the slow speed they had been travelling had saved all three from decapitation.

Finding the right tools and cutting the thick cable free of the cab took nearly an hour. Finally, it was almost eight p.m., and they had to travel another four miles to reach their destination.

The vets and residents were already gathered at or near the station. Most had to wade through waist-high seawater flowing swiftly across their path. Then, the cruel, lidless eye passed over the six-mile stretch between Windley Key and Tea Table Key. All Upper Matecumbe, Islamorada and Lower Matecumbe islands were about to surrender and hope for mercy. Mother Nature, in this mood, knows nothing about mercy.

Missing

Kimbo, Zella, Myron, and Zakari clung to each other, but Sengo was missing. Competing currents had swept him away. His scared, panicking eyes were unseen by his family; he disappeared into the eternal darkness.

The family steadily progressed against the strong wind, torrential downpours, and swirling knee-high water. Peering into the blackness, they had to walk bent at the waist, head butting the wind. Then, the weather calmed. Zella relaxed. Suddenly, she saw stars, the temperature warmed slightly, and she started to let go of Kimbo's shirt. The ruthless eye of the hurricane stared down greedily at its target.

"Keep hold of me! Don't let go, Zella! This is the eye passing over. The back part of the eyewall is coming. It's gonna reach us in only a few minutes. The worst part is about to come for us. We must hold on. Hold on!"

She heard every word of his warning but became helpless as the dark wall of spinning air and moisture rushed towards them. The deep black, evil wall came for their lives. It took them up into its vortex and spun them around. Kimbo tried to hold onto all of them, but it was impossible. The blasting roar of the wall was deafening. They were in mid-air, spinning and spinning. Kimbo and Zella looked at each other for the last time. Zella lost her feeble grip on Kimbo but still instinctively gripped her terrified young daughter Zakari. Kimbo clasped Myron and held on to what he could of Zella. Then Kimbo screamed as Zella and Zakari were ripped from him, high up into the sky. They jerked away and were gone, their faces disappearing into the black night. Zella and Zakari were dropped four miles out to sea; their bodies would never be found.

The raging, whirling vortex took Kimbo and Myron up even higher and spat them out. They fell, still barely clinging to each other, spinning downwards, some three miles from their scattered packing shed home, onto a patch of shallow water, sand and mangroves. The wind left them silently together in a timeless void as the searching eye moved on. The thick cloth covering Myron's head had saved his young life. Kimbo was knocked unconscious and lay still. Myron had shut down in shock; his eyes were open, unblinking. He was concussed and bruised but quiet, still as stone, lying in his father's arms. Father and son were just two pieces of debris; jetsam ripped upwards and tossed out when the monster had finished with them. The only certainty in their lives was destroyed in moments.

For Kimbo, Zella and Zakari's absence would be a powerful presence for the rest of his life. The dead don't leave you; they stay with you if you let them.

Hundreds died that night, mostly from drowning – nobody drowns with dignity. Some perished from being lifted high into the sky and dashed against something immovable. Others were killed by flying debris smashing against them. They all lived their last moments helpless and terrified souls.

But this nightmare was not finished for all those still fighting for their lives in the Middle Keys; they would face one more evil, equally as terrifying as the hurricane's vortex but many times more destructive.

Jack Root, unable to see the little Islamorada station through the flying spray and storm-thrown missiles, drove his train several car lengths past where his passengers were ready and waiting. The crowd shouted, but no human voice could be heard over the engine's noise or above the never-ending shriek of the storm. It was difficult for the three men in the cab to breathe, with sand driving into their faces. They had to cup their hands over their mouths and noses, allowing only air into their lungs. The passengers were still screaming at the train as it dashed past them. Their mouths were open now, but nothing could be heard above the din.

It took another twenty minutes for Jack to reverse his train to allow the men, women, and children to board. They couldn't run or even walk. They crawled alongside the track, just above the waterline, as it crept upwards. It took ten minutes for them to struggle into the carriages, with waves crashing on the track and rain coming at them with horizontal force. Jack could not see how many lives he saved, but he was sure it was in the hundreds.

Suddenly, Jack felt the grip of the fireman on his arm. The grip spun Jack around, making him look out to sea. Then he felt the whole train engine, all one hundred six tons, rumble and vibrate as the growl of a new beast overwhelmed even the roar of Jack's old 447 engine. His disbelieving eyes saw a black wall of water, twenty feet higher than the swollen ocean, screaming towards them quicker than his engine could ever thrust his train. The wave stretched from one end of the horizon to the other, greedily feeding on itself, increasing in size as it did so. The train track was six feet above normal sea level, but the train was now two feet below it. Jack could see that the train would be swallowed whole. It meant nothing to the mountain of otherworldly water surge as it focused on its single mission.

"Please, God, save us! Save us all!" Jack pleaded with his Lord.

A Lord who must have been busy somewhere else that night.

As Jack's hand instinctively went to the throttle, the whole world went dark.

Disgusted with himself
It was the day after the storm in the Hotel Florida, Havana, Cuba. The sky was a clear blue colour. With his nightmares fading to

whispers, they eventually disappeared from his head as airman Joel Biggs started his daily work schedule. He had a throbbing headache. Maybe getting busy would help him resist imagining what had happened further north of Havana, across the Straits of Florida, but he knew better. Joel found his boss in the aircraft hangar, smoking and slurping his thick, molasses-style coffee at his desk.

"Senior Miguel, I'm quitting. I need to go back to Key West and Miami. I need to see how my buddies have survived that storm. I'll return in June next year."

"Senior Biggs, you leave now, before the end of this season of storms and hurricanes, and you will leave us forever. We get someone else tomorrow. Don't bother coming back to us. You wanna go or stay senior?"

Joel stared at a future of scratching around for a job as a pilot in Florida. How many jobs would there be? He stood still, considering the disruption to his current lifestyle – half his year in Havana and half in Miami and Key West – and saw the half smile coming from the other side of the desk. Defeated in every way, Joel Biggs left the office and resumed his daily maintenance and instructing routines. He wasn't a man who could throw away this easy life, even when it was the noble thing to do. He was disgusted with himself.

A Gentle Hand
Now conscious and still holding Myron as tightly as possible, Kimbo realised he was tangled in a mangrove clump. Most of his body was entwined below sea level, and severe cramps had set in. Although stunned and temporarily deafened, Kimbo had been freeing them both when the colossal wave tore through the Windley Key area, three miles from the storm's giant centrifuge. The wave smashed into Kimbo and Myron, propelling them out of the mangroves, as the sea angrily snatched debris that didn't

belong in its waters and tossed it aside. Kimbo fought with all his strength to keep them both afloat. He was gulping seawater, his arms thrashing, left then right, as he desperately fought to keep Myron's head above water. Although exhausted, he was determined that Myron was going to live. He felt asphalt under his feet as he was dragged along, a road skimming his flesh. It was soon to be over. Fate would either leave them to die or, somehow, leave them to survive. Fate didn't care which; it just continued its path, sure of itself. Father and son were swilling around with no control, scraping knees, elbows, face and any part that touched the ground. Suddenly, the surge stopped. It was gone, and the surface of the sea was flat. It was over. The strength and power of the wave had moved on. The flood bled slowly away.

Kimbo didn't know, but they had landed in the middle of a stretch of the newly built highway, just north of Snake Creek and next to the railroad embankment. It was a stretch of road he had helped lay and was the highest point on the Windley Key. The water level continued lowering its hem back into the sea mass. It was as if a hand had guided Kimbo and Myron through this hell and then gently set them down in the best place it could find among the mass destruction. Kimbo sat bolt upright, trying to make sense of something that didn't make sense. His eyes were open, but his mind could only see Zella and Zakari. Their faces faded into the black night. Ripped from him, from his life, and tragically ripped from life itself.

He frantically looked at Myron.

"Son, are you okay? Are you awake? Speak to me!"

Myron lay still.

Chapter Four
Purvis Helps Elizbeth

New York City, 1935
The early morning sun pierced the pocked and thin curtain, squeezing inside his eyelids. Like every other morning, Juan Sanchez woke in the middle of his sagging mattress. He had no idea that later that day he would be the trigger for ten thousand people rioting for two days with one hundred and twenty-five people arrested, more than one hundred injured, and three people lying dead. Juan was twelve, a black Puerto Rican and a petty thief. It was a way of life, and he knew little else. As he left and walked past his mother's doorless bedroom. He checked and found that, as usual, she was absent.

The dime store owner had seen Juan before, and although he couldn't prove it, he told police later that he was "dam sure Juan had stolen from my shop on at least three previous occasions, but I got no evidence."

That morning, he'd watched Juan slip a small penknife from a shelf to his pocket by a swift, practised method. He grabbed the boy's collar and took Juan into the backroom, locking him in. By the time the police arrived, a large crowd had gathered outside. Fearful of what the crowd might do, the owner asked the police to let Juan Sanchez go – with a warning. Reluctantly agreeing, the officers took his name and address, making clear what would happen to him should he be in trouble again. Juan fled as fast as his legs could run after the police slipped him out quietly through the backdoor into the alleyway. That was their big mistake.

No one told the crowd he'd been quietly released, and a rumour spread quickly that the all-white police officers had killed Juan. The swollen crowd erupted abruptly and violently, smashing shop fronts and looting their goods. Fuelled by economic hardship, racial injustice, and community mistrust, a riot started as residents fought the police. Thirty years earlier, Harlem had been a highly desired area, housing many affluent, prominent families. Now, it was a multicultural society, mainly African and Puerto Rican. Resentments had grown on both sides, and Juan Sanchez had unintentionally provided the spark that ignited the flames.

Racing away from the scene, Juan was shocked to see his ex-schoolteacher as he hurried to the park in Washington Heights to find his like-minded friends. No one was rioting in this park, but he knew parks weren't safe places for women. She was sitting alone, and he was immediately concerned. She was the only person who had helped Juan learn to read and write, and she had given him more caring and attention than he'd ever had from his absent father, self-indulgent and shameless mother, or any of his five older brothers.

"Miss Mitchell, please, you better get home from here. This ain't no place for a lady, and there is trouble in Harlem. It's gonna spill over, I reckon. Why are you crying, Miss Mitchell?"

"I'm okay, thank you. Please don't concern yourself."

Juan pointed to the best, safest way out of the area and escorted her out of immediate danger.

When Harlem and the surrounding area were under control the following day, Elizabeth Mitchell got the money she needed for the train fare and initial apartment rent for her to teach in Miami. Elizabeth had never experienced a sense of dread, economic hardship, or impending harm. She knew much more about children like Juan Sanchez than her social peers living nearby, wealthy Washington Heights. She understood how their limited lives played out every day. As a result, she was an outstanding teacher.

Elizabeth grew up in the sparsely populated and luxurious neighbourhood of the New York borough of Manhattan, with middle-class parents of Irish-Scots heritage. They were proud of their daughter for pursuing a teaching career and, in theory, having socially responsible views. They would have preferred her teaching at a private school but admired her… "willingness to help educate the less fortunate…" as her pompous father would say to his friends. His attitude started changing when the growing Hispanic and African American populations overflowed from Harlem, slowly integrating with the rest of Manhattan. Whenever Elizabeth overheard her father talking pretentiously about her, she would tackle him later. She had a mild, easy-going temperament but wouldn't tolerate this.

"These children are as bright as any, anywhere, Father. What they lack is opportunities, and those opportunities come from education and acceptance. This is what I think my purpose is. I want to help them see opportunities and behave in a way that will allow them to get accepted. My job is not to be righteous and self-congratulating about my helping the less fortunate, as you so patronisingly put it!"

"Look here, my girl, you are gifted and well-educated. You could go into business and make so much more money than drifting around thinking you can help these people!"

She looked at her father without uttering another word. She knew he didn't understand her or her ambitions. He probably never would. He didn't understand why money wasn't the driving factor in her life. *Why couldn't she be more like me?* he thought as they stared at each other without blinking.

Elizabeth had been left to fend for herself when the Mitchell family moved to Long Island. She was happy in Washington

Heights and wholly dedicated to the school where she taught. She knew how much joy it gave her to teach children of low-income parents. She knew this joyfulness was the most fulfilling emotion she'd ever had. Whether the children had Polish, Puerto Rican or African backgrounds, she could see that providing primary education gave life-enhancing opportunities. It was clear to her that reading, writing, understanding and using numbers created opportunities for them in their district. She had seen some success, although limited, with several of her students landing jobs that they would not have got otherwise. Problems started to grow when those chances died out for everyone. The Great Depression meant that black people would be the last to be hired and the first to be fired. It laid bare the inequalities in most parts of New York, festering barely under the surface.

Elizabeth had lost her job and was walking, taking time to think, when she saw a fast-moving Juan Rodriguez. At that time, she had been angry at the state government for routinely neglecting public schools and the associated neighbourhoods. They were often the last on the list to be repaired or funded fully, but "times are hard," they repeated. Yes, for the poor of the neighbourhood, she stated in her letter to city hall.

Now out of work, Elizabeth saw an advertisement for teachers in Miami and wrote to the contact, given simply as "Purvis." She didn't know much about Florida, only vaguely thinking it was multicultural. That appealed to her, from little she knew, and sounded like an exciting opportunity; how different could it be? Purvis wrote back, saying she could start immediately after arriving in Miami. She was excited!

She knew the discussion with her parents would be difficult. She had to endure the "I told you so" lecture her father gave her about how "Washington Heights was going to the dogs" and "Public schools were no place for a well-brought-up and intelligent young lady like you." The Harlem riot shocked her father. A silence hung over their relationship. She loved her parents but hated their reasons for moving to Long Island, as it exposed deep prejudices she hadn't seen in them before. However, she remained tight-lipped, aware of needing them, especially now. The conversation became complicated when she asked if they could lend her money. Her mother was secretly supportive but didn't say so. She knew her father was irritable and difficult but never mean. Eventually, he conceded, granting her a "loan." He swallowed his desire to force Elizabeth into his world of money-making.

Miami

On April 15th, Elizabeth arrived at the central Miami train station as arranged to meet the man who had offered her the job. Walking out into the warm and humid late afternoon, she saw a man holding a poorly written name painted on a torn piece of cardboard. It was upside down and read 'Elissabet Mischell'. She waved. He took her to another street corner, where a tall, bulky man stood holding out his hand in a warm welcome. His eyes flashed quickly. His skin was dark ebony.

"Pleased to meet you. I am Purvis."

Nobody would ever know his last name, and if anyone thought of trying to find out, they would discover he didn't have or need one. Elizabeth smiled warmly and shook his huge hand.

"Well, Missy Elizabeth Mitchell, how would you like me to call you?"

"Please, Elizabeth will do just fine. Thank you, Mister Purvis."

"Okay, well, it's just Purvis. Everybody knows me as Purvis."

They sat on a street bench as the noisy traffic passed by.

Purvis outlined the job and the basic rate of pay, which was considerably less than she had hoped.

"I can see you a little disappointed, Elizabeth. I want to explain. You'll be teachin' just black kids."

"That isn't a problem for me at all." She quickly wanted to put his mind at rest.

"Elizabeth, you get paid by me after I get donations from folks you'll never meet. I can never be sure just how much I'm gonna raise. You'll be teaching in 'Colored Town' here in Miami. That's a black-only part of town..." Purvis paused, "...it's against the law for a white person to teach black kids. I'm doin' my best to find ways to get kids some education here. I ain't intendin' to trick you, Elizabeth."

Purvis explained why it would be against the law. In her conversation with him, she realised Purvis was involved in many facets of how Miami worked. However, it became clear that his well-intentioned activities were mainly illegal. Elizabeth needed clarification. How could teaching children be unlawful?

"Wid respect Elizabeth, this ain't no New York. City. You find there's maybe a lotta things you don't know about livin' down here. I can pay you, and I've told you the minimum I can pay, and, sometimes, it's gonna be a lot more. I just can't promise more."

"Purvis, it's not the money. I can't live in Miami with laws like this. I could never do anything against the law. But, Purvis, how is it you can read and write? How did you get taught?" She asked politely.

"I know people, big-shot white people. Let's say they know what I know about them. It's a sorta partnership. They do things for me, and I return the favour. They got me learning. It was in their interest. I do things in their interest, and they do the same."

He smiled in a friendly but also slightly unsettling way. It was a complicated facial expression, but he did not aim to scare Elizabeth. Instead, he used his usual well-practiced expression to reinforce an important point.

She thanked Purvis but explained that she would not break the law.

"The job you offer genuinely appeals to me, but I couldn't see it would last long. If there were ways I could teach without breaking the law, then I would surely do it. Anyway, how long would it be before someone, somewhere, would discover me?"

She smiled gently. He respected her point and honesty but noticed her uneasiness as she spoke.

"Now, I have no money to return to New York. I have nowhere to go anyway, even if I did." Immediately, he saw her problem.

"I have some ideas for you. There's a place a short ride away where I know they are always looking for teachers, and they'll pay better than me, that's for damn sure! Oh, I'm so sorry, Missy."

After giving her the details, he smiled in that slightly unnerving but friendly way. He shook her hand and walked to his favourite bar in the black part of town, still thinking about how to employ a teacher. She had known Purvis for less than an hour, but somehow, strangely, Elizabeth trusted him.

By May 1935, Elizabeth had begun to teach at an all-white school in Everglades City. Too proud to tell her parents of her mistake, she had surprised herself at taking risks and began to like where she now lived and the poor white children she taught.

Elizabeth was determined to find a way to circumvent the law and the system of racial segregation without breaking the law. She could not possibly have guessed how positive an influence she would be on many people's lives. Her determination would change their opportunities.

Everglades City
By Monday, September 2nd, everything changed anyway.

Mercifully, the eye of the storm had passed more than sixty miles south of Everglades City. Elizabeth Mitchell peered through her window. There was stronger light pouring in than she was used to. She noticed the Gumbo Limbo tree had a large branch snapped at the joint with the trunk. Several palmetto clumps looked like wrecked scarecrow figures. Pushing her door hard against bush fragments, loose coconuts and a mess of every kind of wilderness foliage, she walked out into the bright, sunny morning. The storm was over, and she was grateful that her house was only superficially damaged. It would only take a day to put it right.

She was relieved. Never had she experienced a storm anywhere near the ferocity of last night's hurricane. New York had extreme weather, hot and cold, from time to time, but the power she experienced last night was another world. She felt proud that she had survived it. Sitting alone in the darkness during the night, listening to sounds she'd never heard before or wanted to hear again, she knew she had to defy whatever would challenge her. She went from being convinced she was about to die and then wanting to return to her parents at the first opportunity, but then realising that if she could survive this storm, she could survive anything. The school had provided her with a house; she was lucky, and it was as solid as they come in this part of Florida. Then she stopped thinking about herself; someone somewhere had had it worse.

Elizabeth immediately looked towards the rear of her house

through what used to be thick, tall bushes and clumps of trees. A black family had been living in a run-down, barely held-together wooden and reed building. It was more like a shack than a house, but it was home to a family she knew well and was fond of visiting. That shack was gone. No sign of the family. It was as if there had never been anyone living there – no trace of anything but a flattened and battered grass patch.

Looking up the road towards Everglades City, she could see that most buildings were damaged but not catastrophically. It was a storm that had battered but not beaten them.

Chapter Five
Natures Mockery

Dawn broke on the Matecumbe Keys. There was silence where birdsong should be bursting out. The sky was clear, clean and unblemished. It was pure blue. The sun rose, covering the barren landscape with heat and gentleness. The sun is always at its hottest immediately after a hurricane.

Jack Root struggled to get up from the locomotive cab's floor. His head was pounding where it had hit hard against the handrail installed at the side of the cabin. He realised his left leg was pinned under his fireman's body. His right leg twisted sideways and next to the train master, whose head lay on the floor, bleeding slightly from his ears and nose. Jack's body was racked with pain, and it was hard to tell where he hurt most. He was dazed and befuddled. Eventually, he pulled his leg away, stirring the fireman to come out of his coma slowly. Jack shouted in pain as he turned his left leg into a more natural position. His knee was in agony. Crouching, he looked out from the cab at the desolation before him.

The island had been fatally cleansed. The colossal wave had swept over the island, clearing homes, barracks, packing sheds, palm trees, mangroves, gulf weed and all human life before it. There were dead bodies everywhere. All eleven train cars had been lifted fifty yards from the tracks and scattered like children's toys. They lay on their sides, some carriages still loosely connected to others, some not. They lay untidily like a cut-up snake, its' body in zigzagged pieces. Only Jack's 'Old 447' stood upright on the tracks, still connected to the train's tender. It had saved the lives of all three occupants of the cab. Designed for workhorse duty, not elegance, the massive engine stood defiantly, as if indestructible.

Jack looked down onto the devastated land. Tears streamed down his caked and smudged face. Eventually, he just leaned and looked. The scene was incomprehensible, with his mind confused and his leg in pain. As a naturally religious man, he found it impossible to understand why this had happened.

After five minutes, the fireman approached Jack and looked at the scene. Then, a minute later, with blood trickling from his ears and nose, the train master joined them. No one spoke. The sun rose further in a cloudless sky, rapidly bringing warmth to the silence.

"The storm…it's over," mumbled the fireman, speaking one clear word at a time. It was over for hundreds of men, women and children. It was over for the inhabitants and habitats throughout the Middle Keys. It was also over for the railroad.

Jack Root tried to walk down the ladder, but his knee was twisted, and he was in unrelenting agony. He wanted to go to the cars to help those that had survived. Instead, the fireman carried him down the steps and laid Jack out as comfortably as he could make him on soft, wet sand, soil, and weed dumped there from a deep part of the seabed.

"Jack, stay there. I'll be back once I've seen what's happened." Bill Walker, the fireman, struggled to speak but did his best to ensure his train driver rested.

Jack dropped unconscious or asleep; it would be hard to tell just by looking at him. The fireman walked to the passenger cars. What he saw struck him so powerfully that he dropped to his knees. The carriages were water-filled coffins of trapped people, hundreds of people. The vast wave had crashed through the glass windows as if it wasn't there. Those poor souls, just moments before thinking they had been rescued, lay tossed around where they had struggled against each other to get out. The fireman frantically searched each car, shaking any bodies he thought might have some life left. They were all dead. All heavy with water, each a heavy, dead weight. He could see that all the railway cars must have been filled instantly with water. The flying glass from the windows had severed limbs from the force of the water. The people perished there, not knowing what was upright, upside down or sideways. They had enough time to inhale a lungful of air before the wave hit. Whichever decision they made to try and save themselves in those precious few seconds ended in futile panic, drowned in the massive volume of smothering, suffocating seawater.

Bill Walker braced himself and walked to the end of the sprinkled line of carriages. Here, in the baggage cars and boxcars, the black wall of water had blasted open the vast doors. Half the vets must have been washed out of the gaping, open sides. They were flushed into the storm-tossed sea, where they died a more hopeless death. Splashing aimlessly for a few minutes, cruelly fooled that they might be saved somehow.

Jack Root woke suddenly. He took a little time to remember where he was and what had happened. His knee was the first thing to remind him. He looked up at the colossal, black engine he loved so much. It stood solidly, defiantly, boldly alone, disobeying nature's power. It was the only thing for forty miles that had stood its ground. Jack saw that the track on either side of his 'Old 447' train had been ripped and tossed away. The seawater had drained, mostly leaving desolation. He could see no bushes, trees, or houses from where he lay.

He called out for his fireman Bill Walker and the train

master. No answer. He lay still, trying to build strength to raise himself. Finally, the train master appeared at the top of the iron ladder and slowly lowered himself, taking each step carefully as if confused by the movement of his legs. The giant wave's impact had muddled his balance, and he felt dizzy descending the ladder. He walked unsteadily towards Jack, seemingly unsure about his direction and dropped hard onto the ground, face first, dead.

Later, Doc Slim would diagnose a cerebral haemorrhage, causing a severe stroke. A blood vessel had burst and flooded his brain following a massive blow to his head, a similar cause of death to many storm victims. Jack saw blood oozing from the train master's ears; his eyes were bloodshot. He could do nothing for him; he knew nothing could be done. He involuntarily shook his head and said a few words: a prayer. Jack's faith was being seriously tested.

Jack saw someone walking towards the engine.

"Bill, thank God you're okay. What's happening? What have you seen? What can be done? We need to find a way of getting hold of our people in Miami. We must help the injured."

Jack waited. Bill was not a well-educated man. Jack could see the white face of a shocked man, his mouth opening and then closing. It took ten full minutes before he started to tell Jack some of the details. It was always the details that conveyed the most. The details about death stay longer in the mind.

Tears were streaming down both their faces. The last train to paradise was a rescue train that had become eleven large coffins spilt over on their sides. They both realised at that point that driving their train down to Islamorada had only provided huge cages that acted as traps, not life-saving help. They had been too late to save anyone. Jack Root and Bill Walker would have to wait to be rescued. They sat close to each other, feeling helpless, with deep feelings of guilt. Uncharacteristically, Bill hugged Jack.

Theirs was a pang of unusual guilt; it brought an unjust feeling. A type of guilt that embeds itself inside failed rescuers' souls.

The full force of nature's scorn was laid bare, waiting for those coming to help sort out the carnage in the next few days. A short distance from the vets' flimsy tents and poorly built shacks stood the Millionaires Club, formed by eleven New York Cotton Exchange members. This exclusive club was limited to just those eleven men. The storm and the tidal wave had destroyed the club, well-built houses, and a water tower. The whole site was utterly wrecked beyond repair and washed clean – as if on purpose. It seemed as if someone had decided to prepare for something new, something different, but without permission.

The vets' tents were torn from their pegs like thin paper tissues and flung upwards to be ripped into shreds. The men too drunk, tired or stubborn to be lured to the train station were sucked up into the hurricane's giant vortex, thrown against any hard surface and splattered like rotten fruit or drowned by the tidal wave's rolling force. That night, nature took the same view of millionaires, the poor, the drunk, the shell-shocked, and the ordinary, everyday people going about their innocent lives. They were all treated as equals for the first time in their lives.

Homestead

Doctor 'Slim' Forsyth rose from his bed in Homestead and, after failing to reach the famous author by phone in Key West, walked over to the Homestead Baptist Church and rang the minister's doorbell. The doctor called people in Miami who would have followed the storm. He listened to them carefully and started forming a picture from the little they knew or had passed on. Doc Slim became deeply worried.

Eventually, the minister answered and saw Doc Slim standing anxiously at the door. The man of God had slept heavily and appeared groggy. He stank of bourbon. He had slept through the early evening and the whole night without waking once. The minister saw some effects of a nasty, late summer tropical storm around the church and the local community. Bushes were uprooted, and tree branches snapped, but nothing severe. The church building, however, was not so lucky. It was built in the classical style of pine shiplap boards. Its roof and sidewall were ripped, pummelled and torn apart.

"Minister, we have been lucky. As bad as it seems here, I've heard talk that the storm will have hit The Keys about mid-way. Islamorada or Marathon, somewhere in that area. As far as I know, there will be no medical people of any use down there, so I will be travelling with as many medical assistants and our residents as I can find whom I know to be useful and can patch up survivors. I'll call my medical contacts in Miami too. I will also ask Homestead folk to help in any way possible. We will have a lot of injured, sure enough. They will need help immediately for the treatment of severe injuries. We will all need to be vigilant in avoiding diseases and infections. We will bring as many injured as we can to our town. I would be very grateful if you could organise food and soup. Hopefully, the farmers who have benefitted from the railroad in our area will see a way to help the people running the railroad. They all know how much they have helped our town over these tough depression years. Can I please ask you to coordinate in town to help with nourishment and shelter for the injured? We'll need bedding or something on which the injured can lie down as they recover. Can you make the church hall and other church buildings available? Is it possible for you to help in this way?"

Shaking slightly, the minister immediately agreed. He was excited that he could do something practical for a change. His job was to teach the congregation what to think, feel and be afraid of. The prospect of helping people was exciting. But he was a little scared, not of the work and messy job of assisting people in healing and restoring their sense of well-being, but fearful of the questions he would be asked. Questions about God, nature and the dead. How would he explain what seemed inexplicable? He knew about the World War I veterans, the railroad maintenance crew and the hundreds of people who had made their homes in The Keys. What can I say about God, faith in God, or the punishment metred out by God's nature?

"I will do my best as you ask, Doc."

Weather Bureau in Miami and Jacksonville
The weathermen in Miami and Jacksonville were only making calls to each other. Thinking his head might be on the block, Fred Povey needed a consistent story from the bureau about what they had known about the storm in advance. The most important questions would be about the storm's direction; *why didn't they know how fast it had been travelling? What about wind speed and the size of the eye, and, therefore, how destructive it would be? Why were no warnings given on the likely loss of life and property?* The answers became embarrassingly obvious to bureau managers. They all agreed to stall the press and government interference – as they saw it. Fred Povey took the lead and started dictating the story and instructions on how they would all react. It was simple.

"We'll say our investigations are already underway. We must

be consistent with everything we say from now on; if you have any questions, refer them all to me." Fred Povey ended by shouting down the phone line from his quiet office in Jacksonville, aiming his comments, particularly at his contact in Miami. It was here that the newspapers would start asking their meddlesome questions.

"Do you all understand?" Nobody said a word in reply. "And you men in the Miami office better get to the storm area to scout for our information. We'd better get ahead of this before the press start making up their bullshit!"

Fred was interested in only one thing – keeping his job. If he could gather and keep all the information himself, he might be able to control the aftermath and public relations chaos that was bound to follow. The Miami weather boys spent the whole of Tuesday, September 3rd, forming a plan to protect themselves.

Still sitting five hundred miles from the action, Fred Povey called the major newspaper editors in Jacksonville and Miami towards the end of the day. He told the bureau's official story, which amounted to nothing.

"There will be a full-scale investigation into all the weather facts relating to the storm. As I speak, we have our best people on their way down there."

Fred knew that investigations of this type would typically take one to two years. He knew this approach was a gamble, but he was sure that in a month or two, coverage of this disaster would fade away, as so many had in the past. He remembered how the devastating hurricane of 1926 hit Dade County and the young city of Miami, which had a population of only a hundred thousand. He wrote on his pad three factors.

First, most deaths occurred in downtown Miami and The Bahamas Islands, where the population was black.

The second thing he wrote down was the Weather Bureau's

location. Just nine years before, storm warnings were centralised in Washington DC and disseminated to field offices like Miami. Many warnings should have been more specific and faster in reaching them, but they were not. Therefore, the local weather staff were off the hook.

Looting was the third and last factor that appeared on Fred's paper pad. The aftermath left chaos on the streets as people became desperate for clean water and food. Two hundred special police officers in Hollywood, Florida and three hundred in Miami were temporarily sworn in to quell rioting. This meant the looting was more newsworthy. Fred Povey looked at how those three factors, at that time, diverted attention from the plain, obvious truth that the bureau was still totally inadequate to forecast and warn the rapidly growing populations of South Florida of looming, catastrophic storms.

Fred needed his own three factors that would once again hide the current inadequacies of the weather bureau in a sub-tropical climate. He wrote down his three on a new piece of paper. Firstly, the destruction of a railroad that had always made a financial loss. Secondly, the political status of the World War I veterans, and third, the relatively low level of property damage. After all, The Keys were the back of beyond and the middle of nowhere. Newspapers would move quickly to these more exciting topics. Weather forecasting wasn't going to be top of anyone's mind, he hoped. Fred Povey's strategy was clear – delay and obfuscate. Confessions and plain truth about the bureau wouldn't help those people in the Florida Keys now. He had to think about the future, his future. It was obvious.

During the immediate future, Fred Povey's phone laid off the hook – for the following three days.

Ernest travels north
Hemingway spent that Tuesday making sure his beloved *Pillar* was safe and undamaged; it was. He started putting his house in

order, taking down the boarding from the window shutters, clearing the ground around the house, and his studio of the flotsam and jetsam scattered by the storm. He found coconuts floating in his swimming pool. Young, green, hard coconuts flung from the bunches nestling at the top of the palms. He could see how fatal these would be flying at over 100 mph. Some he found smashed against his newly built walls. They had knocked out chunks of mortar and brick as they hurled through the night air. The side separating his house from next door, consisting mainly of huge tropical vegetation, had been wrecked. The giant leaves of his banana trees, silver Bismarck palms, and giant rhubarb plants were torn to shreds. He looked around and felt shocked; his lips moved in a whisper.

"If this is what the storm has done here, what horrors will we find in the mid-keys?"

He wanted to do something rather than sit around wondering and listening to radio broadcasts that would be pretending to know what had happened. He'd tried to call Doc Slim in Homestead, but all the phones were dead.

Before dawn that Tuesday morning, Hemingway walked around the old town, finding as many people as he knew, asking for news about the storm. He was primarily interested in the conditions between Key West and Key Largo. He convinced ten volunteers to prepare to go north with him the following day, Wednesday.

"And we need your boats; the bigger, the better."

Word got around, and by daybreak, he had twenty more who volunteered to go with them.

"I want you to be prepared to be shocked," Ernest told all of them in his attempt to warn them.

His war experience told him there could be no preparation for what they might find.

No shelter from the storm

In Miami, the Florida East Coast railroad's Ben Coleman didn't sleep that Tuesday night. Questions were running through his head. Finally, he got up from his dishevelled bedding, most tossed on the floor, from Ben's restless mind and his bedroom's humidity. It was early, but he immediately organised a gang of FEC railroad workers with pick-up trucks to go down to The Keys. He sat in the cab of the first truck. He wanted his men to be first on the scene. He had an overwhelming sense of responsibility for Jack Root, Bill Walker and other crew members he'd sent to rescue the vets and residents. Even in Miami, he had heard the howling wind and thrashing rain all night. He tried not to think about how the veterans' flimsy tents and appallingly frail sheds would have fared overnight.

Ben Coleman's convoy found themselves following Doc Slim's Homestead helpers. Some miles behind them were the agents from the weather bureau getting ready to fill in their special weather charts. Their anemometer, wind vane, pressure sensor, thermometer, hygrometer, and rain gauges were all in place along the main islands of The Keys. The weathermen were excited about what readings they would find, as crude as they might be. Will we find that extreme weather records were broken? Will we find destruction not seen or documented before? It didn't dawn on them that most instruments would not have survived. Sent to perform a weather audit of the tragedy, they were excited about what they might find.

It took most of the day for Doc Slim's party to reach Snake Creek and the bridge to Windley Key. What delayed them was not only the trees, bushes, roofing, building parts, dead pelicans, buzzards, turkey vultures, racoons, heaps of fish, and an odd dolphin on the road but also every other kind of storm debris found in this part of the world. The dead bodies caused the most delays.

At first, and at a distance, there seemed to be only broken

rock, fallen debris, rubble, and twisted rail. But when doc got closer, he saw the dead. Some were lodged high up in what trees were left standing. The corpses were lying face down or face up along the shoreline. Doc found one man alive with a piece of 'four by two' timber from a house somewhere sticking out from beneath his ribcage. It had missed all his major organs, but he could only take short, rapid breaths, sucking them into his chest.

"What can I do for you, son?" asked Doc Slim. "I have some morphine to help you with your pain. I'll get this out for you, but don't move."

"Don't pull it out yet. No morphine. Save it. I want two beers, Doc."

Doc got two beers from the supplies they had brought with them. The fatally injured man drank one beer and passed out. Doc didn't even know his name. At least he had to try and save him. As doc pulled out the splintered wood, the man died. The nameless victim knew he had no chance of surviving his wound. Doc looked at the sheer humility of that man.

Doc's convoy had stopped instinctively every time they saw a body or cluster of bodies. He started to smell the dead and watched as the blowflies massed in swarms around them, the humidity fermenting the corpses. Decomposition started, accelerated by the day's heat rising past ninety degrees. Doc Slim decided he had to move on quickly, knowing he needed to be where most survivors were – stopping at every prostrated body holding up his convoy. He would be needed everywhere, so he decided to press on. He began to expect mass carnage. He steeled his mind to deal with whatever he found; he knew he would soon have to start setting priorities for himself and his medical entourage – prioritising would be the toughest part.

Ben Coleman's FEC convoy caught up with the medical

team from Homestead, and the whole convoy of vehicles moved together with a single purpose: to reach Islamorada train station. Doc Slim, the first medic in South Florida to respond, led the way.

All told, five convoys set off for the middle keys that day: Doc Slim and his medical assistants and volunteers from Homestead; the Ben Coleman FEC railroad team; the weather bureau's agents; the individual collections of newspaper reporters; and Ernest Hemingway's small boating fleet heading north from Key West. Only three of the five groups had the mission to save life or find as many bodies as possible for dignified committals. They were loaded with medical supplies, freshwater containers, and food. The mission of the other two groups was to provide information about what had happened. No one in any group was prepared for what they saw, what they heard and what they had to do.

Doc Slim's leading vehicle approached Snake Creek. He knew a small hospital had been set up primarily to care for the vets adjacent to the work camps. The physician, Dr Albert Ross, was an overworked general practitioner dedicated to patching the vets after drunken brawls and work-related injuries. Their mental state had always concerned 'Doc Alby' as the vets had dubbed him. The hospital was gone, and Doc Alby was nowhere to be seen. As he stood briefly staring out to sea, Doc Slim whispered to himself,

"Only God knows where he is, but if he is alive, we must work together."

As they came close to the gap between Plantation Key and Windley Key, unintentionally blocking the middle of the road was a big, powerful-looking man sitting bolt upright, holding a limp child in his large arms. He had no shirt or other clothes except ripped work shorts and no shoes. The child had a shirt and shorts torn to shreds but still worn over his body, making him look like a rag-doll; he had no shoes. About twenty yards behind them were two men lying together, arms wrapped around each other, seemingly unconscious. Doc Slim halted the line of vehicles and stepped onto the road.

It was Kimbo who sat upright with Myron in his arms.

"What's your name, son?"

Kimbo stared ahead into space, occasionally and slowly, blinking.

"Son, what's your name? Who are you? Where are you from?"

No response.

"Don't you even know your name?" Kimbo just stared at Doc Slim.

The doc put his hands out to examine Myron, and Kimbo jerked back to life. He snatched him away and held him tightly but stayed sitting as though he was immovable. All the others in Doc Slim's medical party stayed back, watching.

"It's okay, son. I'm a doctor. I want to look at your boy to see if I can help."

Kimbo had never had any contact with a doctor. He didn't know whether to trust him. Nobody except his family – no white man for sure, had helped him in his life up to that moment. Kimbo looked at his rag-doll son. He then looked at Doc Slim. He saw an honest, good man and handed the inert Myron over as softly as possible. Doc first looked at the boy's vital organs, looking for obvious signs of damage. He checked for breath, heartbeat, and eye movement. He gently pressed his kidney and liver to see if they were causing pain; they didn't. He signalled to a female medic to bring fresh water. Kimbo was offered it but signalled for Myron to take the first sip. Myron opened his eyes, and Kimbo opened his mouth and shouted silently.

Doc asked the woman to stay with them while he hurried over to the two men locked in mutual protection. The men were conscious and talking while slowly and gently separating their bodies. They told doc their story, the older man, first. He spoke gently and quietly, as though he only wanted doc to hear his words. His irrational thoughts warned him that if he spoke too loudly or forcefully, the storm might come back to finish them off. His mind was numb; his head was ringing. He couldn't think straight. He told his story very slowly, as though he had rehearsed it, which he hadn't. He just knew what to say.

"Our whole family, includin' cousins and their folk, fifteen of us decided to stay in our house and see this son-of-a-bitch out. But the walls were shaking; the roof started to vibrate. Then, the water started coming under the door and through the gaps in the walls. Because that goddamn howling wind was tearing everything apart outside, we decided to wait. We could hear all hell breaking loose out there. The house started to fill up, so Hank, here, my son, lifted one of the children so the water didn't swallow her up. I lifted another, and so did Jim-Bob and Lenny. We held them up for maybe fifteen or twenty minutes. It takes a lotta strength, I can tell ya. The water kept coming in and coming in, so we decided to risk the wind as we were all goin' crazy. We reckoned we'd all gonna drown anyway. We all got out, and then some crazy things happened. The wind whipped us up in the air, all of us folks. The child I had was gone from my grasp. The next thing I knew, black as ink everywhere, and I got spat out into a tree. I was upside down and tangled in the top somehow, lodged, but I couldn't move. Then this goddamn crazy wave came, faster than any train, straight at me. I didn't know where Hank was or any of our folks. That child I was holdin' could have gone anywhere. I couldn't do nothin'. That wave washed me here. God knows where my family is. I'm tellin' ya, there were fifteen of us all gathered in that place. Have you seen any of 'em?"

Doc Slim shook his head. He didn't know what to say. He asked Hank's father his name – something the father hadn't mentioned.

Hank's father looked blank.

Hank babbled, only trying to fill the difficult moment, worried at his father's confused state.

"My dad's name is Ed. Ed Watson. I'm Hank Watson. The folks in the house were all Watsons of some sort. I got sucked up in the vicious twister inside that fucking storm. Sorry, fer ma language doc. I don't know much about storms, but I tell ya, that ain't no normal goddamn storm. I got spat out like Dad but was on top of a clump of mangroves. I was knocked out for a while, but then this fucking…"

"Hey, Hank, hold your goddamn language in front of the Doc an' all!"

"Well, sorry, Doc, but this huge wave, I can't tell ya how big, but it was higher than the bushes, even the trees. I saw men who had tied themselves to the trees using their belts, halfway up or even some as high as the top. But this wave was maybe six feet higher than all of the trees. It smashed into me, took me; it felt like it hit at a hundred miles an hour. Anyway, it was goddamn moving apace. I had only just come to. I had to swim and fight to keep my head above the water. Eventually, I got washed up. Men were calling out to me for help. Some were shouting at me; some didn't have the strength even to do that, just waved limp arms as they were so weak. I wandered around, and then I saw this man barely able to walk coming along this road here. He was shouting at me for help. We looked at each other, and after a minute or two, I could see it was my dad. We hugged, and then he realised it was me, his son, Hank. We fell onto the roadside here and passed out where you found us. Doc, can you look and see if my dad's okay?"

Doc Slim quickly checked them both. Ed Watson needed treatment for bad cuts and a possible broken wrist. Hank needed treatment for a concussion, deep lacerations, and a fractured nose. He asked the woman medic looking after Kimbo and his son to put all four of them into the first vehicle. It was big enough only for the driver and those four survivors. The doc told the driver to put them in the Baptist Church hall. He said he'd attend to them later.

"In the meantime, give orders to someone in the hall to make them comfortable – food, water, and rest. Make 'em hot food and as much rest and sleep as possible. Their bodies need rest. Their minds will need peace," he said. "And then get back here, ready to take more to Homestead."

Doc realised he could not stop at each body he encountered. It took too long to check them and listen to every story. He needed to make quick and brutal assessments immediately and then send them to Homestead, where all the survivors would be treated. He had to make it to the Islamorada railway station to assess the anticipated carnage and try to save those from the brink of death.

Kimbo was hesitant, still in a shocked state of mind. Still clinging to Myron, it took the gentle medic more time than she had to convince Kimbo that, eventually, they would not be sent somewhere he didn't know or had no choice over. Kimbo wanted to walk around and look at everyone's faces. He wanted desperately to find his beautiful wife and daughter. Suddenly, a surge of emotion ran through his huge body. He stood still, involuntarily sobbing deeply into his massive chest, his chin almost touching it, his head nodding. His mind was spinning as if in its own swirling vortex, with visions of Zella and Zakaria appearing and fading.

Questions beat in his head like a mantra. He shouted, "Where are they? Why can't I find them? The sun shines, the sky is blue, and the sea is calm. They are missing. They are gone. I gotta find them. Where should I look? They must be somewhere; everybody gotta be somewhere!"

He looked at the beautiful, idyllic scene around them but only saw the devastation. Kimbo, a giant man, fainted; Myron saw his father crumble and start crying. What he saw frightened him. Myron's mouth opened as wide as it could, and the small boy screamed as hard and as loud as he could. He was calling out for his father to be helped, calling for his mother and sister in the only way he understood.

"Where is my sister?" His indecipherable scream pleaded with the sky. "I am missing half of me! Where is Zakaria? Where have you taken her? Why did you do it?"

His scream stopped, and he strained to listen for the answers that would never come.

The car took the four survivors away from the scene. The bruised and battered Kimbo, the shocked and frightened Myron, the injured Ed, and Hank Watson travelled northwards towards Homestead.

As his staring eyes watched the miles pass, Kimbo pledged never to set foot in the Florida Keys again. That pledge would be severely tested.

The bridge to Windley Key at Snake Creek was gone. The rail track was gone. There was no road to take the four southbound convoys onto the work camps, the packing sheds and

Islamorada residencies in the island's village. They could not reach the train by road. They would need boats to take them over the first significant open waterway to Windley Key and beyond.

Meanwhile, the rescue party from Homestead found every dead body on the north side of the missing bridge and lined them up in the area known as Little Snake Creek. Just two days previously, a picturesque place thick with sub-tropical vegetation, seagrape and mangroves. It was now scrubbed clean by the storm; not even a blade of grass was left. Now, it looked like an empty seabed.

The boats arrived, sent by the weather bureau, FEC railway offices and FERA authorities, and were immediately confiscated by Doc Slim and his medics, who were then bombarded by loud and threatening abuse.

"Our offices authorised these boats, and we are paying for them. We should be allowed to go about our business immediately!" they shouted their case to Doc Slim. "You can't just take our boats!"

The doc, getting short on patience, shouted, "I don't give a flying fuck. We are using these boats to save people, not to gather information about what fucking killed them! Or, come to that, I ain't worried about an old shit of a train either! Unless you want to add to the number of dead, I would step aside if I were you and let us go about the business of helping the living. Are any of you interested in helping?"

All the medics gathered there, and all the Homestead volunteers were stunned. They had never heard Doc Slim speak in anger, let alone curse words.

"OK, Doc, we'll be right behind you," one of the FEC teams shouted, and a group of helpers joined the medic team from their FEC boats. "Tell us how we can help."

No one from the weather bureau raised their hands. They

knew the newspaper boys would soon be swooping down like vultures, and no one wanted to answer their inevitable questions. Shell Dawkins would "go ape-shit" if that happened, and the weather crew was sure of that. They melted feebly away.

The doctor ordered the medical helpers onto the boats. They loaded as many supplies as possible and set off around Windley Key and onto Upper Matecumbe Key. Watching the weather bureau's boats launch themselves with the volunteer helpers aboard, one of the weather bureau men called after them.

"Yeah, well fuck you, we're just trying to do our jobs," but only loud enough for his weather bureau colleagues to hear him. The comment was like hissing in a thunderstorm.

Although he despised their attitude, Doc Slim briefly thought it was a great pity the weather bureau people were not on board and the first people to see the storm's destruction. Perhaps this might have focused them on improving their capability to forecast more accurately and save more lives – he knew it was needed.

"But now we must do our job. We all must do as best we can," he said out loud for all to hear.

Hemingway's flotilla arrived in the Lower Matecumbe Key, loaded with as much as the boats could store securely. They had packed food, fresh water, and medical items. Both sets of rescuers, now in the Upper and Lower parts of Matecumbe, set about identifying those who could be saved; many were close to dying. Those that were dead were to be dealt with later. Hemingway's group didn't have a doctor with them, but they did their best to stop bleeding and ease the survivor's pain until better help could reach them.

Sailing north from Key West, Hemingway's flotilla had expectations of helping people recover from a bad storm – mend buildings, supply food and nourishment, and help restore life to normal. Their expectations were quickly adjusted. They saw two women high up in a tree. Their bodies were naked. Their breasts were swollen abnormally. Flies were doing their unsightly worst. Hemingway recognised them as the two lovely women who ran the sandwich place and gas station three miles from where they were found. It had been a massacre that no witness had seen before. They just stood staring. The experience lived long, etched in everyone's mind, including, indelibly, in Hemingway's memory. Even the Nobel Prize-winning author had not seen atrocities like this; his time in Italy during World War 1 had not exposed him to such intense devastation of humans in one place. Nor would his experience later, as a war correspondent assigned to the Spanish Civil War, be as shocking as this. Widely regarded as conservative politically, Hemingway shocked a few people by writing a no-holds-barred description two weeks after the storm in *New Masses,* a left-wing magazine with politically left leanings within highly influential, intellectual circles. In Hemingway's article titled *"Who Murdered the Vets?"* he attacked both President Hoover and Roosevelt for personally knowing not to visit Florida in the summer months but, in turn, sent the vets to do "coolie labour" for low wages to keep them out of Washington, where they couldn't make trouble. "...all they had to lose were their lives," Hemingway's article said. The article, containing graphic and vivid descriptions, was the only detailed publication of this human disaster. In the magazine's opinion, no other mainstream newspaper would publish it because it was too real and challenging for readers. Hemingway left his home in Key West in 1939, four years later.

On arrival at the beach nearest to the Islamorada station, Doc Slim noticed about twenty bodies floating in the swill of the small docking area. They had already become bloated with seawater. The flyblown bodies were grotesquely swollen, making the remaining clothes on the bodies rip at the seams. Those bodies were beginning to stink badly. No one could tell if they were bodies of residents or vets. What did it matter? Some had their faces stripped down to the bone by the wind blasting sand into them as they lay dying or dead. Nearer to the Islamorada station, they saw limbs that had been torn from many torsos. Coconuts hurling through the air like cannonballs had smashed people's heads clean off their shoulders. Men were decapitated by flying tin from roofs and walls. Bodies tangled in knots, their bones snapped in many places, their limbs dislocated, seemingly elasticated by the wind. Everyone arriving in Doc Slim's first boats recognised the scene they were staring at; it was like a battlefield after the fighting. They felt as though they were standing in an open-air abattoir.

After half a day of intensive toil, Doc Slim's workload eased. More doctors and medical volunteers eventually arrived from the more affluent parts of Miami, such as Coconut Grove and Coral Gables. On arrival, doctors felt a deep despair at the human catastrophe that had enveloped the Matecumbe Islands. Their shock was palpable. They could see the survivors' distress and anguish and the profound shock of the volunteers' arriving at the various horrific scenes of destruction of people and property. They also saw the effect it had on Doc Slim. A weaker man than doc would have been overwhelmed by the sight of the storm's cruel slaughter. Occasionally, he just stood and cried and then got on with his tasks.

Trauma can visit anyone sooner or later.

PART TWO
Decisions

Chapter Six
Acceptance Comes in Different Forms

Kimbo and Myron found themselves in the large Baptist church hall next to Jack Root and Bill Walker. Hank and Ed Watson were on the opposite side of the hall. That Wednesday night, everyone in that hall slept more deeply than at any other point in their lives – all except Kimbo. He fell asleep with his eyes open, causing Jack to panic, thinking he had passed away.

Jack thought, *is he asleep or dead?* As he touched him to take his pulse, Kimbo jumped bolt upright onto his feet in one powerful movement. He was hallucinating. In his head, yet again, were the images of Zella and Zakari being pulled away from him into the darkness. Kimbo was clawing the space before him, trying to hold on to them but snatching at the air instead. As physical and mental exhaustion hit him once again, he slowly folded himself to the floor, softly but securely, gently clutching the sleeping Myron in his arms. The Baptist Hall fell silent once more. Praying for the missing was the only thing left for them to do.

Myron was still sleeping, curled foetus-like. Kimbo twitched and muttered on the floor, suddenly waking in panic. His instincts returned, and he looked around the hall for food and water. They had shelter, but they had nothing else, not even clothes. Two volunteer helpers, women, had been watching and cautiously approached. Myron had been miraculously spared bad injuries but was traumatised. He repeatedly asked his father for his mother. Kimbo didn't answer. The two women calmly and gently gained their confidence. They fussed over Myron and spent the rest of the day getting him enough of the right food. He looked longingly at them, but they weren't his mother.

Over three days, Doc Slim's rescue workers searched and recovered those still alive and every dead body within sight. Some dead were still lying on the ground or in the denuded trees. Some tangled in shrubs or mangroves. Some lay in seawater on the shoreline, the bodies being investigated and gently nibbled by rays and hogfish snapper. The fish had returned. Some people were found alive, their heads held above seawater by the web of mangrove branches and shoots. Some were found drowned, their heads held under the seawater by the same mangrove branches. It had been a game of chance. The mangroves themselves were stripped clean of the tree crabs and marine organisms. Doc Slim was the last to arrive back in Homestead.

Kimbo asked everyone who entered the hall if they had seen Zella or Zakari. He described them in detail, giving their ages and features. With tears streaming down his face each time, the answer was always the same.

Doc Slim took it upon himself to immediately walk into the church hall. There was no need to delay what he had to say. After asking for quiet and the attention of all those conscious and awake, he raised himself on a table to make an announcement. He felt he should say something. It was something nobody wanted to hear.

If not me, then who will say it out loud? It must be said.

Doc spoke in deafening silence.

"Folks, all survivors have been found. The folks we have found who have passed on have been laid out ready for coffins to be brought from Miami and other nearby towns. This will take a while. Meanwhile, the Federal Government will take the deceased vets to Washington for internment in the Arlington Cemetery..."

Doc was cut short. Shouts went up, "Where is Jake?"

"I want to know about Maisie..."

"...I have five brothers. Are they safe?"

He was drowned out by the injured, wanting to hear about each missing family member...*Were they safe? Were they injured?* Kimbo was among them; he was the loudest voice. Kimbo knew it would be a miracle, and, as far as he knew, miracles never happen; for sure, he knew they didn't happen for him.

Doc held his hand up and waited. Eventually, the shouts died down. The only sound came from people whimpering and sobbing at a low level.

"By my reckoning, roughly two hundred survivors were brought here to Homestead – those of you in the hall now total one hundred and eighty-six. The rest are being treated and cared for by our local folks, who are looking after them in their homes. They are the survivors with the most severe injuries. Some will make it through; some won't. The Lord is watching over them."

Doc looked at the Baptist minister, crouched over someone, pretending to help with their wounds and be seen as busy. The minister ignored Doc Slim's opportunity to speak, giving solace and comforting words from his preaching. After a long pause, looking directly at the now-frozen minister, Doc spoke again.

"Other survivors who were pretty much unharmed have drifted off somewhere. Who knows where? As far as I can make out, the people organising the funerals have an impossible job of knowing how many were killed or, I'm afraid to say, even who they were. Maybe five hundred have died, maybe more. We know the bodies of the vets piled up for shipping to Washington roughly total about two hundred. It could be a lot more. No one knows for sure yet. So far, folks who were Keys residents have a body count of about the same. From what I can gather, some important people in the state capital reckon it'll end with more than half the population between Miami and Key West being lost to this storm. My guess is we'll never know, and I'm sorry, folks, but my thinking is perhaps…" Doc paused… "and I know this will be tough for each of you to come to terms with, but…" He paused again and took a slow but full breath in. "My guess is we'll never find those good folks who are currently missing." He stopped talking.

The room went deathly quiet. Jack and Bill looked at Kimbo. His head hung so low that his bristled chin nearly brushed his breastbone. Three or four children were breaking the silence. They were crying out from pain or trauma or just missing a Mum, Dad, brother or sister and didn't know where they were. Doc Slim walked out of the Baptist Hall. There was nothing more he could or wanted to say – and the severely injured needed him elsewhere.

Kimbo sat submerged in silence. He thought of Zella and Zakari. He looked up at the high ceiling and started whispering out loud.

"Lord, are you there? If you are there, can you find a way for me to do this? Tell me now. How am I supposed to live without Zella? Without little Zakari? I bin lovin' them for so long, Lord. They were what I bin livin' for. How can I live now they gone? How am I supposed to carry on?"

He continued to whisper out loud, prayer-like, as if God might happen to overhear and help him – help all the folk suffering loss or pain. His thoughts flowed as clearly as a freshwater stream.

For Zella to die is bitter and cruel. But the idea that Zakari should die without having lived is unbearable.

He talked, his words coming as if God were encouraging him...

"I just can't escape my feelings, but we can somehow live lives for both. Myron got his whole life to live. We are obliged to live our best lives. This is how I want us, Myron and me, to live. I will find a quiet place. Somewhere where nobody gonna hurt us. I will do this for Zella and Zakari. They gonna be proud of Myron. God, if you are there, show me my way."

Kimbo continued to look up at the invisible heaven. "Zella, I pledge to you that I will give Myron the best possible life I can provide."

As he stared upwards, with the images of Zella and Zakari repeatedly disappearing into the black void, Kimbo Hopper didn't realise that his pledge was overheard. Jack Root was awake with his eyes closed. Jack Root had never known the responsibility that comes with deep love. He opened his eyes and looked at Kimbo. He could see how much pain he was in. Witnessing such deep love was both beautiful and rare in Jack's life. But he also saw how its loss was indescribable torture. Jack, a hard-working, God-fearing and even-tempered man, felt angry that God had gone missing for so many people during that storm.

Bill Walker also overheard Kimbo's soft, painful words, but he wasn't thinking beyond what he should do next. Kimbo was in deep emotional pain; even a callous man would have acknowledged that.

Then, both men watched Kimbo Hopper's reality hit him – a new storm but familiar turmoil. He opened his lips to scream, but as usual, he kept his emotions trapped inside as prisoners. His massive shoulders moved up and down, his head nodding in suppressed grief.

Washington DC

The tragedy of the storm, particularly the destruction of the vets' work camps, filtered through to Washington and the Roosevelt administration. Accurate information was difficult to come by. *How many are dead? How many were injured? Who knew what? What could they do?*

The administration had already decided that all the vets killed by the storm would be buried in the Arlington National Cemetery as a fitting place to honour them. One of the top officials in the White House stood before the president. Both knew there was a major political embarrassment to avoid. The irascible press would feast for weeks on this catastrophe.

"Mr President, we have put together an announcement. This announcement would be a good distraction from uncomfortable questions about why around 650 World War I vets," he paused, "…and I can predict what some will latch on to…were sent to live in mosquito-infested, vulnerable and inadequate work camps, huddled together in flimsy tents and old wooden shacks, in a hurricane-prone area. When the press starts to dig, they will discover these vets had psychosis, self-destructive behaviour, sleep loss, and nightmares, leading to aggression, guilt and shame. From what I've managed to find out, the strong sense of survival, naturally present in almost all humans, was weak in most of these men and non-existent in some. We do not yet have the stats on the numbers…the dead, injured and missing. That is the first thing they'll expect us to know. We must divert attention away from why they were sent there and switch focus on how we now treat the victims."

The official delivered the reality they were facing with grim and pointed words. It took a few minutes before the president spoke. A plan was concocted, and it fell to the Department of the

Army to remove the bodies and prepare for their internment in Arlington. Washington wanted this tidied up quickly and relatively quietly. It had been a messy political sore for over a decade; it needed swift and delicate handling. This remote planning was to backfire.

In the end, five hundred and seventy-seven bodies were reported found, but, as Doc Slim had predicted, the total number of dead was never known. Like Zella and Zakari, those missing had been blown out to sea or dispatched to rot away on one of the hundreds of small islands of coral and islets of mangroves surrounding the middle keys. Their bodies were never recovered. Some were inevitably eaten by surviving alligators, crocodiles, barracuda and sharks. Even the alligator-snapping turtles gorged themselves with their powerful jaws. Most official figures coming from Washington and Tallahassee quote somewhere between four hundred and fifty and six hundred dead. Those figures were laughed at locally. Everyone knew that the number of vets posted to The Keys was never recorded accurately in the first place, and nobody knew how many people, like Kimbo and his family, had gone to work with the vets and lived alongside them. The number was probably around a thousand, but compared with other category four or five hurricanes, Washington considered it a stroke of luck that these casualties were not considered significant. It was the strength of the storm and the height and force of the tidal wave that the statisticians and press were excited about. What was accurately recorded were the thirteen vets who went AWOL in Key West. Staying away that Monday saved their lives. Lives that were to be constantly haunted by guilt. Survivors guilt.

A few days later, a hastily new meeting was arranged in the White House.

"Sir, Mr President, word has reached us that the bodies of the vets are rapidly decomposing from the heat and humidity. We now have the dilemma of what to do with the dead. The bloated bodies are too hideous to ship back on long train journeys, even in refrigerated trucks for interment in Arlington."

The meeting erupted.

"Is it possible to identify the vets separately from the locals?" came a question. The answer became obvious. The meetings' discussion leaked out. There was an uproar in the media. The newspapers pronounced their disgust. Afraid of an epidemic breaking out and further public outcry, one hundred and sixteen bodies were sent to Miami to be disposed of, issued by further decree by the federal government. But this move turned into another farce as the dead were burnt – heaped on large funeral pyres instead of burying them in graves. Repugnant and distraught, local Florida Keys relatives hopelessly tried to identify and then pull out their loved ones from the unlit pyre to give them a civilised way of laying them to rest. In the chaos, several clashes with police broke out. Headlines with photographs were sent to national editors, magnifying the revulsion the bureaucrats were trying to avoid. It could not have been handled any worse.

To add to the official's worries, Hemingway castigated the administration for sending the vets there in the first place. It was revealed why Jack Root's rescue train was not authorised until four thirty p.m. on the storm day. The devastating details all leaked out.

"The train could have been sent the day before," the headlines screamed. Fingers were pointing everywhere. Cover-ups were swiftly created. The FEC said it was because Washington's authorisation had come too slowly. The administration in Washington claimed it was because of budget arguments inside Congress. A spokesperson said the authorisation had run into admin "Snafus" – an obtuse politician's word for bureaucratic chaos and confusion. Fuelled by this rich tapestry of government nonsense, yet again, the press had a field day.

Sitting in his office in Jacksonville, Shell Dawkins was delighted with himself for anticipating what might happen. With silence and obfuscation, he avoided any fingers being pointed at the weather bureau and, more importantly, at himself. Shell kept his job.

The remaining bodies, primarily vets, were stacked into a series of funeral pyres at Snake Creek. Nobody wanted to take stinking bodies to Miami. Strangely, a military guard performed gun salutes over the coffins as the bodies lay waiting. Funeral pyres were considered the most practical way to dispose of the rotting bodies in a sub-tropical climate at its most hot and humid time of year.

Chapter Seven
A New Beginning

Jack Root looked at Kimbo's dazed eyes. Myron's face was vacant. The two men had talked over the three days they had lived side by side. From how Kimbo whispered his prayer just days previously, it was clear to Jack that vast and heavy guilt had set into Kimbo. It was intense, buried deep inside of him. Jack's guilt at surviving when his mission was to save hundreds of those people was a heavy burden. People lost or planned to be burnt or buried.

Kimbo had gradually assessed these two railroad men during this period. Jack Root was not quite as tall as Kimbo and not so muscle-bound, but he could see that the train driver had done much hard physical work driving trains for several years. He was weather-beaten with weeks' worth of dark beard but clear, naturally smiling eyes. But he wasn't smiling. When he talked, Kimbo saw an honest shame at the failure of his mission. Jack's expressions revealed his distress. It would be tested, but Kimbo thought he could trust this man. As Jack told his story, Kimbo watched the gentle and sensitive way he described the vast responsibility he was given, the horrific nightmare journey and its toll on the lives he was sent to save.

Bill Walker was a different type of man. Short, stocky and unusually going bald for a man of around thirty. Bill had quick, brown eyes, a week's growth of white beard, and orange hair coiled around his head like a monk. He had a high, squeaky voice.

Kimbo assessed Bill but came to no conclusions. He would wait to see. Until he had worked people out, he was always cautious. He thought Bill couldn't have been very good at his job as a train fireman – his hands and arms had many burn scars on them. Towards the end of Jack's tale, Bill occasionally added the odd comment. Jack admitted they had set off so late that the train arrived in Islamorada at the worst possible time.

"We had so many obstacles slowing us down," he said, describing the effect of the storm on his powerful train. "Kimbo, I could not believe that wave could just toss around the carriages." He then spoke of his pride in the Old 447 engine withstanding the wave's blast.

Bill Walker repeated what he had seen in the passenger cars but was expressionless. It wasn't that he didn't care, but Kimbo noticed how strangely unemotional he was describing the carnage. "Well, that's what happens when a hurricane takes you by surprise, I suppose." He just shrugged. "How 'bout you, Kimbo?" The train driver and fireman were curious about what happened to the father and son.

Kimbo realised he wasn't ready to tell someone else. He may never be ready. To tell someone would mean describing those last moments of horror and intimacy. It was private. He also knew that, as an uneducated man, he didn't have the right words to describe what had happened adequately. What he felt could not be explained. To describe what losing Zella and little Zakari meant was beyond his capability. For Kimbo Hopper, their loss had no words, even if he had known what to say.

"I don't recall much," he said quietly.

Jack had been watching Kimbo. He was afraid he might go into deep despair. He had seen plenty of men go that way when faced with a tragedy. In a lighter moment, Jack asked what Kimbo planned on doing next.

"Here's what I ain't gonna do. I ain't never goin' back to The Keys."

Jack left it a while before asking, "So you'll be looking for somewhere to settle?"

"I gonna give Myron the best life I can make for him. I'm reckoning that my Zella and Zakari are lost to me. They are lost to Myron. They gone in the storm. I'm gonna show Myron how to live off the land. I know how to do that. Done it all my life."

Jack responded, "I ain't got no folks nor Bill here. We ain't got no job either. Railroad ain't coming back in my lifetime; probably ain't never coming back ever. I don't think I can get back to driving no trains again. Things I saw. Things I should have bin helpin' with – the faces of the folks an' all at Islamorada. I can't get them out of my mind. I got to do something else. The fuck am I gonna do? I ain't no clue. Bill here is the same. Wanna team up?"

It was to be a pivotal moment for them all.

Kimbo realised Jack wasn't talking to a black or poor man. He is looking at me. He's judging me, Kimbo Hopper. Here was a man just wanting to team up and get a new life. Start afresh. He barely knew Jack, but Kimbo thought three men were better than one if you were all going the same way. More importantly, Kimbo knew travelling with two white men was safer for him and Myron. He grew more confident, looking to find their few next steps.

"Where you figurin' to go, Jack the Train Driver?" Kimbo's nickname for Jack Root made Jack smile, and he could see that the big man before him had a sense of humour, even at the darkest point of his life. It had been Kimbo's typical response to try light-hearted talk, even when depressed, downhearted and at a very low ebb. Kimbo then called over quietly to the fireman.

"Hey, Bill the Fireman, what are you thinking?" Kimbo was looking at them both, but Jack spoke about his thoughts. Bill said nothing.

"Okay, Kimbo, you're a road builder and used to be a

railroad man – from what you told me. You have been building and maintaining both. I'm an engineer. As you know, Bill here is a fireman. I guess we all know how to make things work, and we sure are used to workin' hard all day. I can make things work and figure things out. What are you goin' to bring to the team, Kimbo?" Jack thought he knew the answer.

Kimbo's eyes smiled at Jack. It was a new experience to be offered to team up with white men; that was the first thing he liked about it.

"I can catch and skin anythin' you want. And I can cook whatever we catch, too. I can build a house. I can make tools. That means the team gonna eat, and, most importantly, that means Myron too. He always eats first, okay?" At that point, they had already accepted the idea of living together, at least for now.

"Of course, when Myron is ten, he can chip in for the team, too," Jack beamed.

Kimbo gave a short snort of approval for Myron's inclusion in the team.

"Ha, I'm aiming to get him in workin' a good deal before that! This boy's goin' to be my saviour." Kimbo's prophetic words made Jack smile.

Kimbo, Jack and Bill all shook hands. Talking this way about plans and how each could contribute to whatever they face in the future was helpful, uplifting and reassuring. They had a near future, and that was essential. It was the beginning of their relationship, but it gave them all a better sense of well-being. Kimbo realised he'd never had friends. He wanted to have these two men as true friends and hoped that time might change many things, but it wouldn't alter true friends. Could he be lucky with these two men?

While his father talked and agreed on what to do and where

to go next, Myron was busy eating something mashed up by his two adoring Homestead volunteers. As with most children, food was always a comforting distraction for Myron – together with the attention of women behaving like his mother. But he had never been spoilt before; he liked it.

The three men spent another three days in the hall. It was cooler there, and they had food and water. They all knew it didn't matter what had happened to them up to this point; it would be a new path they would take. Kimbo and Jack had a clear idea about how to tackle the next few steps in their lives.

Bill understood what Jack and Kimbo were planning but was unclear about his next steps. As usually happened in his life, he let others figure things out, and then he'd make the most of it. He did like to follow others, but only up to a point.

Across the hall, Ed Watson and his son Hank talked about similar things. What to do next was taking shape in their discussions, too. Both were practical men in their work and their thinking. From what doc said, they realised that they had lost every other family member as far as they could tell. All gone. They had no house, no tools, not even their clothes. Many would look at their situation, lying there with cuts, bruises, a broken nose and a fractured wrist, and say they should have no hope either. It would be easy for them to feel sorry for themselves. These men didn't, not for a second. Ed looked at his son. "What do you want to do?"

"Pa, we have land. The house is gone, but we have the right to the land. Pa, it's ours. What I want to do is start over. I want to rebuild. I want us to dig in, Pa. I want to start to build, to start our lives over. I want to fight against anything that stops you and me livin' a better life than the one we lost."

Ed Watson looked back at his son. He was proud of his son; amid the chaos and depression, he saw a way through, a way to be better. Ed thought Henry Flagler, who built the impossible rail track over the sea to Key West, would have approved of Hank's attitude.

They all sat together the following three days. Kimbo, Jack, Bill, Myron, Ed, and Hank remained in the hall. They talked about building a house from cypress trees, palm tree fronds and sawgrass reeds for long periods. Kimbo had the most knowledge, but Ed and Hank were very well-educated about the Florida wetlands. A bond grew between them all. Kimbo noticed that they talked to him and included him in the discussion. *Maybe it didn't matter to them that he wasn't a white man,* he thought for the first time in his life. *Everything is new. Maybe the storm has given us a fresh and cleaned-up world. Everything has changed. Maybe Myron and me can live a better life in this changed world. Maybe it won't matter any more that I'm black, with no schooling.*

Ed was a devoutly religious man. He told his son Hank he wanted to talk to the Baptist minister. Hank went to fetch him. One hour later, the deflated minister arrived behind Hank, slowly dragging his feet like a child.

"I found him, Pa. He was so busy I didn't know where to look. I eventually found him alone in his lodgings next to the church. I've told him you want some private words."

Ed Watson's upturned face was lit by sunlight. He beckoned Hank to sit with him while the minister was present.

"Minister, we have nothing but what you see us wearing. We have a small piece of land on Islamorada, wiped clean by the storm, no doubt. What would God be saying to us at this moment? What guiding light should we follow?"

The minister was a diminished man, enduring insufferable doubts about himself for the first time. He spoke slowly.

"I don't know what God would say to you. But this is what I will say to you. Never expect an easy life. I hope you and your son here have the strength to live through the difficult one you will inevitably have. One way or another, we all have. It is that strength you will need more than any other aspect. There is no such thing as an easy life. Some live a comfortable life, maybe, but nobody has an easy life."

The Watsons looked at a dispirited minister who seemed to have no joy, no temperament to lift others in dire need and no direction for his own. Later, when it became known what had happened to the minister, Ed and Hank agreed that the preacher had chosen the wrong job.

"I dunno, Pa. Maybe we all get into the wrong job."

Leaving Ed Watson's side, the minister rose and walked out of the hall, never to return. His body was found three miles away along the Anhinga Trail outside Homestead. He was propped up against the trunk of a Gumbo Limbo tree. A dusky pigmy rattlesnake had bitten him. They are aggressive and quick to bite but have small fangs and only release a small amount of venom. The bite is rarely fatal, that is, unless it is not treated. It was later agreed that the minister could have returned to Homestead and been treated and survived. It was clear to most that he didn't want to be treated.

Ed and Hank Watson offered Kimbo, Jack, and Bill to join them on their Islamorada plot. Ed thought combining skills and knowledge would help him regain all he and Hank had lost. It wasn't much, but it was theirs.

Kimbo looked in turn at the four men as he spoke.

"I'm sorry I can't live again in the Florida Keys. That life has gone. Losing Zella and Zakari is too much, too real in my head and too hard for me to take and get over. Me and Myron, we're gonna get a fresh life. I got ideas already, but I don't know what's gonna work for us yet. We can't go back."

Looking only at Jack, he continued, "The Everglades is

gonna be a natural place for me and Myron, and I'd get it if you and Bill decided that these decent folk's offer was a better future for ya both. And well, in truth, Jack, it's most likely a much better future. I don't know how we'll do in the swamp. Skeeters will be a hundred times worse. Least in The Keys, you got the gentle wind every day to blow them goddam skeeters and pesky no-see-ums away. We've got free food in the swamp, and we can make a livin' outta hides and plumes, but it ain't gonna be easy."

Jack knew what he wanted. "Well, mister Watson, your offer is mighty kind, and we appreciate it, don't we, Bill." Bill nodded expectantly; his face froze as Jack continued. "But, no offence, we've already made a deal with Kimbo to start a new life with him in the Everglades marshlands and the Big Cypress Swamp. If things don't work out for us, maybe we will come down to you. Or, of course, if things don't work so fine for you and Hank, you will always be welcome to come and stay with us."

They all took turns shaking hands. Kimbo was thrilled that Jack had chosen to be with him and Myron. Bill was sure it was a bad thing. He was disappointed but went along with Jack for the moment. Let's see what happens, he thought quietly to himself.

The sun had risen when the three men and little Myron started packing and preparing to leave the hall. They took what they were allowed to take – some water, food, and clothing. All three men slept slightly better but still had vivid night terrors revisiting their worst storm moments. Kimbo had built Myron a cart from wood scraps and an old child's bike he found thrown into the scrubland. The Homestead residents had shown enormous sympathy and generosity to the survivors in their care; it had made a significant impression on Kimbo, and he would remember them. For their part, like Key West, the Homestead folk had dodged a bullet, and they all knew it. Helping those who came to them was the least they could do. They treated them as they would also want to be treated.

Kimbo thanked the two women who had looked after Myron so well for nearly a week. He asked their names.

"I'm Freida, and this here's Mary. You have a beautiful son. If you leave, we will miss you. If you stay, you can be sure we'll be coming to see this young man as much as you allow us."

This was another unique moment in Kimbo's life. *I won't forget these wonderful women.* But he needed one last favour. He took Freida aside and said, "Look, I don't mean nothin' by this, but I need a knife. If we're gonna survive, I'm goin' need to kill some wildlife. I'm gonna need to cook some food. Will you help us?"

The woman looked at Myron, sitting in his new cart, smiling and waving at her. She slipped into the large kitchen at the back of the hall, wrapped a large, sharp knife in a cloth and a small paring knife, and beckoned Kimbo into the kitchen.

"You didn't get these from me," she said and smiled. Kimbo looked at the knives. The large one was for killing and filleting, mainly for fish, but a perfect shape for hunting all types of food in the wilderness. The blade was long and sloped upwards into a sharp point. The paring knife was ideal for small bones and fruit and vegetables.

He wanted to hug her but knew it wouldn't be right. A black man and a white woman – a move she might misinterpret and one he'd have a mighty big cause to regret.

With Myron in his cart, the small group of three left the Baptist Church Hall and thanked everyone, excluding the reclusive minister who couldn't be found. They found doc behind a bush of florescent pink bougainvillaea in his garden. He was slumped against its prickly stems. He was crying silently. His shoulders and head were moving, almost imperceptibly, as he sobbed. His kind, sunburnt face was drenched in tears. Jack and then Kimbo bent down, kissed the top of his head, and said goodbye. Everyone had their horrors, but none knew what the doctor had endured. Finding the dead, the nearly dead and parts of the dead. What he had seen, heard, smelt, tasted and touched were etched in his memory and gnawed his every moment since. He was exhausted.

Two days later, Doc Slim had a stroke sitting in his house, the phone constantly ringing as his author friend in Key West tried to reach him. He lived another six months, after which he had a second, more violent stroke and passed away.

At no point had Doctor "Slim" Forsyth ever been at peace with God or himself since the night of the storm.

Chapter Eight
By Any Means Available

Although benefiting from the week of rest, Jack's knee had caused the slow progress along the hardtop road going north from Homestead. In 1931, the road had been 'defined', as they had always described the first stage of Florida road building in those early days. William Krome, an engineer from the FEC railroad, had researched where the best train track to be laid was when Flagler started planning his railroad to go from Miami to Key West. Jack had briefly met Krome once and was aware of all the maps he had produced, the first for the Everglades area. All the train engine drivers were familiar with Krome's maps, and Jack knew this was the best route to reach the most famous pioneering road in South Florida: the Tamiami Trail. Usually, the straight, twenty-two-mile route north out of Homestead would have taken about seven, perhaps eight hours for three fit men, but it was two days before they reached the Tamiami Trail – which would take them due west. The food and water they had been given for their journey lasted only these two days. Kimbo knew he would have to trap something edible at some point. Freshwater was his primary concern. He suggested Jack would be the one to carry the water and ration it between them as needed. He had already sensed that Bill couldn't be trusted with allocating it fairly. Kimbo started to lead.

The heat and humidity were unbearable. Sleeping on flat, grassy stretches alongside the road, they were thankful for the fences. Although not in perfect condition, they mostly protected the travellers from the swamp on either side. Kimbo felt confident that the gators wouldn't come for them at night. He knew enough about them to be sure they would stay in the shallow water after dark. They liked to lay out in the sun during the day; it helped with digestion, gaining temperature and providing energy. However, he was conscious that if the water level was too deep or a temporary drought had dried up the muddy bed, the reptiles would venture out for food during the night. Whatever the conditions, he knew they could wander in the dark; no wildlife in this wilderness was predictable; nothing was certain.

Kimbo had tried to rotate a night watch. Jack took the first turn, Kimbo the middle turn, and Bill the last. Bill struggled to keep awake, and when Kimbo woke at dawn on their first morning on the road, Bill was fast asleep, sitting bolt upright. The fencing had been helpful, but there were many different types of wildlife to worry about. Only one incident, on the third night, disturbed them. A family of four racoons came sniffing around Myron's cart, where he slept. During Kimbo's shift, he caught and killed two of them. Using Jack's matches and Bill's know-how, they were the main meal the next day, served with some bracken fern Kimbo had gathered whenever he saw it and collected fresh water from clear streams. Useful as green food when the leaves were young, he knew the fern could be used to clean or dry their bodies. He knew racoons looked cute to people unfamiliar with swamp, but he knew they were vicious when cornered or caught – they almost always carried disease.

"But," Kimbo said smiling, "they taste better than a hungry man's bile."

Around eight in the morning, they reached the intersection

of Route 997 and the Tamiami Trail. From Miami to Naples town, on the west coast of the Florida peninsular, the trail had been finished in April 1928, seven years before, and had taken many lives to complete. Kimbo marvelled at what it would have taken for workers to have built this road – slogging through water waist-deep, battling alligators and snakes, sometimes snakes seven feet long – dealing with a sweltering sun, raging natural wildfires caused by lightning strikes, tropical storms – or worse, the occasional hurricane. Mosquitoes would have swarmed around the road construction teams in black clouds day and night, and panthers would have attacked their camps now and then, drawn by the odour of freshly cooked meat, the odour of these men, or their food. The trail's construction workers would have been a mixture of Seminole and Miccosukee Indians, escaped or freed African slaves, prisoners and men who had lost their jobs when the land boom collapsed. These disparate groups worked alongside others who sought jobs as refugees from the looming, catastrophic Great Depression. Kimbo didn't know who they were, but from his experience helping build the railroad and later the highway, the vast majority would be poor men with nothing to their name. Kimbo felt privileged to walk along this luxury afforded by many lives and dangerous work. A combination of man's brilliant engineering and sheer determination. Those souls would have battled all these elements just to lay down the surface they now walked on. He felt he didn't deserve such privilege. *Where would this privilege take them?*

The three men now stood and looked west. The road stretched to the horizon. The small group started to walk along the straight road, silent but for wildlife calls. The sun on their backs was already hot, rising in the cloudless east. There was nothing to see ahead except swamplands and sawgrass.

Further along the trail, many Cypress hardwood hammocks grew on either side of the road. Kimbo knew they would be infested with alligators and numerous species of venomous snakes. This was a true wilderness, where men who had nothing were nothing. Nothing that is, except for their skills, attitudes and ambitions.

These three men would have to create their opportunities. Jack Root had no idea what life would be like the next day, week or month. He had faith in himself and God. God, who had saved him where so many had perished all around. Jack had confidence in his new friend. He was sure Kimbo could guide them in establishing the basics of living and safety in this seemingly treacherous place. Perhaps God, in time, would guide him to find love, esteem and morality to fit his circumstances. He was naturally optimistic.

Kimbo Hopper also felt optimistic that he could provide the life for Myron that he had promised in his whispered prayer to the vanished Zella. To stand against or work with, whatever comes their way, to build their own independent lives. To start again, maybe even start a family. To weather whatever new storms came their way by any means available. He was going to deliver his pledge to Zella, come what may. He wanted to find a quiet place if that was possible.

Bill Walker, however, had deep insecurity and strong doubts. He looked around at every step since leaving Homestead.

"This place gives me the creeps," he whispered to himself.

Each man walked towards the future, leaving nothing behind. The three men together, but for how long, and what may separate them? Each man thought, *How should I lead my life now that I have been given a second chance?*

Sitting in his cart singing to himself, little Myron would

eventually, in years to come, decide about his life, too. Thankfully, it would be a while before a sudden, harsh reality would confront them. It lay in wait for each of them. Each had been thinking about the answer to the same vital question since they survived the storm.

Who am I, and where do I fit in this world?

Chapter Nine
Getting Acquainted

The road seemed endless to the three men and a boy, as did the boundless river of grass. The slow-moving river running through the marshland, laced with ditches and natural canals, was blown by a wind that made it look like giant, soft brushes were lightly sweeping over the landscape. The three men and a boy had never experienced such a stark-looking, pre-historic terrain. The unhurried mass of clear water gently washed over sawgrass, deep-rooted reeds and sedges. It was a massive freshwater slough, harbouring and nourishing a wide and overflowing variety of wildlife and vegetation as it moved imperceptibly down to where the Gulf of Mexico meets the Caribbean. A fragile world delicately balanced between nature and ever-encroaching and expanding humanity.

Before they saw a sign for Everglades City, the small troop passed through the beginning of the enormous, moist, hardwood forest of cypress trees. To Myron Hopper, this was a place of wonderment and fascination. Kimbo Hopper and Jack Root saw it as offering a new life and a chance for solace and healing. Bill Walker saw it as a place to escape from – as soon as an opportunity arose.

Entering Everglades City
They eventually stumbled over the bridge on Collins Avenue and entered Everglades City. The three men had taken turns pulling

the cart since they left Homestead, with Myron sitting happily, watching the landscape drift slowly by. Although this place they happened upon was called a city, its registered population was a meagre two hundred and twelve people. The previous week, the number amounted to one more, but he'd gone missing – now presumed dead. A sizeable section of the population was honest, hardworking white folk who lived mainly on the land and from the sea. The mayor knew the actual population wasn't known, nor was anyone willing to try and record who lived there. People, mostly men, came and went. Some stayed for a month, some longer, and some stayed for a year or more but then left or just disappeared. These were outlaws, cheats, or men just keeping out of sight for one reason or another, hiding until the heat was off. One man was fleeing a charge of murdering fifty of his farm workers to avoid paying them the months-owed wages. It was that kind of place.

Despite the city having a bank and a large Rod and Gun Club that ran lucrative hunting and sporting activities throughout the Ten Thousand Islands, it was a quiet town. It was also hot and humid, making people tetchy and volatile, especially when the mosquitoes and no-see-ums were most abundant. Most people eked out a barely sustainable life – not much more than a daily existence, but they were settled, and life was stable.

The small group led by Kimbo found a pool bar next to a grocery store. It had a window with iron bars instead of glass, preventing uninvited guests from trying to enter when it closed. The sign over the door had the words "The Swamp Buggy Tavern" on a piece of wood hacked from a cypress tree. The name had been burnt into the wood by a metal poker heated in a fire. The three men and Myron could hear four, possibly five, men inside. It was obvious from their loud voices and cussing that they had been in there quite a while, drinking steadily.

"Best let me go in an' do the talking, Kimbo," advised Jack. "I'll get some fresh water and see if we can find some work."

Bill followed him inside. Kimbo waited with Myron on a grass verge on the other side of the road. He noticed one or two faces come to the window. The shadowy heads looked out at him. He stared back, meeting their glare with his own. He was well-practised at that.

Jack emerged about fifteen minutes later, fuming. Bill followed shortly after. "Well, I got some fresh water for us, but we gotta keep movin' on," Jack said, looking long at Kimbo, meaning for him to do just as he said and quickly.

Kimbo caught on quickly. As they walked briskly, Kimbo said, "Okay, well, Jack and Bill, it looks like Myron and me are gonna cause you some problems. It's probably better we walk on so you and Bill can get acquainted with local life and settle in somehow. Looks like we've discovered the centre of the town."

"You ain't goin' nowhere without us. I don't think you can get rid of us that easily. We need you to teach us how we can live off the land. I'm not sure this city is where I want to settle anyway or how much payin' work there's gonna be. How about you, Bill? Wanna stay here?"

"Er, nope," said Bill. "Guess you're stuck with us for now, Kimbo." Both Kimbo and Jack noted the unenthusiastic tone in Bill's voice and the put-on, expressionless look.

"Fella in there reckons that men with talent like you, Kimbo, maybe best trying Chokoloskee Island 'bout four, maybe five miles further down the road and then a short boat ride. They got a few Indians still hanging around and maybe a few fellas, same as you scattered about, and some local white folks; they call them 'Crackers' for some reason. These crackers have been living around here for a few years. They'd moved down south after raisin' cattle. So, they say." The way Jack looked at Kimbo indicated he didn't believe anything about what he had been told inside the pool bar. Jack was still angry at their very clearly expressed opinions about Kimbo and "that black kid."

"Reckon, we should try that island. Whaddaya say?" Jack was doing his best to smooth out the wrinkles of the conversation he'd just had. Faces were still coming to the window to look out at them.

Kimbo paused and then said, "Chokoloskee? Hum, yeah, nice name. I like the sound of that. Look, I'm used to this kinda treatment, but you and Bill might do better staying here in Everglades City. Should be plenty of work for fellas like you. The way I heard it, it was the Seminoles who called the early white folks 'crackers'. I heard the term comes from the sound of the whip those first settlers used on the cattle they herded. This town looks like it has crackers mostly settled in here after failing at cattle ranchin'. Must be some truth in there somewhere. You and Bill would find it easier to live among these folks. Me and Myron will be just fine down in Chokoloskee."

"We're sticking together, and there ain't nothin' you can do about it, Kimbo Hopper!" stated Jack in his most stubborn way. "Besides, I think there are more to them fellas in there than wanting you to move on, Kimbo. It doesn't take much to see why this town, and this part of Florida, has that well-known reputation. People talk about it in Miami bars and along the East Coast railroad route. I think all of us will be better off down the road a-piece. I heard that people come down here to hide from the law. Cracker is a name they like to use about themselves, but there ain't no ex-cattlemen in that bar."

Chapter Ten
Life at the End of the Road

Every road going south in Florida will eventually travel to the Everglades. Barron Collier, an advertising entrepreneur and the largest landowner in Florida, had paid for the Tamiami Trail to be finished. He negotiated with the Lee County and Florida legislatures to create Collier County to recognise the investment he had put in to develop this vast area of the state. He also built the road from the Tamiami Trail to Everglades City, which he developed from a small hunting and fishing village into the Collier County seat. The town was the last mainland urban area that ran out of land just before the island of Chokoloskee. However, Collier didn't put any money into a hardtop road for the four miles from the city to Chokoloskee. He didn't see any return on his capital to be had. Consequently, the road to the dock and crossing was just a dirt track leading to the short boat ride to the island.

It was evening by the time they got there. Kimbo had often heard about this area in the Florida Keys. Named "Ten Thousand Islands", it was an immense wilderness with a vast cypress tree swamp with abundant wildlife. Living off the land and water would be dangerous but bountiful. If a man had a canoe or a comprehensive "alligator catcher" boat, he would always eat if he knew the edible plant life and how to catch fish and skin alligators. But the main threats to life also came from panthers, many snakes, and an occasional black bear.

Sources of food were everywhere if you knew where and how to look. It was like the upper keys in many ways, but here, Kimbo assumed they would be away from other people, with no threats or disrespect aimed at them. He was sure that Myron would be happy here. It didn't cross his mind that his son would want any other way of life than the one Kimbo would create for him. Kimbo convinced himself that this was always what he had wanted for himself and his family. He was confident they would be fine, but knowing Jack and Bill would look out for them when needed gave him greater confidence. Jack especially.

At that time, the primary residence on the island was the "Penecott Trading Store," set up in 1906 by a pioneer called Fred Penecott. The Calusa Indians had occupied this part of Florida for nearly two thousand years and built shell mounds to raise the land to twenty feet above sea level to minimise the risk of flooding. They also created a network of canals, allowing dugout canoes to pass through rich, fertile fishing waters. After Europeans started to populate the area during the 17th century, the Calusa tribe had all but disappeared, mainly through diseases brought by the new inhabitants. Seminole and Miccosukee tribes, subsets of the Creek Indians, settled here, pushed down south by the white man from Oklahoma and Georgia. They were being moved around without their consent, provoking a vicious and bloody war.

On arrival at the Chokoloskee dock, Kimbo looked around and felt good about where he had brought his son and his friends. The island had some positive history to it, he could tell. It offered protection and safety from the social alienation he'd felt in working with the vets and the barely restrained aggression he'd felt in Everglades City. The respect he'd had gained in The Keys was hard-fought. Surely, Chokoloskee would be different, wouldn't it?

The three men quickly found good, solid ground to build the

walls and doors of their cabin, mainly from wood. It took them most of the first two weeks. They built it just north of the Penecott Store and near another, a less grand trading post with a sign declaring "Jim Tigertail's". To get a roof on their new home quickly, they weaved three types of thatch together: palmetto palms, reeds and sawgrass. The thick thatch kept the rain at bay, making inside much cooler and bearable, if not perfectly dry. Kimbo explained that cypress shingles would be the best type of roof, and within three weeks, they had finished the job, "and with no leaking roof!" said Jack, pleased with their work and progress. The mosquitoes were the main problem, and they would be particularly unbearable through summer's hot and humid coming months. The oppressive weather typically stretched well into November. The new cypress roof would help keep the 'skeeters' away, at least the great swarms of them commonly found in South Florida's swamp areas. By the end of the second week, Kimbo had shown the other two some basics on how to trap, kill and skin raccoons and otters. Jack was a quick, enthusiastic learner, but Bill was not.

Jack, Bill in tow, traded the skins, fur, meat, and fish at Penecott's for tools. Kimbo noticed Jim Tigertail's store wasn't as busy, although his prices were better. He asked Jack about it one evening as they watched the reddened sun set over the mangrove islands looking west.

"Why do people shop at Penecott's mostly and not at Jim Tigertail's place?"

Jack showed his worldly side. "Well, this may not make any sense to you, Kimbo, but some people like to pay more if they think it's better, more reliable, giving peace of mind. They would talk about what they had bought to show how they made a good purchase, a good decision. If you bought from Penecott's, I've heard folks say you can't go wrong."

Kimbo looked puzzled. Jack added, "Well, all those things

and the fact that Jim Tigertail is a Seminole." Jack looked at Kimbo, and Kimbo stared back at him. Jack continued.

"I buy our goods at the Penecott place because he gives me a higher price for what we sell."

Kimbo tried to understand whether that made sense. It didn't. "Besides," said Jack, fumbling for justification, "only Penecott carries much of what we need since we arrived here. Maybe we should do a bit more at Jim Tigertail's store." Without speaking, Kimbo thought he had just put Jack right on something.

The tools from Penecott's most certainly allowed the men to build what they needed. The most helpful outcome of this was the dugout canoe. Their new cabin home had a shoreline and a deep-water inlet that allowed their boat to access in and out right up to the cabin door. The palmetto clumps were everywhere, and the hearts from these and the cabbage palms provided food and allowed the men to install two new large storage trunks quickly, shielding their hunting catch from direct sun and rain. Most importantly, the trunks kept the smell of meat and fish out of the cabin. Salt was put over the catch. Kimbo had become even more convinced that he and Myron could live somewhere like this, but he still wasn't sure about his friends Jack and Bill. His skills and upbringing were well suited to this environment, but a train driver and fireman? Jack seemed to revel in learning new things. He liked fishing and catching raccoons and the occasional otter. He enjoyed learning about living on the land. It gave him a new sense of freedom. For him, it was bringing him closer to his religious spirit. Bill hated every day.

The main task of finding food fell to Kimbo. He met and befriended a Seminole Indian family of five. They lived a little further north along the Chokoloskee island's coastline, past Jim Tigertail's place. 'Bad Hand Billie' taught Kimbo new and better ways to hook, kill and haul alligators into a boat; sometimes, they were twelve feet long or more. They were much bigger than he'd been used to handling. Alligator hides fetched excellent prices in the Penecott Store and the Everglades City market. Kimbo used Tigertail's store for more everyday items and got to know Jim. Now and then, when Jack and Bill were out, Kimbo would sit with Jim and Bad Hand in the evenings, Myron at their side, whittling some wood or making up a game with stones and shells, as young children often do when they don't have others to play with.

Kimbo was naturally curious, but he had no reason to ask Bad Hand Billie what gave him his name; it was plain to see. He was missing the last three fingers on his right hand, but luckily, he still had his thumb and forefinger. Kimbo knew that Billie would tell him how he lost them over time. It would not be right to come straight out and ask; besides, he had just met him. Often sitting together at sundown, the three men created a strong bond, sharing the history of their different lives. After a while, it became apparent to Kimbo that their lives weren't so different, just their background and culture. Jim and Bad Hand talked mainly about the Seminole and Miccosukee history in the Everglades. Kimbo was engrossed as he listened intently to both Seminole men tell their stories and that of their people. He didn't share his stories, and his new friends noticed.

Chapter Eleven
A Deep and Nagging Remorse

Kimbo listened intently as his friends gave a brief history of Seminole and Miccosukee Indians. They explained they were an association of clans inhabiting areas later given the names of Alabama and Georgia. Bad Hand said there were essentially two clans: upper Creeks, who lived in the mountains and spoke the *Muskogee* (Creek), and lower Creeks, who lived at the base of the same mountains and spoke *Hitchiti* (Mikasuki). Bad Hand pointed out that although the two languages were closely related, they were mutually unintelligible. It made Kimbo laugh. When it was his turn to speak, Jim Tigertail recanted tales of how the language barrier had led to misunderstandings and difficult communication between the two groups. Kimbo was shocked at the depth of knowledge Bad Hand and Jim had about their nation's history. They told him why the Creeks initially filtered into northern Florida and the Lake Okeechobee and Tampa areas, eventually being driven into the Everglades. Kimbo also could not believe that they knew so much detail about the different European tribes.

"The arrival of the white Europeans put the Creeks in the middle of the land grab between the English coming south from the Carolinas, the French pushing east from the Mississippi Valley, and the Spanish pushing north from the Florida peninsular. At that time, the Spanish controlled this area and tricked the Creek Indians into moving to Florida to use them as a buffer against the English and French."

Bad Hand smiled. "The Creeks were as stupid as the white man had thought. They played the three encroaching powers against each other but gained nothing from it. The Spanish sold Florida to the United States government. The Creeks didn't think the white man would sell what they had never owned. But they did. After the sale and, eventually, recognising the brutal wars fought between them, the American government recognised the rights of all the Indian tribes in Florida.

"Well, Kimbo, you won't be surprised to hear this was soon ignored. The white settlers got agitated and greedy. They forced a new 'Indian Removal Act', which dictated that all Indians should leave and go west. Many did, but many defied this and moved further south to the wetlands. There were constant conflicts with Europeans and between other tribes, causing both Seminoles and Miccosukee to seek new lands to live in peace. We wanted peace and land to call our home."

Kimbo marvelled at the extent of his two new friends' storytelling and was glad their forebears had retained their history in such a detailed way. With his Bahamian background, the story's tragedy and the level of deceit did not surprise Kimbo. Now he knew why these tribes now lived in the vast river of grass called the Everglades and the dense land of what was being called "Big Cypress". Kimbo was astonished at how similar it was to his own Gullah history. Feeling he should be open with them, Kimbo immersed his new friends with his personal stories and heritage. One evening, he described to them what had happened in the storm. That evening, when Kimbo had finished speaking, silence fell, and the three men each walked away in the evening twilight, walking softly to their own homes without another word.

The next evening, the three men met again as if there were still things to say and things to explain. Kimbo had wondered why Bad Hand and Jim Tigertail had left the tribe. He knew it must have been something very significant. He knew most of the Seminoles and Miccosukee preferred to live their lives away from the white man, to live their lives by their traditions, no one else's. They firmly believed in their way of life and did not intend to change it or where they lived. They should have foreseen that they would be forced to do so by the US government to accommodate the land-hungry settlers. Bad Hand knew that if you are ignorant about those who mean you harm, you will have difficulty foreseeing what actions they might take. The white man had a phrase they had used for many years: *keep your friends close and your enemies closer.* Bad Hand didn't know that saying, but he knew its meaning.

The conversation from the previous evening restarted. Both Bad Hand Billie and Jim Tigertail professed deep and nagging remorse. Leaving the tribe in Big Cypress was a profoundly personal trauma for them both. Chief Wildcat Billie was an unlikeable leader who was subtly forced upon the Seminoles living in the Everglades by the white man. Bad Hand Billie had sensed something was wrong even before Wildcat Billie was appointed chief. One day, he appeared in their village with undeserved confidence and unwarranted arrogance.

Bad Hand said that since the end of the three Seminole wars, successive governments have tried and failed to force the Seminoles out of the Everglades and Big Cypress forests. Treaties have been signed and then voided as the government attempts to remove the tribes and relocate them to barren land in Oklahoma. Those who resisted hid in the Everglades and Big Cypress forests after many violent conflicts provoked them. There was a defiance and collective strength that the new white settlers couldn't break.

Bad Hand continued, "The next move by the settlers was to

create just one reservation in Florida for all natives – in a place called Brighton. This barren land was northwest of the town of Okeechobee, located on the north shore of Lake Okeechobee. This is a huge freshwater lake and has become precious to the tribe. Knowing freshwater would be an attractive bait for the tribe to relocate, it was another deceitful attempt to trick us into eventually relocating to Oklahoma or, better for them, out west. In the settler's mind, it was just a stepping-stone in a bigger plan to eliminate us. Kimbo, this Wildcat Billie, a misguided man who only sought power and recognition, had been sent from the Brighton Seminole Reservation, northeast of Lake Okeechobee, to fool the Everglades Seminole Tribe Council into nominating him as chief. The council realised it was essential that any chief needed to understand the white man, the white man's ways, and the white man's ambition. They didn't see that although Wildcat Billie understood many things about the tribe and the settlers, he could easily exploit both camps. He was devious; he knew more about each side than anyone else. The man with one eye is chief in the land of the blind."

Bad Hand paused for this statement to take effect. He continued to explain that the Seminoles thought Wildcat Billie could help keep them safe from the US government's attempts to terminate their right to tribal status and federal benefits.

"We," he said, "didn't know that Indian tribes in Oklahoma had their land allotted, but their right to the land title had been extinguished. We no longer had any white man's legal rights over our reservations. Moving us to Oklahoma was an unspoken objective. Once there, the tribes would have no land to call their own."

Between them, Bad Hand and Jim Tigertail continued to tell Kimbo native history over the next two evenings. "The white man's authorities thought Wildcat Billie could help persuade and lead us to the Brighton reservation. They wanted to move all the tribes out of the Everglades. The settlers wanted to convert wetlands into farms and communities. They had building and drainage projects. There was money to be made. Many of these projects had altered the wetlands and damaged many wildlife species."

Kimbo said with simple sincerity, "Well, my good friends, if God gave me the power, I would take this land from the settlers and give it back to the Seminoles. I've known you for almost no time, but I don't yet see why you're not with your tribe. There is too much land grabbin' and greed comin' from these settlers, that's for sure. Your people know how to use the land without hurtin' the land. Nobody could farm the land better. You understand these lands. The settlers want to change it so they can live as they always did elsewhere, and as they change it, they destroy it. Why are you here in Chokoloskee?"

Bad Hand was an independent and instinctive man. "We were sent a new chief from the north by the white man. For me, it was clear he was sent to take us all out of this area to the land the white man had given for a new reservation. I saw the deceit in his eyes as he talked to the tribal council. I tried to tell the council this was another trick, another attempt to rid us of this land so they could drain the water for the settlers along the coast. Places such as Miami keep demanding more and more fresh water. Here, our tribe live next to the best source of fresh water in the south, this slow, clean river. We have freshwater from Lake Okeechobee to the tip of our land. Jim Tigertail, this man sitting with us now, stood up for what I said. The new chief cast us both out. No one accepted my thoughts except Jim Tigertail. So, I left with my family. I want to go back, see my people, and see how they are dealing with the white man's wishes. One day we will go back. Maybe it will be our honour to have you come with us to see how we live. You will be surprised at what you find. How different, yet how similar we are. Kimbo, you, me, and even old Jim Tigertail are brothers. The three of us, brothers."

When he left the tribe, Jim had no family. He was one of the oldest in the tribe and knew where Bad Hand had gone. He explored the area the settlers called Corkscrew Swamp in the northwest but then followed him south to Chokoloskee.

Jim told Kimbo stories about the value of the Ten Thousand Islands to the ever-intruding settlers. It was well known that the area had increased its population through an influx of bank robbers and outlaws. As they all sat together during these special storytelling evenings, Kimbo carefully watched Myron to see if he was taking in even a little of these tales. Kimbo hoped he didn't, as his son was too young to start worrying about killers and desperate men.

"We get white men on the run from the north and hide in the hundreds of places in this wilderness. The white man's law enforcement officers would pursue these men, but then they disappeared without a trace. The most talked about and notorious thug was "Bloody" Ben Jones. After killing fifty farm workers, the local law officers were angry that some of the workers were white. This prompted Ben Jones to take off south, ending up in Everglades City. He was vigorously pursued. Each time Jones got wind of a lawman looking for him, he would vanish into the wilderness hideaways until the heat was off. It was calculated that about ten lawmen disappeared in the wilderness trying to find Jones. They were never found, but neither was Ben Jones."

"Do you know what happened to them, Jim Tigertail?" Kimbo asked.

"Kimbo, it doesn't take much to surprise a man from behind in these swamps if they don't know what they are doing. These men would have no experience with this type of landscape. They would get hit on the head and let nature, the alligators, take care of the rest." This was a short description of what must have happened one way or another. To Kimbo, this was important information he didn't know he would need later.

Upon arriving in Chokoloskee, Jim saw that Bad Hand had built his own house and looked after his family well. Jim asked him how life was for him here. Bad Hand had asked for his children to go to the Everglades City school but had yet to receive a reply.

It was no surprise to Bad Hand Billie that he'd struck up such a good and warm friendship with Kimbo. Now three years old, Kimbo would often take Myron to visit the Billie family and have fun with his two sons, Naama and Tocho, but he mainly played with the youngest child, a girl his age called Tehya.

Towards the end of one of their evenings together, Bad Hand Billie winked at Jim Tigertail, turned and said, "Okay, Kimbo Hopper, I know you are a gentle and respectful man, so I'll tell you – because you haven't asked. It was something that looks like an alligator...but isn't." He smiled, waiting for Kimbo to catch on. "My fingers, you've been wondering why or how I lost my fingers. Yes?"

Kimbo was a little embarrassed. "Yes," was all he could manage to say. He wondered what looked like an alligator but wasn't.

"It was an alligator snapping turtle. Don't put your hand or anything else near an alligator snapping turtle when you pick it up." He laughed, and Jim Tigertail roared at the "anything else" comment.

Jim then asked Bad Hand, "With you missing those fingers, would you be able to learn to write with that hand?"

"Probably, but I wouldn't count on it!" They both roared with laughter at a well-practised joke.

Kimbo Hopper smiled, but he was a little embarrassed and very uncomfortable. He had rarely had a light-hearted exchange with anyone. He felt ignorant and suddenly conscious of how little he knew about where he was living.

Chapter Twelve
Missing

His life had taken a good path. He had friends and new and enriching experiences unthinkable a month earlier. Bad Hand had shown Kimbo new and clever ways to capture alligators, boosting income. The strange family of three men and a boy weren't eating well, but well enough. Myron didn't complain. He just ate what he was given, and when he asked for more, his father and Jack gave him food from their plates. Kimbo appreciated his son's peaceful and mild temperament.

The Penecott trading post had become a profitable focus for selling their 'coon skins, 'gator hides and bird plumes. The three men sold meat and fish to Jim, helping him hugely. Kimbo trained Jack and Bill to hunt, fish and trap, and within a year, they had built a good reputation throughout the Ten Thousand Islands. Their alligator skins were highly sought after, especially when the buyers had customers waiting impatiently in Miami and "up north". The demand for fur, alligator hides, and plumes along the east coast grew dramatically.

Docking at the shoreline alongside the Penecott Store, boats came from Key West and other South Florida islands. People drove from Miami and the west coast of Florida to Everglades City to buy as much as Kimbo, Jack, and Bill could offer, although they weren't the only ones selling goods. It became clear that white folks were inclined to buy from white sellers unless the Seminoles or black folks were selling a lot cheaper, but even then, they tended to buy from "their kind". When Kimbo noticed this, he spoke frankly.

"Bill, you ought to be the one to meet the cars in the city to sell our skins an' all."

Jack looked at Kimbo and realised he had weighed the situation well. He turned to Bill.

"Bill, you're good at hunting, but you'd be better at selling and getting a better price than Kimbo. Just look at him. Most would be afraid even to ask the price!"

Kimbo beamed a big smile, and Bill, unsurprisingly, seemed to relish the job entrusted to him. Kimbo and Jack knew Bill hated hunting and lacked the right skills and motivation. Kimbo realised, and Jack knew, that the white retailers resented the 'coloureds' under-cutting them, and the 'coloureds' resented the white folks getting better prices. This could be lucrative. Jack became the prime contact for Fred Penecott's, Kimbo for Jim Tigertail's Chokoloskee stores, and Bill was the trader in Everglades City. Jack focused on developing his trapping and fishing skills. He wanted to rival Kimbo, but he knew that wouldn't happen, so he spent his spare time watching Myron. He liked the responsibility of that role.

"Well, Myron is such a great kid," he said to Kimbo whenever he looked after him.

They made a good life together, and for his part, Myron was growing and contributing, if only as entertainment for the three men. He had developed an effortless sense of humour and often mocked each man, including his loving father and doting "Uncle Jack". He poked fun at Bill's limp. He imitated what they said and how they said it. He particularly liked to mimic Jack. He knew he used to drive a train, even though he didn't understand what that was. What he did know was that it had a whistle, and he imitated the whistle's sound that Jack had taught him every time he came into the cabin. Bill was getting edgy, restless and irritated by all this, and Myron's response was to mock Bill's irritability.

All three men missed the company of women. Myron still suffered deeply from his mother's and Zakari's absence. Now and then, he'd ask his father where they had gone and when they were coming home. They were missing from his life, and he ached for them.

Then Bill went missing.

By the time the sun had set behind a cluster of mangrove forests, Jack was loading the gun the three of them had bought to share, and he put a knife into its holder under his left armpit. Bill had left early that morning with an enormous pile of skins, stuffed animals and the largest set of plumes he'd ever taken to sell in the city. The money from this day's trading would be plentiful and put with the rest of their savings under Myron's bunk. The money was missing.

They were planning to build their trading post. It would be erected on the mainland, in the city, as near the Rifle and Gun Club as possible. They knew that rich folk from both coasts of Florida, particularly Miami, liked to come down to have an exotic and sporting vacation at the club over a weekend or longer. They went fishing and hunting with locals and then bought skins or fancy hats with feathers to take back and pretend they were trophies from their trip. Bill had been trusted to sell goods to this market, but his absence before sundown was a bad sign, no matter what happened. To Kimbo and Jack, it was ominous.

"You want me to come with you, Jack?" Kimbo said, very concerned for Jack's safety. Jack, a quiet, peaceful man, guessed what had happened. Kimbo saw anger and exasperation on his face. The clues were there. Bill had been noticeably reluctant to make the best of who they were and where they were.

"Jack, we can always get more skins and money. I don't want you to risk your own life or be arrested for shooting Bill. I treasure our friendship more than revenge," he said passively. Jack looked at him.

"You gotta look after Myron, Kimbo – no good you helping me. You can't leave the boy or bring him. I should go and find out what the hell happened. He may have been robbed. You know there are enough bandits on the run around here for someone to figure out the cash he would be carrying on his way back home. But if I find he's been spending our money in that buggy tavern again, I'm sure gonna let him have it!" Kimbo looked surprised at this statement about the tavern. Jack thought it was time to tell Kimbo some truths.

"I thought you didn't know much about Bill's drinking. It didn't seem to me that it mattered much until now," said Jack, looking a little awkward at telling Kimbo. "Truth is, Bill is dealing with his troubles his way."

As Jack disappeared into the darkness, Kimbo stood looking out of the open door. He thought Jack had grasped what had probably happened to Bill and would be unforgiving, whatever it was. Jack had a strong sense of justice and an intense loathing against injustice.

Bad for business

Jack burst through the door with his pistol waving, shouting, "Where's that bastard Bill Walker?" Jack was now convinced that he and Kimbo had been betrayed. No doubt at all.

As Jack had made his way from the cabin in Chokoloskee to the Swamp Buggy Tavern, he turned everything over in his mind about what Bill had been saying to him over the last few weeks.

Bill had never been committed to living off the land in the Everglades or anywhere else. He was more interested in having the most fun possible in the shortest time available. It had become clear to Jack, but not to Kimbo, that Bill had been building up to something. The effects they experienced in the storm had made a different mark on Bill. Jack had made the foolish assumption that Bill was angling to move to Everglades City and find an independent life from the one he undoubtedly didn't like in Chokoloskee. Jack was afraid he'd sold the bundle of skins, stuffed animals and animal outfits and blown it at the tavern and on the small brothel at the Riverside Turn-off, where visitors enter the city from the Tamiami Trail. Inside the tavern, he quickly discovered what had happened that day.

"Whoa there, Mister Pistol," responded the massive man behind the bar, a deep scar from the top of his cheek to his chin glistening in the dimly lit bar room. He looked carefully at Jack and the gun he held at waist height. "If you lookin' for Bill Walker, he left first light with Zip Thomas. I heard old Zippy tell Will Tulskaya last night that they would be heading to Miami. From what I heard tell, they ain't coming back."

Jack sat down hard on a bar bench. Some other men sat at a table, looking warily at Jack until he put the pistol away in his coat.

Jack took a minute to think and then said, "Bottle of whisky to the man who can tell me where he went!"

"Hell, and Miami knows, but we don't," said one man who looked like he'd sell his children for a bottle of whisky. "Zippy ain't the kinda guy to let no one know where's he goin' or come to that, where he's bin. They took the two gals from the whore house too. I guess the guy yer lookin' fer ain't comin' back anytime soon, mister."

Another said, 'Hey, ain't you that fella who lives with that big black son-of-a-bitch?" Jack ignored the last comment.

"Anyway," said another, "that Bill already had a ton of money with him. I didn't think it was too good an idea to go flashing that kinda money with the kinda folks we got in this town. Know what I mean? And I guess they'll be up to no good in Miami before they head somewhere else."

The colour drained from Jack's tanned face. He knew that bastard Bill Walker had also taken all their savings. Jack asked where he might find Will Tulskaya. He was the only man Zip Thomas spoke to in the bar. After Jack tracked down his house, knocked on the door and spoke briefly with Will, he realised he would learn nothing from him or the good people of this city, and certainly not from the villains he found in the bar. The barkeep knew everything that went on, but he wouldn't talk; it would be bad for business. *Assessment.*

Myron was asleep when Jack returned to the cabin. He immediately double-checked under Myron's bunk; it was all gone. He sat down at the big table where they usually ate. Jack shared some crab soup with Kimbo. The way Jack spoke, it was clear that he felt personally responsible for what Bill had done.

"So, now we know exactly what Bill wanted to do since we arrived here. The question is, what are we gonna do about it?" Jack was seething.

Kimbo gave his assessment. "Here's what I figure. Ain't no good telling the city sheriff or finding the county sheriff; they're the same fella anyway. He ain't gonna go chasing after nobody, 'specially if it's me telling him. What's more, we're Chokoloskee folk, and he doesn't care too much about us on this island anyway, as I hear it. We ain't in his, what's the word, er, territory? Best we get on with our lives, Jack. Money's gone, but we're gonna be all right. We both better off now than we were with our asses hanging out of our britches down from the storm. We gonna skin a lot more 'gators, 'coons and the like. We will get to start that business we wants in the city if we keep workin'. It just gonna take a little longer."

Kimbo, who was used to mistreatment and luck going against him, was immediately resigned to the fate dealt them that day. Jack was not. He wasn't going to live with Bill taking their money. He spoke his mind.

"Kimbo, this ain't right. I can't leave it like this. There ain't no justice in this. I should have seen what was comin', and now it should be down to me to put this right. You and Myron goin' to be ok, set here in this cabin. You know what you're doin' with huntin' and catchin' stone crabs an' all. You got good at stuffing and mounting the animals, and Myron's comin' along. Folks up north love that your boy makes good stuff, too. You gotta get someone to look after little Myron while you go catchin', but you be okay for a while on yer own. I'm goin' after that bastard and will get our share of the money back. He can keep his share, an' that's fair. I might want to beat him up a little because I'm so mad about what he did. But I gotta keep it fair."

Kimbo looked at Jack and knew he was a good man to think that, even to say that, but Kimbo knew he didn't live in a fair world. He didn't want his friend to believe that the world was waiting to even things up. *It doesn't*, he thought to himself. Kimbo wanted Jack to know his feelings about this.

"Bill's gotta pay for this, Jack, but I 'spose I ain't the fella to chase after him. You right; little Myron needs me. Jack, I know somethin' you don't yet. It's that things ain't fair, and nothing gets evened out, not for folks like me, that's fer sure. If you go after him, go first light tomorrow. Don't leave the trail cold. Take the pistol; you will need it. I'm sure you will. This other fella, what's his name, Zip? From what I hear tell from Bad Hand Billie and Jim Tigertail, he's one of those men who comes to this city; we can guess why. He done somethin' wrong up north somewhere or Miami, and he come here to hide out. You know there are ten thousand places to hide, and they can also do that for a good while. You can live well off the crab and raw fish out there in the small islands until the heats off. Bad Hand told me this fella Zip has been around fer a few months. I'm guessing, but I reckon Bill got his head turned good and proper with the girls and drink. Wouldn't be surprised if he ain't settin' somethin' up in Miami or somewheres else similar. I don't want you to go, but if you fixin' to go, then first thing tomorrow would be right. If you find Bill, I'm askin' you don't hurt him. It might feel right, but Jack, you don't seem the kinda man to go around beating on people, no matter how angry you get. You a God-fearing man, and I'm sure God don't want you to go hurtin' Bill. I'd be happier knowing you didn't hurt him, Jack. Please find another way. If we gets our money back, all's well and enough."

Jack knew Kimbo was right, but it started him thinking. *Do I want to leave? Do I really want to hunt down Bill and this other fella and then get in a fight that maybe I don't win? Do I want to risk my life and go after Bill? This is a good life here, and we plan on improving it with our own business, and we will. Maybe this is just a blip, as Kimbo says. Or is it? If I stay put, will I regret it? We need to get that money back, but I'm beginning to love it here with Myron and Kimbo.*

Jack could not sleep that night. He tossed, turned, got up, walked outside, and looked at the clear sky, twinkling with ten thousand stars in the night sky above the Ten Thousand Islands. "How wonderful it is here," he said quietly to himself.

When Kimbo woke the next morning, Jack was gone.

Chapter Thirteen
The Dice Are Loaded

With Jack gone, Kimbo took Myron to Bad Hand Billie's place. Myron was always happy to go there, and Bad Hand's wife, Halona, greeted them with a hug, as she always did. With Myron in tow, the children went to play in the area created for them by Bad Hand. The fencing made it safe from "critters", as white men called them. Kimbo sat down with Bad Hand and Halona and told them, in as much detail as he thought they should know, about what happened with Bill – and Jack's subsequent pursuit. Bad Hand listened attentively, without emotion or interruption. Halona sat with them, slightly shaking her head occasionally as she listened. Bad Hand gave Kimbo his thoughts.

"Jack is a good man. A good white man. He knows how to treat people, judging them by noble standards. But he is chasing dark shadows by going after these men, and they'll be mixing, maybe, with others like them. Jack has a good life here with you and Myron. My people hunt only for food. We would hunt men if it helped the whole family, perhaps the whole tribe, but we would not hunt them just for money. This is a disease in people. Revenge for killing or harming, yes, I understand that. Revenge for stealing is only hurt pride. Jack is suffering from hurt pride. Jack feels he has let you and Myron down badly; it's become personal, which is dangerous. But he could stay here and work to build something better, sweeter. If he brings back the money and his life in one piece, it will speed up your lives, but he stands to lose both. He chooses to gamble, but the dice are always loaded. Your friend, who you call Bill, has passed into a new world of greed. Maybe this is right for him, but it is a world in which it is difficult to return. Bill may have decided he would rather live a short and pleasurable life than what he might consider a barely survivable existence. Kimbo Hopper, we are lucky men. We know ourselves better than anyone. We know what makes us happy, but there are consequences to every path, as with all things. Kimbo, Bill took his path, and now Jack has taken his. Don't be too hard on them. As you did, they also suffered in that storm but had different horrors to overcome. Many would look into their souls, trying to discover why they survived, while others didn't. Sometimes, the dice are loaded. Sometimes, people must throw the dice and find out."

The three sat together, talking for an hour. Halona spoke her mind during the conversation, making it clear that whatever the two men thought was the right or wrong thing to do, nothing should be undertaken that would put the children in danger. Bad Hand looked at his wife. "Kimbo, this woman, Halona, would do more than just bite the hand of Holata, her husband, if I put our children at risk. An alligator snapping turtle would be nothing if Halona turned on me." He showed half a smile.

Halona spoke. "Yes, it will be more than dice that will be loaded," she said, looking at the rifle above their bed. Her look was unusually grim and severe. It went silent. This was the first time Kimbo had seen her this way, and he tried to lighten the mood and steer the exchange between friends in a better direction. He picked up on something inconsequential.

"Bad Hand Billie, was Holata your original first name?"

"My father named me after the famous Seminole chief, Holata Micco. My father waited a long time before finding a nickname for me." He held up his hand to demonstrate his following comment. "When I was eight years old, I foolishly picked up an alligator snapping turtle; as you know, I lost my fingers. But my name, Holata, in our native tongue, also means 'alligator'. Being a man with a sense of humour, he wanted to give me a name that was in keeping with an important part of my life. So, he called me 'Bad Hand'. I also have a sense of humour, so I married Halona." His wife kicked him hard in the shin. "Ow, what I mean is Holata marries Halona. Very funny. But the funniest thing is that Halona means 'fortunate' on our tongue. Very funny, yes?"

This time, Halona swiped at his head but missed as he ducked. He was used to ducking out of the way when Halona reacted to one of his jokes. She gave the impression that she was annoyed with her husband, but it was obvious to Kimbo she loved him very much.

Witnessing this domestic play-acting, Kimbo realised how much he missed Zella, a woman like Halona. He watched Halona's movements and how she swayed her hips as she checked on the children playing outside.

I must try to forget about Zella. I must put these thoughts away. He knew he was a man, alone and missing a woman. He missed their intimacy. He didn't think he would ever have that happiness again. He would be wrong, but he could never have guessed his future. He was going to take just one day at a time.

Chapter Fourteen
Drink Talking

Jack Root knew he was taking a risk by entering Miami's 'Colored Town', especially a white man sitting at a bar first thing on a humid morning. The southern state laws, nicknamed "Jim Crow Laws", compelled Miami to segregate a part of the city to house the black population away from the white areas. The black people of Colored Town spent most of their day working in the white-dominated parts of Miami, primarily the new and booming downtown and Coconut Grove areas. The white parts of cities at that time, not only in the southern states but also in some places in the north, were nicknamed "sundown towns", sometimes known as "sunset towns", "grey towns" or "sundowner towns". You had to be out by sundown if you were black and working in white municipalities or neighbourhoods – or suffer the consequences.

Jack had hitched a ride to Miami, a city he had lived in for many years and knew well. People who travelled east along the Tamiami Trail were generally good-natured and easy-going. Almost anyone, especially white men, would be guaranteed to get a ride, as most drivers had been in that same situation at some stage in their lives; the drivers were white men anyway. It was, however, unsafe for women to travel alone. And never safe for a black woman.

Jack had guessed correctly that Bill and his cohort, Zip Thomas, had headed for the street markets of downtown and the upscale market on Lincoln Road, a well-known spot for wealthy northerners from New York or Washington to shop. He had learnt all this from a man called Purvis.

Asking discreet questions of the drivers along the trail, one had slipped Jack a piece of paper with the address of a rum shop and bar with a person's name written on it.

"BUT don't ask for this man. Don't say his name out loud. He will notice you."

Jack found the bar and sat quietly, staring straight ahead most of the time, until a man slipped onto the stool beside him. They sat together in that bar in the middle of Colored Town, talking while Jack shared a bottle with him. Jack knew that if you wanted to know what was going on, people in this part of the city were sure to know. He realised that he had struck lucky the day he met Purvis. Fate had dealt him an ace for once, the dice in his favour so far.

Although Purvis lived in Overtown, another 'black-only' part of Miami, he liked to drink in Colored Town. "Because," he would say to anyone asking, "I don't like to shit on my doorstep."

As the teacher, Elizabeth Mitchell, discovered, Purvis was straightforward and full of local knowledge and gossip. Jack realised that Purvis was very well connected. He knew all about Zippy, as Zip Thomas liked to be known. Purvis knew Zippy was a thief, a murderer and a brothel owner who was in Florida escaping from somebody or something in the north. Jack slowly revealed to Purvis the story of Bill and Zip Thomas stealing money and skins from his home in Chokoloskee, and Purvis snorted. "Boy, you sure didn't see a snake like Zippy coming, now did ya?"

"Can you help me find him, Purvis?" It sounded like he was pleading. He didn't want to discuss more detail of what had happened, only what he could do about it.

"I only visit that part o' town when someone pays me. I go

when I'm workin' or else police gonna throw me in jail if I don't got a paid reason to be there. By the look of yer, I'm guessing you don't got no money, so I can only tell you two things. Go to those markets I told ya 'bout and ask real gently 'bout ol' Zippy's whereabouts. And two, watch yer back. He gonna shoot yer as soon as look at yer. He's a mean white man – real mean. And if yer don't mind me saying, you too nice to be goin' hunting down a fella like that."

Jack thanked Purvis, paid for the bottle and left.

Within two days, Jack discovered that Bill and Zip Thomas had sold most of the stolen alligator and racoon skins, stuffed animals and plumes at Miami's Lincoln Road market. It made sense for them to go there first. The rich folk gathered there, looking for something exotic to take back north. Bill and Zip then took what they didn't sell to the downtown street markets. Everything they had was sold, and they moved on. They had disappeared from Miami a day before Jack would have caught up with them. No one would talk to Jack beyond simple facts of what they did. Even if they did know where he had gone, nobody would tell Jack. Talking about someone else's business only led to bad things.

Jack went back to the bar in Colored Town and waited for Purvis. He might have helpful suggestions for his next step.

"Ha, so that son-of-a-bitch didn't shoot ya like I thought he would, eh?" Purvis burst through the door, looking pleased with himself about something. Jack didn't want to know what. He'd learnt not to ask, just let information slip, creep, and spill out.

"Purvis, you were helpful to me the other day, and I don't have much money, but can you help me work out where they went after the markets? They sold all my stuff and disappeared." Jack wasn't optimistic he would get even a hint from Purvis, but he had to try the only link he had to work on.

"I don't want yer money, white man. 'Tis easy. They

hightailed it down to The Keys. From what I can tell, they aim to set up a new whorehouse and gambling den down there somewhere. My bet would be Key West; there's much more action there with tourists and boats up and down to Cuba. I can't see them coming back here for quite a while unless it's for a particular reason, not even to shoot you." Purvis smiled, revealing a gap between his two front teeth and the smile Elizabeth Mitchell had seen when she turned down the teaching job Purvis had offered her.

"Purvis, I'm grateful to you. You've helped me get a direction. I wanna ask you how you know all these things, but it would be wrong for me to ask." He waited before continuing, just in case Purvis made the mistake of telling him. Purvis never made that kind of mistake. Purvis just looked at him wryly, almost smiling again. He had a profoundly sardonic but gentle way about him.

"When you got something to offer, then we can talk. Not before," he said.

"Anyway, Purvis, thank you, and please thank your contacts too." Jack left.

Purvis shrugged and finished Jack's bottle; it would be a shame to let it be resold, as he knew the barman would. It would be quite a while before they'd meet again, and next time, Jack would make sure he had something to offer.

Jack gets a job
The last place Jack wanted to go was the Florida Keys. He had almost no money and no friend like Kimbo Hopper to help him catch and cook his meals. He hitched rides from Miami, through the familiar city of Homestead and onto Key Largo. He saw no reason to stop and meet anyone in Homestead. He couldn't

remember anyone other than Doc Slim and the Watsons; they would be back at home in The Keys. He thought about his predicament. At twenty-eight, Jack had nothing to show for his life, and after two days of very little food and hard travelling, mainly in the back of vehicles, sometimes riding with pigs or cattle. He was penniless and homeless once more. He'd returned to the hand-to-mouth existence he'd endured as a sixteen-year-old before his railroad years.

Travelling south, he sometimes sat in the back of a truck transporting black and Hispanic migrant workers down to the middle keys. Since the storm, they worked hard on the highway to Key West, but it wasn't finished. The renewed road-building project through The Keys meant back-filling the jobs of the dead vets and others, typically employing men who were desperate, shunned or lacked ambition of any kind. Jack thought these men would be grateful they had a job to go to, whatever the conditions. They knew they would be getting fed; their meals were provided at the worker's camps on Pigeon Key and Islamorada. The camps would be Jack's first opportunity to find his feet and determine what's next.

He stepped down from the truck alongside the work-seekers who flowed into the hut marked 'Canteen'. Jack peeled off the line as the wretched men trudged in for an eagerly anticipated meal. Chancing his luck, Jack knocked on the door marked 'Office'.

"I'm Russ Porter, the overall Keys road works manager. What can I do for you?" A polite and professional Russ Porter looked Jack up and down and wasn't sure what he saw. Jack appeared dressed like a road worker but held himself differently from those he was used to seeing. He had an itinerant appearance but intelligent eyes and an immediately engaging manner. Jack put on his best-educated train-driver accent and vocabulary. Jack had learnt early in life to fit in and act like he was naturally part of whichever situation he found himself in.

"Mr Porter, I am very pleased to meet you. My name is Jack Root. I was one of the train drivers for the Miami to Key West line until the storm took it away."

Jack was now using instinct to guide the conversation. "I heard many good things about how well things are organised here, Mr Porter. With the recovery work and highway building, you have achieved great things. I was hoping to get a job with you using my engineering background and, of course, my experience with the terrain and weather in these parts. I miss working in this important part of the world." Jack was hoping he hadn't overdone the compliments.

"Well, Jack Root, I always regard flattery as chewing gum. Enjoy it, but don't swallow it," said the worldly works manager. Jack smiled, and so did Russ Porter. The ice had been broken between the two of them.

The two men talked briefly, and Jack discovered Russ Porter had an opportunity on an automobile ferry service connecting the forty-one-mile gap between Lower Matecumbe and No Name Key. He was in luck. They needed an engineer who knew what he was doing. He didn't mention that he was the actual train driver that fateful day in September 1935. He just told Russ Porter he had driven trains to Key West for many years and knew The Keys, its engineering challenges and, at times, the unpredictable, brutal weather. He got the job.

Jack knew he needed to slow down his pursuit of Bill and Zip Thomas. He needed to regain personal energy and feed himself better. At this point, he needed to accumulate a little money and much strength, not speed. He needed to think and have a clear plan. He needed to ask around. Many questions needed answering before he would confront the two thieves, wherever they were. He was sure the stolen money would already be spent in many ways. The cash from under Myron's bed would also be gone. He asked himself a difficult question. *Was he chasing revenge, or was it repayment or both?*

He didn't yet know. He wondered if he should return to Chokoloskee or refocus on recouping the loss he and Kimbo had suffered. He wasn't concerned about Kimbo and Myron; he knew they would continue to thrive. The life Kimbo and he had created in Chokoloskee was sound. He had arrived here, an ideal place to work things out carefully, not rush. He knew Zip Thomas would be dangerous but didn't know how Bill would react. Would Bill turn on him, his old friend Jack, when he appeared – demanding his and Kimbo's money? He was sure that charging into a lair occupied by Zip Thomas would be a fatal mistake. This needed thinking about; he needed to know much more.

Rushing to a decision may hurt me, but so will it if I wait too long. I'm in danger of being obsessed with making the right decision. It could be that good luck will produce a reward, but also it might punish me as a result. Destiny has a fixed plan, or does it? One step will take me to another, no matter what.

"So," Jack muttered, "what do I do next?"

Jack Root was in an ideal situation to do that thinking. After a month, Russ Porter knew he had a sound, solid engineer in Jack Root. He appointed him chief engineer of the car ferry, shipping people both ways, down to the lower Keys or bringing them to the upper Keys. The ferry was highly reliable, and Jack had little to do as an engineer. The ferry job gave him time to talk to travellers, learn about life in The Keys since the storm, and ask detailed but careful questions about specific places. It took six months before he had a complete picture of where those two men were, what they were up to, and what he should do next. Six months well spent, in Jack's opinion.

Unwavering from his righteous objective, he now had a plan.

Chapter Fifteen
Watson's Visitors

During those six months, Jack visited Ed and Hank Watson, who had successfully returned to Islamorada and rebuilt their lives. He knocked on the door marked 'The Watson Family's Place'. When the door opened, Ed immediately slammed it shut. He shouted to Hank to get his shotgun, and suddenly, both barrels poked out at Jack when the door cracked open again. He was shocked to learn that Bill and Zip Thomas had visited the Watsons.

"Whoa, Mr Watson. It's me, Jack Root, the train driver. We were together in Homestead after the storm. Do you remember?"

"I sure do. You got that good fer nothin' bastard Bill Walker with ya?"

"No. He stole my money, and I'm looking for him. Did he come to see you?"

Bill Walker remembered where the Watsons lived and came calling. He convinced Zippy to rest a little in The Keys to understand how things were after the hurricane and to see what opportunities they had to start a new bordello business. Realising Jack was being straight with them, Ed told their story.

"They knocked on our door and were welcomed into this house. Although the other fella didn't give his name to us, we heard it right enough. They stayed two nights. This Zippy fella knocked Hank out cold and tied me up on the third day. They found the money we had stashed away under the bed and disappeared. Hank ain't been right since, and he was lucky he didn't die. He sometimes gets bad headaches and is very confused..." Ed was about to go into many details already explained to the town sheriff, but Hank stopped him.

"Enough, Pa. I don't want to hear it all over again. You finds 'em, Mr Root, you gonna tell me 'cause I'm looking to get our money back. Ya hear?" Hank Watson spoke with a slight slur to his words.

"I do hear, Hank. Don't you worry! It's the thing that gets me going every mornin'. You and me ain't the only people they done wrong to. I ain't gonna settle again until I put it right, or I'm six feet under God's earth." Jack's voice tightened, and both Watsons could see he was genuinely emotional about what they had just told him.

Ed burst out, "Now don't go getting yerself killed for this! You're a good man, Jack Root. Now I see you more clearly; you wanna stay and have a bite with us tonight? Be interested to know what happened to you and that black fella…what was his name?" Ed lowered the gun, put it away, and welcomed Jack into their house.

"Kimbo, Kimbo Hopper. He is also a good man. He was robbed by those two bastards as well as me and you. We got a good life out there on Chokoloskee, 'cept fer them skeeters."

Jack slid into the local way of speaking; he thought it would help. "Man, them skeeters, they'd eat you alive if you don't know what you're doin'. I must say, Mr Watson, you and Hank rebuilt your house real nice. Someday, I'm gonna have somethin' like this and maybe get myself a big family."

Jack surprised himself by saying these things out loud. The Watsons were good men, too, bringing out feelings he hadn't realised he had. Things were changing for Jack. He wanted to put things right with Bill Walker and Zip Thomas but didn't want to die doing it.

As Jack spoke to Ed Watson, he noticed that recently, he'd slipped into the vernacular of the people he was mixing with. He'd done it with Kimbo, Purvis, Russ Porter and now the Watsons. *Was this a good thing, or was it insulting? Did it help communicate, or was it stupid?* So far, it wasn't stupid, but he must be more conscious of it. He noticed that it did put them more at ease. He thought, as long as folk don't think I'm being funny with them. Jack had supper with the Watsons but didn't stay overnight. Neither he nor the Watsons wanted that.

It would be quite a while before Jack would return to Ed and Hanks's place.

Chapter Sixteen
Key West

Business booms

Following their visit to Ed and Hank Watson, Bill Walker and Zip Thomas found what they sought in Key West. The house on the corner of Angela Street and Thomas Street needed some work but was ideally situated and for sale at a reasonable price. Within three weeks, it was turned into a bordello and gambling hall. The locals preferred to call it a bordello as it sounded French or Italian and, therefore, much more sophisticated and cultured than the brothels and whorehouses of Miami, New Orleans or Havana. Zip Thomas was trying to provide an image of the most up-market brothel south of Miami. They discovered it wasn't a difficult challenge. Between them, they decided to put the women upstairs, with gambling downstairs. It became popular with the local men and merchant sailors, naval sailors and boat people from the other islands of the lower Keys. Visitors from Havana and other Cuban towns started coming to Key West to gamble. Of course, they had brothels and gambling in Havana, but this was attractive, presentable, American, and, most importantly, more fun. Zippy had provided everything they could think of.

In a short time, the business of the Bill Walker and Zip Thomas partnership was booming, and they were looking to expand. Bill was having the time of his life and turned a blind eye to Zippy's brutal treatment of the girls if they didn't make the money he set for them. His rules were fixed, and Zippy knew what business income, expenses, and profit should be, right up to the last cent. Failure by a woman to make the specified amount of money twice meant a beating. They were thrown out if it happened a third time, regardless and no matter what.

Bill often sat alone with a beer or whisky, but he never wondered or cared what might have happened to Jack. He certainly didn't think of Kimbo or little Myron, not once. They were black and not his people. It was plain to see that the horrific storm had a truly different and indelible stain on Bill's thinking. He didn't care about anybody. It was apparent by the way he drank and womanised that he didn't much care for himself or his future either.

Accumulating knowledge

At last, the entire one hundred and seven miles of the hardtop overseas highway, from the mainland to Key West, was opened for traffic. The road builders continued the tradition Henry Flagler's railroad established by fixing markers spaced one mile apart and starting from Whitehead Street, Key West, just three blocks from Zippy and Bill's bordello. There was some nervousness about installing toll booths along the long route as armed robbery was feared. However, it was pointed out to the highway authorities that given there was just one road for a hundred-mile stretch, it would be difficult for the criminals to make a fast and clean getaway by car. The local Keys residents had a good laugh about that. Eventually, one tollbooth was located on Big Pine Key and one on Lower Matecumbe Key. The income helped convince some doubters that the road was worth building, bringing tourists fishing and boating on frequent vacations.

Before the new highway made the car ferry redundant, all

kinds of people had boarded the boat Jack managed. The mixture was highly diverse. Wealthy people on vacation were hoping to reach Cuba from the ferry port in Key West – police in pursuit of wanted criminals, work migrants, artists, or those who wanted to view a famous author's house. They all liked talking to Jack while taking the ferry up or down The Keys. From easy chats and gratuitous gossip, Jack's accumulated knowledge helped visitors understand how to get the best out of their vacation in The Keys. It was even more valuable for Jack, as they were happy to repay his help with the information he wanted on their return journey. He was careful not to ask too many direct questions of Key West residents. He didn't want any word to get back to Key West that a man was asking about the bordello and who was running it. Jack began to build a picture of what happened to Bill and Zip and where precisely they were located. When he knew where they were and had enough money saved up, he planned what he should do next, and he was ready to carry it out with the new highway finished. Over that year, his anger had turned to guile. He was determined to recover their money and retrieve Ed and Hank Watson's stolen cash. He was obsessed but prepared to do whatever it took. He hoped Bill Walker and Zip Thomas would hardly know what hit them. He was a little surprised at himself and his unwavering determination.

But now, out of a job, he didn't go to Key West. Instead, he headed to Miami.

Chapter Seventeen
Elizabeth

Myron was six years old and ready for schooling. He knew how to skin racoons and snakes, and although his products were not yet of the highest quality, they still sold well. He also started to learn taxidermy and animal mounting skills, but, reluctantly, his father knew it was time for him to read, write and know his numbers. He thought it was time for Myron to mix with children his age more than he had. School was the right thing for him at six years old, but Kimbo hesitated. His fear of how Myron might be treated dominated his thoughts.

"He would probably be the only black boy in his class, probably in the whole school. Hell, there's no more than twenty, maybe thirty, kids schoolin' there anyhow," Kimbo muttered to himself. Since Jack had left, Kimbo muttered to himself a lot, and, in his mind, he still felt it was a joint decision between him and Zella. He was waiting to hear her opinion.

It was the night before he planned to take Myron to register him. He was worried about how his son would deal with the next part of growing up: *How would he cope with bullies? Would the principal even register him for school? Would he be accepted?*

It had been a long time since the storm had taken Zella and Zakari. With just Myron now, Kimbo had developed a constant habit of talking to Zella. It helped him with his decisions. In his head he could hear Zella answering him.

He didn't expect Jack to return, and even if he did, he didn't think he would recover anything stolen from them. He had developed a strong relationship with Bad Hand Billie, Halona, and Jim Tigertail. Myron felt Naama, Tocho, and Tehya were part of his family, too. Kimbo told Bad Hand that he was going to Everglades City the next day to register Myron at the school. Bad Hand was curious.

"I wish you the best of luck, Kimbo. My two boys should be readin' and writin' by now, but those people at the school just ignored me. If you get young Myron in there, I'll march right through the door the day after and get my children registered. Good luck. Just one thing to remember – don't get angry. Be prepared to be disappointed."

Going to School
Kimbo and Myron put on their cleanest and neatest clothes, crossed the channel between Chokoloskee and the mainland, and walked to the small school north of the city. It was the furthest point for them to walk from the dock; residents stared at them as they made their way along the roadsides. Kimbo knocked on the door marked 'Principal' after being guided there by one of the teachers. She didn't give her name.

Kimbo spoke in the best way he knew, using his best English and manners. "Good morning! I am Kimbo Hopper, and this is my son, Myron Hopper. I would like to register my boy in your school. Can you help me understand what I do next? Unfortunately, I cannot read or write, so if you have papers to write on or whatever needs to be done, would someone please help me to write them?"

Mr Andrew Clemens looked at them and immediately knew he had a problem. The man before him was huge, with his son's hand buried deep in his enormous, gnarly fist.

The principal answered Kimbo with a soft, cruel, but academic voice. He stood unblinking, a man in his mid-fifties with an ill-fitting, well-worn light grey suit. There was a hidden smile in his words.

"Good morning to you. My name is Andrew Clemens, and I am the principal of this school. Mister Hopper, you say. Thank you for asking us to admit your son to our school. You should, however, know that I would be breaking Florida's laws if I allowed any of my white teachers to instruct pupils of another race in this public school. It is a criminal offence, and you are technically breaking the law just by asking me to do it. It was written into Florida law in a 1927 statute. I'm sorry; there is nothing I can do about that. If you want to look at it, I have a copy of that statute in my desk drawer. But then again, from what you tell me, you cannot read."

Kimbo was confused. *Is this man tricking me? He knew I couldn't read, so he could show me anything or say anything to fool me.*

"Mister Clemens, sir, I don't want my son to grow up to be dumb like me. I want him learning readin', writin', and doing his numbers. I want him to have a better life than I could get. Is there anything you can do to help me with this or advise me on what to do?"

"I'm afraid there is nothing I can do. This is a public school, and, as I said, it'd be breaking the law if I did what you asked, and I'm sure you wouldn't want me to do that. We wouldn't want to get the sheriff involved – a vile man. If you find a school with teachers of your colour, that will not break the law. Do you see?" So, Kimbo realised that was the trick. Black children can be taught, but only by black teachers.

Kimbo's next question was to the point. "But, Mister Clemens, how do black teachers learn enough to be able to teach?" The question hung in the stale air and was left unanswered by the Principal. His weasel words and hidden smile were already enough answers.

Kimbo stood still. This school was the only one in at least forty miles. Probably Homestead was the nearest, or perhaps Naples. He thought about all these things as he looked blankly at Andrew Clemens. Even if he moved to Homestead or Naples, he couldn't see how any of those places would have black teachers. He now understood what Bad Hand meant.

"Don't get angry, but be prepared to be disappointed," he'd advised Kimbo. These words were given to him by a true friend. But Andrew Clemens was right about one thing: Kimbo knew not to get the sheriff involved. He'd heard why from Jim Tigertail and Bad Hand.

Father and son took each other's hands, turned their backs on the principal and walked out through the office door, trying desperately not to be angry. Kimbo clenched his jaw hard.

Outside, they quickened their pace along the corridor and were about to leave the school building when a woman called softly. "Say, mister, come in here. I'd like to talk to you."

The same teacher had guided Kimbo to the principal's office, and it appeared she had waited for him to re-emerge. The woman was probably younger than Kimbo, but not by much. Beckoning them into an empty classroom, she spoke warmly and rapidly.

"I'm guessing the principal has told you the law. He may delight in it but is not trying to fool you. He is right – that is the law in Florida and plenty of other places. In Florida, the law says you can't have, let's say, me, a white woman, teach your lovely son, a black boy, in a public school. But if I were to teach your son at my house or yours, it wouldn't break any laws. It wouldn't be in a public school, do you see?" Kimbo wasn't following very well; his anger was getting in the way.

She continued, "Some people won't like it, but that's too

bad. I already teach three Seminole children at my house so that another child won't hurt. I won't ask you for money as I can't spare as much time as I'd like to, and I don't want money anyway; I'd like to do it. Would you want me to do that for your son? My name is Elizabeth Mitchell."

Kimbo was stunned. He took a few moments to collect himself.

"Missy Mitchell, that is right kind of you, but I don't want you to get into no trouble. I see that it would not be a problem if you were black. But the way Mister Clemens was talking to me, it was plum obvious he plain didn't see teaching black children as the right thing to do. You can tell many things from the way folk talk. You'd get into a lotta trouble, and I don't want to be the reason to bring trouble to your door."

Elizabeth Mitchell attempted to reassure Kimbo.

"He doesn't need to know. But let me put your mind at rest on this law business and emphasise what I'm saying to you about this. The law says someone from one race can't teach children of another *in public schools.* We'll not be doing this in public schools, will we?" She smiled at Kimbo Hopper and Myron. Kimbo paused, thinking, and then spoke.

"I can't tell you how much I 'preciate your offer. But I can't take it."

It was Elizabeth's turn to be stunned. "Why?" she asked, puzzled.

"Well, I can't take your free time; it ain't right. I don't have much money, but I have skins, hides, or coon hats. Maybe you don't want a lotta dead animals crowdin' out your house, but if you can wait 'til I sell some of these, I can give you some money. But, Missy Elizabeth, taking your free time wouldn't seem right and proper. I will pay what I can when I can. Also, I can't accept your kind offer unless I can add three more children to your private schooling. Myron here has three Seminole friends who need schooling, too. Would you teach them alongside Myron? And would you please accept my offer of a little money…er, for all of them?"

Elizabeth Mitchell stood in admiration. She said, smiling, "Yes, of course, I would be delighted."

Even though Kimbo Hopper had somehow taken full advantage of her generous offer because she knew she would never take any money to teach these children, Kimbo had sensed that, too. A delicate negotiation had taken place.

Kimbo and Myron returned to the dock and arrived at their house in Chokoloskee. Kimbo had an unfamiliar feeling that something very significant had just happened, and he had made it happen – just by trying to find the right way, to do the right thing.

Within three months, Myron, Naama, Tocho and Tehya had learnt well enough for each of them to read. Reading without speaking the words aloud had yet to be mastered by Myron or Tehya. Naama and Tocho were older, more advanced and now confident, and they read quietly to themselves without their lips moving or making a sound. Tehya was Myron's age, but she had been learning for longer.

Elizabeth Mitchell lived on Copeland Avenue, a road leading out of Everglades City, just outside the city limits, on the unmade dirt road to Chokoloskee. The school had provided the house, and Elizabeth was delighted with where it was. She had privacy to hold her classes. She was confident no one would see the children coming and going.

She held daily classes for six Seminoles and the young, delightful Myron Hopper. She had wanted to do this since she moved to Everglades City from New York via Purvis and Miami. She wanted to help educate children, no matter their background. Elizabeth also knew precisely the first thing the new classmates would learn. Once they had practised it, they would always remember it.

The proudest moment in Kimbo Hopper's life came when young Myron came back from class with Missy Mitchell and announced to his father that he had something he wanted to read to him. Kimbo's eyes brimmed with tears as Myron looked at a thick piece of parchment and started reading. He stuttered once or twice, but it was the sweetest, most beautiful sound Kimbo had ever heard – the words and who was reading them.

We hold these truths to be self-evident, that all men are created equal, that they are endowed by their Creator with certain unalienable Rights, that among these are Life, Liberty and the pursuit of Happiness.

When Myron had finished and looked up at his father for approval, Kimbo lifted him and hugged him so lovingly that they were both surprised at how much each was weeping and how hard they hugged each other. Elizabeth appeared in their lives, which would be a pivotal moment. Kimbo would always remember what she had done for Myron.

Chapter Eighteen
A Deal Is Struck

Jack Root sat at the rum bar all morning, waiting for Purvis to arrive. The barman had told Jack that Purvis still came in every morning rather than the afternoon, but it was around two o'clock when he finally walked through the half doors and took his usual seat. Jack sat in the chair next to him, and a drink was poured for him on arrival. Purvis looked hard at him.

"Hey, you that white guy comin' asking questions, what, maybe a year ago or summat?"

"You were helpful to me, Purvis, and I haven't thanked you properly. Share a bottle with me?"

"Fella, like you comin' in a place like this takes some guts once, let alone three times. Yeah, I remember you now. You wanted to know where Zippy Thomas was and some fella. Can't remember his name now; must be gettin' old."

"Yes, Purvis, you've got a pretty good memory. You told me to come and see you when I had something to offer. Well, I have. Wanna hear it?"

"Well, you'd better tell me 'cause now I'm curious that a white fella comin' in here after a year is still huntin' down that mean son-of-a-bitch. What's taken you so long, and why ain't he, or you, dead by now?"

Purvis wanted privacy and cleared the bar. It wasn't polite, but everyone, including the barkeep, understood that Purvis and this white man wanted the room to themselves. Purvis always got what he wanted. He could be very persuasive. He listened to what Jack had to say and who else would be involved. Jack told Purvis what he had found out and the plan. He asked Purvis straight away if he wanted a part in it. If he said "No," then all Jack's planning would be for nothing. The plan depended entirely upon Purvis.

Jack had discovered whose name appeared on the title of 302 Angela Street, Key West, and it wasn't Bill Walker's. The owner's name was Zipporah Thomas, which puzzled Jack. Not because Bill's name didn't appear, but because the name that did appear was strange. He didn't know the Bible inside out, but he did know the name Zipporah. She was the wife of Moses, and therefore, Zipporah was a female name. Purvis nearly fell backwards from his bar stool when he heard that. He didn't know what to do with this new and curiously amusing discovery, but he thought it might be helpful. Purvis was delighted with this information and said he could sell it to one of his contacts downtown. "And we could all get a good laugh out of it!"

"No, wait, Purvis. I think we can do better than that. Here is what I think we should do. We will both get more outta this than we've been thinking, and it will be all above board and legal… well, sorta. Certainly, a sorta justice."

Purvis was more than a small-time thinker. He listened, and he could see the logic and the so-called legality of Jack's plan. The legality was a little questionable, but who exactly would question it? That amused Purvis. All he needed to do now was find the right woman and a forger who could keep his mouth shut. Jack continued to describe the best type of woman for the job.

"She'll need to look wealthy…and white," he explained hesitantly. Jack laid his plan out but was less convincing than he should have sounded. As he talked it through and out loud for the first time, it now sounded like wrong-doing. He wasn't sure about doing something wrong to settle a wrong. Purvis noticed this hesitancy.

"Now, don't go coy on me, Jack. This is a job – it ain't no social debate. So, from what you're sayin', I need to get an actress and a forger lined up. But we ain't discussed money. I want half of the property sale. I'll have to pay out before I get any pay in. So, I want half." Purvis was serious, but so was Jack. This could give them both a big payday. They continued to discuss the details of the house, along with which real estate lawyer and agent they could use. It was essential to Purvis to use only the people he knew and whom he could "reach" if it went wrong. Jack asked what he meant by "reach".

With a thin smile, Purvis said it meant "hold accountable" for any "activity" taken outside of the plan. Jack wasn't sure if this was a threat to him, too. Purvis explained that being held accountable was normal and expected in his world.

"How else would this kinda thing work?" he said. "Look, I got a big question. How quick can we sell it? It seems to me people don't got lotta cash these days. Everyone's talking about 'The Depression'. Folk, these days, are short of cash. We gotta be quick. If it takes a while, ol' Zippy's gonna get wind of what's goin' on. Fella like that always got his ears wide open…and an itchy trigger finger."

"Yeah, I get it, Purvis. But I'm confident. The road's finished now. It goes all the way down from Maine to Miami, and from there, you can get in a car and drive the one hundred and sixty miles to Key West. It has opened the whole east coast to travel down. What's more, if you're tradin' with Cuba, then ninety miles southwest by boat, you're there. Seems to me that's havin' a place in Key West is gonna appeal to a lotta folk," explained

Jack. "Purvis, even better, this house is just three blocks from the world-famous writer Hemingway's house. In what those realty fellas call 'prime real estate territory'. I called one of them, you know, just askin', and they reckon they already have people asking about property around that area. Folks from Miami and New York and the like. Should be fast, they reckon, a day, maybe two, but at most a week."

"Weeks gonna be too long," Purvis stated.

Purvis asked a few more questions, paused, and told Jack about the dangers. They agreed that there was only one serious danger: a predictable Zippy Thomas. Purvis thought he could handle that, "but I'm not sure you could, Jack." It was a risk Jack always knew would be there. He looked at Purvis and held out his hand.

Jack asked, "Deal?"

Then Purvis smiled and said, "Yes. Deal." They shook hands.

They were beginning to understand each other, and trust was starting to bind them. Purvis could see this as a nice payday, a very nice payday. He would use some of his best connections. People he already knew he could trust. Jack didn't know how much he could trust Purvis, but his instincts were usually right. He had no choice but to go with his instincts.

Chapter Nineteen
To the Sound of Music

Jack sat at the back of the Sanchez Grocery store, Whitehead Street, Key West, sipping a "cold 'nuff" beer, as it was nicknamed. Jack's face was in shadow. Each evening, Cubans and Bahamians would gather in the small back room and start an impromptu Latin or Caribbean music session. Word had it that Bill Walker got in there almost every night. Jack sat patiently, waiting for Bill to walk through the door.

Jack saw him trip slightly as he entered. Bill looked fat, burnt by the sun and drunk. Bill had always been a happy drunk, and Jack hoped he still was.

"Mister Walker?" With his face still in shadow, Jack called out before Bill entered the back room, already throbbing loudly with Latin sounds.

Bill heard his name and came over to Jack's dark corner. "Yeah, what is it to you, buddy?" he slurred.

"Let's just keep this chat to the two of us, Bill." Walker was startled as Jack moved his face briefly into the light. It took a second for Bill's addled brain to recognise Jack Root.

"What the hell...? How did you know I would be here? What are you doing here? What the hell have you been up to? Are you mad at me for hightailing it outta that shithole?"

"I ain't mad at you, Bill. Shit, every man gotta do what he thinks is best for him, don't he? It's part of being free; a person gotta be free to make his way. This ol' country is all about being free. Let's get a bottle o' rum and go outback. I need your advice."

"Sure, Jack, it's great to see you. Glad there's no hard feelings and all. I got a real good life here in Key West. I got a business partner, and he's set me up real good here. I'm the boss of the place on the corner of…" Jack stopped Bill as he continued to slur his sentences. They were still in the store's open area, and their conversation might be heard. It would be best at the back of the grocery store, where a wide variety of tropical vegetation would screen them from view.

"Yeah, Bill, lots to catch up, but it's so noisy here with the music; let's go out back and catch up. See, I've got a bottle of rum right here." Jack took Bill by the arm, leading him out of sight and hearing. Bill looked at the rum bottle rather than Jack as they walked; it looked like a good brand.

A downed Gumbo Limbo tree lay conveniently across the back of the store, framed by bright red poinsettia plants. It was clear that many people had sat here for many different reasons. It also looked like couples had taken advantage of the vegetation screening, as there were places where the grass and plants had been flattened. The music was now low enough for them to talk easily.

Jack talked in a friendly, calm and unconcerned way, telling Bill the basic facts of his life since Bill had disappeared from Chokoloskee. He didn't mention the stolen money and merchandise. He didn't tell him he had called in on the Watsons in Islamorada. He made his life sound as matter-of-fact as possible and then turned to Bill and asked him how he had become such a big shot in this rich and busy town.

"Yeah, as I said, I have this partner now. He and I own the place on Angela Street, near Duval Street, which, if you don't know Jack, is the heart of the town. We call the place a Bordello, and we have gambling downstairs. It's a long way from running trains, but boy, does it pay big time!"

They sat drinking and remembering some of the good times

they had together before the hurricane had changed everything. Jack was drinking more slowly and with less in his glass.

"You know, Jack, I still get nightmares and flashbacks from that night. I know I drink too much as a result. I know it. But I'm gonna make my life just pure fun; that storm taught me not to wait for things to happen, go out and grab whatever you can, Jack, that's my philosophy."

Jack switched topics. He wanted to see Bill's understanding of his partner, Zip Thomas.

"You haven't told me about your partner. When did you meet him? What's he like? Would he give me a job? Would you give me a job here in Key West?"

"What's Zippy like? He knows what he wants in life. I like that, Jack. He's got some business interests in Miami, and he helped me set up in Key West. He can be very tough on people who get in his way. He chose the place I run here and recruited the girls and croupiers. I used the money I got from calling on the Watson house on our way here; they...er, lent me some. You remember them, Jack? Nice folk. So that money plus what I raised in the street markets in Miami from selling hides and stuff, I bought the house outright. Zippy set me up with a guy who does the numbers, you know, counting the money. He also got a lawyer to make everything official and above board. The lawyer keeps all the documents and stuff."

He then unwittingly gave Jack the name of the lawyer. Jack looked sideways at Bill. "So, exactly what is it you do every day, Bill? Do you own the Bordello? Have you signed your name on the paperwork?"

"Not exactly. I leave all that to Zippy. He's had these Bordellos before and explained that letting the lawyers sort the paperwork was best. I have good wages, and Zippy calls me once a week to see how things are. It's a real good life here, Jack. Next time he calls, I'll ask him about a job for you."

Jack realised Bill was in big trouble and wondered if he had any real job at the Bordello. If he toed the line, Bill would be okay. Bill wasn't necessary to Zip Thomas, but he was convenient currently to keep the Bordello ticking over. Convenient for now. Jack responded to Bill's offer.

"A job at the bordello? No, don't bother your partner with me. Thanks, but no. Let's see what job I can find first, but thanks, Bill. I'm not sure I'm cut out for the kind of work you're doing. Of course, there's nothing wrong with it, but it sounds like it's all sewn up already. I might try to get a job on those private boats running to Cuba and back. I think I'd be more useful doing that."

"Be careful, Jack; those boats are running some things. Things that might get ya killed at the drop of a hat. Be real careful who ya team up with. Rum running, drugs, you name it, them Cubans got an eye for all kindsa business in Key West, especially now we got a road through to us. Those Cuban boys are thinking they gotta route to wealth now. East coast folk think they got a route down, but the Cuban boys see it the other way round."

Jack continued to discuss life around Bill's bordello while offering him the rum bottle. Jack had stopped drinking early in their discussion, but Bill hadn't noticed. In the end, Jack extracted the names and addresses of all the people he needed for his plan to start working. It was clear to him that he could get his, Kimbo's, and Ed and Hank Watson's money back and, he thought, maybe a lot more. There were a few dependencies; he would have to be very careful. Purvis was to play a vital part, but they all needed to take each step exceptionally carefully.

Getting it wrong would be catastrophic.

Chapter Twenty
Fire and Gator Bites

Miss Elizabeth Mitchell's private school was going well. All the children were making good progress in the three main subjects. Myron liked numbers. He could add, subtract, divide, multiply, and make his father groan in the evenings before bed as he recited his math tables. He was becoming so good at them that he sang them in a tune he had made up.

"My, now aren't we the big shot, mister Myron Hopper! Showing off to your papa all your numbers and the like." Kimbo teased his son, but Myron knew his father was very proud of him. That was just part of the unbreakable bond between them.

"But, Papa, I can teach you the numbers, and it would help you when you takin' the skins and hides and plumes to sell."

"Son, I got you to do that now. It'll be good for you to do the numbers for me, and then we won't get no white folks tryin' to fool this old man no more." Kimbo's pride was a factor in this response. He wasn't ready yet for a son to teach a father anything. He was also afraid of making mistakes with the white folks. Having his son handle the numbers was a sign of pride and showed people that a young black boy who knew his numbers was as good as any other boy.

Their subsistence level of living was still all that Kimbo wanted or needed. However, he struggled with his promise to himself and Zella after the storm – that he would provide the best life for Myron. He was being schooled, and they were never short of food.

Myron had other children his age around him, and they all got along well, but is Chokoloskee the best place to live? What opportunities will he miss if he is condemned to just a life of trapping wildlife and selling it in its different forms? Should they seek a life where they lived with people who looked like them and shared their likes or dislikes?

Kimbo wished he had more knowledge and was as clever as Jack.

The spirit of the law

Solomon Bass became suspicious when he noticed Myron arrived at Elizabeth's house with a small book.

"What's a black kid doin' wif a book?"

Bass spoke out loud. Solomon Bass usually spoke his thoughts out loud. It was an annoying habit to the local Klan faction. The Ten Thousand Island faction was a splinter group calling themselves the "Knights of the Cypress Fire".

"Hum, I'd better report this to da boss," he said. It was another annoying habit that he called the Grand Wizard of the splinter Klan 'boss' when convention demanded more of a military-style and respectful way of addressing the head of the group. The Grand Wizard instantly tried to correct Solomon Bass by shouting at him repeatedly,

"Look, I've told you not to call me boss!" Solomon forgot every time.

As Myron entered Elizabeth's house, Bass watched him and spoke aloud.

"I'm goin' to take me a look so I can reports back wif details an' names. I'm gonna prove my worth to all 'em 'glades, good ol' boys."

Bass moved slowly toward the house, listening and

watching, his beady eyes and sullen face frozen in an evil grin. If this were what he thought it was, he would get high praise and greater acceptance from the group, something he desperately wanted. Elizabeth saw him as he clumsily peered through the side window and saw six Seminoles and the black child he'd seen going through the door. Her heart thumping, she ran to the door, opened it quickly, and asked, as calmly as possible, if she could assist this strange man. He stepped back in surprise and then looked at her breathing anxiously; he stared at her heaving breasts.

"You teachin' them? You ain't allowed to teach no injun an' black kids. You teach in the school, don't cha? I seen ya teachin'. I'm gonna tell the, er, the er, sheriff. He gonna arrest ya. Yer gonna be in big trouble."

"What you see here is me minding the children while their mommas and papas are out working."

Elizabeth had told the children that if anyone other than their parents saw them reading books or writing at her or their own house, they should pack away everything out of sight as quickly as possible. They did this as she was tackling Solomon Bass outside. She deliberately talked slowly, distracting him. She gave the children enough time to hide their books.

"Here, you can come in and look, Mister, er, Mister...what was your name again? It would be very nice to know your name."

"Bass. M'names' Solomon Bass. Well, I don't mind if I do come in."

Bass looked leeringly at Elizabeth's slender figure and her full breasts. It made her inwardly shudder. He then strode across the scrubland and burst through the door to see all the children playing games he didn't recognise. "Ha, injun games, eh? Well, maybe these kids are just playin', an' maybe they ain't." He said, thinking aloud, making him sound slightly foolish to everyone except himself. Even the children thought hearing someone talk aloud to themselves was strange. "I say yer teaching 'em. That black kid, ain't he that Hopper boy, over yonder in Chokoloskee? Well, I knows fer a fact it agin' the law ta teach that boy!"

Elizabeth knew immediately that it was pointless to argue the rights and wrongs of Florida law with Bass. She knew that the 'Jim Crow' rules dominated everyday life regardless. No one should teach "coloureds" in any place, school or house or come to that in the middle of the Everglades, regardless of the letter of the law – it "didn't mean diddly squat." The spirit of the law was enough for most settlers in these parts.

"Hum, look, lady, black kids don't get no schoolin'. I'd better report this anyway, just in case. I might get a lotta credit for reporting this," he continued. "Sheriff's gonna hear, and so's Mister Clemens at the school. The whole town's gonna thank me for this." He started walking away but then, with a cunning look, turned to speak to Elizabeth again.

"See here, missy. You got anythin' to say to me, or perhaps, do fer me? I like the way you look. If we was, you know, doin' it, maybe's I could forget what I seen."

That made Elizabeth shudder for a second time. "Please leave," she asked politely, her heart thumping harder. Bass thought that was a weak response for someone facing big trouble. He spoke his mind again. "I sure bet you want me to come back again, maybe a little later tonight? You know, when the kids are gone back to their mamas. Yeah, I'll come back. Don't cha worry. I'll see ya later!"

"Please leave," she asked once more. She knew he would still tell all who wanted to listen what he had seen, regardless of whether he raped her or not. Rape was rarely brought to justice in this part of the world unless it was a black man accused by a white woman. *Blood in the water.*

Kimbo waited patiently behind a palmetto clump. His heart was thumping in his chest. He hadn't ever set out to hurt anyone badly in his life; he'd dished out a few sore heads but not serious injuries, just fistfights, and he wasn't sure he could hurt someone badly now. However, he knew that rape was on the mind of Solomon Bass, and he had seen and identified Myron as carrying a book. Consequently, something had to be done, which probably meant more than a fistfight. There was everything at stake. Protecting loved ones was always prominent in Kimbo's thinking and actions. Bass was threatening the two most important people in his life.

He watched Solomon Bass standing alone outside the house. Bass stooped to light a small fire of grass, cypress twigs and branches, sending flames licking light onto the trees. Bass then moved forward in his long white robe, covering his head with a white hood. He talked out loud. "She'd better be ready for me when I come in there. I'm gonna rape her, and there ain't nothin' nobody gonna do about it."

Elizabeth was not at home.

Solomon Bass glimpsed something coming at him in the darkness as he approached the house. He caught a glimpse of a large man just a split second before a giant fist hit him straight in his face. He went down like a sack of rocks. His nose was broken badly, and his bottom lip split open. Kimbo had hit him so hard that he was unconscious immediately. Kimbo dragged him into the bushes and heaved him into his two-man skiff. He handled Bass as though he was a ten-foot alligator but a good deal lighter. He then paddled through the small channels to the open water that took him south past the Chokoloskee shoreline and Turner

River. The mosquitoes were swarming over Kimbo's head and arms, infesting his chest and stomach, finding different ways to get inside his shirt. He was used to 'skeeters', but they were eating him alive out here just after dark. They were almost unbearable, but they wouldn't stop his plan. Jim Tigertail's stories about men disappearing in the wetlands were etched in his mind.

He knew these waters better than the back of his hand; he didn't need maps. Miles of small islands and small rivers inevitably flow into the Gulf of Mexico. He paddled the skiff with speed and skill through Liquor Still Bay and past Watson Prairie, eventually coming to Gator Bay after twenty miles, wedged between two swampland masses. He knew the bay had earned its name. Alligator caves and holes were stretched along the shoreline, where the swamp met the water, the mangroves hiding their entrances.

During the journey, Solomon Bass started moaning and speaking his drowsy thoughts. It wasn't clear what he was saying, but Kimbo thought he'd muttered the word "teacher." Kimbo hit him with his fist again, and he was quiet again. He tied him to a single, lonely, stunted cabbage palm tree and propped him against the trunk. Kimbo gagged his mouth with Solomon's hood still pulled over and around his head, preventing him from seeing who this big man was, just in case. The gag prevented him from speaking his thoughts out loud. Bass was out cold until the first daylight. Kimbo then put him back in his skiff and paddled deep into a channel where he knew alligators and crocodiles had their nests. It was the nesting season, and plenty of hungry reptiles would be there.

The brackish water allows both types of these reptiles to mix easily, and Kimbo knew the nesting season was the time of year to stay away from both. As in all of nature, these creatures protect their young aggressively and forcefully. Humans are not usually the first food they seek, but they seek and eat their flesh if hungry, particularly this season and when the taste of blood is in the water.

Kimbo Hopper took hold of Solomon Bass's white robe and ripped it off his limp body. He left his hood covering his head and, most importantly, his eyes, shielding him from sight, just in case. With blood oozing out of his mashed nose, Bass was still unconscious as Kimbo tipped him overboard into the salty water inside a large mangrove thicket. Kimbo noticed new ripples on the water's surface, maybe twenty feet away, sending mini-waves ahead of the approaching mouths.

Shared unwillingly
An average twelve-foot alligator will open its mouth slightly while searching for food in the water, using its integumentary sensory organs to detect disturbances and differentiate objects. Once the alligator finds and bites the object, it can examine it with its mouth to see if it's edible. Once the decision is made, they are swift and accurate in the attack. Alligators kill their victims after clamping their powerful jaws onto their prey and dragging them underwater to drown them. The drowning, coupled with violent shaking, breaking and munching bones with its teeth, squeezes the life out of their victims. That is, if terror and shock at what was happening hadn't already killed them.

Crocodiles are much larger than alligators, with longer snouts up to five feet long. They differ slightly by clamping down on their prey with their massive jaws, tasting it, crushing it, and then swallowing it whole. Nature gave them longer, sleeker snouts more suited to chomping large prey and swallowing.

It would never be known whether it was an alligator or a crocodile that consumed Solomon Bass, or even if it were only one. Whichever reptiles they were, they had tasted Solomon Bass and decided he was edible. It was also never known whether he was awake or still unconscious when the first bite was made or whether he was swallowed whole or dragged under, taken to a nest and left to rot before being consumed in smaller bites later. There may even have been a fight among a bask of reptiles for his edible body. He could have been ripped apart and shared unwillingly.

To Kimbo Hopper, it mattered that Solomon Bass was never seen again. Kimbo hadn't ever thought he had it in him to harm anyone truly. In his mentally stressed state, coming from his need to protect Elizabeth and his son, he convinced himself that he hadn't killed Solomon Bass, not personally. He had persuaded himself that justice had been done and terrible things were avoided. He thought avoiding what would have happened to Miss Elizabeth, Myron, and Bad Hand's children was much better. In his mind, Kimbo saw what was right and what was wrong. He justified his actions to himself but wasn't used to being a judge, jury and executioner. He was to feel this discomfort again, more than once, but there would be a time when he was not truly in control of himself or his fate.

At this horrifying moment, he suddenly realised he was a murderer.

The biggest hug
Myron woke to find Elizabeth Mitchell preparing breakfast. His father was not there. It was the first time in his life that his father wasn't in the house when he woke. Elizabeth said, "Good morning, Myron. Can you show me where Bad Hand lives when

you've finished breakfast? I can take you there until your father returns. He had to go somewhere to help someone. He should be home sometime today. I must go to school now."

Bad Hand used his small motorboat to take Elizabeth to the landing dock for Everglades City. She walked the dirt track to her empty house, washed, changed her clothes, and, after noticing a small fire had burnt itself out the evening before, walked to school at about the time she would typically do on any school day. That is as if this was a typical day, which it wasn't.

It was around midday when Kimbo arrived back at Bad Hand's place. Elizabeth hadn't told anyone why she looked after Myron overnight or where Kimbo had gone. Bad Hand knew better than to ask. If he should be told something, Kimbo would tell him. They had mutual respect and mutual understanding. Bad Hand offered conversation when Kimbo appeared.

He said, "The only thing Miss Elizabeth said to me was that it would be better if we found somewhere on Chokoloskee to continue the schoolin'. I got some ideas. You wanna talk? Now?"

Bad Hand could see Kimbo wanted to talk, which would allow his friend to unburden himself. Bad Hand could always tell when someone needed to get something out in the open and talk it through. Kimbo knew that Bad Hand was the only person he could completely trust. They had a special bond, the type that neither of them had with anyone else.

Kimbo said, "Let's go up the Turner River. I know a good place to sit and talk. I want to tell you what happened last night, but please tell me if you don't want to hear bad things. We can sit. Just sitting with you will help me a lot anyway."

For the rest of the day, the two friends sat and talked. It was as though they were close brothers. By the end of daylight, as the sun sank beneath the mangrove forest around them, they made their way home. By then, Bad Hand knew what had happened and why.

Myron skinned a racoon during the day, and the meat was available for the evening meal. He had meticulously scraped the fat off the underside of the hide and then rubbed it with a crude and local form of borax and cedar sawdust, knowing it helped the hide dry quicker. He used wood wool to stuff the animals, just as his father had taught him and Kimbo's father before that. Myron was becoming very proficient and skilled. He was sewing up the animal when his father walked in. He ran to him and gave Kimbo the biggest hug since the storm. Kimbo broke down and sobbed; it was less dramatic than crying in front of his son.

It had been madness for twenty-four hours. The best thing to come out of the chaos was that Kimbo Hopper and Holata Billie had a plan. They were both determined that their children would continue to be educated.

Sheriff Jeffries shouts

"I don't know where the hell that goddam idiot has got to. Fer one thing, he don't amount to a pile o' shit anyway. Fer another, I don't know why I even allowed him in!"

Sheriff Jeffries, otherwise called 'boss' by Solomon Bass, shouted at his second-in-command of the Knights of the Cypress Fire.

"I reckon he's been done by one o' them bandits hiding out in the islands, or a gator's got the son-of-a-bitch. Whatever, he's no loss to us. An' don't anybody go askin' if I'm gonna look for him. Cuz I ain't."

Sheriff Jeffries referred to the criminals as bandits, escaping from their previous lives. The locals saw their arriving, disappearing, re-appearing and then leaving again as an entertaining game; just an amusement if they weren't threatening anyone. Sheriff Jeffries knew mostly where these hideaways were but did not venture out to look for Florida's – and sometimes "America's most wanted" – villains on the run. The sheriff reckoned he had enough to do where he was and had good pay for very little work. The courthouse was only troubled with cases of drunkenness, assault, small-time robberies and the odd, very rare rape case. It was rare, not because it rarely happened but because it was seldom reported.

"Look, people disappear all the time here. I ain't goin' to look fer him, okay? I look fer him, and then I gotta go look fer every stoopid moron who wanders or runs away into the swamp."

Chapter Twenty-One
The Best Man

One of Purvis's strengths was his connections for printing authenticated documents. He employed someone trusted with previous dealings and was confident they knew what they were doing. This forger could fool most people. Fooling a small-town registrar in Key West should be straightforward. If not, a few bucks will help.

Jack spoke to Purvis by phone. It was no surprise to him when Purvis said he knew who the registrar was. A former employee of Miami City Hall, Ben Dugan, had disgraced himself by being drunk at work, and not just once. He had been sacked after he was found under his desk for the fourth time. However, he obtained a reference from the mayor, an old school friend, who helped him get the City of Key West job as its Land Registration and Recorder of Deeds. Purvis knew all about him, so he called City Hall and spoke to the mayor personally. The mayor knew about the connections Purvis had up and down the social strata of Miami. Next, Purvis called Ben Dugan.

The second part of Purvis's plan was to recruit an actress for the demanding role of Zipporah Thomas. He had connections with the Tower Theatre on SW Eighth Street and Fifteenth Avenue. It was housed in a splendid art deco-style building with a forty-foot steel tower piercing the sky. It wasn't in the black part of the city, nor was it in the strictly white part, either, but predominantly populated by Hispanics from Cuba. It was, however, a very lively part of town where theatre and music thrived.

Over several years, Purvis found he could operate as an agent for black actors wanting to be part of the Tower Theatre's performances. He was the deal-maker and made a small income from recruitment, helping both sides. His contact suggested an actress who turned out to be perfect. She was dumb enough to think it was a live audition; she only wanted a small fee and someone to drive her to Key West and back. Purvis organised the drive and the small cost, and his contact coached her on acting out the part. She thought it was exciting and such a great opportunity. An audition and a trip to Key West! She was warned, however, not to mess up this vital key role. It could lead to some other very important roles for her in the future. She was told she would be guaranteed important parts in New York and perhaps London. Blinded by the honeyed words, the actress rehearsed her lines and expressions repeatedly until everything was going to be perfect.

Registrar Ben Dugan's phone call with Purvis had been short but not sweet. Previously arranged, Purvis spoke to Jack, calling him on the telephone at the back of the Sanchez Grocery store, using the secure phone he always used in Miami. It was a safe phone in a secure area for Purvis and, likewise, for Jack. The plan was at the point of execution.

Mrs Zipporah Thomas walked into a realtor's office in Key West, and her house was on the market three days later. It was to be a low-key, "no signs up" transaction. Mrs Thomas signed all the relevant paperwork with the agent, proving who she was to the well-briefed registrar. The house was sold for a good price after four days. The purchaser didn't need to view the property personally and had outbid two rivals for the title. He lived in New York, and it was fortunate that all he wanted to see were photos mailed to him. It was enough for the purchaser to know it was only one block west to Whitehead Street and then three blocks south on that same street to the house of Ernest Miller Hemingway. The house on Angela Street was in a prestigious location, and the buyer knew the property was bound to increase in price now that the road to and from Miami was open. He thought he might even extend his business reach to Cuba, and he asked the agent to make sure the house was emptied as soon as possible after the purchase had gone through. The money had been split evenly and sent to the two bank accounts Mrs Zipporah Thomas had stipulated that same day.

Jack and Purvis had set up accounts in Miami for the money transfer. Jack was happy that he had recovered much more than the total stolen from Kimbo, himself, and the Watsons – a considerable amount more. Purvis was delighted with Jack and invited him to stay in Miami "anytime you goddam want!" Jack felt his instincts were right, and his trust in Purvis was repaid. Although technically the deal was fraudulent, he knew two wrongs didn't make a right. But he thought God might forgive him, just this once. For his part, Purvis found that he liked a white man for the first time in his life – a man who had not tried to cheat him, a man as good as his word.

Before Jack could leave Key West, he had to see Bill Walker the day the purchase went through and before word got out. He knew Bill should leave quickly before Zippy came storming down to create hell for him or worse. The same day the money was paid into the two Miami bank accounts, Jack waited again at the back of the Sanchez Grocery store while musicians were tuning up. The unsuspecting, already slightly drunk Bill Walker came into the store, but before going to the back room, he spotted his old friend Jack smiling at him in the dimly lit entrance.

"Jack, great to see you! Let's have a drink. Ah, I see you have a bottle with you again. You're a pal."

"Bill, let's go behind the store. You know where we sat before. I need to tell you something, which might save your life."

Bill didn't take on board immediately the importance of his words, but he did look twice at Jack and frowned. Jack's words then sank in. They sat on the same felled Gumbo Limbo tree, with Bill swigging the rum bottle. Jack didn't even pretend to join him this time.

"Save my life? Jack, the fuck ya talking about?"

Jack spared him the details of Purvis and his contacts, but he was keen to get the hard facts understood by Bill Walker. "Bill, you'd never owned that house on Angela Street. The name on the title deeds was Zipporah Thomas. In other words, Zippy! He took all your money, and by the way…" Jack looked at Bill without blinking, "…the money you took from Kimbo and me, Zippy bought the house with it under his name."

"Holy Fuck!" Bill suddenly understood what had happened.

Jack thought it was best not to give too much away, but he needed Bill to understand that the house had somehow been sold, but not by Zippy. Most importantly and urgently, Jack needed Bill to realise that he should get out of town fast before Zippy Thomas came down from Miami "with all guns blazing," as Jack put it. He went on to say that in his opinion, from what he had heard, Zippy would see he had been cheated and would assume Bill would have had a hand in it.

"Look, I'm not telling you what to do, but if I were you, I'd get on the next ferry to Havana with whatever money you've got and stuff you can carry that's of any value and leave this place for good. Don't ever come back. If I were you, I'd get out tonight. The new owner will clear that bordello from everything tomorrow and the next day. I'm leaving town myself right now. From what you tell me about good ol' Zippy, he won't like this one. Bill, I fear for you!"

Jack ensured Bill was sober enough to walk to the ferry dock via the Bordello, picking up all he could of transportable value. Bill was sobering up fast. *It was amazing how quickly fear can sober you up*, Jack thought, watching his fireman from the Old 447 locomotive quicken his step towards Angela Street.

Ironically, two days later, just as Jack was welcomed into the Watsons' house on Islamorada, his path crossed Zippy Thomas's as he passed in the opposite direction. They were within ten feet of each other at one point, but they didn't know what each other looked like.

Ed and Hank stood waiting for Jack to speak and wondered why a big smile lit his face. Then they knew. The first act of Jack's intended redemption of the consequences of the "Storm of the Century" was completed. Ed and Hank Watson had never experienced such honesty and integrity. It took a while to sink in. They were going to get back every penny stolen from them. It would transform their lives.

Jack used a telephone in the post office on Key Largo to call Purvis. He told him he would not return to Miami but would look him up if he ever went that way again.

"Dam right! You da best white man I ever met," Purvis confirmed, saying it out loud for the first time in his life. He then realised it was the first time he meant that about any man, black or white. "But where you goin', Jackie boy?"

"Best not tell you, Purvis. No insult intended. But I do know where I can call you or where I can buy you a drink." At the other end of the line, Purvis grinned, showing the gap between his front teeth and that trademark smile.

Jack put down the phone and took the first steps toward the new life he wanted – a new life he had planned ever since he realised he had a calling.

That realisation had been the day after the storm in Homestead.

Chapter Twenty-Two
God Arrives in Chokoloskee

They had finished the church building by September 1939, funded by Jack and Kimbo. Jack had given his name for the Land Registry documents, and the land they had bought was secure. Establishing that fact by law was very important to everyone. "The Chokoloskee Church of God for All" was established, and Jack underwent the ordination formalities. They had "planted" a brand-new church. Most people had failed to understand how much legal paperwork was needed to complete the church commencement process, but Jack did not underestimate it. It had taken him months to get legal property and church bylaws laid out and certified by law, using an easy-going lawyer in Naples, nearly forty miles away. Jack and the lawyer set these laws down on paper, and then Jack wrote them on two large painted boards, one to be placed on the outside next to the church door and the other on the wall inside the door. This was done so that anybody curious about the new dwelling could see them, and any folk leaving the church would be reminded of them. It was, however, only meant for the consumption of those who were entirely against the idea. It read more like a constitution by the time Jack had finished.

The church bylaws signs showed definitions for the following areas:
- Member qualifications and expulsion rules.
- Worship times and places in addition to other regular meetings.

- Qualifications for church board members and leadership positions.
- The procedure for amending standing bylaws.

The definitions first caught the attention of the sheriff of Everglades City. He checked with the three lawyers in his city and didn't like their answers. Jack Root's definitions may have come from a minister of the church who followed the letter of the law, but Sheriff Jeffries decided that they very definitely didn't follow the spirit of the law in his neck of the woods.

It wasn't only the definitions that had made him incandescent. It was who was behind them and who made the decisions on these definitions. According to the painted boards displayed, that meant anybody who sat on the church board – no matter their skin colour. Elizabeth Mitchell was proud of what Jack had achieved. It was both clever and simple. It provoked her to think of what she could do to help educate the people in the area who most needed it.

Unfortunately, it also provoked Sheriff Jeffries in an entirely different way. He was a simmering pot about to boil over.

"This preacher man, Root, needs to be reminded of who runs this place. Around here, I'm the man who makes the goddam rules."

The sheriff became obsessed with reasserting his authority, one way or another.

War

The news of war in Europe reached the Ten Thousand Islands surprisingly quickly. Bad news travels fast. The origins of settlers in Florida were from countries coming down on one side or the other. Some direct European immigrants, some first and even second generations. However, that it was happening four thousand miles away meant most people in the area "didn't give a hoot". Most didn't care about what happened miles away in Naples or Miami, big cities on opposite sides of the Florida peninsular, let alone in Europe. It wasn't until the Japanese bombed Pearl Harbour two years later that anyone took notice. When the European war turned into a world war, like most places in the USA, it touched many people in many ways.

It would have some surprising effects on some Everglades inhabitants.

Elizabeth Mitchell held school classes inside the church each day of the week, from seven until noon, except Sundays. She had left her job working for Principal Andrew Clemens as soon as the church was ready to hold classes. The original seven children attended, but seven new Seminoles and three other black children joined to boost the numbers. Many Seminole and Miccosukee natives lived around the Ten Thousand Islands area but not in Chokoloskee or Everglades City.

There had been much discussion between the tribes about whether sending their children to this settler's school was a good idea. The traditionalists in the tribes resisted it. They were wedded to their own culture and saw no good coming from a white man's school and certainly not their church. Most remembered stories from the wars with the encroaching white man. They knew the attacks aimed only at taking land, moving the Seminoles, and exploiting the natural resources of fresh water, abundant wildlife, and fertile land. Some of the black children were descendants of freed or escaped slaves who had fled to the cover of the Everglades, the Florida prairie or swampland. They were naturally cautious about their children being taught by white people, no matter who they were.

Those who did send their children knew that opportunity would come from learning to read, write, and use numbers. Most fathers were proud that their sons would learn and use numbers like the white man, but not all. One Seminole father had learnt to count to a dozen; a friendly white trader taught him a technique and method. His limit, however, was a dozen. He amused his children when he adopted his own way of counting. Once he got to twelve, he'd say, "One dozen." Then he'd say, "One dozen two," when reaching twenty-four. Then, "One dozen three," and so on. After three days of schooling, his son taught his father to count to one hundred. Both father and son were proud of each other. It was a simple yet powerful bonding.

Elizabeth knew of these stories and had heard of the pride their parents felt. This gave her a gem of an idea that inspired her to formulate a plan.

The Sunday church services were held at ten o'clock and again an hour before sundown to avoid the monotonous emergence of the thick mosquito clusters. By the beginning of 1940, Jack and Elizabeth had worked well together. Jack knew immediately after he had arrived back in Chokoloskee that she was a woman who was attractive in many ways. Intelligent, knowledgeable and beautiful. He'd heard Myron's story and knew about her operating a school for local children barred from attending school in Everglades City. Kimbo told him she had been astonishingly brave in the face of threats from a man who had mysteriously disappeared. Jack looked sideways at Kimbo; it was something in the way he told the story. Kimbo looked away.

Elizabeth was feminine, but Jack could tell she was not to be threatened or trifled with. He liked that. It meant to him that she stood up to and against anyone or anything that wasn't right in her mind.

For her part, she saw a straightforward, honest, handsome

man in Jack but, importantly for her, a worldly man. She admired that he worked out how to provide a school by establishing a church, thus avoiding the so-called 'Jim Crow Laws'. She admired him because it didn't matter who he was talking to or helping; they were all people to him: white, black, native or biracial. Jack was only interested in their self-respect and how they treated their families and their community. He was a very different man from any she had met before. He'd become a different man than the train driver once ordered to rescue people from a storm.

One Sunday, after the late service, his whole world changed. Elizabeth took Jack Root's hand in hers. She looked at him and smiled. In his shyness and hesitancy, Elizabeth took the initiative. "Will you marry me, Jack Root?"

He smiled a toothy grin and said gently and with love, "Hey, what took ya so long?" She laughed, and they kissed long and lovingly for the first time to seal their pledge to each other. They walked together, hand in hand, to find Kimbo. Jack told him he couldn't believe how happy he was. He said that he owed Kimbo a debt of gratitude for showing him how to take opportunities, for helping him find the right way, his way, in this life. Kimbo was startled that someone would say that to him.

"Kimbo, truly, without meeting you, I may have drifted and begun a life similar to Bill Walker."

Kimbo looked at him and said, "No, you wouldn't."

Elizabeth kissed Kimbo on the cheek. He was struck dumb with shyness and embarrassment. Not one of them considered that the kiss had broken the law. Elizabeth only saw a man. A man who risked his life to save hers.

Jack had trouble finding a minister to perform the service. No minister in the area, or even out as far as Naples, was available on the dates Jack gave them. He gave fresh dates and got the same response. He guessed why this was happening and knew exactly what to do next. He called Purvis.

Interestingly and surprisingly to Jack, Purvis was a church-going man, which gave him some advantages. The ministers he knew well were all black, but he suggested a white minister whom he had "connections" with. Purvis remarked that he would test the ministers' promise to God to treat everyone equally. Jack at first resisted his suggestions, but Purvis was quite clear.

"You want this to be regarded as legal, right and proper and let no man question it? Sure, ya do! Now get off yer high hoss, and let me get things movin'. I know who I want and how to get him."

Purvis used his connections and arm-twisting tactics until he was referred upward to the person he wanted. When faced with Purvis' persuasive directness, that "high-up" person agreed that the sensitive information he held on him was best kept out of the Miami Herald. In turn, a well-regarded and connected man of the cloth was contacted and told to perform the wedding vows.

"Make yourself available, is that understood?"

The Reverend Richard Green of Coral Gables was driven along the Tamiami Trail by someone called Purvis; the two contrasting men travelled across the southern tip of Florida, eventually reaching the dock to Chokoloskee. Smiling all the way, Purvis paddled the Reverend across the water on a hollowed-out Seminole canoe, especially decorated for the wedding. It still smelt of dead alligators, and the Reverend noticed the stench. He smelt it but didn't recognise it. Of course, now in his most mischievous mood, Purvis informed him it was alligator blood and innards, which caused the Reverend to retch slightly. It was Richard Green's first time outside the Miami area, and he was amazed and frightened by the terrain. He had been recruited as the first minister of Coral Gables by George Armstrong, the founder and developer of the city. Armstrong wanted an Englishman. It suited his idea of social standing and added to the upscale nature of his imposed European revival style of architecture. Purvis was aware of the "highfalutin ways of the big shots", as he liked to put it. On the drive from Miami, he had a little fun with the Reverend but disguised enough so the minister wouldn't know he was being teased or made to feel foolish. Purvis took greater delight in poking fun at him; he enjoyed every minute.

"Well, ya see over ther' Minister? That's where the twenty-foot-long alligators live. When ya see one fer the first time, ya gonna feel it hit ya stomach real quick if ya don't mind me bein' direct an' all. Soon as ya seen one of those and have recovered, you might see a thirty-foot crocodile comin' at you. Boy, you'll know then you ain't in Coral Gables no more!"

Purvis continued exaggerating to the minister about the snakes and vicious, rabid racoons, speaking as casually and matter-of-factly as he could manage without bursting out laughing. The minister had immediately regretted complying with George Armstrong's request to perform this ceremony the minute he saw and smelt Purvis. Sitting next to him in his car was every bit as challenging as he anticipated. The Reverend put a scented handkerchief to his nose frequently. Purvis's exaggerations about the reptile sizes were believed, and the minister was already figuring out how quickly he might escape Chokoloskee.

"Now see here, Minister, if you find yourself running from all these critters, the next thing ya gotta worry about is quicksand. Don't go sprintin' away through the swampland without bein' real careful." Purvis knew there was no quicksand in the Everglades, but the Reverend didn't.

The Reverend had been asked to go there by the most important man in his world. He thought Mr Armstrong owed someone a lot to make him perform this service. From what little he knew about George Armstrong personally, Purvis believed that the great man would be highly amused at this pompous minister conducting his business in the middle of the largest swamp in America whilst being chaperoned by a sweat-soaked and smelly Purvis.

Elizabeth had regularly written to her parents and sister once a month, describing what she had experienced since she had arrived in Miami. Nothing was detailed, and she barely mentioned the perils of Florida society and wildlife. In her last letter, she told them of her love for minister Jack Root and that they were to marry. She would be honoured, she said, if her father would give her away. Elizabeth was proud of the life she had created and happy with the man she loved. The only letter she received from them arrived two weeks before the wedding. It was from her mother. She wrote in dispassionate prose, telling her that her father had died six months previously. A heart attack, she said. He had been working too hard.

Elizabeth was devastated and had strong feelings of guilt that she wasn't close by or at hand to help her mother with the funeral details. Two days following the arrival of that dreadful news, Elizabeth's younger sister, Mary, had written to her with the truth. Their father had committed suicide after every one of his business interests had collapsed. The Great Depression had hit his banking and shipping investments. They were now as poor as the people he didn't want to mix with. Elizabeth's mother and sister could not afford to attend her wedding even if they wanted to. It was, in fact, only Mary who wanted to. She missed her big sister badly.

Jack asked Kimbo to be his best man, and seven-year-old Myron Hopper walked Elizabeth Mitchell down the aisle to give his teacher away. A smarter-looking and prouder boy could not be found south of Lake Okeechobee. Bad Hand had organised the colourful decorations, and many Seminoles had come to celebrate the marriage of these two well-respected and loved people.

Purvis was as happy as he had ever been and as rich. This day, he felt pleased with life; he was repaying Jack a little for the trust he had put in him, not just the cash he put in his pocket. He also felt proud to have been the person to lure Elizabeth to Miami and, consequently, the Ten Thousand Islands. He beamed every time he told someone. Some less charitable people thought it was more gloating than beaming, not that Purvis cared either way. But Purvis had something else on his mind that he wanted to unburden.

He was keen to find time to tell Jack about what happened when Zippy Thomas arrived in Key West.

Information Sharing

The party went on most of the night. A small Cuban/American band arrived late. Purvis had arranged for some Miami music, but the "Stetson Sid Seven" had missed the turning for Everglades City and then, when they found their way, had, unfortunately, stopped at the Swamp Buggy Tavern for a beer or two.

A fight started almost on arrival when a local man took offence at a black band member standing at the bar. Stetson Sid was no slouch when a bar fight was in progress. Three local men were dragged outside unconscious, but it was lucky that only one of the seven band members was hit. Bartolo Genaro was the band's singer and was punched hard in the mouth. With his lips and cheek swelled and one eye starting to close, he sounded heavily drunk when singing all the usual set numbers they performed. His thick and tongue-filled crooning added immensely to the fun and laughter of the evening's events. Elizabeth giggled uncontrollably, watching Bartolo, the cavorting guests dancing, and children running around like headless chickens. She was the happiest she had ever known. Even Myron danced, resisting his natural shyness, which he shared with his father. Bad Hand's wife Halona asked Kimbo for a dance, but he couldn't. He had not been physically close to a woman since Zella had vanished into that spinning night sky.

It would be a betrayal, wouldn't it?
Purvis and Jack moved outside to get some fresh air and catch up during the evening. After a few minutes, Jack had to ask if Purvis had any news of "events in Key West?" He knew that Purvis would not only have the story but many details. He took ten minutes to tell him what had happened.

"Jack, it wasn't pretty. I will tell you all I know, only if you refuse to feel guilty. They found the land registry clerk tied up in a chair in the back room of his office on Duval Street. It looked plain that he'd been made to talk before he was stabbed through the heart. They reckoned he was stabbed six times. Zippy wanted to make sure he didn't talk no more and, for sure, that hombre ain't talking no more to nobody. Whatever he kept in the safe was gone. Ol' Zippy then hit Angela Street. He set fire to the Bordello – it was burnt to the ground with three people inside, and then he went to the Sanchez grocery store to find Bill Walker. It was clear that ol' Bill had high-tailed it outta town days before. Zippy was madder than a wet hen. He cornered several of Bill's regular drinking partners and eventually discovered that ol' Bill had disappeared on a ferry to Havana. Well, guess where our desperado went next?"

Purvis didn't wait for the answer. "Yep, ya got it, Havana! Eventually, ol' Zippy tracked Bill Walker down to a casino in that big, famous National Hotel or whatever those Cubans call it. Ol' Zippy made a big mistake. He walked into the casino where Bill was working and pulled a gun on him. Zippy didn't know that those mafia gangsters, 'Lucky' Luciano and Meyer Lansky, were close by, gamblin' in the casino then and had their protection watching over them. Jack, Zippy got zapped."

Purvis laughed at his own words. "Bill slipped away. Nobody knows where he went, but as far as my sources tell me, he's still in Cuba, down in the southern part. Probably the city down there called Santiago de Cuba..." Purvis paused. He looked hard at Jack and raised his voice for emphasis. "I know you...don't get ideas, Jack. You wouldn't last two minutes, and for what? You think you could turn around that son-of-a-bitch Bill? Nah, he don't got it in him."

Purvis wasn't going to pull any punches. He didn't want to see his newly married friend's life end just as it was beginning. Jack reassured him he wasn't that stupid any more.

"Thank you, Purvis. I'm glad I warned Bill. And I'm glad he's away somewhere. It's clear he's following the life he wants, and I'm happy for him... well, if he doesn't cause harm to people. I can't help feelin' bad about the clerk. He was doin' his job. I guess he got caught not payin' enough attention. Thank you for telling me, Purvis. That closes the book for me on my previously trusted fireman, Bill Walker."

Purvis didn't ever think books got closed unless someone died, and as far as he knew, Bill Walker wasn't dead.

Good news

Sheriff Jeffries was fit to be tied. On his doorstep, but outside his official jurisdiction, was a school teaching black and native children just the same as white kids. He knew that, technically, it wasn't against the law. He'd always said things weren't as clear-cut as they should be. He'd also heard about Elizabeth and Jack's wedding, with "all kinds of people strollin' around, drinkin' and having fun – no matter who they were."

Chokoloskee was a lawless island where he didn't have recognised authority. What was going on was against his rules. He had twelve men signed up and under his command in the "Knights of the Cypress Fire" Klan, and he'd had a few discussions about what to do with the Chokoloskee church and school. Only three wanted to join him in a raid when the sheriff suggested – "burning down the church one night and hanging the big black bastard named Hopper and his son for good measure." He also told them they should "string-up an injun, maybe that Bad Hand no good son-of-a-bitch. Jim Tigertail would be good, too, but he's old and no real problem for us. I think the message would be loud and clear to everyone that this schoolin' ain't to be tolerated." He would need more than three men to help him, however. They knew Kimbo and Bad Hand would handle themselves well in a fight – too well if the odds were near even.

The news that Elizabeth was pregnant was everywhere on Chokoloskee Island, and Jack Root was overjoyed. After the news broke, a small party was held following the Sunday evening service.

With the money from Jack's trip to Key West and his thriving fishing, crabbing, hide, fur and taxidermist business, Kimbo felt that his life was almost fulfilled. He rarely went to Everglades City and was extremely grateful to Jack for going to the market twice a week to sell his merchandise for him. Kimbo didn't like that side of the business and thought he would provoke Sheriff Jeffries just by his presence. It had already given the sheriff a problem when Jack was there. Although Jack Root was a white man and a church minister, he was an enabler of wrongdoing in Sheriff Jeffries's mind.

Chapter Twenty-Three
A Father Teaches His Son

With Jack's experience, Kimbo now understood outboard engines. Life was much easier once he acquired motors for his three boats: a small skiff for Myron, a much larger skiff for him, and his biggest boat, for which he now had an excellent outboard motor. He could catch, kill and even skin up to three alligators at a time with his outboard boat, but he knew enough not to hunt crocodiles in the brackish water. They were vicious and quicker than alligators and could leap at prey and jump many more feet higher than their reptile cousins. Gators can push themselves up by their tails and leap five feet out of the water to snag their dinner. Crocodiles have much more power in their legs and tail and can propel themselves clean out of the water. They can almost outrun a fit hunter on firm ground, travelling nearly ten miles per hour. Catching alligators was much easier, but Kimbo always respected their danger. He would cut a piece of bait, perhaps a giant catfish or grouper and hang it from a good-sized triple hook, then tie it to a branch a few feet from the water's surface. Blood would drip down and attract the alligators. He would haul them along in the water and kill them before dragging them into the boat. His preferred method to kill an alligator would be thrusting a spear into them, no loud gunshot to warn the hunted. Bad Hand had taught him the old Seminole techniques with knives, spears and clubs, but it left no room for error. In rough weather, a high wind could easily unbalance a boat with a man standing upright, so he would use a harpoon gun, speargun or when it became too risky, and if he really had to, shoot it with his rifle – a single rifle-ball shot, in the head, between the eyes.

Kimbo decided it was time to take Myron on the hunt for gators. Kimbo had given him a single-shot .22 rifle to learn to shoot. Kimbo had a .22 pump action rifle for those times when crocodiles decided to charge at his boat. He knew that only a pump gun would reload quickly enough, and one bullet would not stop a surging, angry crocodile. Myron was tall and strong at eight years old and developed the same physical attributes as his father. He was a good and patient student and keen to learn. Myron had advanced so well and quickly that he had matured into a highly accurate marksman. Kimbo was quietly pleased. He knew Myron was ready for the hunt, but first, he had to have an important talk with his son. He had decided to only talk about using a rifle; he had not yet developed enough physically to handle a spear, knife or club.

"OK, Myron, you need to listen to me. I gonna tell you about gators and crocks. First, don't bother with crocs. They're meaner and faster than gators, and you don't wanna be messing up with a fifteen-foot angry croc snappin' atcha ass! Anyway, they fight and tear around so much that their hides get scarred up, and they ain't no good for sellin'."

Myron started to laugh because his dad had used a curse word, but he saw from his father's expression that this was a serious discussion.

"No laughin', it stops ya listening, son. That was my fault for using a cuss word. Now listen carefully, cuz I ain't gonna tell you all this again. If ya, go huntin' best to get a headlight. Their eyes are gonna shine backatcha, but as you get closer, you've got to turn your headlight upwards slowly. It fools them into thinkin' ya moving away. When I'm about thirty feet away, I shuts the motor off and creeps up to the bow of the boat with my rifle. When he's 'bout fifteen feet away, I usually shoot him. Now listen to me. The gator's skin is as tough as bullet-proof armour. To kill him, ya gotta get the bullet behind the brain. You gotta aim roughly in the direction the gator's nose is pointin' and shoot at an angle above his head. With a little luck, the first shot is the killer shot. If it is, he usually rolls bottom up with his front foot stickin' out the water. I then paddles like fury to get to him with my gator hook; otherwise, he's gonna sink to the bottom of the water and into the mud. Ya don't want that. You gotta keep that long pole with the gator hook close to hand. It'll make it ten times harder to haul him up and into the boat if the critter sinks into the mud." Kimbo was looking at his son's eyes getting bigger as he continued. Myron was listening harder to his father's words than he had at any stage of his life.

"Now, don't think becuz I just 'splained it this way makes it easy. It ain't always that simple, it's never easy, and it's always dangerous. Sometimes they hang out under large thick branches so ya can hardly see 'em or even make out their eyes. My rifle ball better be perfect, or he'll know I'm there and sink himself to the bottom so I can't get him. Or, if I ain't real quiet paddlin' around, gators are gonna get scared and go down to the bottom and hide." Kimbo looked at his son. "Yep, believe it or not, son, gators can get scared too. They can hide away for maybe thirty minutes before comin' back up. Mostly, the water's too muddy, and I can't see 'em, but if it's clear, I can put my gator hook under his chin and raise him up that way. Now, Myron..." he paused. Myron was transfixed on his father's every word, and the images were forming in his mind, "...once ya got him, ya gotta haul him up onto ya boat, or he'll splash around for hours, even though he's dead. They'll scare away all the other gators you'll wanna be catchin', so get him up by the snout, push the snout down hard onto the boat and then chop the spine in two at the back of the neck. If he's still wrigglin', then chop him again on the back between his legs. That usually puts an end to the fight. Just when you think it's all done, you gotta watch out for the blood. These critters bleed more than any other critters I cut up, except maybe the sea turtles. Them turtles also got lotta blood."

Kimbo looked at Myron as his son rushed outside to be sick. After about ten minutes, Myron walked back in with his head up and sat beside his father again. Neither said a word, and Kimbo paused long enough to see if he could continue. He needed to reach the end of his lecture. It was important.

"Now if all what I been sayin' don't hush that ol' gator down, then it ain't no good cuttin' his head off, makes no difference. You gotta run a wire or long piece of saw grass or reed down his spine. Gives ya hell for a little while, and then he slows right down and stops. Then he'll be dead." Myron was getting scared now, not sick.

"You also gotta know the three different sounds a gator makes. One is the grunt. Young gators in distress call their mothers with a grunt. I want you to listen to the way I do it so when you're a man, 'bout fifteen or sixteen, you can use it to fool the mothers into comin' to you. Then, there's the blowin' sound when the gators feel cornered. When they got no place to run, they get real mad and angry, and then they blow. The third sound they make is the one that spooks you real bad – a bloodcurdlin' bellow. The sound can be heard for miles across the 'glades. You get a special kind of scare when you out in the swamp gator huntin' at night and hear that bellow from big boar gators. They do it in the mating season, and suddenly, in the stillness of the night, if a twelve-foot boar gator bellows a kinda growl nearby, you can sure get spooked. First, if one bellows, then another will answer. They tryin' to find each other. It's natural but hearing all the other weird animal sounds can be real creepy when you're out there. If you're in the middle of gators bellowing, and then a panther roars out near you, too, you know it's time to come home real quick. Your hunt is over. Your luck is gonna be out that night."

Kimbo felt he had instilled enough in his son to make him not take hunting in the Everglades and Big Cypress lightly.

Eight-year-old Myron did not sleep a wink that night.

Ghost Orchids

Myron went hunting with his father for the first time in his life. The trip was going to last about four or five days. The best gator holes and caves in South Florida are near the beginning of The Keys, so they had to steer their large, eighteen-foot outboard past some of the significant milestones of the area. The route took them past 'The Stevens Place' at Chatham Bend, through Gator Bay, past Lostman's River, Cape Sable and finally, to Alligator Creek. The two Hoppers knew they'd hit the jackpot when they saw gator eyes everywhere they looked. It was their first night out camping in the wild together, but Myron didn't sleep for the second night in a row. He was both excited and scared. He'd notched up four gators himself and killed each with a single rifle ball shot from his .22 gun during the first day. By the third night, he was so tired he just ate his supper, curled up in a thin bedroll with a seat cushion from the boat for a pillow and passed out until an hour after Kimbo had finished his breakfast the next morning.

"Well, good news, son. We done so good together this trip that we can leave later this afternoon and head for home. We'll be travelling some of the journeys in the dark, but there's gonna be a full moon tonight, so all is good."

The two sat together all morning, skinning the alligators they'd caught so they didn't have to carry back anything they didn't want or couldn't use. They did take back some of the gator meat, which they knew was a delicious and nourishing meal, cooked with corn and naturally grown leafy greens. Kimbo was well-practised in using salt to cure his gator hides, but he also used it to preserve the gator meat he'd brought back from a hunt. He told Myron to rest while he cleaned the boat before stocking it with the return fuel, gator hides and remaining food. He had to work hard at cleaning; there was always a lot of blood – and they had caught a lot of gators. Kimbo had to clean it out regularly over the period of any hunt because the blood dried hard, and with the hot daytime sun beating down, it would make everything stink.

As he cleaned and scrubbed, he looked across onto the bank where Myron lay, fast asleep, exhausted. The love in Kimbo's heart nearly overwhelmed him. Myron's perfect face, resembling Zella, blistered hands and dirty clothes. He wondered how similar his twin sister, Zakari, would have looked. It suddenly occurred to him that this was another wonderfully proud moment since the storm. It was even close to matching the moment when Myron, returning home from school, first read to him out loud.

The sun was setting when they set out for home. The first half of the journey was difficult and slow, loaded heavily with gator skins, travelling through narrow channels with large red and black mangrove clumps and low overhanging seagrape bushes and brambles. Kimbo sometimes had to get out and push the boat as the water level was too shallow to use the outboard motor. Eventually, they came to more open water as the black night fell sharply and the moon rose over the sparkling bay. Myron could see starkly white birds on the rookery, abundant night herons, and feathered egrets everywhere. On one tree they passed, he counted eight snowy egrets perched roosting high up, away from the jaws of alligators. Myron was in a wonderland of natural beauty that he hadn't known existed at night. As they got nearer home, their passage became narrow again, with the thick vegetation and heavily wooded sections of pond cypress, bald cypress, water tupelo and black gum trees dominating the terrain. Myron was suddenly scared as there were ghost-like white images on some of the trees, making them look like they were lit with glowing, tiny lights. Seeing Myron's alarm, Kimbo touched his shoulder and whispered, "Ghost orchids, Myron. We are lucky to see them. So few of them are left now."

"They are so beautiful, Papa." It was Myron's turn to be overwhelmed by what he saw.

They arrived home in the early morning hours of the night. Myron insisted he helped his father unload and secure their gator catch from the hunt before going to bed.

Myron had turned from a boy to a brave young man in less than a week. Most importantly, he had become a crack shot. That was to be very important.

Chapter Twenty-Four
There Is No Quiet Place

It was sudden, but it had been expected, sooner or later. Bad Hand asked Kimbo if he would return with him to visit his village and asked Jack Root to come along. Jack had heard from Kimbo most of the background reasons for Bad Hand leaving his tribe and building a life in Chokoloskee. Bad Hand had assumed that his words would have been shared; the three had very little they didn't know about each other. It was essential to Bad Hand that both his friends went with him. He certainly had the courage to return alone, but it would help him see things better if his close friends were beside him. Somehow, perhaps, it would help them in some way – Kimbo because he was a black man and Jack because he was white. Whatever they were to find might tell them something about their heritage. It might help shape their future, of that, Bad Hand was sure. His instincts were usually right.

At the break of another day, the warm orange glow of sunrise slowly lit the black sky, wiping the clouds away, and the huge dome of stars started to disappear. The sunshine lit the dancing, waving and swirling wetland. Bad Hand, Kimbo and Jack set out together. Individually, they all had felt a strange trepidation, but for entirely different reasons. The three men took enough food and clean water to last that day, planning to return home at sunset.

Word had reached Bad Hand a few weeks before that there had been trouble in his old tribe, but no details were given. Hearing that there was trouble worried him constantly, and his sorrow had persisted since he'd left. Recently, it had flooded almost his every waking hour. He talked about it to Halona over several days since the news had reached him. He appreciated her sharp words.

"Stop wallowing like a buffalo. Just thinking about something will never help you. You must either bury it and forget it or... do something that will stop your agony. I say you should do something. So, get on with it!" How I love that woman, he thought.

What will I find? How will they treat me? What is it I could do, in the words of my Halona? Bad Hand repeatedly worried about these questions, churning them over and echoing in his head. *I must stop wallowing*, he muttered and smiled at those words.

Kimbo was unsure how the tribespeople would regard him. He was not a white man, not a native. *Might they find me too strange to accept? Would they ask me many questions that I'm unsure how to answer? Would they ask me to stand outside their camp, or would they ask me to join them in sharing food? Would some people look like me? Would he and they have shared experiences?*

Jack had the biggest fear. He knew a little about the effects of the constantly encroaching white man on their traditional land and customs. He knew little about the white man's lies, deceitfulness and reneging on signed agreements and treaties. *Would they have hidden anger and suppressed resentment, which he might provoke just by his presence? Would he be attacked?*

Bad Hand was proud of his travelling companions. They did not hesitate to agree to accompany him. He judged that Kimbo was the most nervous about how he would be received. Kimbo had no personal experience with the Floridian natives, not

Seminole, Miccosukee or other derived Creek tribes. As they travelled together, he would try to put his friends at ease by explaining a little history.

"Kimbo, you will meet people in my tribe who are like you." Kimbo looked surprised. "They are descendants of enslaved black people. They came down to us from the north, Georgia or the Carolinas, as escaped people or freedmen looking for peace away from the white man. They have lived among us for many years and have mingled and raised families with Seminole men and women. They will look like you and Myron, but their ways will be Seminole. They will be curious about you but not hostile. We are defensive people, not aggressive. You will see, and you will hear what we are."

Bad Hand looked at Jack and tried to set his expectations.

"Jack, you will represent the white man to my people. Be prepared to hear and see things that will make you cry inside. Please do not feel this is aimed at you, but it will be about your people as mine sees them. Remember, they have suffered from the white man's unquenchable needs. It will not be aimed at you as a person but at how the white man's ways have affected my people. Try and remain quiet and unemotional, at least outwardly."

As they approached Bad Hand's tribal land, tucked away in the Big Cypress forest, they saw an open platform with the remains of a body on top exposed to the wilderness elements. Turkey vultures and large-sized, buzzard-like raptors were pecking rapidly, feeding on the rotting flesh. Also, on the platform, the dead body was surrounded by its favourite possessions. From this evidence, Bad Hand realised this must be a recently deceased chief. Immediately, his spirits soared. Most bodies of deceased Seminoles would be placed in a small open-sided chickee, away from the tribal settlement. Possessions of that person would sometimes be thrown into the swamp. This must be the body of a dead chief, perhaps the body of Wildcat Billie. He dared to hope.

Chief Sammy Bowlegs stood at the entrance where the Chokoloskee men first entered the village. It was an enormous relief to Bad Hand to see him standing in full chieftain clothing, legs apart, feet firmly balanced, and his strong arms crossed. The chief spoke "Istonko," a neutral greeting, a passive face. Bad Hand was overjoyed to see his beautiful friend, a man he had grown up with, a person for whom he would give his life.

"Istonko, Chief Bowlegs," Bad Hand returned the neutral, passive greeting. Kimbo and Jack stood still, waiting. After what seemed an eternity, the chief walked forward with his arms outstretched and hugged Bad Hand warmly, kissing him on each cheek of his beaming face. As they hugged, Jack Root noticed that Chief Bowlegs was tall but with long, thin, straight legs. This was the first of many beguiling things Jack was about to see and hear. Chief Bowlegs spoke in his native language.

"My brother, you have come back to us. I hope. We must sit and talk. As you see, Chief Wildcat Billie is no longer here. He perished by the cottonmouth, the water moccasin. You spoke out against him and suffered rejection. I saw this. I watched like the screech owl waiting for its prey to weaken, wearing a scowl under my face. You knew he was from the government reservation. You knew he was a threat to us. But he had lost his knowledge and fear of our wildlife and its dangers. He has departed us now. We start again. Come, we must talk; you must eat with us, each of you who come to us today."

"Chief, before we enter your village, I must allow you to meet my friends. This is Kimbo Hopper. He is from the southern islands, not far from here. Originally, his family were from the Bahama Islands, in the Great Sea. Before him, his father and all his forefathers were either blacks from the north, black Seminole, Seminole Maroons, or Seminole Freedmen. Maybe his blood comes from all of them. Before living on the islands stretching to sea, his fathers were in the north before him. From Georgia and the Carolinas. This man is good, Chief Bowlegs. He is my friend."

The chief greeted Kimbo in the same way he had Bad Hand: with a hug and kiss on both cheeks, calling him "Brother." As he released himself from Kimbo, he looked at Jack and waited.

"This is Jack Root. He was an engineer, which means he rode the big iron horse. I have witnessed him perform many good things. Good things for people and good things for our earth. Chief Bowlegs, this is a good white man. He is a man of God, and he is my friend. His God is our God, the same for all of us."

Suddenly, there was an intense, uncomfortable silence. Chief Bowlegs looked at Jack Root. Jack saw the chief had ebony black, impenetrable eyes and spoke slowly in Maskókî, the Seminoles' language. They all stood still, strangely transfixed. Chief Bowlegs could speak English, but he wanted to be as eloquent as he could; he wanted to express what he felt, what his people had felt. He wanted his people to hear what he had never expressed to them. Bad Hand knew how to put the chief's words on the white man's tongue and spoke in translation for both his friends. Both men spoke at a slow beat. It was a powerful combination that struck a beautiful tone. The chief singing in warm, baritone notes, with Bad Hand softly accompanying him.

"Jack Root, the Seminoles of the Everglades, this land we are in, we call ourselves the unconquered people. Our fathers, and father's father, numbered just three hundred when they escaped the white man's army. We live because they cannot defeat us here. They have tried. They continue to try in many ways. We do not fear the white man, just what they are doing to this land. You, Jack Root, are greeting us for the first time, and we do not know each other. Much distrust lies on our side. I am a savage and do not understand the white man's ways. When I was in the north, land of the Sioux, I saw a thousand rotting buffaloes on the prairie, left by the white man who shot them from a train, your iron horse. We, the red man, are savages; we do not understand how the big smoking iron horse can be more important than a thousand buffalo. These buffalo, our brothers, the Plains Indians, kill only to eat, to stay alive. But you are a friend of my brother Bad Hand and a man of God. This earth we all live on is precious to God. Even the white man cannot be exempt from our common destiny. We may find that we are real brothers after all when we pass. We shall see."

Chief Bowlegs paused, walked forward, hugged Jack Root and kissed him on both cheeks of his anxious face. "Welcome, brother," he said in English with warmth in his eyes. Bad Hand didn't have to translate the welcome kisses.

The three men had been tracked since nearing the village, and preparations were made for how they would be greeted and welcomed. The three were split up once Chief Bowlegs had made the greeting and initial traditional welcome. The plan was to show Kimbo and Jack the Seminole way of life to learn individually without reference to, or influence from, each other. Bad Hand was encouraged to spend his time as he wished.

The most significant effect was to be on Kimbo. He was shown the Seminole fishing methods, trapping, skinning and preserving. He saw that they only killed the wildlife to sustain their living standards and support their traditions. There was no hunting for fun. What jolted him was the existence of black Seminoles. He sat most of the day listening to their stories and, to his surprise, sometimes speaking in Gullah. He learnt they were blood descendants of both freed and runaways from slavery. Kimbo Hopper sat concentrating on many astonishing tales of people a hundred years ago – thirty years before the Civil War – who secretly channelled black slaves to freedom. 'The Underground Railroad", as it was to be known later, was very well organised. Mostly, they went to the northern states and sometimes as far north as Canada. Still, some slaves thought it safer to escape southwards into a place considered by the white man as hostile swamplands infested with dangerous wildlife and warrior Indians. He learnt the fleeing people settled with the Calusa and, eventually, the Seminoles and Miccosukee. Some went further, over the sea to the Bahamas. Their intermingling and intermarriage brought about the emergence of black Seminoles. Kimbo Hopper was stunned to hear the history of his ancestors, who had brought him to this spot, to this place. He was overwhelmed when he thought of the pain and anguish that would have dominated their lives – the sheer terror of being caught and returned to their owners. Jail would face the brave people who had helped the people on the run. The less fortunate of these courageous organisers would be killed without the law intervening. The law just looked the other way.

 Kimbo was welcomed with warmth and understanding. One woman, Yuchi, particularly stood out. She was about the same age as Kimbo but lived with a daughter, Hachi, roughly the same age as Myron. The woman had a look that Kimbo liked without realising it. Then he noticed her body, her sweet voice, her calm manner. Yuchi stirred his long-suppressed sexual urges. She had maturity that he appreciated. Her soft, dark brown eyes were both weary and bright simultaneously, sad yet smiling. In the easy conversation he had with her, he discovered with horror that she had lost her man and their son in the hurricane of 1935. It hadn't occurred to Kimbo that, after sweeping over The Keys, it ripped northwards to the Ten Thousand Islands and along the coast, passing through Whitewater Bay and skirting along the east side of the Gulf of Mexico and the west coast of the Floridian peninsula. Her husband, Dosar John, was fishing with their son, Abraham. Their boat was found in pieces, washed up on the shoreline of Ponce de León Bay. Their bodies were never found.

Kimbo was startled by the similarities in her tragic story. *How is it possible that this woman, Yuchi John, had the same loss during the same storm?* It felt like he had found the last piece to his life's jigsaw – a mirror image. The same but reversed. He had lost a wife and daughter; she had lost a husband and son. It was as though Kimbo was coming out of a dense fog of buried grief and loss. The fog was lifting, and the sunshine streaked through. His life seemed to change when she told her story of the storm. They looked at each other and knew what should happen next. The same question ran through both of their minds but went unspoken. It was too sudden. It was right, but at the same time, it felt wrong. Both felt the same but went unspoken.

Yuchi asked Kimbo to sit in a place generally reserved for a husband. She sang quietly while she made him pumpkin and potato soup. It took quite a few minutes for her to be sure the moment was right to serve. It wasn't a big bowl, but it filled Kimbo not with food but with warmth, attachment and fondness. It was a cleansing soup. It washed, bathed and rinsed through his body and mind. He looked at Yuchi. Yuchi's soup had captured something he had forgotten was inside him. The soup brought something alive in him again. It was the first time he had looked at a woman and not compared her to Zella. Yuchi looked at

Kimbo being nourished by her soup. She saw in him something she had not seen for a long time.

He spent the rest of his day with her. Nothing was rushed, and they spoke very little, but what little was said was worth saying. Even the trivial things had power, not bright sparks but small, powerful lights. He walked around the village again, but this time together with Yuchi. Sometimes Kimbo asked a question, sometimes Yuchi. He was fascinated with daily life. She told him of the extraordinary spiritual events of purification and manhood ceremonies. She explained the fun of stomp dancing, where a medicine man leads a single file of dancing men, chanting and stomping through the village with women dancers following, quietly shuffling with shakers tied to the legs and quietly singing sweetly. Kimbo was astonished to hear so much about the traditions and stories he'd heard about his own Gullah heritage. He thought it strange, but it sounded like fun. He craved fun.

As Kimbo thanked Yuchi and reluctantly said goodbye, he surprised himself by bending to kiss her on both cheeks, regrettably avoiding her lips. Yuchi was not surprised, but she was disappointed. He left her, watching him walk away to find Bad Hand and Jack. She watched this man from behind and noticed how much she enjoyed his stride. He was embarrassed by his obvious erection. He was facing away but wished she could see him. The last touch was his hand on her back. That touch remained tingling on her fingertips for days.

He had three questions echoing in his head. *Could this be love? Is this love that I'm feeling? Is this what destiny had for Myron and me? How will I choose? Is this the right path for us to take?*

For Kimbo, it was a truly transformational day.

Walking among stars
Bad Hand had spent the day finding men and women he had

grown up with and caught up on what had happened since. He reflected on his experience since he left the tribe and how his varied life had provided him with different challenges. He thought how difficult life would be for him and Halona if they returned to the traditional ways and lived again in the village. He was attracted to the village life, but at the same time, he felt he would find difficult the seemingly narrow existence it offered. He doubted returning would be a good step for him and his family. He would have to discuss with Halona what he had seen and what life would be like if they returned to live under the leadership of his boyhood friend, Chief Bowlegs. Bad Hand had his own questions from that day to answer.

Jack had quite a different experience. He wanted to be accepted but wasn't. It was hard for him to see that it wasn't a rejection of him but what he represented. The Seminoles were polite to him, instructive in their ways, and passive in their communications. It felt like an armed truce. For the first time in his life, he realised he wasn't being accepted for who he was; he was being rejected because of who he wasn't. He wasn't a Seminole. He was a settler. He had white skin. He knew nothing of their ways. These thoughts filled his mind. *Maybe they think I'm the savage?*

The three men returned and sat with Chief Bowlegs and the tribal council to eat the day's last meal. The sun was setting; the scattered clouds against the deepening blue sky gave it a canopy of space, an opening into infinity. At the end of the meal of squash, cornbread, soup and alligator stew, they sat together, ready to engage but waiting for Chief Sammy Bowlegs to speak. The chief started looking each visitor in the eye, pausing for a few seconds. He stood and addressed them one at a time.

First, he looked at Kimbo. "Kimbo. I see from your eyes that you have had a transformational day. This will be either a burden or freedom. It is your choice. God will guide you, but you will have to take a new path at some moment ahead. Your path. You know that this earth is sacred to my people. To us, every black, red or white mangrove is the same. They are mangroves. Every shining cedar leaf, shoreline, mist in the dark woods, clearing and humming insect is holy in my people's memory and experience. The sap that courses through the trees carries our memories. The land is sacred to us. The shining water that moves through this land, in the streams and rivers, is not just water but the blood of our ancestors. It is all sacred to us. Each ghostly reflection in the clear water of the lakes speaks of events and memories of our lives. The rivers are our brothers; they quench our thirst and carry our canoes, which, in turn, feed our children. You must think if this is your life or another. For you, these are important choices. You know how fortunate you are to have choices. You have never had these at any time in your life. Now you can choose. When you go from here, think carefully. Whatever you decide, your son will make his own decisions when he becomes a man. Kimbo Hopper, you already know these things are true."

Chief Bowlegs looked then at Jack. "The great chief in Washington has sent his word to me. He wants to buy our sacred land and move us to the north. How can he buy what is not owned? The red man has always retreated before the advancing white man. We have brutal wars; we kill you, and you kill us. Then you take our land because you are stronger. The white man takes our land, the land of our father's ashes, their graves, this consecrated, holy ground. We retreat as the mist of the mountain runs before the morning sun. Each portion of land seems the same to the white man. He comes in the night and takes what he wants. He thinks the earth is not his brother but his enemy. When he has conquered a place, he moves on to the next. He does not care.

The white man's dead forget their place of birth when they go to walk among the stars. For our people, this earth is part of us, and we are part of this earth. The perfumed flowers are our sisters; the deer, the horse and the great eagle are our brothers."

There was complete silence as the chief spoke. Although not sitting with the group eating the meal, the village had gathered around, listening to every word and understanding every meaning. Chief Bowlegs continued.

"The advancing white man treats his mother, the earth, and his brother, the sky, as things to be bought, owned, plundered, sold like cattle, beads, or useless objects. His appetite will devour the earth and leave behind a desert. Just the sight of the white man's cities pains the eyes of our people. Perhaps it is because we are savages and do not understand. There is no quiet place in the white man's cities. There is no place to hear the unfurling of leaves in spring or the rustle of insect wings. There is no quiet place. What is the life of people who no longer hear the lonely cry of the northern mockingbird or the frogs arguing around a pond at night? A people who are blinded by purpose. Our ways are different. We prefer the soft sound of the wind brushing over the face of a still pond and the smell of the wind, cleansed by the midday rain. The air is precious to us, for all things share the same breath, but the advancing white man does not seem to notice the air he breathes. Like a man dying slowly, he does not notice the stench of his own rotting flesh. Whatever befalls the earth befalls the people of the earth. If men spit on the earth, they spit on themselves. This is what we know – all things are connected. Man did not weave the web of life; he is merely one strand of it. Whatever he does to the earth, he does to himself. So, I told the messenger from the great chief in Washington that it matters little where we spend our last days. Our children have seen their fathers humbled in defeat. Our warriors feel shame and spend their time in idleness, contaminating their heads with strong drink. We could mourn the passing of our peoples, but tribes are made of men and women, nothing more. Men and women come and go, like the waves on the sea, like the waves breaking on the shore. You, Jack Root, are a man of God, a man of righteous law with your people. This is your destiny. God is your destiny. I know this to be true."

There was a long, silent pause.

He then turned to Bad Hand. "Holata Billie. I have said nothing more than you know, think or feel. I know you, and you know me. After today, you will have the biggest fight of all to win. You have experienced the world each day outside our people. You have children who know little of us but have our blood and soul. The life you choose to settle on is both difficult and easy. When you look inside yourself, you will see who you are. And when you do, and you will, it will be easy."

Chief Bowlegs turned to address the council and his listening village to speak his last words of the day. "When our animal brothers and sisters, the deer, the bear, the birds, the fish, the buffalo far away, are slaughtered, the trees and flowers cut down, what then? Where is the forest? Gone. Where is the eagle? Gone. I ask all brothers and sisters who breathe the same air, will it be the end of living and the beginning of survival? I say to each of you, preserve the earth with all your strength, with all your mind, with all your heart, for your children. And love it as God loves us all. We all know that when we are silent and have our soul talking to us, our God is the same. Like the mangroves, the red man, the white man and the black man cannot be exempt from the common destiny. When the storms rip through, they treat us the same. Walking among the stars, we may find we are brothers after all. We shall see."

The chief then kissed Bad Hand Billie, Jack Root and Kimbo

Hopper on both cheeks and walked to his chickee. The council and the Seminole people dispersed. They went to their homes, and the three visitors left the village and walked home in the pitch black of nightfall. There was no moon that night. It took them four hours to arrive home from the Big Cypress all the way to Chokoloskee.

All three men heard every night call of every northern mockingbird along the way.

Jack told Elizabeth everything he had seen and heard. He mainly talked about the speech Chief Bowlegs had given the three of them, with the village gathered around, listening. She understood for the first time why the Seminoles and Miccosukee were reluctant to let their children come to Chokoloskee and learn in her school. Listening to Jack retell the chief's words fed her ideas. She began to plan. She had a calling now.

Chapter Twenty-Five
Decisions Determine Destiny

Gordon Filippo, Joseph Wolensky, Freddie 'X', Sammy Earl, Pete Hughes and Joel Briggs put on the white robes and hoods for the first time in the backroom of the sheriff's office. It was about midnight. The brooding Sheriff Jeffries had erupted yet again. He had been stewing over the continuing provocation of the situation in Chokoloskee, and he had been raging all that day. He needed to stamp his authority on those offending his beliefs. That island was like wearing a hair shirt with glass embedded in its fabric. He had recently recruited the six new Knights of the Cypress Fire members standing in front of him. All were on the run from the law "up north." Usually, these men would be the last people to team up with a local sheriff, but word got around in the Swamp Buggy Tavern that the Klan was recruiting. After more than several beers, Wolensky said earlier that night, "I reckon the sheriff is a real smart guy, and he ain't gonna worry who he has in his posse. He wants to get a job done, so I'm saying if the sheriff is the Grand Wizard in these parts, I'm in!"

Sheriff Jeffries had persuaded another three current members to come along. The ten white-robed and hooded figures set off behind the sheriff's office building with guns, three ropes, matches and torches soaked in oil for slow burning. They crossed the water at the Everglades City dock in a large shrimp boat borrowed from close friends. Each held a flaming torch as they marched together to Kimbo's home. Kimbo had seen the light from the flames flickering on the wall as the group got closer. He jumped up and looked out the window.

"Myron! Wake up! Go to Bad Hand and warn him. Then go hideaway safe. Go, quickly." Myron fled in the direction of Bad Hand's house.

Kimbo looked for his pump action rifle. He remembered he'd left it at Bad Hand's place the day before, following their return from the Seminole village in Big Cypress. He heard the sheriff's voice bark, "Okay, boy. We gonna teach you and that son-of-a-bitch, Injun, a lesson. A lesson all the folks around here ain't gonna ferget."

Five of the group split off and headed towards Bad Hand's place. Kimbo stayed inside. The men lit some oily rags and threw them onto the roof of Kimbo's home. They caught the cypress shingles and dried sawgrass and palmetto thatch. "Come out, boy! You gonna git a whoppin' and then a stringin'. Yah, got it comin'."

Kimbo stayed inside as long as he could, but he realised he'd perish in the thick, black, poisonous smoke long before the flames would get him. He thought his best action would be to come out swinging. He'd hit two of them hard with his sledgehammer fists, and they had gone down. He charged at the other two to his left, and as he swung at them, a pistol cracked the back of his head, and they grabbed him as he kicked out.

The Grand Wizard held the gun to Kimbo's head and said, "Hey, settle down, big boy, or you ain't even gonna make it to the end of ma rope!" Kimbo stood still.

"Hey, Sheriff," shouted one of the returning five outlaw thugs, dragging Bad Hand by his feet so that his face was turned onto the ground as they ran with him. Bad Hand was unconscious. "We got the Injun, but the little black boy weren't nowhere. Guess tonight we just need the two ropes."

"I told ya not to call me sheriff! You wanna swing here too with that spare rope?"

They found a medium-sized cypress tree and slung two ropes on one of the two strong branches, low enough to secure the ropes but high enough so a man's feet wouldn't touch the ground when swinging. They tied Kimbo's hands behind him. They did the same to Bad Hand while one of the gangs dragged the unconscious Seminole onto his feet. They put the rope around their necks and started to pull the two helpless men upwards.

A single shot rang out.

The rifle ball hit the Grand Wizard precisely between the two eye holes cut in the large, white-pointed hat. The pointed hood flipped off his head, revealing blood oozing from his forehead. Inside the skull, the rifle ball tumbled around, doing maximum damage. It didn't do any external damage as it didn't exit the skull – a completely normal activity for a rifle ball. Blood and brains were mashed and minced together, but almost nothing showed outside the fat head. It was a perfect, marksman-quality shot. It was the kind of single shot good enough to stop an alligator from coming straight at you. It wouldn't damage an alligator or crocodile's skin, and it hardly noticed on the Grand Wizard's skin, except for the round, black, blood-sodden hole. That's why it's a favoured weapon for the Everglades hunters. A .22 has no recoil, makes low noise and does not damage hides. Perfect for a young boy to train with.

The remaining nine Klan recruits stood in shock. It occurred to the brighter ones that they were next. Anyone could be next if someone shot the sheriff, the Grand Wizard. More importantly, there would be all hell to pay now with the sheriff shot dead. The law would be swarming all over.

"Best get the fuck outta here!" shouted Wolensky. They all fled to the shrimp boat, and as it took them back to the city side of the stretch of water, they all stripped off their robes and hoods and flung them into the water. It was pathetic to see, but there was no one watching.

Myron Hopper ran to his father, cut through the ropes with his gator skinning knife and did the same for Bad Hand. His father sat dazed, oxygen flowing rapidly back to his brain and trying to make sense of what had just happened. Myron looked at the head of his hunter's bounty, the Grand Wizard. It was as white as his gown, blood draining slowly from his ears, nose and eyes. The face was still easily recognisable.

Jack was the first to arrive to see the carnage. Band Hand slowly gained consciousness, but his face was severely cut, bruised, and had a nostril split open. Kimbo was sitting, looking at his son. With his well-trained and steady hand starting to shake a little, Myron held his single-shot .22 rifle out for Jack to take. He was only nine years old, however his unformed character had dramatically started to take shape.

The Klan posse was correct in thinking that the law would come in large numbers. By the end of the following day, the Miami-based FBI had set up in the Gun and Rifle Club of Everglades City to investigate who shot the sheriff. It could not have been Kimbo Hopper or the Seminole. Their rope burns around the neck and wrists were convincing enough to show that. The shot would have come from some nearby bushes where it was clear someone hid there watching the attempted lynching. There were brambles and grass that had been trampled underfoot.

All the residents of Chokoloskee were either asleep or in their houses at that time of night. No one had seen or heard anything except the single shot splitting the night air. Jack was the only person to be interviewed under suspicion. During the short interrogation, it became clear that Jack Root was a man of God and very believable. He told of the scene he found: Kimbo and Bad Hand with a rope around their necks and wrists and the dead sheriff, but he mentioned nothing and nobody else. Jack said that it looked to him like the sheriff's killer used a knife to cut the two men down and free them. Jack made sure he wasn't lying, just withholding some details.

"He or she must have disappeared pretty quickly after that," he said. No one believed it was a "she". Possible, but unlikely.

The FBI headed back to Miami, completely satisfied with their findings. It had been suggested by Jack Root that, in his considered opinion, possibly one of the Klan "must have chickened out, hid in the bushes, shot the chief Klansman in the head and high-tailed it out. The rest panicked and went with him. Everyone knew it was the sheriff, and my guess is that someone saw an opportunity to pay him back for something or other." That was the truth.

The head of the FBI investigation team was happy about Jack Root's summing-up. However, it did seem implausible that one of these outlaws would be carrying a single-shot rifle, let alone cowering in the bushes, waiting for a chance to shoot the sheriff in the act of lynching. However, the chief investigator was happy to go along with the conclusion because of other matters. Whoever aimed and pulled the trigger was doing everyone a favour, including the FBI. Nobody knew that the FBI themselves had been aggressively investigating the KKK in Florida. The state had the highest per capita lynchings in the country, and it was an objective at that time to clamp down on it. J. Edgar Hoover, then the head of the FBI, was not driven by an abhorrence of racial murders; more likely, he needed to offset the negative publicity that the Bureau was receiving in the wake of some recent unsolved Florida bombings. It had been these events that motivated him rather than any personal commitment to racial justice. This incident and the riddance of a Klan leader would be welcome news to the newspaper proprietors, and they all ran the story. The agents heading back to Miami were pleased. The problem of Sheriff Jeffries, Grand Wizard of the Knights of Cypress Fire, had been solved locally. The fact that they had been associated with the death of a Klan leader, getting the agents photographed with his body showing a dark hole in his forehead for the front page of the Miami Herald and Naples Daily News was such a gratifying coincidence.

The FBI agents drove home to Miami along the same Tamiami Trail that Kimbo Hopper, Myron Hopper and Jack Root had taken a few years before, in September 1935, hoping to start a new life.

As Kimbo looked at his home razed to the ground, the strong smell of burnt wood, reeds and smoke filled his head. He held Myron's trembling hand, and with Bad Hand's scarred and bloodied face strangely smiling at him, his head spun in a maelstrom of confusion. Kimbo knew he would have to start a new life once again, somehow – but it would have to be different. It had to be a life where he wasn't always on the edge of destitution and fear. Bad Hand also knew he had to do something new for his family. There was a compelling need to make changes, and both men realised that their lives must alter fundamentally, in some way.

This stark reality hit Kimbo Hopper hard. He stood with the stink of his burnt home in his nostrils. No money, no clothes, no home, yet again. *What will I do now?* The question came spinning in his head. He wanted to live but also to retreat, to hide away somewhere safe from the crushing reality of people and their complicated prejudices. Retreat from a world of death and hatred. Of constantly being at the endpoint of other people's violence, greed and the settler's need to dominate.

He was illiterate and carried deep-seated guilt and a hopeless feeling of worthlessness. It had become crystal clear that even though he was surrounded by people in his life who were poor and trying to make it day by day, sooner or later, he always seemed to be at the end of the poverty pecking order. But deep within his quiet head, a familiar voice spoke to him.

This is different. Not only do you have Myron, my son who saved your life, but you also have true friends. This time, you have great skill, and you love where you live. Your life is as full as it has ever been. And I think you are in love. Follow love.

It was Zella.

Kimbo's spirit swelled, and he had a fresh feeling of joy. Zella knew and accepted that he needed to move on to new things and bring new people into his life and his love. Bad Hand Billie stood smiling at Kimbo, his friend. As bloodied and hurt as he was, he spoke to him clearly but not loudly. His words were of a man who thought he knew what was next in the chain of events. He was now quite convinced, but it wasn't what Kimbo had expected.

"Kimbo Hopper, I want to show these settler people that we, the Seminole people, are worth something – worth something more than just ourselves, our beliefs, and our traditions. I don't know how, but I will look for it and know when I see it."

It wasn't until early in 1944 that Bad Hand Billie saw he could prove his worth.

After the fire at their house, with all their belongings and hides burned to the ground and every dollar of their hidden cash turned to ashes, Kimbo and Myron set out again, homeless and penniless. Jack Root and Bad Hand Billie offered immediate shelter and food until Kimbo could start his life with Myron again. His friend's offers were generous, appreciated and accepted.

In their way, each said to Kimbo, "You may live with us as

long as you want to. You will be welcome in our house always." Kimbo knew this was genuine, but he wanted to ensure that he and Myron were making their own way, contributing in their own way, and fulfilling these friendships as independent people. He also knew that arrangements like this would mean problems sooner or later, in some way or another. He didn't want to put friendships at risk.

It took only a few weeks for Kimbo to make his decision. He was visiting Yuchi and her daughter, Hachi, when Myron fell ill with a fever. He shivered, burnt like fire and then lay listless. Yuchi used a cold compress and put large, warmed stones near where he lay to cuddle when he felt cold. After two days, his fever broke, and his sweating ceased, but a cough started. His right ear was swollen and painful, and he began to wheeze and progressively cough fluid. There was no doubt that Kimbo thought his son would die. Yuchi stayed with him night and day, bathing, cooling, and keeping him warm. She provided him with steam from boiling water mixed with herbs to inhale. Kimbo was beside himself with worry and grief. After five days, it happened.

Myron woke early that morning, sat up and looked at Yuchi. He saw Zella at first, and then he realised it was Yuchi. She was half asleep, sitting upright. He knelt, put his arms around her, and said, "Thank you, Mother."

After a respectful period and with tremendous emotion on leaving Jack and Elizabeth Root, it was natural for the two Hoppers to move into the home of Yuchi John and her daughter, Hachi. Kimbo knew he would be accepted and welcomed by Chief Bowlegs, but he asked permission anyway. It was the right thing to do, and their acceptance was formally granted in front of the village. That first night, and every night they lived under the skins and blankets together, Kimbo made Yuchi dance inside.

Chapter Twenty-Six
March 1944

Holata Billie arrived in Liverpool, England, with his unit; the only other Native Americans were to be his closest friends for the next few months – Virgil Brown, known as "Chief Falling Cloud", from an Arizona-based tribe of Pima's, and Woody Akee, known as "Little Big Foot", from the Navajo nation. Unlike African and Asian Americans, Native Americans did not serve in segregated units but served alongside white Americans. Holata joined the army when the country was rapidly recruiting for what was known later as D-Day. They would have refused to enlist him if they had seen his right hand, but it was a cold recruitment day in Atlanta, Georgia, and he was wearing mitten gloves.

    The three Native Americans proved great value to their unit, serving as scouts and trackers, and they excelled in the role of snipers; Bad Hand used his well-practised left hand for his trigger work. The lives they had led meant they needed very little training for warfare. Daily hunting in the wild had given them as much training as needed. They were billeted in a small village near Portsmouth, on England's south coast, where the D-Day launch was planned. All three men loved the lush, green countryside with its different wildlife. They had never heard the sweet twittering of the skylark above the summer meadows and hills or the beautiful singing of the song thrush. The lush fields and a thick yew tree forest brought a scent they had never before inhaled. Virgil Brown rigged up a squirrel trap and cooked two for his unit comrades. Only his two friends, Bad Hand and Woody Akee, ate his offering. It was sweeter than the tree rats they were used to. The variety and gentleness of the landscape and wildlife compared with the swamp, plains, and desert were welcome and delightful to each of them. For these three Native Americans, the English countryside was a different and wonderful place to be.

Each of them, however, kept in mind that it was 'the quiet before the storm' of war.

The allied army of mainly British, Canadian and American soldiers landed on the Normandy beaches on 6th June 1944. As Bad Hand's unit poured out of the amphibious landing craft on Omaha Beach, a bullet ricocheted into Virgil Brown, killing him instantly. Bad Hand dragged him out of the shallow water and stumbled several times as he carried him forward over the soft sand. Another bullet sunk deep into Virgil's breathless chest, a shot that otherwise would have hit Bad Hand. The dead Virgil Brown had saved his life. Bad Hand and his unit suffered hours of fighting on that beach, but they slowly and dangerously made their way through heavy gunfire from the gun emplacements looking over the beach. These emplacements were perched high on the cliffs, picking off the invading Allies as they painstakingly moved up the shoreline. The beach was mined and covered with obstacles – wooden stakes, metal tripods and barbed wire – making the work of the beach-clearing teams brutal and murderous. This, in turn, resulted in heavy casualties.

Bad Hand and Woody Akee immediately saw what was needed. They carefully climbed the cliff top and disabled two major gun emplacements. It took them more than an hour, during which they escaped death by a whisker many times from a deluge of bullets. This allowed a considerable section of the invading army to push through more quickly, thus saving many American lives.

As an integral part of the Allied Forces between December 1944 and January 1945, Bad Hand's unit helped storm through occupied France in bitterly cold conditions. Eventually, it was part of the vital victory against the German attempt to split Allied lines in the Battle of the Bulge. The Germans were forced to retreat, and on 7th May 1945, Germany surrendered. Bad Hand and Little Big Foot were winners of the Bronze Star, Purple Heart, three battle stars, European Theatre Campaign ribbons, a sharpshooters' badge and a Good Conduct Medal. Bad Hand and Woody Akee returned to their tribes and communities in New Mexico and Florida, and each enjoyed a glorious hero's welcome. Virgil Brown, "Chief Falling Cloud" from Arizona, was buried in the American Cemetery and Memorial in Colleville-sur-Mer, Normandy, France, along with nearly ten thousand other US military dead. *Coming home.*

Bad Hand was greeted in a ceremony led by the newly elected Everglades City Sheriff and respected minister – Jack Root. The mayor had put him forward for the position unopposed. Most of the residents of Everglades City and Chokoloskee joined a large group of Seminoles to see Holata arrive home. A huge cook-out was organised with guitars, banjos and tribal music long into the night. Jack Root had appointed, in a new position, an Everglades City deputy sheriff, Chucky Chisholm, and he was also prominent that day. On this occasion, some of the less visible or liked residents of the Ten Thousand Islands were nowhere to be seen.

Jack now had two children, a packed Sunday church, and good pay to go with his shiny sheriff's badge. He and Elizabeth Root were at the core of the community in both Everglades City and Chokoloskee. A young Chucky Chisholm was happy to take some of the irksome night shift patrols and spared Jack the more onerous everyday tasks. Jack's prayers for a safe return of his friend Bad Hand had been answered. Elizabeth Root continued the Chokoloskee schooling for those children whose parents wanted it. She was pleased to see a few new children who came along without their parents initially knowing. The class swelled to twenty – red, black and white children. Everyone knew this type of school wasn't allowed in Everglades City. Some more traditional townsfolk weren't yet ready to ignore the so-called Jim Crow Laws, which were still strongly upheld throughout all the southern states. Jack had to tread the fine line between federal, state and Jim Crow laws. Then he had to apply his moral judgment. All this in an emerging county, growing in respectability that had been absent since its lawless development. This balancing act was to test him more than anything he had tackled so far in his life. It was to test the basis of his deep friendship with Kimbo Hopper.

Bad Hand had seen war and peace in the white man's world. He had seen and admired the ingenuity and technical inventions of the rapidly developing world. During dangerously tough battles, he looked into his soul, as predicted by Chief Bowlegs. He knew then that he wanted the life of a Seminole for his family and himself. He knew what he wanted for their future.

After celebrating his safe return to the Ten Thousand Islands territory, Bad Hand Billie took Halona and his three children to live in the Big Cypress, in his old village, among his tribe, under the wisdom and leadership of Chief Sammy Bowlegs. He built his chickee near, but not too near, Kimbo and Yuchi Hopper. Myron, Hachi and Bad Hand's children spent their childhoods and young lives growing up together.

Bad Hand Billie became his boyhood friend's principal advisor and assistant chief. His advice about how the Seminoles could survive and thrive in a white man's world proved priceless. Between them, they knew they had to use the settler's weaknesses while establishing strength and respect for the tribe. This was their leadership challenge.

Kimbo and Yuchi shared their lives. Their courtship was slow and gentle. Their intimacy grew from the initial lust that had laid dormant in each for so long to tender but strong love-making. Kimbo had felt guilt initially, but the voice in his head disappeared. He saw that as a positive sign. They married in front of the whole village. He promised himself not to compare his life with Yuchi to his life with Zella. Yuchi also committed to Kimbo. In the first few days, Kimbo asked himself, *How can one woman be compared with another and decide the best? What is the point? Is it impossible to love both women as individuals and not compare their beauty? This must be love. At last, I think my luck has changed!*

It was to be false hope.

Part Three

Purpose

Chapter Twenty-Seven
The Maelstrom of Law and Order

Suddenly, things changed. They changed dramatically for everyone who lived in the Ten Thousand Islands and without their consent. If a vote was ever taken anywhere about this change, it most certainly did not include the people who lived there. The Everglades National Park was established in 1947, and the consequences, put politely, were either unforeseen or disregarded.

Following World War II, America rapidly changed almost every aspect of its way of life, culture, and technology. One change can possibly affect about everything. As war so often does, it can innovate almost every aspect of society. Almost.

For most communities, innovation means the past will not be repeated. The speed of change is determined by who has the power, who has the enthusiasm and, most importantly, who will benefit.

Collier County decided it was time to build a causeway connecting Chokoloskee with the road into Everglades City. By that time, Elizabeth had a full, thriving, integrated school, which irked some city residents but was increasingly, and surprisingly, recognised as precious, by many. It was accepted by those who had initially dismissed it. Even Seminoles started to see education as valuable for their children, and the number of school pupils grew too big for the small dwelling on Chokoloskee Island. With the retirement of Andrew Clemens, the newly-elected Everglades City school principal, Elizabeth Root, moved the school from Chokoloskee and integrated it with the one already established in Everglades City. The schoolhouse was conveniently located next to Sheriff Jack Root's office. For two years, there were disturbances. Small groups came down from north Florida and Georgia to "disrupt" the school's programme. Elizabeth had trouble recruiting additional teachers locally, but the growth of pupils was outstripping her ability to give sufficient time to each child. She needed more teachers. Her vacancies were filled when enlightened newspaper editors gave her free job advertising in Delaware, New Jersey and New York. Miami, however, wasn't so ready; at that time, the city didn't care about such things. Elizabeth was delighted with one recruit, Connie Bloom. Almost immediately, Elizabeth could see that if anything happened to her, she was confident that Connie could step up and run the school. Without knowing it, she was thinking ahead, just in case.

The Fred Penecott store continued to thrive, but Jim Tigertail's outlet faded and closed after Jim had a fatal heart attack. His diet was both his main pleasure and his downfall. Every Seminole living in the Everglades and Big Cypress area came to his funeral. Kimbo was devastated. He mourned deeply the loss of someone he loved and who had taught him so much – from practical skills to his invaluable and life-influencing storytelling.

Kimbo was forty-seven, and Myron was twenty-three. He was now stronger than his father. They worked well together on their hunts for alligator hides and plumes despite the potentially devastating constraints placed upon hunters. The change of status to a protected national park did not affect them until the causeway was built, as nobody was bothered to check and enforce the new restrictions.

Havoc came to the newly reachable Chokoloskee as all

wildlife hunting and fishing within the park's boundaries had to stop. This now included the island. Someone, somewhere else at a desk job in an office building, had calculated that alligator numbers had dropped dramatically throughout the USA. A few years before the war, they said, the alligator population was between three to five million and had now been reassessed at less than one million for the whole country. This prompted the new National Park authorities to apply for alligators to be officially listed as 'endangered', and a new power had come their way. Although this application would take another nine years to be enacted throughout the nation, it was immediately and enthusiastically outlawed in the Everglades. Hunting and commercial fishing were against the law. This was catastrophic for Kimbo and Myron and the whole economy of the Ten Thousand Islands area. The residents became angry and defiant. What were they supposed to do? It wasn't just them that it affected, but all the people living between Homestead and Naples. What were all the residents of South Florida supposed to do? Hunting and fishing were their life, and the economy was founded on it. They had always done it; it was how they survived, their purpose, and their primary source of livelihood. Everything was built around it, and at the behest of local, state and federal bureaucrats, it was taken away by law. It was hard to imagine that those who enforced this law didn't understand or care about the impact it would have on the people who lived there. The red, black and white – not mangroves but people.

Although Kimbo saw he was facing life with nothing, once again, this time he was going to ignore the change that threatened to destroy what he had built with Yuchi. He took no notice of the new legal arrangements for the Everglades National Park with its imposed regulations and laws. He carried on as usual and learnt ways to avoid the hurriedly established Park Rangers, who were authorised to arrest, charge and bring to justice anyone they caught breaking the law. He heard the rangers were new to the job, and most of them were new to the environment. Kimbo thought he would easily outwit them in the labyrinths of the wilderness, at least for a few more years, and he did.

To stop hunting was hard for the whole community but harder on some more than others since fresh meat and fish only came from their efforts. The authorities deliberately omitted the city limits of Everglades City and Chokoloskee in the newly defined park territory, but all areas outside of the two small city limits were included. They thought it might look better. Of course, it had no positive effect as the restrictions applied to all Ten Thousand Islands down to the Florida Keys, near Long Key. The territory restrictions encompassed the area identified as the Everglades, the area bordered by Miami in the east and Marco Island, near Naples, in the west. Commercial fishing rights only allowed two miles from the coastline into the open Gulf of Mexico. Many fishermen in the area, including The Keys, could not afford the extra expenses of owning much bigger boats needed for Gulf fishing and had to give up the one trade they knew. Who could afford new open-sea fishing boats?

This was a huge blow to everyone. Those with property deeds within the new park boundaries were given next to nothing and told to "clear out". The same treatment was dished out to old squatters and poor folk who lived on the ancient Calusa shell mounds. These vast mounds had been created from conch, oyster, and clam shells by the Calusa Indians, using them to separate private and community spaces, establishing high ridges, mounds, crescents, platforms, canals and courtyards. They were utilised by poor and drifting white migrants, making themselves homes and shelters with local seafood readily available. Now that it was classified as a national park, they were driven out without compensation or consideration. Their resentment grew into anger. They asked themselves fundamental questions about why this was happening. Why were they being isolated, deliberately cutting them off from the rest of the trading world? Was it so that tourists from the north could sightsee in their homeland, their territory? People were thrown out, and what they had left behind burnt down. A life that had taken them a lifetime to build had to be abandoned, to become wilderness once again. Just the way the new national park regulations wanted it. Some residents were defiant.

"I ain't taking this no more! I gonna show them that Kimbo Hopper ain't takin' this. I'm just tellin' ya, son. Every time I get established, someone takes it all away. God damn it!"

Myron was shocked. He'd never seen his father curse or get angry, and never this angry. Kimbo punched the air in practised violence. It was a pathetic demonstration, and he knew it. "What are we gonna do if we get caught doin' what we always bin doin'? If we only gets a fine, we probably can't even pay that, damn it! What will we do if we can't pay?" he shouted.

"It's okay, Pa. We can carry on. We're too smart to get caught." Kimbo was encouraged by Myron, but he was inexperienced in the ways of the world. Kimbo started to have doubts already.

"These rangers don't know what they're protecting, but we'd better watch out for ourselves when we huntin'. Son, somehow, we were born into a world we can't control. Most folks can't control their lives, but we're the kind that gets bad luck dished at every step. People always tell me we gotta take it, or else it's gonna get worse. Some folks can keep taking it, but I ain't. I ain't not gonna take it any more. We're gonna be okay but we gotta keep our heads down and be on the lookout."

These words were to stick in Myron's head for a long time. The words were like a magnet pulling him back into an unwanted, troubled world, and he didn't want more confrontation. But, at the same time, they were an impetus pushing him forward. An ambition instilled itself in Myron, which was to shape him and a good deal of the future of South Florida. But that ambition was to emerge later, much later.

Looking at the situation from the outside and the plight of the good and bad people of Everglades City and Chokoloskee, no one could have guessed what would happen over the next few years. Developments were both good and bad.

The assessment of good and bad would depend on whether you were thrust into the maelstrom of Florida law and order.

Chapter Twenty-Eight
Caught Saving a Life

It was nearly dusk when Burt Sadler saw the father and son Hopper floating slowly in their skiff, Kimbo pushing on his pole, and Myron busy skinning a ten-foot alligator. Sadler was a week into his new job and his first day in the park. He was from New England and a lousy gambler. Burt had lost all his money, his house and his girlfriend. He saw a Park Ranger's job advertised and applied. He was shocked when he was almost instantly offered the job. He saw he had a chance to rebuild his life.

Burt wasn't sure of himself in his new job. He wasn't trained or briefed, and consequently, he didn't know what exactly he was supposed to do if he caught anyone trespassing and hunting illegally. His boss sat behind his desk in a building that controlled the entrance to the park. The chief called to Burt as he was leaving for his first day in the Everglades.

"Well, Burt, you just gonna learn on the job because there ain't no teachin' on how you gonna deal with the likes of the folks round here. Ya got the CB radio, but it don't always work, even if ya keep the batteries charged. But make sure ya do anyway. Ya gonna be all right...er, but anyway, try calling, maybe every two hours, just to let me know you ain't been eaten yet."

Burt Sadler didn't return his boss's smile. An hour and a half into his first visit to the wilderness, he was in at the deep end. He didn't know his boss wasn't serious about calling every two hours. Chief Ranger was just covering himself, as usual.

"Hey, you two! What ya doin' here? Is that a gator I can see the young 'un skinning?" Burt had seen two men.

Within a few seconds and with great skill, Kimbo had switched the skiff into a narrow channel behind some clumps of buttonwood trees and a large patch of mangrove islands. They were racing against a ranger for the first time. He had a gun, but they didn't know he hadn't fired one in his life, not even at a practice range.

"Stop!'" Burt Sadler fired in the air, expecting the two hunters to stop with their hands up.

Wherever had they got to?

All Burt Sadler heard was the fading but rapid plop of Kimbo's pole entering the water each time he thrust downwards to move swiftly out of sight and out of reach.

Which direction did they go?

The tall sawgrass screened Kimbo and Myron's rapid movements. Both father and son were breathing heavily, mainly from the fright of suddenly being discovered. They had never been challenged before. They were east of Flamingo, in Alligator Creek, at the end of the thirty-eight-mile trail from the park entrance, a place they both knew well – Burt Sadler not at all. It was a favourite spot for Kimbo, and this hunt had paid off spectacularly, yielding a good bounty and a huge income for the family and would last them for months ahead.

Burt was inexperienced but brave. He guessed which direction the skiff had gone, but he didn't yet know how to focus his enthusiasm or manoeuvre his small motor launch through the myriad of channels and at the same time give an update to his boss on the CB radio. Just as he entered Crocodile Creek, travelling northwards, he fell into the water headfirst. The boat went one way, his CB radio another. The radio sank, cutting off the remote possibility of communication with his Chief Ranger.

Both son and father knew what the sound of that big splash meant. The ranger was about to be supper for the crocodiles and alligators, and there would be a terrible competitive fight to get at Burt's chubby fresh meat.

"We gotta rescue him, son. There ain't no two ways to look at it." Kimbo and Myron returned and found Burt Sadler standing up to his neck in brackish water with complete panic written across his New England face.

"Stay right there. Don't move an inch. The water don't get much deeper than you in already. We're coming for ya." Kimbo took control.

Kimbo flashed his light across the waterway, and the light returned two monstrous, red eyes heading for the ranger. It was a giant crocodile heading away from under a bird rookery and swimming straight towards something very different to eat – Burt Sadler. Kimbo didn't understand why the bulk of the croc's body seemed to change in size as it rushed through the water. What was troubling Kimbo was that the body was snowy white! It was as if the reptile was a ghost. Both father and son could not believe what they were seeing. The closer it got to Burt, the whiter and bigger it got. Kimbo stood upright with his .22 magnum pump action and shot the creature in the head, aiming straight between the eyes and behind the brain. As the reptile reacted to the bullet, Kimbo realised he didn't get the shot off perfectly in the dim light, he'd missed the spot behind the brain. The gator grabbed Burt's right hand in its mouth and started to do a death roll. Kimbo and Myron realised it was just an old, colossal grandpa alligator that had held a live pure-white wood ibis in its jaws, deciding to let it go for a bigger prize. Burt was in big trouble.

Instinctively, as the alligator rolled over, he tried to take Burt down with him. Although badly injured, the gator's intent was to drown Burt and stash him in a lair somewhere close. As he rolled for the third time with Burt helpless, the gator exposed his head above water, and another shot rang out. It was Myron who'd made the killer shot, hitting him perfectly, as he'd been taught. Before the beast could sink to the bottom, Kimbo sunk his gator hook into the soft belly while Myron freed Burt and, like he would a gator, dragged his dead weight into the skiff.

Twenty minutes later, Kimbo pulled into the natural rise of a favoured hammock, where he had another skiff securely hidden. He'd always kept an extra skiff in his main hunting areas in case his hunt had yielded more hides than he could manage in one skiff. He'd hide them away and come back on a day when rough weather had set in, and rangers wouldn't be out looking for the likes of him.

Both Hoppers looked at Burt. He was more in shock than badly hurt. His right hand had been bitten hard and was missing two fingers. Both of Burt's rescuers cleaned his several wounds and laid him down with his feet raised. Kimbo found some sugar in an emergency bag he always took with him. Burt was in deep shock.

After a lengthy discussion, Kimbo said, "Enough, Myron. I've decided I will take this ranger to the ranger station at Flamingo, and you will take this skiff home with our hides. The ranger needs immediate attention." Myron was about to disagree when he saw the look in his father's eyes. "Let's bind his hand to stop the bleeding and get him resting."

"Okay, Pa. But first, we should skin this old grandpa gator because we should nail him up somewhere at home. We should name him 'The Grandpa Ghost Gator'." The two men exchanged their normal soft and gentle smiles. It was a moment after which things were not to be normal again.

Burt Sadler lay quiet and unconscious, unaware that his life had been saved.

It was at the break of dawn when Kimbo got to the ranger station. He helped a now-conscious Burt out of the skiff, across the scrubland, and onto the bench outside the small, locked office. It was a good deal too early for Burt's boss to be present. Chief Ranger had to get out of bed, make himself a pot of coffee, freshen up, dress in his smart Chief Ranger slate blue uniform, put his day bag into the national park vehicle and then drive the forty miles to Flamingo to check on Burt Sadler. The day bag, containing his lunch and reading material, was very important to the chief. Around eight-thirty, he pulled up to see his newly recruited man lying down, quite unwell, his right hand bandaged with what looked like a shirt. Next to Burt sat a black man without a shirt.

Chief Ranger listened to the whole story from Kimbo while they loaded Burt into the park ranger's vehicle, ready to take him to the doctor in Homestead. As Kimbo was about to wish Burt well and a speedy recovery, Chief Ranger pulled out his pistol and told Kimbo to put his hands behind his back. He handcuffed him and put him in the front seat next to him.

"Any trouble, boy, and it'll be a pleasure to shoot you."

When Myron arrived back home, expecting to see Yuchi and Hachi and tell the story of last night. It was empty. No sign that anyone had prepared and eaten breakfast. He stashed the gator hides safely and looked around inside and outside the house. Nothing. No sign of anyone. Myron ran to Bad Hand Billie's place and found Halona busy.

"I can't find Yuchi and Hachi. Do you know where they are? I must tell them what happened last night down there in Crocodile Creek."

"The last I saw of them was yesterday. They were going north into Corkscrew swamp. They mentioned surprising you both by bringing four ghost orchids back – one for each of you. You know how she likes to do some unusual things to please you both."

"But Halona, they don't seem to have returned from Corkscrew. There is no sign of breakfast or that they slept there last night. Where could they be?"

It took Myron three hours to arrive at the place in the swamp known to have the best leafless ghost orchids. The rare species mainly thrived fifty feet up, clinging to the cypress trees and drawing in the moist, humid air. Hachi would climb up to gather them into a woven basket before lowering them down slowly to her mother, a practice she had learnt early in life. Myron spent a lot of time calling, looking and eventually tracing where they had been the day before.

He then found their bodies lying on the ground like rag dolls.

Chapter Twenty-Nine
Deep within Us

Chief Ranger sat passively, listening to Burt Sadler's version of what had happened in Crocodile Creek.

"Sounds like we got 'im. Ain't no doubt that this boy was trespassing with at least an intent to do illegal hunting. We don't got the evidence yet, but we will. You say he had a young 'un with him? Probably another black fella from up there in the Seminole place. Well, what we got now is good enough to get the big man. I ain't lookin' for trouble with them, Injuns. He'll be in court in five days when the judge comes on by."

"But, boss, he saved my life! He didn't have to do that. He coulda got clean away, and I'd a been gator meat. We shouldn't do that to him, boss. Why don't we just give him a warning?"

"Hey, just forget about it, Sadler. You'll probably get a promotion outta this, capturing an illegal hunter despite your severe wounds. Not bad for your first day. I heard from the doctor that you're missing two fingers, eh? A hero, I'd say. Ever heard the expression, 'Never give a sucker an even break'? My old daddy used to say that all the time. He'd say it was one of W. C. Fields's best films."

Chief Ranger was feeling pretty good about all this and thought he'd probably get some recognition too. After all, it was their job to protect the wildlife. Burt Sadler couldn't believe what he was hearing. A man saved his life and would most likely get time in jail for it. Burt thought he might be new to this job and certainly new to the territory, but he wasn't totally naive. He suspected Chief Ranger was going to bask in the glory of capturing what would be considered by the district judge and the Miami authorities as an intruder who had no right to be anywhere near the Everglades National Park, Big Cypress Grove and the Ten Thousand Islands. What's more, the intruder was hunting wildlife. The arrest and conviction of Kimbo Hopper would sit well with those who ran and funded the park rangers and would be a lesson to all those who were no longer welcome in this area. Chief Ranger felt good that evening while driving home in his official park vehicle. He was looking forward to his supper of bonefish, gifted to him by one of his park rangers who regularly did some covert fishing.

Burt Sadler was feeling confused and lay in the small hospital in Homestead, nursing the part of his hand where, just one day ago, he had two fingers. He turned the events over in his mind. Many different thoughts came and went. He speculated about his missing fingers. *Did the gator eat them? How stupid of me to think of that,* he told himself. He knew there were more important things to consider. *Do I want this life? Do I want this job? Do I really want to work for a boss like Chief Ranger? What can I do to help the man who saved my life?*

He may not have been from these parts, but he knew he should show some New England compassion and Christianity. He lay thinking about what he could do, and then the realisation of what he should do became obvious, and the answers to his questions became clear.

Falling

Kimbo Hopper sat in Miami's dim and filthy cell, his mind numb. He couldn't quite understand what had just happened. His biggest challenge was to stay sane. He had six other men in the cell with him, but he felt totally alone. He made the mistake of thinking about all the events of his life after the 1935 hurricane, a storm that had not stopped roaring through his life ever since. He wept as the other men laughed or insulted him for what they took as weakness. The pent-up anger burst out of Kimbo, and he hit one greasy and unshaven white man so hard that even the guard outside heard his jaw snap, broken with a single punch. Four of the other five men jumped on Kimbo and beat him until he was quiet, lying still and unconscious. Hours later, when he regained consciousness, he felt pain in most parts of his body. Blood was oozing from his lip and nose. He saw himself locked in a cell, stinking from an unwashed body, sharing the same existence with other desperate men who found themselves imprisoned here for God knows what. He decided to 'play possum' until the food arrived. He thought his life had reached rock bottom. It wasn't until Myron arrived the next day that he realised he still had further to fall.

Recovery

Myron Hopper was back in his now silent home. The silence was soon broken by his crying out. Shock and anger had passed through him, perhaps too fast. He was wracked with grief. He cried louder than he had ever done.

He had run as fast as he could from the rape and murder scene to Chief Bowlegs to report what had happened. He arrived after taking only short breaks for rest. He was breathless, panting and unable to speak. His urgency was not about finding the murderer so much as recovering the bodies before panthers, bears and a multitude of wildlife creatures – from the largest to the smallest red ant – started to consume them. Within minutes, he was on his way back to the place where he found them. He had Chief Sammy Bowlegs, Bad Hand Billie and ten of the strongest men in the village with him. Also, Chief Bowlegs chose two women to go with them; whatever they found, Yuchi and Hachi should retain as much modesty and respect as possible. The group recovered the bodies, showing no sign of what they felt inside. They showed no anger, no boiling revenge, no emotions at all. It was just a respectful and gentle activity; emotions would flow later. They carried the two bodies on rapidly made frames and quietly sang traditional songs of grief as they walked, tears streaming. Canvas had been brought from the village and stretched between poles, which had been selected, cut and trimmed. It was a homecoming with as much honour and respect as was possible, considering the savagery that had dispatched the women. What they had found at the scene would shock even Chief Bowlegs and Bad Hand, people not easily distressed.

They had also found an abandoned CB radio in the bushes, lying alongside an Everglades National Park Ranger's hat.

Bad Hand showed the hat to Sheriff Jack Root. It was unmistakable, as was the park ranger's CB radio found ten feet away from the bodies. The question was now, what could Sheriff Root do about it?

"You know that area is not in my jurisdiction. I have no power to follow this case and find the perpetrator." Jack Root was just stating the facts.

"You have no power except your influence." Bad Hand made his point short. He looked at the man he thought he knew.

Sheriff Root drove to the Chief Ranger's office, not the coastline office at Flamingo, but at the park entrance, Southwest Homestead. It was a five-minute drive from the chief's home.

"The Seminole could have planted these." The chief snorted.

"Nothing to say they haven't been stolen by the perpetrator to distract our attention!" the ranger's boss shouted in defiant rejection.

"I found a name inside the brim, 'Jacques de Lors'. Do you have a ranger called Jacques de Lors in your team, Chief?"

Fuck, thought Chief Ranger, *it's that French Canadian bastard from Louisiana. I knew we shouldn't have hired him. They told me he could be trouble for us.*

"We do. A thoroughly reliable and professional ranger. I'll have a little chat with him to see if he'll confess to having his hat and radio stolen."

Sheriff Jack Root already knew what would happen next, but he was not prepared to sit and do nothing.

"I'm holding the evidence in Everglades City. It might be useful to someone," Jack faked a half-smile and left Chief Ranger's office abruptly.

An unfamiliar address

Jack had found out that Kimbo was in a Miami jail and thought he'd kill two birds with one stone. He carefully planned his trip to the East Coast, and once he knew when Kimbo's court hearing was scheduled, he kissed his family goodbye and drove along the Tamiami Trail. Elizabeth had insisted on going with him; she had a strong emotional attachment to Kimbo. But as husband and wife discussed the reasons for his incarceration and the conditions he would now be in, there was a robust disagreement. Jack wanted to make clear the reality of what they were arguing about.

"Kimbo broke the law, and he knew he was breaking it. His capture was outrageously harsh, given he saved a life, but that was part of the risk he took. Probably, he hadn't thought or cared too much about that part. Of all the people we know, he would have known about the severity of the risk a black man had if caught. Now, Elizabeth, he will acknowledge his punishment quietly without any fuss, like the calm, gentle man he is. He will almost certainly get a fine. There is nothing I can do for him, probably, but I'm sure there will be nothing you will be able to do either. We can help him raise the money for the fine, which I'm pretty sure we will get. You should not go to see him in the Miami jail or wherever they take him afterwards. He will be ashamed and humiliated if he sees you, someone he loves. He will feel deep shame. We should not add to his distress."

Elizabeth was extremely frustrated with that reality. She looked at the husband she loved and spoke words she didn't know she had. They poured out of her soul.

"Jack, in keeping quiet about injustice, in burying it deep within us – that no sign of it appears or shows itself – we are implanting it. Sooner or later, it will appear many times stronger. I'm afraid that will happen with our dear friend Kimbo. It may destroy him altogether."

She sat down hard on the family sofa and sobbed for a very long time.

Jack took that old familiar route to Miami, but he was headed in the direction of two unfamiliar addresses. One address was on Coral Way, in the middle of the old district of Coral Gables, and the other was at the courthouse on West Flagler Street.

Chapter Thirty
Reduced to Nine

With tears streaming, Myron drove himself in a borrowed Ford pickup truck. It was the day before his father's court hearing, but what he had to tell him was the worst news possible. He arrived at the Miami Police Department, where Kimbo was located. It was on NW 5th Street near the Miami River, situated ironically on the many old Tequesta, Myaamia and Shawnee Native American settlements. The Tequesta were quiet, peaceful people. Myron noticed how things had changed since then. The irony didn't pass him by. He was maturing rapidly.

Kimbo was pulled and pushed through the door of the small visiting room. He stumbled rather than walked, but after much pleading, Myron was reluctantly allowed to meet his father. Myron stared disbelievingly. His face was swollen, his right eye had closed, and his bottom lip bulged. He had never seen him so battered; alligators, crocodiles, panthers and bears had never hurt his father as severely. He now looked to have been broken. Myron was temporarily stunned.

Through his stinging eyes, Kimbo saw his son and went to grasp him in a bear hug. The police officer pushed him back with his stick and tapped his gun holster to remind Kimbo who was in charge. There was a small table with one chair where Myron sat. He rose to offer his father the chair, but the officer ordered him to sit back down.

"You sit. The prisoner stands. Those are the rules. You should keep well apart," he barked, tapping the chair back.

"Hello, son." Kimbo's soft voice showed his love for Myron, evident in those two words. He tried a rare attempt at humour to help his son.

"If ya think I look bad, ya should see the other four." He attempted to smile, but it hurt, and he winced.

"Father, it is so good to see you. Can we touch?" he pleaded with the guard.

"No."

"Father, I know you have a court appointment tomorrow. I want to tell the judge about what happened."

"No, son." Kimbo held up the flat of his hand and pointed it at Myron.

"But…"

"No, son. They'll lock you up too. You'll not say anything to anyone. Not tomorrow or ever. That is my wish. Will you honour my wish?"

"I will honour your wishes, as always."

Before Kimbo could ask about life at home, Myron started to tell him the horrific news. He had practised the words many times on the journey to Miami. He started slowly, telling him what he had done with the 'coats'. This was the agreed code word for hides and any other wildlife bounty. He then plunged straight in, telling him about finding their bodies and what had happened to them, sparing most of the gruesome details. There was an audible intake of breath from Kimbo, as though a blade had thrust into him. Myron told of the eight men and two women Chief Sammy Bowlegs led to reclaim their bodies and how an organised traditional funeral had been held with the medicine man. Their bodies lay on the traditional chickee, with open sides and a thatch roof made from palm fronds and cypress poles. Once the small ceremony had been held, with quiet, beautiful songs, the bodies were left for the deceased to make their journey into the spirit world.

As Myron was telling the story, Kimbo was swaying. At the end of the tale, after listening to the last word, the mountain of a man crumbled into a heap on the filthy floor. After a long, silent pause, Kimbo looked up at his son and spoke words that seemed to come from deep within his soul as though someone else was speaking. He needed to show his son strength and give him some guidance at the very time he, Kimbo Hopper, felt lost. He spoke unforgettably to his son with uneducated words, a wavering voice, and a quivering body.

"Myron, we are all gamblers one way or another. Nobody gets dealt a perfect hand. It ain't a matter of holding good cards, son, but ya gotta play a poor hand well. Ya gotta be who you are and do ya best, son. To become what we are capable of becoming. It must be our purpose." After a slight pause to catch a sob, he continued.

"None of us can help most things life does to us. Son, they're done before ya realise it, and once they're done, this is the most dangerous time. They make ya do other things until, at last, everything comes between you and what you'd like to be, and if ya don't watch out, ya lose ya true self forever. My life so far ain't been fair. It ain't fair now, and I can't see it changing. But, son, never think you are some kinda special victim. You're not. I'm not. We are just livin' our lives like everyone else. Ya gotta take things as they come. We get treated by people who see themselves as different or better than us. They try to make themselves feel better by making you feel worse. I know this only now. Now, I lie on this filthy floor, beaten by strangers and in prison for doing what I did before when it wasn't against the law. Think about what I said to you today, son. It may help you in every step you take each day. Find your purpose."

Myron flung himself onto his father to give him the biggest and most loving hug a son could give a father. He looked into his father's eyes and spoke.

"Father, what you got cannot be taken."

The police officer didn't move or say anything. He just stood with tears streaming down his cheeks, and his stick dropped limply to the floor.

A tragedy, told sincerely, can penetrate any human shield.

A new friend

The four men who had beaten Kimbo saw him weakened by his son's visit. The fifth man, who hadn't joined in the previous beating, sat still, watching. It was Kimbo who anticipated the first move. As they went for him again, Kimbo grabbed two of the attackers and banged their heads together hard, producing a sickening, ear-splitting crack. The other two rushed Kimbo. He hit one in the face, smashing his nose open and causing blood to spurt everywhere. On the last tug, he brought his knee up into the man's crotch as hard as he could. All four were helpless and in extreme pain.

The guards rushed to see the carnage scattered on the floor of the small cell. "What the hell happened here?" screamed the one in charge.

In a slow and unconcerned manner, the fifth man remarked that these men had had an argument and had "beat up on each other". Not that the guards cared, dragging the four men out to get medical treatment. Later, the doctor diagnosed two cracked skulls and another man whose nose had all the small bones broken and the nasal septum permanently displaced, lodged at an angle. The doctor declared that the man would have a flat nose for the rest of his life. The fourth man would probably not be able to have children. This final diagnosis got the biggest laugh in the Police Department that week when the officer on duty declared, "Well, thank God for that!"

When Kimbo and the fifth man were alone in the cell, he muttered thanks through his swollen lips. He politely asked his name.

"I am Juan Rodriguez, and I think I can change your life."

Kimbo paused and looked at this man again.

"I don't have a life any more," he said.

"Amigo, I know you think that, but I can show you how you can survive in this world, how you can rise above whatever shit has been thrown your way and stuck. I hear you come from the Ten Thousand Islands area in the skeeter-infested swamp you probably call home. I'd like you to tell me all about where you come from, as I think I can help you, and I think you can help me."

Kimbo's life had reached rock bottom just at a time when he thought it could not go lower, but he didn't intend to tell this stranger about his life, his family or his friends. However, he started talking slowly at first but was gaining confidence. It was beginning to help him. He proudly explained how beautiful and complicated Everglades City, Chokoloskee, Big Cypress Swamp, and the Everglades were. He described how there were thousands of inlets and places to hide from park rangers, how criminals and outlaws on the run hide away for months without being caught, surviving on an abundance of fish, crabs and all types of shellfish.

Kimbo looked at Juan Rodriguez. He wasn't a white settler, but he wasn't a black man or Native American. He'd never encountered a Hispanic man before, but as they talked together for hour upon hour that day, Kimbo was sure he would get along with this man. With just a few questions, Juan had a way of listening to bring Kimbo out of his caution. Without realising it, Kimbo strayed into talking about the people he loved and who had helped him. He told Juan about Jack Root and Elizabeth. Instinctively, he referred to Jack as the train driver; he didn't want him to be identified as a sheriff. With Elizabeth, he couldn't help but explain how much she meant to him. She had educated Myron and other Seminole and black children, and apart from his son, Elizabeth meant more to him than anyone else. She had treated him and his son with respect and dignity.

"It's her kindness and consideration of other people," he said. "I've never known anyone put themselves at risk as she does. I would do anything to help her if she needed it." Kimbo's breath started to jerk in and out as he suppressed a sob.

Juan Rodriguez's face was passive, but he took in every detail Kimbo outlined. He had taken a deliberate and sympathetic interest in Kimbo without telling him anything about himself. The attention Juan Rodriguez had given him had made Kimbo feel a little better about himself that night, although both men slept fitfully. Sitting and talking to someone was reassuring – a stranger with no apparent or devious plan to exploit or harm him. A rare experience indeed. He didn't notice that Juan hadn't told him how he could help him.

Both were in court the next day, with Juan first on the schedule and Kimbo the last case of the court day.

Jack's influence

After arriving at the Miami FBI offices, Sheriff Root was ushered into a room with two agents sitting at a well-worn table. He explained the current situation, his evidence, and the Chief Ranger's rejection. The FBI head of the Miami Division looked at Jack, loaded his temper into both barrels and let him have it.

"So, let me see now. You say there were two native women raped and murdered at Corkscrew Swamp, way out there on

Seminole land. There are no witnesses to this, but you found a hat and radio belonging to, let me see, a ranger named Jacques de Lors. The rangers say they were stolen, though this was not reported anywhere backing this claim. The bodies of the two women have been left to buzzards, turkey vultures, and God knows what else to be consumed over time. No doctors can verify what these women died from or whether they had been raped…as opposed to just having sex with a person or persons unknown. All this at a time when all these various tribes, Seminole, Miccosukee, and whatever other swamp creatures are living out there in remote and uninhabitable lands, are asking for formal recognition as a distinct self-governing political entity. What's more, they are demanding land-and-water-rights-related claims. I am reliably informed that this will probably be granted within the next year. So, let me get this straight, Sheriff, er, Root. You want me to divert scarce resources from our Miami bureau to this crime, as you call it. You want me to do this when we are chasing every badass South American rum and drug-running hombre currently swarming over South Florida?"

Jack left the bureau offices shortly after this tirade, feeling that his influence was not worth the money spent on the gasoline to take him there.

It was the day Kimbo was scheduled for his court hearing. Jack was seething, and Myron was in despair. Sitting in the jail cell and disconnected from the reality of his situation, Kimbo had no idea what would happen next. The court was ready, and Juan Rodriguez said farewell to Kimbo, leaving him alone with dreadful fear consuming him. Strangely, he immediately missed the calming influence of Juan Rodriguez. When his time in court came, late in the afternoon, he followed the court officer into the room where the decision would be made about his future. The judge looked at this massive black man with a badly beaten face and instantly made some assumptions. He'd given the guards a lot of trouble.

Judge "Hatchett" Hoskins was tired, hungry and in a nasty mood. It had been the usual long day. This day, however, was a little unusual in that one of the accused, someone called Juan Rodriguez, due to be put before the judge, had had his case dismissed, apparently, through lack of evidence. That evidence had mysteriously vanished from custody. The main witness had also disappeared two days before the hearing. Anyone appearing before Judge Hoskins always got a sentence, so he felt particularly aggrieved at this setback. Looking at Kimbo Hopper, he didn't think this case would take very long.

Kimbo hadn't noticed Chief Ranger, Myron, Sheriff Jack Root, and Burt Sadler sitting behind him in the courtroom. Chief Ranger stood up, took his assigned place before the bench and told the story of "this man Hopper brazenly stealing wildlife and trespassing on the property of the Everglades National Park."

"What evidence do you have?" said a bored "Hatchett" Hoskins.

"Well, my man, Ranger Burt Sadler, captured Hopper just as he fled the scene of his discovery. Your Honour, Sadler, is here today, standing in the courtroom behind me."

"Okay, come before me, Ranger," Kimbo turned to see Burt, Myron and Sheriff Jack Root, and his spirits lifted. Ranger Sadler did not acknowledge Kimbo but kept a straight, passive face. Burt walked forward, was sworn in and stood before the judge. He began his testimony.

"This man was in marshland, in Crocodile Creek, when I spotted him. I pursued him, but as I was focused on my pursuit and failed to steady myself, I fell from my boat into the alligator-infested waterways…"

"Wait, as I remember it, Ranger, he pushed you in and tried to make his getaway." Chief Ranger was trying to correct Sadler and put his preferred storyline across.

"Judge, Your Honour, I have sworn on the Bible here to tell the truth to you about what happened. I fell into the swamp water through my lack of experience. This man, Kimbo Hopper, tackled an enormous alligator. It may have been a crocodile, but I'm not sure of the difference… er. Anyway, the beast had my hand in his mouth and started a downward plunge to drown me. This man, Kimbo Hopper, shot him in the head and pulled me out of the dangerous water so that other reptiles could not reach me. I lost two fingers, but it could easily have been my life. Mister Hopper brought me to safety by putting me in his boat and floating me as fast as possible to get me medical help. That is the truth about what happened. This man saved my life, and I want to thank him for it." He looked at Kimbo; this time, Burt Sadler smiled warmly.

"Yes, all very well, Ranger, but by your testimony, this man was trespassing in the National Park and is found guilty of that. Now, what evidence do you have that he was hunting illegally?" The judge looked hard at Ranger Burt Sadler, hoping he had something else to say so he could sentence this man and go home.

"I have no evidence, Your Honour. There was nothing in the boat he used to bring me in. No hides or anything else." Sadler felt good about that. He thought trespassing in the National Park was an offence but was never custodial. Without evidence of hunting, Kimbo would be fined and go free.

"No, wait, Judge, Your Honour. We have evidence." Chief Ranger had a very smug look on his face. "The skiff this man

Hopper used had a huge amount of alligator blood inside its hull. This is quite common when these poachers and illegals hunt for gators and crocs. You find blood all over the skiff, as it was, in this case, Your Honour." The chief beamed a crooked smile at Kimbo.

Kimbo, Myron, Burt Sadler and Jack Root were utterly downcast. Judge "Hatchett" Hoskins immediately tapped his gavel lightly – he had no energy for a bigger thud on his bench. "Hopper, for trespassing, you get a fine of fifty dollars. I sentence you to a year behind bars for hunting and killing wildlife in a national park." Kimbo and Myron were stunned. The shock of the judge's cruel sentence silenced the room.

"Your Honour, may I approach the bench?" A uniformed Sheriff, Jack Root, walked forward, took the Bible, and waited for the judge to permit him to speak. The judge gave a weary nod.

Jack told Judge Hoskins how they first met and how they had made a life together and supported each other. He gave a brief history of how he became a minister and was voted by the good folk of Everglades City to be their sheriff. He finished with the statement, "…and I could trust this man, Kimbo Hopper, with my life."

A bored "Hatchett" Hoskins commented briefly, "How very nice of the sheriff of a so-called city, somewhere in the middle of a nowhere-swamp, known for outlaws and criminals on the run, to come all this way, to a thoroughly modern and well-regarded city, such as Miami, to plead for a man clearly guilty of all charges. Sheriff, this man's character is not on trial here, but his crimes are. However, I'll reduce the sentence to nine months if this man Hopper can hold his temper and not get into fights or other problems while he is incarcerated – which, by looking at him now, I can't see being avoided. Twelve months, reduced to nine if he stays out of trouble." He banged his gavel hard this time, rose and went home for his longed-for supper, his usual three glasses of beer, and an early night in bed on this long, tiresome day.

As Kimbo was being led out, he turned to Myron and said, in that brief moment, "Myron, my son, make your own life now. You may not see me for a long time. You will survive because you are skilled. You are a strong man now. I love you." Myron opened his mouth to say something, but those last three words his father spoke to him left him without any of his own. Kimbo looked at Jack Root and Ranger Burt Sadler and mouthed "thank you" to them. He was led from the courtroom with his head hung low, his heart broken, and his life crushed.

Chapter Thirty-One
Crossroads

The United States Highway 1 stretches from Fort Kent, Maine, near the Canadian border, to Key West, Florida. It is 2,370 miles long, and as Kimbo travelled along a small part of it in the back of the caged part of a pickup truck along with seven others being transported, he began to sweat. He was sweating not from the sweltering heat and humidity of midday Florida but from emotional trauma. It was not only what had happened in court but mostly because he was headed to the Monroe County Detention Centre on Marathon Key in the middle of the Florida Keys. He had pledged never to return to The Keys after the hurricane of 1935. It was going to be another humiliation.

He'd lost Yuchi. He was incarcerated for doing the only thing that had provided a living for him and Myron. He lost his freedom to save a man's life instead of saving his own skin. He was picked on in his prison cell for being black and vulnerable.

As the pickup travelled, Kimbo realised he was travelling on a road he had helped build. With his eyes closed, he realised that he had built every road that had brought him to this point. This seat on this pickup was heading to jail. He was a man who barely wanted to mix outside his family group. A man who mostly took a defensive attitude toward people and situations. He allowed Zella to dissuade him from being cautious and acting before the storm. He took too long to show the veterans why they should not mess with him, assuming they would eventually leave him and his family alone, but they didn't. Kimbo's passiveness sometimes made them step up their efforts, that is, until he flattened two or three of them, and the message got out. He had been too passive with the school principal, Sheriff Jeffries, and Bill Walker. He had ignored the encroaching dangers of men assigned to the Everglades National Park who had powers to do what they liked. *Am I so unworldly that I'm a danger to others as well as himself?*

He constantly turned it over in his mind – how his personality had caused many of his problems. He decided that he had arrived at this point because he didn't take the initiative; he didn't do what he should have done, so he should stand up for himself and improve his life. He decided from that moment, sitting in that truck with toughened criminals, with sweat seeping out of his body constantly, that he would take control of his life. It was precisely at the instant he was about to be incarcerated for nine months – when his life took an entirely new direction. Although the road was as straight as a die, it met a crossroads. Card Sound Road crossed the main route to Key Largo.

He would make decisions rapidly from now on, without someone telling him what to do.

A New Road

The pickup truck slammed on its brakes. Kimbo picked himself up from the truck bed. The tailgate flew open, and Juan Rodriguez stood there with a big smile, looking directly at Kimbo Hopper.

"Kimbo, welcome to the rest of your life!" Juan's accent now sounded more Hispanic than before. He was with three others, all holding rapid-fire guns. Two had their weapons pointed at the driver and guards in the cab, whilst the third trained his guns on the other prisoners.

"Out you get, amigo Kimbo. You other hombres can either

run or stay in the truck." They all sat frozen by the choice. It was so sudden. There was no violence to jerk them into running or joining in any brutality. They had never suffered at the hands of these particular guards in any way, so they didn't have any instant motivation to take revenge. It took about five seconds for Juan to wait for the prisoners' decision, and then he crashed the tailgate shut. He and his fellow compadres backed off, pointing their guns and waving the truck to drive onwards to its destination, the Detention Centre on Marathon Key. The vehicle immediately accelerated away from the high-tension scene, and the ambush squad watched as the dust billowed and then faded onto the ground. The whole kidnapping had taken about three minutes.

Kimbo stood shocked. "Okay, amigo, take all your clothes off, I mean all, and hand them to Pedro." Juan pointed to a man about his size who was already stripping down. "You'll switch clothes. Don't worry. His clothes will fit you, and he has a change of clothes for when he needs them." Kimbo followed Juan's direct command.

Pedro, dressed in Kimbo's clothes, handed his to a naked Kimbo, put a rucksack on his back and headed in the direction of the area known to the settlers as Southern Glades, due west of where they had ambushed the pickup truck. Kimbo was confused, and his eyes glowed in fear.

"Hey, Kimbo, amigo, don't worry. We have a plan for you, my lucky friend. Pedro will go as far as he needs into the swamp to ensure they think you are heading back home. The search party will have dogs sniffing you out, so we must leave your sock here for them to find and use. We'll see Pedro in about two days. Ok, my friend, we are going to Miami. Have you ever been to Miami?"

Kimbo hadn't said a word during the snatch. *What had just*

happened? Have I been kidnapped, captured or set free? He was confused. *Do I have a choice? To follow these men, to follow Juan, who has made me a friend? What do these men want in return?* He chose not to ask any of these questions. He thought he should wait.

"Juan, I am afraid for Pedro. Does he know this country, these Everglades and the dangerous wildlife that live here? Is he familiar with finding direction from the stars, the sun, the wind, and the changes in the land and water as you walk? Does he know these things?" Kimbo was genuinely concerned, as he knew Pedro would be risking his life, as he was unfamiliar with the terrain.

"Hey, don't worry, Kimbo, my friend. He has found his way out of tougher spots than a swamp. We've got to be convincing, so they think you're dead. You will now become a dead man in the eyes of the law. He'll leave your clothes near alligator nests somewhere out there. How hard can that be? He's a big, tough hombre." Kimbo just hoped he had some experience and knowledge of this area, no matter how tough and big this hombre was. Nothing felt right.

Juan led them east through a wetland to a soft shore beach, where they found two boats with motors. They boarded and headed through Little Card Sound Bay and on towards Key Biscayne, just south of Miami. From there, Kimbo was told they would be crossing into south Miami via the newly completed Rickenbacker Causeway.

Kimbo assessed the preparation that must have gone into springing him from his journey to the Detention Centre, on Marathon. *They want me for something. I am now in their hands, and at this moment, I have to wait and see. What have I got to lose?*

He was taking new steps in his life. He was travelling a new road. A new unclear path. He had no way of going back now. He started to feel both thrilled and frightened.

But now he would be a hunted man. He had taken that new road without looking back.

It took three days.

Pedro was lost. It was getting dark. He heard a rumbling, guttural growl, which sounded like an angry panther. It was. He had a handgun but wasn't well-trained in its use over distance. He'd only had to shoot people at close range, not animals twenty yards away. People were predictable in his experience, especially when a gun was pointed at them. The light was fading, and he hadn't seen any place that looked like it housed gators, but then he didn't know what that would look like. He'd been assured it would be obvious – he'd know when he saw it.

He stepped off some hard ground into clear water. Surprised at how cool it felt, it briefly took his breath away. His footsteps squished as his feet sank into the muck. He immediately thought of quicksand, but he remembered vaguely that someone had told him there was no quicksand in South Florida. He didn't know that the biggest threat to walking through this terrain was sharp spires of limestone rock. Some are visible, and some are just below the soil, mud or water level. He noticed a cypress dome rising from the water and decided that would be where he would spend the night. He didn't know these domes would typically have a deep-water hole in the middle, favoured by nesting alligators. As he walked toward it, his left foot stepped on a limestone spire, which penetrated his boot and slid into his foot. Blood oozed into the water.

With his mouth slightly open, the twelve-foot-sleeping alligator sensed Pedro approaching from the blood leaching from his foot. The gator lay still, then rapidly grabbed Pedro's left foot;

he sank his powerful jaws into the flesh and bone, crunching as hard as possible. He then began to shake his head vigorously. As big and robust as Pedro was, it was no contest. Kimbo's clothes were ripped to shreds and scattered over a wide area. Pedro was unconscious when he was submerged in the deep-water hole. He either drowned or died of shock; it would have been difficult to tell even if a doctor had examined him – which was never likely. It took the vast gator three days to consume Pedro completely, but even then, he had help from his neighbours. It was a hearty meal shared by the community.

The day following Kimbo's escape from the pickup truck, the Miami search party burst into where Myron was sleeping – the home he had shared with his father, Yuchi, and Hachi. He was alone. Very quickly, it became clear, even to the doubting police, that Myron had no idea about his father's escape or whereabouts. After a thorough search around the unwelcoming Seminole village, the search party came to the uncomfortable conclusion that they would have to use dogs through the swamp, starting from where he was freed. Every one of the police officers was reluctant to do this, but they knew their boss would give them no choice in the matter.

It took them two days to find the cypress dome with Kimbo's ripped clothes strewn around the water hole. There was no sign of a body. The dogs convincingly confirmed they were Kimbo's clothes, and the case was closed. They were slightly puzzled by the unopened rucksack with a fresh set of clothes stashed for him to change into as part of the escape plan. One of them nervously looked around and then announced the end of the search. He yelled, "Let's all get outta here." Most of them half-ran back the way they came, and they all jumped into their trucks and headed back to Miami, relieved. The hunt leader shouted so all could hear him.

"See. What did I tell ya? Not even an old swamp creature

like this black guy Hopper would be safe from the critters livin' in these parts. Makes my blood run cold!"

Kimbo Hopper was now considered officially dead. Jack Root had been told via a phone call what had happened on the road to Marathon Key, what was subsequently found in the Everglades, and how Kimbo had obviously perished at one of the many cypress domes with a deep-water hole in the middle. Elizabeth was inconsolable for days.

Jack felt it was more than just his duty to tell his son, Myron. With heavy, heartfelt grief, Jack Root visited Myron Hopper with the tragic news of his father's death. He sat with Myron, Bad Hand Billie and Chief Bowlegs. It was like a shockwave hitting all three. They sat together, quietly thinking of the qualities of the man.

Recovering slowly from the shock of Jack's information, Myron became curious to know more about those men who had hijacked the pickup truck. Sheriff Jack Root had no details because the police had no details. The officers taking Kimbo to the Detention Centre said there were three, maybe four men. Nobody noticed precisely, but they heard an accent – they couldn't say what accent. They didn't want to be known as officers who could identify the ambush party.

Myron knew his father better than anyone alive. He knew his father enough to believe Kimbo would never be a victim of an alligator. He wasn't the only one sitting there with those thoughts. All four were thinking the same questions.

But where is he? Will he show himself to me, or will I never see him again?

Chapter Thirty-Two
Yes, to Death in the Darkened Room

He sat in the darkened room. It was hot and humid. The one window was shuttered and locked. He was waiting for something to happen, and he knew, yet again, it wasn't something he could control. Yet again, he didn't know any words for what he felt. This situation was entirely outside of Kimbo's experience. He felt an overwhelming feeling of bitterness, a feeling he didn't recognise, an alien feeling. Here he was, a penniless, worthless man once again. But it was worse than that. He was a criminal, a fugitive, and as far as the world knew, he was dead. He had lost his wife and his daughter to a storm. He had lost two people he dearly loved to rape and murder and, for all intents and purposes, his son Myron, who would now think him dead. The bitterness of these losses and his helplessness took over Kimbo's soul. If the Lord had asked him then, he would have said yes to death. He wasn't asked.

He had been sitting in this stifling, stinking room in a timeless stupor, his hands tied behind the chair. Something changed inside him; it wasn't a snap-change or a fleeting flash. It was a profound realisation that he had to do something different in his life, or he could see no point in living.

Am I going to keep living like this? Living a life always determined by somebody or something else? Another storm, a thief like Bill Walker, a new law, a rapist and murderer, a judge, a gang member? He could only wait to see what was next. *How can I live with this constant pounding?*

At this point, he decided his next choice would be his. Nobody would determine what he would do next; only he would decide. He would be the one to choose whether he wanted to live at all.

He knew he was in Miami, but he didn't know where. The only person he knew was Juan Rodriguez, but he realised he didn't even know him. What he did know was that Juan must have organised his escape and taken him to Miami, a place unfamiliar to him except by name and stories he'd picked up from Bad Hand, Jack Root, Jim Tigertail and others. He felt alienated and vulnerable, but in a different way than before. These men obviously wanted him for something, but what? It can't be money and won't be because they need more men for whatever they are operating. There obviously were enough men. Even enough to send one into the Everglades to fool the troopers sent out to recapture him. Then it became clear. It was a realisation that confused and unsettled him. They wanted something no one, except Jack Root, had ever sought from him. Knowledge.

Chapter Thirty-Three
Seeking a Better Path

The village was numbed. Yuchi and Hachi were raped and murdered, and Kimbo dead. They performed their traditional funeral without Kimbo's body. Instead, they used the body of the largest alligator they could find as a tribute to Kimbo. Birds of prey swooped down to feed over three days. Myron had taken the sacrificial alligator's hide to hang alongside the grandpa ghost gator he had caught with his father when saving the life of Burt Sadler. Red-shouldered hawks, turkey vultures, barred owls, osprey, bald eagles and even snail kites, all of which had suffered badly from the sudden, unknown decline in snails, gorged themselves until a week later, the clean alligator's skull and skeleton had been stripped bare. A vast array of insects had swarmed over the last remaining parts of the carcass. High up on the roof of that chickee, it had been a rare chance for the birds of prey to feed well on the familiar flesh of an alligator without looking around for approaching danger. It was a feast for all, and they gorged.

The villagers' spirits were at their lowest ebb for a week when Chief Bowlegs called a meeting of six of his closest confidants. He wanted to change the mood and overcome the disastrous turn of events. At the chief's request, Bad Hand and, for the first time, Myron Hopper joined him in his chickee.

"Our water is dying. Our fish are dying, and our crops are drying. The water from the big lake, Okeechobee, is drying up.

The settlers are taking our water before it flows through our land. They grow sugar crops and use the water in their huge cattle ranches, and we cannot fight back. The settlers will tell us to move north into Oklahoma, Georgia or the barren lands next to their ranches, where they say we can live peacefully from the white man. We think of ourselves as free people, but remember, we are called 'The Unconquered People' for a reason. This land we live on here is our home. It is where our ancestors survived the wars with the white invaders. This is where we will live and grow as a people, or this is where we will pass into the spirit world." Bad Hand, Myron and the others looked proud. Chief Bowlegs looked at them and shook his head. "Our pride is one thing, but our action is vital. What we do next is what will save us. I request you all, including Myron, son of Kimbo, to provide me with counsel, advice and ideas on how we can survive and grow. I want you to go from here and seek ways we can and will live. To beat the white man, we must play the white man's games or at least gain his respect so that he treats us as equals. Maybe that will never be possible, or maybe it can."

Bad Hand, Myron, and all gathered rose together to walk out. Chief Bowlegs gestured for only Myron to stay. He sat down again, and the two men were now alone together.

"Your father is not dead, and I think you may know that. He is hidden from us. I don't know where or why. Your father is too clever and knowing to be eaten by an alligator in a water hole. Somehow, he escaped the life he was ordered to have by the white judge. We know that, and Bad Hand Billie knows that. We do not know how or when, but I am sure we will see him again somehow. We will meet him along the path. He will seek a better path. A path we all hope to take, and… we will meet him. It will be joyous, and it will be on this beautiful earth or with our spirits. Myron, Kimbo's son, know this as you journey along your path."

Myron left the chief's tent an inspired and focused man.

Chapter Thirty-Four
Mapping the Future

Juan Rodriguez followed his boss into the dark, humid, stinking room. Sal Blanco immediately assumed control and beckoned two others into the room. "Si, El Baygon, immediately," and the two hurried in. He indicated that one of them should open the window, and fresh air and sunlight flowed in on a fresh sea breeze. It was a merciful relief for Kimbo.

Their discussion was direct and to the point. Sal Blanco told Kimbo that he and his pandilla were in business, a profitable business, importing marijuana from Columbia. Still, he said he was being hurt by informers and "outsiders", as he called them. His new strategy was to have a small, trusted set of amigos as a core part of his business. Those who broke his trust would not live very long. Sal didn't like to mince his words.

After describing his business, he told Kimbo he would be taken to live in Overtown, a part of Miami designated strictly for black people. Kimbo didn't know what this all meant, but he remembered it was where Jack Root's friend, Purvis, lived. Kimbo instinctively knew he needed to be very cautious if he would live to see Myron again. His instinct told him to address the boss as the others had done. Kimbo had assumed a submissive role for most of his life, so it was easy to quickly adapt and find his first few words.

"I am grateful to you, El Baygon and Juan Rodriguez for providing this new life. You know I have nothing to give you, for

I have nothing. How is it that I can help you, El Baygon?" Kimbo was finding his best words and a straightforward way to speak to someone whose second language was English.

"We like new names for our trusted amigos. Yours will be 'La Noche'. It means 'the night'. That is when you'll be doing most of your work with us, and you also have the right colour for it."

They all laughed at El Baygon's poor joke, even Kimbo. It was the beginning of what he needed to understand the mentality of his new accomplices. He needed to adapt to his new existence.

"But first, we have to draw some maps."

"El Baygon, 'scuse me, but I do not have words to write or be able to work with numbers. I have no schoolin'."

"La Noche, this we already knew or guessed. We are prepared to have you describe and draw, with my two hombres here, detailed maps of the Ten Thousand Islands, Everglades City, Chokoloskee area and the land right down to the Cayos. This is the first part of our plan for your new life. For the second part of the plan, I will explain that when I'm happy with your work on the first part. But for now, let's eat together. Tonight, you sleep here. Tomorrow, you work with these two, Paco and Waco." They all laughed again, and everyone except El Baygon and Juan left the small room.

"There is one other thing, La Noche. I want you to always keep in mind that if you try to leave my business, I will track you down, and you will be killed. But, amigo, you may be tempted to risk your own life because you want freedom. I understand this, but you should know that two other people will die if there is any disloyalty to me – your son, Myron and your dear friend, Elizabeth. Leave me or betray me – be clear. They will die and not, my friend, quickly." His reddish lips, around the corners of the slit that was his fat mouth, creased his dark brown skin. It was chilling. Kimbo looked at Juan Rodriguez. Juan's face was passive, and he avoided eye contact with Kimbo. El Baygon and Juan left the putrid room. Alone, Kimbo stared at the walls and saw images of Myron and Elizabeth. He no longer would trust Juan Rodriquez.

As Kimbo got up from his chair, he noticed the light from the previously closed, shuttered window shining down on the blood-stained concrete floor. This is where he would sleep that night.

Myron's new friend

He knew he was taking a risk, but Burt Sadler approached the Seminole village with enough caution and openness that the scout tracking him allowed him to walk through the entrance. He then stopped him suddenly.

"White man, what do you want? We live here in peace, away from you, settlers."

"I seek the son of Kimbo Hopper. I want to thank him for his father saving my life. I owe a debt of gratitude. I come from a land in the north where we repay debts. I am unarmed and do not represent the law or any government. I only represent myself."

The scout told him to stand still, not move for any reason. He immediately informed the chief. On his return, the scout found Burt Sadler surrounded by village children. They were laughing and having fun at seeing this white man standing bolt upright, sweating profusely and looking petrified. The scout shooed the children away and led Burt to Myron's home. Myron immediately recognised him from his father's court hearing and the swamp rescue. He greeted Myron, and after Burt gave his genuine and heartfelt thanks to Myron, he expressed deep regret that his rescue in the swamp had ultimately led to his father's death. He told Myron he wanted to repay this debt somehow and had some ideas that might help him and the whole village. Myron listened with intelligence, not anger. They talked for hours, during which Myron had turned Burt Sadler's ideas and information into a plan; he realised what an advantage Elizabeth Root's school had given him over the life he otherwise would have had. Myron asked for and was granted a visit to Chief Sammy Bowlegs for a discussion. Another hour later, Chief Bowlegs called for a council meeting and briefed Bad Hand Billie beforehand.

Myron stood before the council, introduced Burt Sadler and talked through ideas they had put together. At first, the council reacted badly. They were naturally sceptical. A white man walking into their village uninvited? This was the same white man responsible for Kimbo Hopper's imprisonment, even though they knew he had pleaded for his release. Were these ideas further attempts to absorb the defiant Indians into white society? To control them and then move them away to Oklahoma or Georgia? Something they had tried many times to such a tragic loss on both sides.

However, they were curious that a white man had come to them suggesting ways for the village to make 'settler dollars'. They wanted to know what this white man wanted in return. Nobody had experienced a settler coming to them with ideas from which the red man could benefit. It was always the other way. Treaties were signed and land allocated, but then taken away with violence. Was this a new type of white man's trick?

Myron talked openly about what the council was thinking. "If this is a new trick, we can shut it down. It will be on our land, now protected by United States law. We may laugh at this idea of law, but it must be our way forward. We can take this path but move away if we decide. It will be in our control and for our benefit. The money we make will earn us respect. Money will give us protection. We should open a few "smoke shops". We will offer discounts and tax-free tobacco products. This will give us a stable money flow and, over time, substantial dollars from the settlers. We can place these on our land, which we control and have been given the right to do with it as we wish. It would be sensible of us to tell the white man before we start. Make them feel they have a say. There is a new mood among some white men to recognise our rights. My father's friend, Burt Sadler, has helped me understand how the settlers can change their attitude toward us."

This last comment, Myron calling this white man his father's 'friend', caused a murmur. Then the meeting settled down, and the Chief, Bad Hand Billie and the council sat listening, without comment or expression, as Myron continued.

"This will be a start only. The first smoke shop should be on our Immokalee reservation, and the second should be on the Hollywood reservation near Miami. Many people will come from the north to Miami and the west for short periods. They like to spend their dollars and have fun. If you approve, I will take responsibility for setting this up, and Burt Sadler will be a comforting white face by my side for the white visitors. He has turned away from his job as a park ranger. The white man likes to gamble and take risks with his money. When we have some success, we should open high-stakes bingo halls on each of our defined reservation lands. We should be a friendly novelty where they can buy cheap tobacco and play a game called bingo. We should learn to be businessmen and build our future on the white man's money." Myron stopped and waited for a reaction.

Chief Sammy Bowlegs waited to let Myron Hopper's proposal sink in. Then the chief started speaking slowly.

"We want our people to be self-reliant. We want our people to have Seminole doctors who are taught by the white man in settler's medicine to fight against diseases. But we want those doctors to be part of us, be Seminole people, know our people and know our ways. We want our own schools that teach about the world and our ways. We want houses that are safe from storms, and we want to control our own affairs. After we see it prosper, I will set up a tribal council and ask all Seminole leaders from all the Seminole reservations to join us in this new future. We will have a tribal council bringing Big Cypress, Hollywood, Immokalee, Tampa, Kissimmee and Brighton reservations together. We have been the 'Unconquered People'. We survived the settlers killing us and taking our land and water. Now we shall become the 'Self-Reliant People'. I pledge to do all in my power to unite all Seminoles under a single tribal council where tribe decisions benefit all who follow our ways."

The council voted with the persuasive voice of Chief Bowlegs singing in their heads. It wasn't unanimous, but the proposal was agreed on.

"I speak for us all in thanking Burt Sadler, a man who didn't have to think of us. A man who didn't know how we would greet him. A man dedicated to repaying a debt to our departed Kimbo Hopper. He has given us a gift of ideas for the next part of our tribe's journey in this life. He will join Myron in helping this village. I want to honour him by giving him his Seminole name."

There was stunned silence.

"From now on, Burt Sadler, you will be known as 'Bad Hand Burt'."

The whole council laughed hard and loud as Burt looked

down at his hand, missing two fingers. Bad Hand Billie had tears of laughter rolling down his cheeks, as did many others. The chief knew the value of laughter.

Chief Sammy Bowlegs rose, and his chest took in as much air as he could manage. He held his breath for five seconds, emptying his mind of small things, and breathed out slowly, a deep humming sound emanating from the middle of his head.

Chief Bowlegs now had the road forward and a way of lifting the tribe from their recent loss, tragedies and gloom. His people had something to focus on, which was in their control, for them to determine. That night, Chief Sammy Bowlegs thanked the spirits of his ancestors for providing the way forward.

That night, some miles away, Elizabeth Root also had some ideas.

Maps

It took two days, but finally, Paco, Waco and Kimbo had the maps at a very detailed level. Throughout their time together, Kimbo tried to assess these men; most likely, they would be part of his future world. They were educated and could speak two languages. He didn't know the word for it, but there was also something sinister about both. Paco had a false charm about him, and Waco had an underlying hint of violence. Their eyes were constantly darting first to him, the door, and the drawings. As their work progressed, they saw it would deliver what the boss wanted. They had created a blueprint for offloading and delivering many tons of pot staring at them from the maps. Kimbo knew that having a map was one thing; knowing where you are, where to go, and what to avoid in the middle of the night was a completely different world. In finishing the detailed maps, there was visible relief on their faces. El Baygon was called, and he looked over the maps for some time. He had questions, many questions.

"El Baygon, we have these maps, but they will not be helpful if you don't know the area. Your men will easily lose their way at night, even if they have a map. The night also plays tricks. Some wildlife only appears when it is dark. You will need guides." The boss appeared to ignore Kimbo's words.

"La Noche, who lives here? What do they do? Do they make a lot of money? How rich are they? How many people live in the Ten Thousand Islands and in Everglades City and Chokoloskee? Where are the natives on this map? Do they mix with the gringos? Do they..." His questioning lasted four hours, by which time Kimbo was exhausted. He had never had to work hard at concentrating on words, drawings, places, or how to describe land areas. The maps were good, but El Baygon realised they were insufficient for his purposes. He was going to need Kimbo for part two of his scheme. Kimbo had realised this and should have felt relieved, but he didn't. He knew what would have happened if El Baygon had been unhappy with his work. For now, he knew that being a guide and co-ordinator would save his life. This was only to be the first of many tests to come.

"La Noche, you have provided the information we need." Again, he suddenly became straightforward, using minimal words to describe the plan.

"I want you to be our guide in the Ten Thousand Islands for importing and distributing our goods. It may be that we recruit local people to be our carriers from ship to shore. I will need you for this also. These new people will be paid well for their efforts, and it sounds like they need the money. But they need to be trusted." He smiled and continued. "Then we need some others, maybe, to drive it to Miami. That's all they need to do, and that's all they need to know, including you, my friend La Noche. I want them to know what will happen if they break my trust. Okay, my friend?" Kimbo doubted that El Baygon considered anyone his friend.

Kimbo may not have been used to this world, but he certainly understood what was happening and what part he was about to play. He would be a critical element of the pot-hauling and transportation business in South Florida. For the first time, he was fundamental to others for what he knew and could do. For him, this was strangely intoxicating. But he knew he wasn't getting a choice, and he knew the alternative. He also knew he should never ask El Baygon a question. He thought *I may not be schooled, but I'm not stupid*. He was learning to adapt to his new life and the different types of people around him. *Was this a better life?* He wondered, knowing it was a pointless question to be asking.

As he was being taken to the Overtown area of Miami that evening, Kimbo started to chat with the only person he knew anything about, his driver, Juan Rodriguez. But what did he know about Juan? He had already had reason not to trust him...he'd passed the boss the names of his son and Elizabeth as people closest to him.

"Juan, when did Pedro return? Was he scared of the gators?"

Juan told him that the police had found Pedro's clothes but not Pedro. "They had made a stupid assumption that it was you that was taken down into a deep-water hole and eaten. Everyone now thinks you are dead, amigo" – another shock. Pedro, a man Kimbo didn't even know, had lost his life for him to survive. This was very different from anything else he had experienced.

As they drove through Miami to Overtown, Kimbo sat thinking about his situation. He could see clearly what he had before him without ever understanding how or when his life would end. Would it be sooner or later?

"Juan, I always wanna know if El Baygon isn't happy with my work. If I hadn't come up with the maps and information about the people who lived there, would he have just released me or killed me?"

"It is time I was straight with you. Paco's nickname is 'Psycho Paco', and Waco is just Waco, for reasons that will be obvious when you see him in action. And you will. They are both brutal. Your work was exactly what I thought it would be and what I told the boss it would be. If it hadn't, it would probably have been Waco to take care of you. Our time together, that day in the cell, and ever since, taught me how valuable you could be to us. You've proved it. Thank you, sweet Jesus! Otherwise, you would most certainly be dead. You are now a very important part of our business, and you will be well-rewarded, amigo. But one wrong move is all it takes for any of us to be killed."

Kimbo then said out loud what he was thinking anyway. He asked two questions. "I know what my name, La Noche, means in Spanish, but what does 'El Baygon' mean?"

Juan looked away from the road briefly and stared into Kimbo's eyes. "Baygon is an insecticide." He could see Kimbo didn't know what that meant. "It kills insects like roaches, spiders, mosquitos and sometimes…rats."

"Juan, what is your nickname from the boss?"

Juan didn't smile or look at Kimbo.

"El Asesino."

Kimbo didn't understand and didn't want to ask. Juan knew he wouldn't. A forgotten sense of foreboding hit Kimbo. He immediately realised he was now riding a different storm.

Chapter Thirty-Five
A New Deal for Purvis

A month went by before Kimbo received new instructions. He was told to leave Overtown and wait at a one-bedroom apartment on 737 5th Street, South Beach, Miami. He would hear from El Baygon or Juan. A message would be delivered between five and six in the evening. If no message was delivered then, Kimbo could do as he pleased until the next evening's delivery hour. Over that month, he kept away from almost everywhere, only going out at night to buy fruit, vegetables and a little chicken to cook on an abandoned grill at the back of his building. He grew a thick black beard to cover his face as much as possible and had his hair cut neatly short, the first time he had paid good money for a haircut. He used cash given to him as a "retainer", as Juan put it. He wondered if he was being watched.

That month made him think about Myron and how or when he might see him again. He thought about his complicated situation, being considered dead but very much alive and living the most leisurely life he'd ever known. But, at the same time, he was on the edge of death if things turned on him.

"I'm not stupid," he'd say out loud, alone in a thriving and bustling city. Many times, he sat quietly, thinking through his opportunities. *I will have to fulfil what is expected of me. Cutthroat thugs control me. If I make one mistake, I will die by their hands or the law.*

Each day, he spent time thinking about what he should do.

He had to consider Myron and Elizabeth. He had every reason to believe Sal Blanco would carry out his threats.

"Above everything, I want to be remembered," he said, looking in the cracked mirror on the unpainted concrete wall in a room that hadn't been adequately cleaned in ten years. *But who do I want to remember me, and for doing what?*

Kimbo remembered the bar where Jack Root had met Purvis; he was restless and needed some company. Safe company. A person whom he thought he could trust and who could help him with his ambition. As he came out into the hot sun from behind 737 5th Street, he noticed, across the street, a familiar figure. At first, he observed how the man walked, then his physique and, finally, his face – a face much changed from when he last saw him in Everglades City. He had put on weight. The man's hair was almost completely gone, tanned but giving him a more intimidating look than Kimbo remembered. He wore expensive clothes. He went into the building next door.

It was Bill Walker.

A giant hand

He walked to the bar in Miami's 'Colored Town', hoping to find Purvis. By the time Kimbo sat at the bar, he had decided how Bill Walker would fit into his future, whether Bill liked it or not. Whether he liked it or not, he was determined Bill was returning to Everglades City.

It was just before noon when Purvis walked in. Kimbo immediately recognised him from Jack and Elizabeth's wedding. Purvis completed his routine scan in every bar, restaurant or closed room he entered. He then came to sit at the bar on his usual stool, next to Kimbo, but showed no sign of recognising him. Purvis looked at the barman and indicated the room to be cleared, including the barman himself. The bar emptied, and no one complained. He turned to Kimbo and spoke.

"Let's not pretend I know you and you know me. I'll not use your name. The reason is I know all about you. I also know where you live and which Colombian you are workin' for…well, nearly workin' for. You haven't quite started yet. I know you live near 819 5th Street, a flophouse and brothel. If you haven't found out, Bill Walker owns and runs number 819. After a few years in Santiago de Cuba, he made enough money and more than enough enemies to high-tail it back here. I think your friend Jack Root told me that the book had been closed when Ol' Zippy got zapped 34, and Bill Walker disappeared down to the tip of Cuba. Unless Bill Walker was going to die, the book ain't ever gonna be closed. Well, my big friend of Jack Root, he ain't dead, right? So, how can I help you? That is why you are here. Jack always knew that if he helped me, I would help him. So, Mister, fancy hair, what's your deal?"

Kimbo realised he was talking to the right person. He decided to tell him his plan, what role he wanted for himself, what role he wanted for Purvis, and, just as vitally, the role he had in mind for Bill Walker.

Purvis wanted to know what his cut would be. It only took a short pause before he smiled wickedly, agreed, and shook the giant hand offered. This was the first time Kimbo had ever worked out a deal and then sealed it, and he was a little shaken by it.

Chapter Thirty-Six
A Wedding and a New Life

It was morning when Bad Hand's daughter, Tehya Billie, opened her eyes to a new realisation. From this moment, her life would take a different path.

She grew up a shy, dutiful girl, and now everyone around her saw she had become a competent, intelligent and beautiful woman. Her friendship with Hachi, a girl murdered alongside her mother, had been strong. They were the same age with similar interests and had grown as close as sisters, perhaps closer. Tehya witnessed the aftermath of Hachi losing her father and brother to the storm of 1935. She helped them recover and repair the damage done to their spirits and happiness. She was overwhelmed with joy for Hachi when Myron and his father moved into their home and provided them with a new life to overcome their grief and insecurity. She had seen how their union had nourished all of them. With both families losing a parent and child, it had been the initial bond they all needed to understand each other and their loss. Tehya had not only grown close to her friend Hachi, but she admired Myron. He was clever, thoughtful and brave. He knew many things about the land they lived on and how to live on it, but he also knew the need to treat it with respect. It was the same respect Seminoles had for the Everglades and Big Cypress.

As she lay there, waking from a deep, fulfilling sleep, opening her eyes to stare at the underside of the chickee thatched roof, she wanted to turn her head to the right to look at what was next to her. She wanted to make sure it was all true.

There he was, Myron, still in his deep, enjoyable sleep. A slight wisp of a young man's beard sprouting hairs in different directions. It was true; she had spent the first night with her friend Myron. He was now a highly respected man, helping to build a new future for their tribe. He used his peaceful manner to persuade, convince, and lead the development of different sources to accumulate settlers' dollars. Last evening, he quietly encouraged Tehya to gather tribal women to discuss how to produce clothing, novelty Seminole dolls, and other items from hides, pelts, and plumes, all lawfully hunted within their reservation land. Myron instilled confidence in Tehya, allowing her to develop her ideas for selling things to the settlers and the growing mass of tourists, using their curiosity about native Americans living on their doorstep. Myron knew the white man was planning a new road across the Everglades. A highway, soon dubbed "Alligator Alley", would pass just a few miles south of the Big Cypress Reservation and would be perfect for luring the traveller to stop and have a break at a Seminole shop. He had an idea that if they could set up a gas station with their own brand and sell their gas a little cheaper than those selling it at either end of the one hundred-mile stretch from the Miami–Fort Lauderdale end to Naples on the west coast, there was money to be made.

Myron broke her dreaming. "Osee hatatki," he said with his large smiling eyes.

"Good morning to you too, Big Chief Myron," she joked.

"Tehya, I want us to be married and have ten children," he said with a serious face. She pushed his shoulder in mock rejection. Then, after letting his words settle down into both their thoughts, Myron felt he had been rejected. He looked at her, slightly shocked.

Tehya said, "Well, certainly not ten. Three at most!"

With considerable preparations, Tehya and Myron were married. They both asked to see Chief Bowlegs after Bad Hand's permission had been sought and given. It was traditional for Seminoles to avoid marrying within their family, so Tehya and Myron's bond was acceptable. In other ways, it was considered a perfect match for Bad Hand Billie and Chief Sammy Bowlegs. Both these young people were emerging as natural, highly accepted tribe leaders.

The wedding ceremony began with a procession headed by Myron. In turn, the same procession was led by Tehya, followed by Chief Bowlegs and then other tribe members – everyone dressed in their best rich, colourful garments and headwear. Myron and Tehya stood before the Chief as he carried out the official ceremony. All were happy about this beautiful and modest couple marrying. At the most solemn moment, the village gathered around the couple as the chief spoke. He ended with the words stated clearly and loudly so everyone could hear them. Words that had permanence stamped by his delivery.

"You take each other for man and wife forever!"

He then leaned forward, softly smiling and joking, and said, with the same clarity and volume, "There are no divorces among the Seminoles." Everyone laughed.

Chief Bowlegs was overjoyed that he could see the next generation willing to embrace the future of 'self-reliance' as he pictured it. He thought this self-reliance would be tested but wasn't prepared for how and who would test it.

Chapter Thirty-Seven
Bill Understands His Role

On the same day his son was married, Kimbo stood outside the room where he had first arrived in Miami and met El Baygon. Bill Walker was tied to a chair, staring into the dim light. He wasn't alone. Juan Rodriguez, Paco, and Waco were standing behind his chair, and all four were looking at the only door. It was shut, and nobody was talking. A sweating Bill Walker knew this was not a good place to be.

El Baygon walked in ahead of the following Kimbo Hopper. There was shock on Bill Walker's face as he looked at both men and thought he recognised them. Sometime before, Zippy had pointed out the Hispanic man with just a few powerful words of advice for Bill.

"Don't ever get mixed up with that man. You do what he wants, or you'll die sooner or later, normally sooner. He keeps real bad company around him." It conveyed everything.

The other, a huge, muscular black man, seemed very familiar, but he didn't know why. The man had neatly trimmed hair, a vast coal-black beard, and stylish clothes. It was the clothes and beard that threw him. Then Kimbo Hopper spoke.

"So, I meet you again, Bill Walker."

It was Kimbo, but a transformed-looking Kimbo. Here, he stood in a modern city, smartly dressed and with no deference in his manner, except to the man standing menacingly in front of him.

"I want it to be clear in your mind, Gringo, if you want to live, if you want to carry on with your whorehouse at 819 5th Street, then you are going to do exactly what Meester Hopper tells you. You will be well paid if you succeed with what you do for El Noche. If you are unsuccessful… well, I've already spoken on that subject."

Although El Baygon's accent was heavily Colombian Spanish, Bill Walker understood every word. The boss turned and left the room with Paco and Waco following. Kimbo opened the shuttered window, and the sea breeze blew in the fresh, salty air. Kimbo was very aware of the symbolism on view. He opened the window to let in the air and sunlight; this time, Bill Walker noticed the blood on the floor. Kimbo was referred to as "Mister Hopper" and "El Noche" by the man who could snuff out anyone's life at any time. Kimbo realised he was valued and had gained some status; how long that would last was another matter.

Juan brought in two more chairs and a small table. He freed Bill from his chair, and the three crammed around the map Kimbo had created with Paco and Waco. They set to work.

Bill understood his role and left for Everglades City and Chokoloskee. He had briefly thought about taking every bit of cash with him and disappearing north, maybe out west, California way, where this Colombian would tire of looking for him. He had already burnt his boats in Cuba. But what could he do with his money? He knew he could set up more bordellos and make a good living, but the only places he knew he could do that would be New Orleans and other large southern cities. He had no real idea how far El Baygon's reach could be or if he would send a lone tracker after him wherever he went. Someone like the three he had met. Paco and Waco were unnerving enough, but he thought Juan Rodriguez would probably be the one to track him down. Instinctively, Bill thought Juan was the most dangerous. He'd met a few.

Bill walked into Sheriff Jack Root's office to make peace with him. He was impressed with Jack's improved status and steady family life. There was even envy, but Bill had realised enough that he could never maintain that life. He was too "restless"; that was his word. Others would say, "too crooked".

Bill intended to make Jack aware of his remorse immediately. He said he wanted to make amends somehow, and it might take a while to work it all out. He'd like to stay somewhere and settle back. Jack Root wasn't convinced, and no amount of Bill's different attempts to explain his behaviour would hold water with him. Never again would Bill trick, hurt or steal from others for as long as he was sheriff. However, he played along; he wanted to know where this was going.

"So, whatever happened to that fella, Kimbo? You know that black guy with the kid?" Bill tried not to let anything show in his words.

"Kimbo is dead. His old enemies ate him...the alligators. Myron, the small boy you remember, lives out in Big Cypress with the Seminoles. From what I hear, he is well respected and is building a nice little business for them. But I warn you, Bill, if you show one little sign of your old ways, I'll come for you. D'yer, hear?" Bill nodded but was highly interested in what he had just learnt. Jack gave Bill an address where he could stay in the city and asked him a loaded question.

"Bill, would you be willing to come and see me once a week, here in my office, shall we say ten o'clock every Monday morning? You know, just for a chat, to keep in touch. Maybe I could help you settle and lead that new life you just told me you wanted?" Bill agreed, but he didn't think what he would be doing could be helped by the strait-laced Everglades City sheriff.

The plan

Kimbo and Bill worked on the plan. They met in places Kimbo chose where he knew they wouldn't be seen together. The plan was in four sections. The first was obviously for El Baygon to organise. This had been underway already. He was cutting off his current ship-to-shore work hands in Miami. His regular routes into the city from the tip of Key Biscayne, Hollywood Beach and the area around south Ft Lauderdale and Dania Beach, called "Colored Beach", were getting too risky.

It had taken ten years of protests and court hearings for Broward County to designate a "Colored Beach" for blacks only. When Kimbo learnt of this, he was surprised. He thought this was a giant step forward somewhere black folk could swim and relax. Somewhere just for them. However, the designated beach was a cruel joke among the black community, as it was across from Port Everglades and, at that time, accessible only by ferry or a long trip over land, making it unaffordable or unreachable. Which, of course, made it a perfect location for Sal Blanco to use to beach his cargo from Colombia.

Too much attention was paid to this previously perfect landing spot for illegal cargo. It had been an ideal place, close to the big nearby cities but hidden from view. No one went there – but things had changed. This southeast area had become a big problem for El Baygon, and Kimbo's arrival and knowledge were welcomed more than he realised. Securing and shipping the cargo to the waters outside the Ten Thousand Islands was now El Baygon's new territory. Kimbo and Bill Walker got the pot from the mothership up from Colombia and brought it through the myriad of channels, mangrove islands and swamp land to waiting trucks. Then, their final involvement would be getting it to Miami and Ft Lauderdale and on to the boss's waiting distributors. El Baygon had the acquisition of the pot, 'part one', as he called it, and the distribution, 'part four' – the landing, securing, and delivering all changed. Kimbo had understood his value, but Bill was still puzzled about his role or, more importantly, why him? He wasn't quick on the uptake, so Kimbo explained that he would have to recruit people in Everglades City and Chokoloskee. They needed trustworthy and willing truck owners and drivers. It would be easy to borrow a truck for life-changing cash. Drivers would be recruited with no risk to the truck owners.

"Bill, if you organise whorehouses, you can organise truck drivers haulin' pot, I reckon," Kimbo stated. Bill laughed.

"Kimbo, I will find plenty of poor and, therefore, willing truck owners. But trustworthy? I don't think so." It was Kimbo's turn to laugh.

"Bill, we must find a way to get people we trust to carry out simple tasks. Lend a truck or drive a truck. It's that simple." Kimbo was adamant. "We can't get a lot of dead people attracting attention from Miami! You gotta get owners and drivers, and El Baygon expects it. Do you understand?"

"I will let you know in a day or two. I have an idea." Bill walked away smiling.

Chapter Thirty-Eight
In Luck That Night

Myron was so happy. Tehya would have their "first of three" babies, and business was developing well. The first "high-stakes" bingo hall was about to open on the Seminole Hollywood reservation, and Myron had provided his chief with the first big bag of money. Chief Sammy Bowlegs was astonished. This was beyond any expectations and estimates they had discussed. Myron was encouraged to do more and faster. He loved that instruction.

He was alone in the Immokalee "Native Seminole Arts and Crafts Shop" when Bill Walker came quickly through the door.

"Istonko, my name is Bill, and I'd like to ask you a question. May I?"

Myron offered Bill a seat, and they talked for about two hours with just two interruptions from passing tourists.

"So, when do you expect you could provide me with the number of stone crabs I'm asking for?" Bill asked the vital question.

"It will take us six months to establish a stone crab farm. The waters around Chokoloskee and the Turner River are ideal. At six months, we can take their claws and ship them to where you want, and within a year, the claws will have grown again. It will be a good business; I don't know why I didn't think of it before. From what I hear, Miami restaurants will love this. But what part do you play in this?" Myron was not fooled by this generous stranger wandering their shop with ideas.

"Simple business for you. You grow the claws; we load them onto our trucks and ship them to Miami. You will get the market rate. We will not undercut you because once this gets going, you could find someone else to do my shipping and delivery job. We will not rip you off and need your loyalty. Deal?"

Myron was young but not stupid. "Can you advance us the money to get started? Creating the stone crab traps and finding the ideal waters will take time and money. And you'll need to give us a while to get it in full swing; then it is a deal...er, Bill, you said your name was Bill?" He was testing this stranger.

"Yes, er, Bill Smith. I'm from...up north." Something was nagging at the back of Myron's mind as Bill Walker walked out of the shop and said he would be back by next week with the advance. This Bill Smith looked familiar; he felt sure he'd met him before. He had, but that was when he was three years old.

As Bad Hand and Chief Bowlegs sat with him that evening, Myron discussed the plan. Making a good business from stone crabs hadn't been done before, but the more they talked about it, the more each liked the idea.

"What is this white man like? His name is Bill Smith, you say?"

"I cannot speak for his honesty or reasons for bringing this idea to us. He could have gone to most fishing men in Everglades City with this, and they could easily have set it up quicker than us, as they have easier access to money and people willing to help them. We will have to...no, we should do all this ourselves. We grow the stone crab claws; they pay us and then take them to the markets and restaurants in Miami. It sounds a little too good and too easy. Like our other business starts, let's see how it goes. We have nothing to lose if they lend the money to begin."

The three agreed to keep a careful and constant watch on

how this new business might work. They also decided it would make good money for them.

A kiss

El Baygon was always unhappy and always impatient. He liked the stone crab plan, but it would take too much time to set up for the cover they needed. It was not good enough.

"Hey, Gringo Walker, what the fuck you gonna do to get the next two shipments from home into Miami? Eh?" He was talking to Bill Walker but looking at Kimbo.

"I have another idea," said Kimbo. "These motherships, as you call them, boss, from what I can see, we could make 'em look like those cruise ships you see in Miami and Port Everglades north of here. Why don't we set up a laundry in Everglades City for the sheets, beddin', and other cotton to be brought ashore for washin' and cleanin'? There are plenty of all kinda reasons for the ships to get laundry done there. Damn sight cheaper, and nobody will ever think it's a scheme. That's our daytime cover, and we do our normal pot-haulin' at night. That way, we get it all ashore quicker and reduce the risk of our being caught with the whole lot at once."

"That's why I love you, La Noche!" And El Baygon walked over to Kimbo and kissed him on both cheeks. Kimbo thought the last time anyone did that was Chief Bowlegs. Then he realised he was wrong. The last time someone kissed him, it was Yuchi, and it wasn't on the cheeks; it was on his lips. He felt it was a very long time ago.

A new truck

Bill briefed Sheriff Root that Monday morning of the plans to attract cruise liners to Everglades City to launder their dirty linen.

"It will provide much-needed money to the city and a few jobs in the bargain. Do I get your go-ahead, Sheriff Root?"

Jack Root knew Bill had a good business head even though it didn't always fit with Jack's approved line of work. Jack wasn't fooled by Bill's over-zealous enthusiasm for this idea and thought there must be something else, but he couldn't think what it could be. He knew prices were higher for almost everything in Miami than the Ten Thousand Islands. The idea did make sense.

"Bill, the minute I think you are building up to disappear with money that's not yours, I'll be chasing after you and getting the Miami FBI involved, so be warned."

Bill ignored Jack's warning. He was over the moon with his progress and the money his role would make. "Maybe I'm cut out for this type of business better than whorehouses and gambling joints," he mused as he jumped into his newly gifted pickup truck from El Baygon. Jack Root looked out his window and wondered where Bill had found the money for a new truck.

It was a Saturday night, and the first cargo arrived along the Ten Thousand Island coast. The laundry wasn't ready for operation, but the stone crabs were still months away. Bill had talked to a few men recruited from the Swamp Buggy Tavern. They, in turn, borrowed a shrimp boat and other medium-sized fishing boats. With the Klan's influence diminished in the area, Kimbo had taken the lead position at the bow of the shrimp boat as he guided it through the labyrinth of medium-sized, small and tiny islands – the smaller boats following the wash quietly bubbling up from the stern. They cruised out to meet the mothership.

Kimbo had requested Juan, Paco and Waco to be truck drivers, but they would drive local registrations to avoid curiosity, particularly from the sheriff. Although Hispanic through and through with accompanying strong accents, Paco and Waco were born and raised in the part of Miami rapidly being nicknamed "Little Havana". Juan Rodriguez and Sal Blanco – El Baygon – were both from Barranquilla on the Atlantic coast of Columbia. Sal was Juan's uncle. All four men were from cities where the night skies were masked by light pollution. They rarely saw the clear, dark universe above them. When they did, as children, they were in the familiar streets of Miami or Barranquilla. Familiar but full of different dangers from those in the swamplands of Florida.

El Baygon wasn't going to be part of the operation; he was too smart to get his hands dirty and had done plenty of dirty work for long enough. *These young sementales need more experience*, he thought, *much more*. He then laughed at his joke of using the Spanish word *sementales* to describe them. It meant *uncastrated adult male horses*.

He was sitting in the Cuban café, "Cartagena", sipping strong coffee with a nip of rum. It was a twenty-four-hour café, and he intended to wait until the first truck arrived from the swamp before freeing his usual seat to anyone else. The Cartagena Cuban Bank and Cartagena Bakery were right next door. They were his other frequently visited places along Miami's well-known carnival street, "*Calle Ocho*". The bank was one of his favourite places, as he was always greeted quietly and respectfully, then shown into a private room by a beautiful-looking young woman. This was a proper bank, in his opinion. He got this welcoming treatment every time a deposit or withdrawal was made, although he mainly made deposits with no questions asked.

More serious
A little after eleven that night, Sheriff Jack Root heard an unusual number of trucks driving around Everglades City. He watched

from his door and saw the taillights of several trucks disappearing towards Chokoloskee. He was about to jump in his police vehicle when he heard a dull thump in the bedroom. Opening the door, he found Elizabeth on the floor, blood running down her legs. She was in agony. He immediately thought it was the regular agony Elizabeth felt during her "monthly cycle", as Jack usually put it. She always had some stomach or back pain, but it would be worse during that one-week cycle. Elizabeth didn't complain or want to discuss it with Jack, although he knew at times she just wanted to stay in bed instead of spending the day at school. But Jack could see from the amount of blood and excrement that this was much more serious than usual.

Jack picked Elizabeth up, put her and the children in his police vehicle and headed to the nearest hospital in Naples, nearly forty miles away.

Kimbo's pick-up and delivery operation was in luck that night.

Chapter Thirty-Nine
Everglades City Gets a New Sheriff

When they got to the Colombian boat, they were shocked to see just how much marijuana was stored under canvas. El Baygon usually arranged for these freighters to haul two thousand pounds, approximately equivalent to one US ton. This was no exception, and given the size of the boats Kimbo had available, it would take about ten to twelve trips to bring them to the outboards. They exchanged pre-determined passwords, spoke phrases, and climbed on board. Kimbo looked at Juan Rodriguez and shrugged.

"Well, Juan, this ain't all goin' to Miami tonight! It's too much for the three trucks we got. It's gonna take at least all night to get this load safely to shore. We gonna take enough for you to load all your trucks fully, and we gonna stash the rest in the islands. I know places where it's gonna be safe to keep it. We can't leave it long. It looks like it's gonna take maybe two more nights to shift all of it to El Baygon's people in Miami."

Kimbo made what should happen very clear. He was taking control, and he liked the feeling. The situation played well, and the plan was going the way he hoped it would. It fitted his longer-term thinking.

"But wait!" Bill Walker's shrill voice pierced the night air. "I've only arranged these trucks to be hired tonight. I ain't sure their owners gonna be pleased to be without them for two more nights."

Kimbo re-took control again just before Juan was going to turn nasty. "Bill, how much you payin' 'em for tonight?"

"Five grand a truck for one night. Tonight only."

"Tell 'em you want these trucks each night for three nights. They'll get five grand for each night. What do these fellas make a year, roughly speaking?

"I reckon...depending...about fifteen to twenty grand a year, depending."

Kimbo just looked at Bill and shrugged again. "So, Bill, what's gonna be their problem?"

Juan watched. Kimbo was growing into his part of El Baygon's plans, and Juan was beginning to be impressed with himself for getting Kimbo into the operation.

The first load was put on the trucks to be driven to Miami. They were covered with a tarpaulin sheet with miscellaneous fishing and crabbing gear scattered over the top. Kimbo then organised several outboards stationed at the west part of Sandfly Island. The idea would be to take the pot from the mothership onto the shrimp boat and the smaller boats and then put it into the outboards nearer the shoreline. It would then be transported through the dense foliage and multiple islets and stored in a place recommended by Kimbo. This was not only out of view from any usually inhabited area but also close to, and very handy for, Everglades City and Chokoloskee. Kimbo stated that it had to be weatherproof for ultimate protection "unless we get a hurricane this week, in which case we ain't gonna know 'til afterwards whether it survived."

When the pot-haulers checked the area and declared it clear of snooping locals or the police chief, the cargo would be loaded later in the week. Kimbo was making decisions without someone else's agreement. It felt very satisfying – uniquely satisfying. He was giving out instructions, and people were following his orders, even a white man. Crime seemed to be a great leveller.

Kimbo had Waco on his outboard as they travelled to the place he had identified to store the load, which couldn't be driven to Miami that night. Kimbo told Juan and Bill Walker that he and Waco would stay with the hidden load until one of them returned, whenever that was. "El Baygon would appreciate Waco waiting with me so I don't make off with all this stash!" Everyone laughed except Waco.

"I don't wanna do that," Waco stated loudly and nervously. Kimbo noticed what he had expected to see. Waco was very uncomfortable when he was out of his habitat. Even Bill Walker caught and understood that feeling. Bill remembered many years before his first feelings about this god-forsaken swamp.

"Hey, Kimbo oversees this deal, Waco, and I agree with him anyway. El Baygon will approve. Do you see what I mean?" Juan spoke to Waco in Spanish. Paco wondered how his close friend would react in this swampland without him.

With the Colombian vessel unloaded and sailing back home to South America, the surplus pot was stored safely, and every truck available was loaded. The vehicles moved out one by one, leaving Kimbo and Waco behind. The trucks were spaced with a five-minute gap between them. Kimbo told them a convoy would have attracted the attention of authorities. They didn't know that the city had no authorities that night.

They'd had been given the complete diagnosis. Maybe too full, Jack thought. As the doctor left the small hospital room, Elizabeth said, "Oh, Jack, I'm so sorry."

Dr P. A. Barrowclough diagnosed dysentery, phosphate poisoning and endometriosis. He didn't say how, why or when this could have happened. He rambled on, taking an academic pose while stroking his chin. He'd talked non-stop, in great detail, for five minutes about the endometriosis problem. He was excruciatingly dull. He cited Carl Rokitansky from Vienna, who first discovered endometriosis, and John A. Sampson from New York, who named it. He was about to talk at length about phosphate poisoning, but Jack cut him short.

"Thank you, Doc, but we'd like to know what this means for Elizabeth's health going forward. We live in Everglades City, and I am the sheriff and minister of the only church we have in those parts. Will we need to change how we live?" Jack had realised this was very gravely serious.

"Mr Root, you need to change *where* you live first." Dr P. A. Barrowclough explained how dysentery is contagious, and children are particularly vulnerable; they have a high risk of dying if they contract it. Please do not get close to your children or those at your school until it has cleared up. I'm afraid, Elizabeth, you must live with endometriosis, a common complaint for women," he remarked a little dismissively. "You must live with the pain…women do all the time, you know."

Jack barely resisted commenting on the doctor's condescending tone. Judging by Jack's look, he realised he hadn't shown enough empathy for Elizabeth's condition.

"I must say any of these conditions would be painful, but to have all three must be unbearable for you, my dear." His words didn't help anyone.

Elizabeth was devastated. What she had created for the children in Everglades City and its surroundings would need continuity. But how? Jack thought this doctor was very well-educated but aloof, detached and rather callous regarding women. *Well, certainly, my Elizabeth*, he thought.

The doctor continued, "It is not well known, not talked about, and certainly not yet well understood, but the fertiliser, high in phosphate and toxic chemicals used by all the farms, concrete works, sugarcane plantations and cattle ranches north of Lake Okeechobee, is being flushed down into the Everglades in agricultural and stormwater runoff. You've probably eaten frogs and catfish. You have also been swimming in the freshwater pools, no doubt, and drunk a fair bit from freshwater streams without thinking except to keep an eye out for alligators!"

He laughed at his joke, but the room was silent. He continued. "Er, well, most people do all these things where you live, I'm sure, but you are more prone to the effects of the bacteria and the high toxicity levels. Elizabeth, you probably have chronic liver disease, and your cardiovascular system will deteriorate unless you change your environment." He looked at Jack. "Can you live here in Naples? This town is installing modern plumbing; we have an excellent hospital here. You will need it from time to time. Perhaps you could get a job at the Naples Sheriff's office?"

Jack became angry as he felt useless and hopeless. Feelings he had not ever felt before, not even after the storm. He briefly thought of Kimbo Hopper and his spiral into despair. Immediately, he knew he had to be positive and think through how to improve his life despite this setback. What is the point of anything if Elizabeth doesn't have her health? He could make his family a new life here in Naples. This town was as good as he had been anywhere, so why not Naples? Elizabeth knew she had problems ahead, but she had a good family and was confident in creating new opportunities. She didn't know what they were going to be.

She couldn't know that her friend, Kimbo, was alive and in a new kind of imprisonment. He was free from prison, but he didn't have his freedom. He had his own problems.

Changing jobs

Everglades City Mayor Henry Bone received a phone call from Jack in his office. "OK, Jack, I'm sorry to hear this, especially as it's Elizabeth." The mayor always had a soft spot for Elizabeth. Everyone who knew her loved the care she showed for all children, no matter who they were or their background.

"Jack, do you have any suggestions for your job? We should act quickly and ask the townsfolk to elect the new sheriff. The trouble is we didn't ever think you wouldn't be there in that job, so we don't have an obvious deputy to set up. Got any names?"

Henry Bone carefully avoided giving Jack his own suggestions. Jack was also reluctant to nominate anyone other than his deputy, Officer Chisholm. Henry Bone continued talking.

"Perhaps we should ask for people to come forward? Should we ask Miami if anyone would be suitable but also willing to take a job with such a wide range of... challenges?" Henry was fishing.

"Surely, Henry, we can promote Chucky Chisholm? He is a solid, reliable and trustworthy officer. He has good experience and is well-liked." Mayor Bone had his own and much better idea, which he kept to himself. He diverted the conversation.

"Jack, what about Elizabeth's job as principal?"

"We have discussed this matter thoroughly, and Elizabeth is confident that Connie Bloom is highly capable and dependable and would be ready to take over from her immediately. She also said that Connie would be better at the job anyway – which I doubt.

"I doubt that too, Jack. Elizabeth is the best thing that happened to children in the Ten Thousand Islands. She will be greatly missed. Look here, Jack, don't go worrying about what's going on here. I will get cracking with a new sheriff and talk to Connie Bloom. Thanks for your thoughts. You've got enough to set up your new life in Naples and look after your dear wife. Tell me when and where you get settled, and I'll keep you in touch with my progress in the city here."

It would be better if Jack took his path and left Everglades City entirely alone, thought Henry Bone. It would be better and healthier in more than one way – for both.

Within a day, Connie Bloom was appointed as school principal, and Mayor Bone commissioned a statue to be erected in honour of Elizabeth Root in the middle of the roundabout, in the middle of the city, in the most visible and prestigious spot. It was a just and proper acknowledgement of all the work and love Elizabeth had devoted to educating children in the area. It was a fitting tribute.

The first thing Connie Bloom did was set up an adult reading and numbers evening class, but a month after her announcement, no one had applied. Pride and embarrassment were significant factors. Connie struggled to overcome these factors, no matter how hard she tried and how sensitive she was. She was good and well-liked, but she wasn't Elizabeth.

One day later, Officer Chucky Chisholm disappeared. He could have strayed into the swamp by accident or just taken an offer of cash to find a new place to live. No one was sure what had happened to him.

Two days after Mayor Bone had spoken to Jack, he had organised the election of a new sheriff. He hand-picked three men to put themselves forward. One was the former school head teacher, Andrew Clemens, now in his seventies, and another was Hank Howarth, the owner of The Swamp Buggy Tavern. The third person Mayor Bone asked to be nominated as a candidate was well-known throughout the area. He was someone known to Sheriff Jack Root, someone who was known to be his old friend and fellow survivor of the 1935 hurricane.

Bill Walker was overwhelmingly voted into the office of Sheriff of Everglades City, and Mayor Henry Bone could not be more delighted.

Chapter Forty
Sheltered by the Storm

For their first day together, Kimbo and Waco just talked and ate. Kimbo made it clear that drinking liquor was a bad idea out in the wilderness. "You gotta have ya wits about ya," he said. "By the way, Waco, ya bin with El Baygon for a long time?"

"A long time? No. Maybe five years. He gives me great jobs. I kill people when he tells me." Waco spoke with a strong Hispanic accent, and his words always sounded like he was boasting to Kimbo.

"Yeah, that sounds like a good job to get. How many people you killed, Waco?"

"Ah, I dunno. Maybe fifty, maybe a lot more. I don't keep score any more. It's just a job, amigo, but I like the life it gives me. Most of these guys I whacked deserved it, ya know. The gringos name for 'em is scumbags. They were causin' all kinda trouble for El Baygon. Normally I just shoot 'em in the head, but sometimes I like to surprise 'em with a baseball bat, ya know?" He gave a sinister smile.

Kimbo remembered all the dried blood on the concrete floor in that dimly lit, vile room near the beach in Miami. He wasn't aware that "psycho" was a commonly used name for people like Waco.

Kimbo felt ashamed of himself and what he had become for the first time, but he'd never had the power he now had, and he liked it. He was organising people around a plan. He liked that, but he still knew right from wrong...didn't he? He still tried to correct and adjust things or situations so that good people would not be harmed. What would Zella or Yuchi have thought of what he had become? What would Myron think of his father now? How would his friends Bad Hand and Jack Root view him? He wasn't dead, but he was spending his life mixing with and assisting murderers and drug smugglers. It was a heavy feeling. After Waco's descriptions of how he killed people and how he matter-of-factly treated the murders with his cold-hearted tone, Kimbo felt deeply disgusted. The fact that Waco didn't even know how many victims he'd murdered was all Kimbo needed to know to judge a man like him.

Kimbo sat in the clearing and thought through what he should do to overcome the conflict between who he was now and his new thirst for control and power. He could make things happen just because he decided it, not someone else. He suddenly had some control over his life, but did he? He knew this kind of life also comes with a cost, sometimes higher than not having any power. Maybe as time passed, he wouldn't feel this guilt, but it was now becoming clear that who he had been all his life, up to this point, was the main reason his family and close friends loved him. When Juan set him free from the journey to the Detention Centre, he'd taken a direction without understanding the consequences. Should he have stayed in the truck?

He realised he was now on an inescapable path that would give him much more than the subsistence living he'd had all his life. Could I do both and still tell the difference between right and wrong? Could I still be Kimbo, who always had love and caring at the centre of his life?

Suddenly, an old, familiar, unwanted feeling returned – a sense of uneasiness, foreboding. He looked at the sky; a tropical storm was coming, and he and Waco would be hiding deep into the Ten Thousand Islands. New ideas emerged as he sat near the murderous Waco. Would it be the start of Kimbo restoring his natural self?

No, he decided to take a new, dangerous path. It would be a path of his choosing, but he would show little love or care along that new route, a route that would make it difficult to see the destination.

Paco appears and disappears
El Baygon was delighted at how the first pot-hauling in the Ten Thousand Islands had gone. The system worked. Kimbo had the practical knowledge to bring and keep safe about a ton of Colombian pot. Now, he thought, if we could get the laundry and stone crab operations going, the second part of the Everglades plan would be executed.

"Hey, Paco. Go and join your amigo Waco today. Drive out, find them and assess how it all went. You should assess La Noche. I want to know if I can trust him."

"But, El Baygon, there is a storm about to hit us. I never want to get caught in a fucking tropical storm anytime, but it would be worse to be caught out there in the swamp."

"Paco, you scared. Are you scared of the dark and the swamp? Get out and return by two days with another truckload and a plan to get the rest into Miami. I'll be getting the distribution organised. Go and get my cargo!"

Juan Rodriguez was listening and watching the conversation.

Paco drove hard into the night. An almighty storm was blowing through, but the wind strength had not yet reached its peak gusts. It was to reach at least eighty miles an hour later that night. By the time he'd got to Chokoloskee and the outboards moored waiting to help move the stored pot, the storm was delivering downpours every twenty minutes. As he got closer to where he knew Kimbo had chosen to shelter the remaining haul, he saw the stash but didn't see Kimbo or Waco. They were nowhere to be seen. This was odd. He decided to follow a channel south of Sandfly Island, where he next had expected to find them both. The small inlets got smaller, and his outboard hit something hard in the water. It was an alligator returning to its nest to shelter from the storm. Paco went over the side and hit the water, causing a big splash. At any other time, Paco would have been in serious trouble. A big splash would have sent at least five or six alligators and probably three or four crocodiles sliding to investigate. The water was salty, which suited both reptiles. Luckily for Paco, they had taken shelter. The wind was howling and sending branches and loose mangrove tufts flying. The alligators and crocodiles would return later if they sensed the smell and taste of new meat permeating the water.

    Paco swam to a raised land hammock. It was one of the largest in the area, and he lay in the branches of drenched, hardwood and broad-leafed trees rising a few inches above the water flow. He heard a scream, or was it? He waited and heard it again – a bone-chilling scream. Paco crawled towards the sound, and there, hanging upside down like a butcher's carcass, was Waco, his clothes ripped open at his chest and stomach. Waco's long-time friend Paco kept still while watching, shocked to his core. He found it hard to believe what he was witnessing. Kimbo had smashed something into Waco's face so that blood was dripping rapidly into the water. Rope tied to his ankles, Waco was waiting to die, to be consumed, bite by bite, by a congregation of reptiles, now ignoring the storm and slowly tasting the blood trail to the hanging meal. This meal was too good to miss, storm or no storm. A few feet away stood Kimbo, also watching and waiting. The storm blanketed any sound Paco made as he crept forward.

Out came Paco's stiletto, his preferred knife to kill his enemies. He thrust the long, thin blade at Kimbo and caught him on his thigh. Kimbo struck Paco hard on the side of his head as the Miami thug passed his left side. Paco lay semi-conscious on the ground. Kimbo turned to see an alligator jumping up at Waco and clamping his powerful jaws on his head to drag him down and drown him. No such luck. It was a worse outcome than that. As the gator crunched, gripped, and wriggled, Waco's head was pulled clean off his shoulders, and blood poured into the swirling water. Another twelve-foot crocodile with a long snout grabbed Waco's torso. Eventually, Waco's poor, destroyed body was dragged down into the water, leaving only the bottom half of his legs still tied to Kimbo's rope. It had taken just ten seconds, and it was a horrific scene.

Kimbo was stunned at the outcome of his efforts. He looked behind him, but Paco had vanished.

A place remembered

It was risky, but Kimbo had to go there. He needed patching up and some advice. Instead of his old friend Jack Root, he was surprised to find Bill Walker opening the sheriff's office the following day. After explaining what had happened to Elizabeth and Jack and while boasting about how clever he had been to land the sheriff's job, Sheriff Walker helped Kimbo clean his wound and bandage his thigh using the medical kit from the first aid box. The box contents were always available in the sheriff's drawer for all eventualities. Jack Root always made sure of that.

"So, La Noche, we have a new sheriff in town, yes, yours

truly. This has worked out very well for both of us. Getting caught pot-hauling off the Colombian boats could not be easier now. I'm calling it my 'Catch and Release' policy," Bill Walker beamed. "I know how to do it, and, what's more, I know who does it." Bill Walker laughed out loud. "If I get my cut and my big buddy, Mayor Henry Bone, gets in on it, we can take it to the next level. I think El Baygon will be very pleased with us!"

Kimbo asked the only question important to him.

"But Bill, what is wrong with Elizabeth? Is she in serious danger? What will Jack do now if he can't live here? Where will he go?"

"I spoke to Jack yesterday before that storm blew through. It wasn't nothing but a tropical storm, so it was no big deal. He's okay. He's getting a job with the Naples sheriff's office, and they will live near the city centre, out there on Rattlesnake Hammock Road. Jack said Elizabeth had handed over the school, and if she ever felt better, she would try to get a teaching job in Naples. Boy, are they gonna struggle! Jack confessed that their hospital and doc's bills are mountin' up pretty good. I feel bad for them, but, hey, we all gotta get by the best we can."

Kimbo just looked passively at Bill Walker. He thought it best to say nothing. Naples was a long way from El Baygon but not out of reach, not by a long shot. Kimbo then explained that he had been waiting with the surplus stash when the storm hit.

"Well, Bill, Waco's dead, and I've lost Paco. He'll be heading back to El Baygon, and I won't last long after that. They'll hunt me down for sure." He looked hard at Bill to see his reaction. "Seems I'm on the run from just about everybody now."

Kimbo hadn't mentioned precisely how Waco had died, but Bill thought it wouldn't be long before La Noche would be gator meat himself. Kimbo was more distressed that Myron and

Elizabeth were in extreme danger. *What could be done? Had I told Bill Walker too much?*

They were talking in the backroom of the sheriff's office when the solution walked in rapidly through the front door. They fell silent, waiting. Bill could see through the crack between the backroom door, and the person who stood poised for action in the front office was Paco.

"Well, Paco, what a surprise." Sheriff Bill Walker walked into the front office. "Hey, you okay? You look terrible. What's happened?"

"That bastard Hopper!" Paco then explained at length what he had witnessed.

Bill was shocked. He had underestimated Kimbo Hopper. With quick thinking, he said, "Quickly, Paco. You can't be seen here. I can take you to Miami in my police car. Go through here to the back. Yes, through this door."

As Paco walked into the backroom, Kimbo punched him hard in the face and knocked him out. He dragged him out to the back of the building, found a stray skiff, and slumped him into it. He pushed off into the dense bushes and undergrowth through a narrow canal and into the large water outlet parallel to Collier Avenue. Bill Walker watched Kimbo disappear with Paco lying unconscious, like a stunned gator, along the bottom of the skiff. Sheriff Bill Walker had to reassess everything he'd assumed.

Kimbo remembered the place where Solomon Bass vanished a few years ago. Paco didn't regain consciousness. It didn't take Kimbo long.

Bill Walker drove a hidden Kimbo to Miami, where he told El Baygon of the tragic circumstances of Waco and Paco's deaths. The storm, Kimbo said, had spooked them into a panic. "They just not used to this place, El Baygon, and that tropical storm just scared 'em shitless. I could hear Waco screaming as the gators took him away. Paco didn't shout out or nuttin', but I'm sure he's gone from us too." Both those statements were factual, without revealing the whole truth. Kimbo was learning to tell a story convincingly while not lying.

El Baygon shuddered, thinking about what had happened to his loyal employees. Employees were how he thought of them. He had no reason to think Kimbo was lying. *How hard will it be to replace them and how quickly? Who was ready to graduate from my pack of keen, younger gang members? T*hat was now his priority. Waco and Paco were already consigned to fading memory. El Baygon had a business to run.

"Well, La Noche, you, Juan, me, and our new sheriff will run the pot-hauling business from now on. I'll deal with the distribution here in Miami. As I see it now, we'll all make more money with less hombre to feed!" He didn't smile, but Kimbo was surprised at the callous tone at first, but then, of course, he knew the kind of people he was now living and working with.

El Baygon's economy was booming. The daytime laundry offloads and the stone crab shipping cover were working perfectly. Vast amounts of money were circulating to all involved. The Chokoloskee and Everglades City locals involved were taking a good cut. Making a truck available rose to ten thousand a night, while the men involved in getting the pot from the ships to the trucks and into Miami were getting rich beyond anything they could have thought possible. *Getting rich quick* was their catchphrase used mainly in the confines of the Swamp Buggy Tavern.

A lack of common sense would be their downfall.

Chapter Forty-One
One Year Later

"Hey, La Noche, I like how the business has grown. You and Bill running the haulin' into the swamp really worked out. I wanna thank the Seminoles for their stone crab cover. Can you fix it? I wanna meet them." Sal Blanco was smiling from ear to ear.

"No, El Baygon, that's not good. They don't know it's a cover for our pot-haulin business. We can't tell them. I don't think they will be happy if they knew we've bin usin' 'em all this time. Chief Bowlegs wouldn't take kindly to us usin' them. He is also very careful about how much his tribe mingles with the white man. He thinks too much mixing will bring too much alcohol to the younger men in the tribe. I'd say we leave them be." Kimbo was being as clear as he could that it would do no good.

"Well, I got a better opinion." Sal Blanco stared straight at Kimbo with a look on his face he had not given him before. "Arrange it for me, or I'll just go find this Chief Bowlegs myself. But, you know, I got you to do that for me. Don't I?"

Juan Rodriguez listened and watched the conversation closely.

Kimbo was in a corner. As far as he was concerned, nobody knew Kimbo Hopper was alive except Bill Walker, El Baygon and his men. And they had no reason to tell anyone. Just yet, anyway.

With Jack Root, now based in Naples, and appointed

Undersheriff of Collier County, his salary combined with Elizabeth's, who was now well enough to teach part-time, meant the Root family were well settled in the Naples area. Their main worry was paying the medical bills that had piled up. As part of his responsibilities, he was given the Ten Thousand Islands area to coordinate and support the local force. It was considered a perfect fit, given Jack's previous experiences there.

"You even know the Seminole chief personally, so there ain't none better than you, Jack, and I believe Sheriff Bill Walker is an old friend…" The head of police in Collier County had been adamant about Jack's promotion to undersheriff, "…so Bill Walker is another perfect fit," he'd said.

It would not be long before Jack would smile at the irony of that statement.

Chapter Forty-Two
The Future Changes

Chief Bowlegs, Bad Hand Billie and Myron Hopper sat in the back room of Sheriff Bill Walker's office, waiting politely. Bill noticed how grown-up Myron was, built like his father but moving gracefully like a Seminole. Myron knew who Bill Walker was and the history between him, his father and the absent Jack Root. Myron had forgotten nothing his dead father had told him over the years. He wondered why Bill Walker hadn't acknowledged his father's death and given him some personal sympathy or comforting words when he had greeted them on their arrival. Bill Walker opened the meeting.

"May I introduce you, gentlemen, to Señor Sal Blanco? He is an old friend, and he wants to thank you personally for providing such excellent stone crabs. They are getting extremely popular in Miami, and we are beginning to ship them up north. There is a new method of keeping things fresh for longer, much better than our old methods. It's called refrigeration... and..."

"Enough..." said El Baygon.

Bill stopped mid-sentence as El Baygon held up his hand. The three senior Seminoles were sitting, wondering why they had been asked to come to listen to a white man talking about something they had no interest in. El Baygon began in earnest.

"Chief Bowlegs, my friend and business associate, I want to give you your share of our huge stone crab profits." El Baygon reached inside a large brown, well-worn leather bag and pulled out four bundles of $100 bills, totalling to at least $10,000. "This is for you. It's your share of our extra profits from the crab runs." He smiled at the two Seminoles and Myron.

"White man, we have been paid well for the stone crabs. You speak of extra profit. What is extra profit? We like this business but know what people pay in Miami's eating houses and rich men's restaurants. There isn't any extra profit, just your profit, not ours." Chief Bowlegs sensed something was wrong. El Baygon tried to steer the conversation back to his blunt agenda.

"Well, my Seminole amigo, you give us the stone crabs. We put a little extra profit underneath the full crates – I'm talkin' about what the white man calls pot. It is very popular with the white man, and we sell it all over Miami and other places. Just look at your share of what I call extra profit. And this is just the start. I have other plans, which I want to tell you about." El Baygon didn't notice the three men staring at him and sitting completely still, stone-faced. The Colombian continued speaking: he didn't read people well.

"Amigos, this money is just the start of what will become a very lucrative business for all of us. I know you have tribal grounds here in Big Cypress, but you also have your reservations in Brighton, Hollywood, Immokalee, Tampa, Fort Pierce and what is now called Lakeland. This represents a huge opportunity, which I know you'll understand, as I tell you, my plan. We bring white powder into the Everglades just like we do the pot haulin'. Our Ten Thousand Islands community operators will continue the pot business but will now add the Colombian white powder. This is where the big money will come from. I have assessed how you can boost your bingo business. In a year, you will make millions of dollars by taking it from the boys haulin' it off the ships, channelling it through to each of your reservations, which will limit our risk and loss through discovery. We..." El Baygon stopped as he noticed faces of thunder staring at him. Chief Bowlegs stood angrily and prepared to rush the Colombian. El Baygon pulled out a pistol and aimed it at the chief's head. It stopped him in his tracks. They all froze; nobody dared to move.

Kimbo Hopper burst through the door behind El Baygon, followed rapidly by Juan Rodriguez. The Colombian drug baron swivelled around to see a massive fist smash into his face, and he flew backwards from the force. His fat, sweating body was almost horizontal before it hit the floor. Juan jumped on El Baygon, stabbed his uncle in the gut with his stiletto, and then slit his throat and neck such that an artery bled out quickly, creating a large puddle of rich, dark red blood. The blood immediately started to stain the wooden floorboards.

It wasn't the blood that made Myron faint. It was the image of his not-dead father, with short, neatly and expensively cropped hair, a full black beard and the smartest, most highly-priced clothes he'd seen anyone wear. Nobody in that room moved except Juan, the assassin, who slowly and with great expertise cleaned his knife and put it in its usual place, tucked down inside his belt and hidden under his shirt.

Chapter Forty-Three
Ostentation

Undersheriff Jack Root decided it was time to revisit the Ten Thousand Islands; it was part of his region to patrol. He had been given a Harley-Davidson to use as his territory was enormous. The bike's economy was good, but, most importantly, it enabled police officers in the southern part of Florida to navigate small, single-track lanes with healthy, green foliage-high-growth areas that sometimes reach over parts of the roads. Most police officers were delighted with being given a motorbike, but Jack wasn't. He'd rather have an automobile so he could use it for family outings and short trips around the Naples area. He'd work on that with his boss when the time was right – one small improvement at a time.

Jack left Naples along the Tamiami Trail and turned right onto Collier Avenue, Route 29. As he rode over the first bridge into Everglades City, Jack was a little shocked to see some of the younger men, just boys when Jack had first arrived in the city, wearing gleaming new leather cowboy boots and heavy, expensive gold chains and watches. He noticed a few brand new, sleek pickup trucks where those ramshackle abodes were used to having old rust buckets sitting on the grass verges. Some houses that were previously in desperate need of repair now had screened-in porches, air-conditioning units fitted in walls, and paved driveways. As he drove through, he thought he glimpsed a swimming pool at the back of one old, well-known, dilapidated house.

Jack stared in disbelief at the sudden, conspicuous wealth. He drove every street he knew in the city before going over the causeway and onto Chokoloskee, where, in contrast, there had been almost no change at all.

He'd seen enough to know something had happened that would be dangerous to tackle. Dangerous for him, Bill Walker, and everyone in Everglades City. He drove to Sheriff Bill Walker's office and walked in without knocking. Bill Walker on the floor scrubbing.

Bill had been left to clear up the pool of blood.

A final resting place

Chief Bowlegs and Bad Hand talked as they walked. They left Myron to be with his father, but once Myron had returned to the village, they would discuss with him what to do about the stone crab business. They had been shocked by events and the unravelling truth about how they had been fooled into participating. Despite having no knowledge of the pot hauling or "smuggling", as it would be called, once word got out into the white man's world, they realised the tribe would be considered just as guilty as the pot-haulers and Hispanic thugs. The image and standing of the Seminoles would be severely damaged. Their growing bingo hall and other businesses would suffer badly. The two men debated soberly as they reached the edge of their village about how this situation could be reversed.

Juan Rodriguez waited patiently in the pickup truck for Kimbo and Myron to finish their extended, near-spiritual reunion. Myron couldn't resist holding his father's hand, stroking his beard and occasionally hugging him as tightly as possible. They had gone out through the back of the office, and Kimbo lifted the fat Colombian's dead body and carried him outside to the same waiting blood-stained skiff he'd used for Paco.

With growing impatience, Juan left the pickup and walked into the office to talk to Sheriff Walker. He was agitated.

"Okay, Sheriff, this is what is going to happen now. I don't know what kinda trouble we're gonna be in with El Baygon's people in Miami now he's dead, but I've got a good idea they're gonna be here in the next few days looking for him. I gotta plan, but I need to get Kimbo on board. You are going to tell our boys here that there ain't gonna be no haulin' for a while 'til things settle down again. I'm gonna manage the Miami end. Gottit?"

Bill nodded eagerly and noticed how easily Juan Rodriguez had moved into the role previously mastered by his uncle, El Baygon. The quick, terrifying way Juan Rodriguez had dispatched him would stay in his mind for a long time.

Myron had reluctantly left his father, standing next to the skiff with the large body of the dead drug baron, waiting for his final resting place. Kimbo didn't want Myron to be associated with Juan Rodriguez or what had happened and asked him to leave the area immediately.

Juan appeared. "El Noche, please take me to show me where and how to get rid of an enemy." Kimbo watched the face of Juan Rodriguez as he punted the boat through the swamp. He showed no fear, quite the opposite. He had a relaxed and delighted manner. Kimbo sensed what Juan had been planning had finally come to fruition.

Kimbo thought about it. Waco, Paco, and now El Baygon were dead, leaving Juan in charge of the Miami end. Now, he, Kimbo, oversaw the Everglades and hauling business. Juan had the contacts, and Kimbo had the risk. Everything will return to normal if Bill Walker is in place, with big profits being shared with even fewer participants. Kimbo had to think hard about what the future should look like now. *How could he get back his life to live with and support Myron? How could he get out of the pot-hauling business and not risk his death and severe consequences for Myron, Elizabeth or the Seminoles? How could he help the only people who had shown him genuine respect, love, and a peaceful, fulfilling existence? How could he do this without the risk of the world knowing he wasn't dead?*

Meanwhile, Juan Rodriguez had already started to think about what should happen next as Kimbo took him to where they would dispose of the fat Colombian's lifeless body.

The burden of truth

Bill had been looking for the four bundles of cash the dead drug baron had offered Chief Bowlegs. He was sure they had all been sitting on the desk, but they were nowhere to be seen. The door opened, and undersheriff Jack Root walked in. He no longer looked like the man who had turned to God as a shell-shocked hurricane survivor. He was unnervingly sure-footed and clear-headed.

"Okay, Bill, the fuck has been going on in this town since I left." Jack deliberately didn't say any more. He thought hearing the first words coming out of Bill Walker's mouth was essential. Jack looked down at where Bill had been scrubbing; obviously, it was a large blood stain. Bill turned and faced Jack slowly, thinking as quickly as he could. They both knew his next words would determine their immediate future and the lives of many others. As Bill prepared to speak, he instinctively decided not to mention the involvement of the Seminoles. He could see no advantage yet in doing that.

"Jack, you can't believe how good it is to see you." Pause. Jack didn't move a muscle or speak a word. *Would this historically untrustworthy man tell me the truth, some of the truth, lies or a complete fairy tale?* Jack stood and listened, increasingly shocked and upset by what he heard.

"This is the blood of a Colombian drug baron, Sal Blanco. You won't have heard of him, but I'm pretty sure the FBI will. He was murdered here in this office less than an hour ago. Kimbo Hopper has taken his body out into the Everglades to be eaten by wildlife." Jack's eyebrows lifted at hearing that Kimbo was alive. He didn't blink.

"The Miami thugs who killed him have gone back to Miami. They have been running marijuana shipments up from Colombia to the Ten Thousand Islands for about a year and a half. Kimbo has been organising it because he knows the swamp better than anyone, and believe me, nobody else is willing to learn what he knows. He had help from plenty of willing hands in this city. Jack, what else will these folks do when someone offers them ten thousand dollars to borrow their truck for a night? These poor people have had their livelihoods taken away by a government that doesn't know about them, doesn't know about their lives and frankly, doesn't care. They put up their "Everglades National Park" signs and then employ park rangers with the power to arrest and imprison folks for just going about their business like they always did. The only way to make a living out here now is to be fishing in the open waters outside the park, and what is anyone gonna do? Buy a big commercial fishing boat? With what? Well, I can tell ya. It's with money for lending your truck or helping haul cargo ashore and get it to Miami. That blood you can see here on the floor is the blood of a South American wanting people to shift cocaine, heroin and the like. It got ugly in my office, and someone – I didn't see who it was..." Jack continued to show no emotion. He knew Bill was lying. "...killed the guy with a knife. Kimbo's cleaning up the best he can. So, you might be thinking – the fuck am I doing about all this? I'm the sheriff in this town, and I've been doing what most sheriffs do in most towns. I check driving licenses, arrest drunks causing trouble, and make sure the kids don't get mistreated by anyone. That's what I've been doing. What the fuck would you do?"

Bill was deflecting and carefully diverting attention. Jack Root sat down on a chair with a hefty thump, and Bill Walker knew he'd made the best speech of his miserable and selfish life. He then tried to continue.

Jack held his hand up. "Shut up!" he shouted.

Undersheriff Jack Root sat trying to make sense of what he had just been told. Kimbo, a friend whom he had thought dead, was alive and, although suffering an injustice, he was officially on the run from the Detention Centre, a fugitive. There has been a murder with plenty of witnesses, but he only knew the names of two, Kimbo Hopper and Bill Walker, a man who was also technically within his, Jack's, scope of responsibility. Probably, half the city at least was guilty of drug smuggling one way or another, and he was sure they had also broken many other laws along the way. Having criminals and fugitives now and then coming into the area and hiding for spells was one thing. But this new situation, now well established, is another. The place where he had found rehabilitation and restored his sense of worth since the horrors of the 1935 hurricane had turned the Ten Thousand Islands into, probably, one of the most crime-ridden and corrupt places in America.

The burden of truth sank Jack Root deep into the chair. He realised that as life changes, people and the truth change. What he had been told about his old stomping ground would be unthinkable, let alone true, just over an hour ago. Jack knew that things could go badly wrong when decisions are taken without recognising how they can affect simple people living straightforward lives. He knew people's lives could be devastated if problems were viewed from a single angle. Ignoring reality would compound problems, not solve them. As a lawman, Jack saw wrongdoing and breaking the law as wrong. There was only one way he should deal with it. Many people will indeed have broken the law, he thought. Murder and drug smuggling were never trivial crimes. Prosecuting one person in Everglades City would inevitably lead to the prosecution of all others involved. That is the way of life, and maybe, he thought, that is the only way, regardless of the destruction it may cause. What was at stake was a moral judgment. Wasn't it? Or should the law always be the absolute determination? Jack Root had more power now than he had ever wanted or even dreamed possible at this moment.

"Bill, I will call you in a week, and you will tell me how this whole town will clean itself up. If it can't, doesn't want to, or can't decide how, I will take charge and do it myself. You'd better talk to your mayor buddy to help get things straight, ya hear?"

Undersheriff Jack Root left Bill Walker's office, left Everglades City, and arrived home to find Elizabeth waiting for him. She wanted to know how everyone was fairing in the Ten Thousand Islands and was eager to hear all the news and a little light gossip, perhaps.

She regretted it immediately. Her keenness for an update on Everglades City and its law-abiding locals, for whom she'd previously had enormous affection, had been badly misplaced.

Chapter Forty-Four
Sooner or Later

"La Noche, I want you to start travelling to Colombia and making the deals. You now know enough about how to negotiate and take no shit from those fuckers down there. I know who they are. I want you to go to Barranquilla and Cartagena to get known, learn the language and learn where and how we get the cargo. We need each other, but I'll have special assignments for you now and then. It will involve taking a few of our Miami partners to where you've taken El Baygon, Waco and Paco. We gonna tidy up some people in our operation, which was always full of Sal Blanco's choices. That's no good for our business now. Ya know what I mean, amigo? We gonna cut the Seminoles out now, too. They can do whatever they want with their shitty crabs. It was helpful, but now I see trouble ahead." Juan spoke his mind.

The two men, Kimbo and Juan, the assassin, were travelling back to Miami. One was extremely happy, and one was in despair. Neither showed it to the other.

"Oh, and I want you to meet a new pack member. His name is Jim-Bob Smith. You'll know him, of course, as he's been living in the Ten Thousand Islands all his life. I think he said it was at a place called Chatham Bend, near the Watson's Place area. He claims he knows that area better than anyone. Ya know him?"

Kimbo said "yes" in a very non-committal way. He knew him all right. He was one of the men in the Swamp Buggy Tavern when he, Bill and Jack Root first arrived in Everglades City, pulling Myron along in his truck. He was one of the men Kimbo knew was a big friend of the Grand Wizard and Everglades City Sheriff Jeffries. It was a surprise that Jim-Bob Smith wasn't there the night the KKK tried to hang him and Bad Hand. Kimbo thought it was lucky for everyone that he wasn't there, including Jim-Bob himself. So, why is Juan bringing him into the "pack", as he had started to call his gang of drug smugglers? Then it dawned on Kimbo.

On the step
What happened when Juan Rodriguez met Kimbo in the Miami jail was the last piece of Juan's bigger plan. The instant Juan had set him free on the road to The Keys, staying silent during the time Waco and Paco disappeared, slitting Sal Blanco's throat, it should have been obvious what his plan had been. Juan, the assassin, followed a path he had carefully worked out and let others, like Kimbo, carry it out for him. Kimbo wasn't clever enough to see what was happening. What was Juan's new plan? Does he want to put me in Colombia, or is it something else? He must know I can't write or read, so how will I learn Spanish to be good enough or quick enough to run that part of the business? He had another strong sense of unease. What was really in store for him now? A final and fatal visit to Colombia?

Kimbo dropped Juan Rodriguez off in Miami and drove back west, towards Naples, with just one stop. The stop was at a gas station, not to buy gas or food. It was to ask someone to perform an innocent request.

Jack had explained everything about the situation in the Ten Thousand Islands to Elizabeth, who initially thought her husband had been drinking. But it became evident he was telling her the truth – all of it. It was with mixed feelings that she learnt Kimbo was very much alive but was now an escaped convict who had been part of a criminal gang carrying out drug smuggling. They had discussed Jack's dilemma together, but without being anywhere near a solution. Even a barely adequate solution would take much thinking.

Jack opened his backdoor the following day, slightly later than usual – it was rare, but he had been drinking. There on the step was a paper bag with four bundles of $100 bills, which, as he flicked through, he assessed that they probably amounted to about $10,000. There was a note with a simple message in appalling handwriting. It read "4 lizbet doctuzz, from peepul of NAPLES". Kimbo had asked the pump attendant at the gas station to write it for him… and he had stressed, "Make clear the word Naples."

Jack was confused. This note was obviously not written by any well-established person, and Jack hadn't made himself that well-known. Most of his duties in Naples had low visibility across the city. This was an act of kindness that seemed beyond anything normal. Jack knew it would transform their lives, but what should he do? When he talked to his boss about the gift, the head of police shrugged.

"I dunno, Jack. I guess you should take it and show the people of Naples how thankful you are. The new incomers here want police like you. You're a regular guy. They hear you used to drive that Flagler train. You survived that hurricane that took so many lives down there in The Keys, and you were a damn good preacher man and sheriff of the swamp lands too. What's not for them to like? They want you to hang around and do a good job. A lot of new money is arriving here every day, and they are looking to you to keep the peace around these parts. You know, they want no trouble with the riff-raff and crooks that we sometimes get. Okay, we used to get...particularly down there in the Ten Thousand Islands."

Jack Root knew he had a serious dilemma, but now he had a looming crisis and had to deal with it. When should he tell his boss in Naples?

Hatched
Kimbo waited until about midday and was just about to leave when Purvis came into the bar and sat down in his usual chair. The barkeep cleared the bar. Purvis looked at the big man perched next to him. They talked for two hours and quickly shook hands; Kimbo walked out. A plan had been hatched. Purvis smiled in his trademark, slightly menacing way.

Another plan
Knowing Chief Bowlegs personally was an essential part of Elizabeth's plan. A plan had been incubated while she regained her health slowly. Her health became more robust and less prone to severe stomach cramps. Being healthy and strong was vital, but Myron Hopper was equally crucial to her plan – critical, she believed.

She drove to the smoke shop on Tamiami Trail, where she had heard Myron spent a lot of time. He was writing in a book as she walked in, enough to make her smile.

"Myron, good morning. Istonko." Elizabeth smiled as she spoke with her familiar soft and warm voice, and with Myron smile even bigger. They immediately sat together to catch up on what was happening in their lives. It was more than a teacher-pupil relationship. It always had been more. For Myron, a part of Elizabeth filled a gap left by Zella. For Elizabeth, an example of what inspired her to teach was sitting next to her.

Elizabeth outlined her offer. Myron said it was a perfect idea with perfect timing. Myron said he would arrange for Elizabeth to see Chief Bowlegs the next day. Myron was so excited that he didn't sleep a wink that night. Neither mentioned Kimbo.

The chief looked at the person opposite, and Bad Hand sat motionless. It was Elizabeth Root, not a contingent from Miami or some other white man's intruding city. To implement Elizabeth's idea, the chief had to decide who, how many, and how often. It was easy to determine, and it was unanimous when he outlined his plan. Bad Hand had sat watching the chief's face throughout the discussion. As usual, there was not a scintilla of expression.

Elizabeth Root would start teaching two days after she had persuaded her husband Jack that they didn't need her part-time income now that he was Undersheriff of the whole of Collier County and, most importantly, that the medical bills had been cleared. She agreed with him that the minute it took any toll on her health, she would stop or slow down. Elizabeth anticipated that Jack would ask if the village could provide transport and a driver so she could go home every night. Myron suggested paying for this rich opportunity would be a small price. It was to be a huge step forward for everyone involved: Myron, the chief, Bad Hand, Jack and Elizabeth, all knew it.

Chapter Forty-Five
Mirror Image

"Bill, I'm telling you this is what you have to do!"

Jack started to shout. He'd felt enormous pressure over the last five days and could no longer wait for the whole week that he had promised Bill Walker. He was jumpy and hardly slept. His boss noticed, and Elizabeth certainly felt the worst of his unusual irritability, dark mood, and bouts of evening drinking.

"Jack, I don't think you understand the nature of the people we're dealing with. If they find out I blew the whole scheme apart, I will be killed sooner or later. And I'm talking about slowly killing me...and you." Bill Walker was running scared.

"Listen to me very carefully, Bill. I am going to the FBI headquarters in Miami tomorrow morning. I have arranged my meeting there for eleven. You will come with me and immediately go into their new Witness Protection Program. They will explain it to you, but as of tomorrow at eleven, you are either under the care of the FBI or the Miami thugs or wherever you've fled, but you know they will both hunt you down. I know what I'd do. Tomorrow, you will tell them everything you know, and I mean everything. If you hold back, they will hold back, and you don't want that. This whole setup is now blown anyway, so what do you have to lose?"

Bill knew Jack was right. "Okay, but what about Kimbo? He's in the thick of it. And he is with that little runt, Juan Rodriguez. He's the boss in Miami now, and that man is ruthless.

His whole gang is ruthless. They are very well-armed. If you go in, there is gonna be blood, and it ain't all gonna be all theirs."

Jack didn't answer the question about Kimbo.

Bill Walker and Jack Root kept their appointment at exactly eleven the following day. The most senior FBI officer stationed in Miami was called into the meeting after Undersheriff Jack Root had taken two minutes to summarise what the meeting should discuss. Although po-faced, the senior officer knew this would be a big bust, and promotions would be dished out.

Completely alone

As Jack Root and Bill Walker were talking five miles away, Kimbo sat in a familiar, small room in Miami, tied to a chair with blood running down his cheeks. He had been cut on both sides of his face by a knife, just for amusement. The shuttered window, this time, was left open, and Kimbo could see the blood on the floor and smell the fresh sea air. He knew it would be his last day on earth and was calm. He had been left sitting quietly for a short while, entirely alone. He had thought about Zella and Zakari, Yuchi and Hachi, and...Myron. His tears, mixed with his blood, fell onto his bare chest. Mostly, he thought about Myron. He'd promised to the empty sky, where Zella lived, that he would give Myron the best life possible. *Had I done that? What was the best life? What better life could I have given Myron if I'd had the power? Was Myron a good man? The best he could be?* Kimbo was at peace when he thought of his son. *What man could have had a better son? As a boy, he had even saved my life with a single shot;* Kimbo sat hoping this was not the end. *How he wished he could be swept up into the sky, to disappear, to be taken and put down wherever* the hurricane pleased.

The day before, he'd refused to take a man to the swamp

who Juan Rodriguez had instructed him to execute. To kill this man and make him disappear in a flurry of vicious mouths. He had forced the assassin to reveal his plans. It became clear, in the increasingly toxic argument they were having, that Juan didn't ever want Kimbo to organise the drug production, routes and shipping in Colombia. His role was just to be one of killing and disposing of dead bodies. Jim-Bob Smith seemed destined to take over his role in the Ten Thousand Islands. Kimbo had become replaceable; Kimbo would vanish.

It was late afternoon when Juan Rodriguez and three of his Miami pack returned to the room. It was to be Kimbo's execution. He tried for the last time to free himself from the tight bonds around his hands and feet. It was useless; these men knew what they were doing and would not take the chance that this huge, muscular man could break out of the room.

"Okay, mi amigo, time to say goodbye. You will have seen that you are the last piece of my plan to fall into place. I considered your value once you had performed on El Baygon in the swamp. What would I use you for if I had you in my pack? You're a wanted man, amigo. You are a dangerous man on the run, no? I couldn't have you running the operation in your home territory. Sooner or later, someone will know and get a reward for taking you in. I think plenty of gringos in the islands would turn you in. Reward money is delicious when nobody can know it was you who told the cops, no? I soon saw that your only value to me was as a 'hombre de disposición' as we say, or 'Disposal Man' as you would say." Juan and his three men laughed.

One of the two men stepped forward to face Kimbo, who was suddenly surprised to see how closely the man looked like him. The man had almost a mirror image of his head, with a coal-black bushy beard and neatly cropped hair. It flashed into

Kimbo's mind that this was also part of the plan. He was going to be replaced by a perfect look-a-like. This man grabbed Kimbo's tufted hair and pulled his head back, exposing his neck. A large, well-sharpened knife appeared in his other hand, but he dropped it in open-mouthed shock as Myron burst through the door, followed by Purvis and four men. The shock was electrifying.

Myron kicked Juan Rodriguez hard between the legs, and Purvis stood watching as his men demolished the pack members in the room and dragged them all outside, including Juan Rodriguez. Purvis untied Kimbo and cleaned his drenched face. He smiled his trademark smile and watched Myron and Kimbo hug. Only Myron wept this time, as his father knew there was more trouble ahead.

The light was fading fast outside. The sun had set, shining its last embers at the top of white, art deco-style buildings that faced the beach and the beautiful, azure blue, peacefully calm Atlantic Ocean.

Purvis's men were tying up the unconscious pack, confident they had them in control. At the precise moment when they were not paying attention, Juan Rodriguez sprang up and kicked the nearest one in the head. He ran through an alley and out along Ocean Drive. He then headed west along 7th Street into the busy Collins Avenue. One of Purvis's men ran after him, but Juan Rodriguez had disappeared. Purvis was uncharacteristically furious. This escape meant others would die before the plan was finished, and he was fearful for the person he thought it would be.

Chapter Forty-Six
Operation Ten Thousand Islands

It was five o'clock in the morning, three days following the pivotal meeting in Miami at the FBI offices. A rumbling, armed convoy of more than two hundred drug agents and police swept down Collier Avenue and into Everglades City. Every house, nook, crevice, inlet and outlet that Bill and Jack had mapped sent officers to find, discover, search and arrest all. Collier County Head of Police and his undersheriff, Jack Root, were part of the raid. Everybody in Everglades City and Chokoloskee over fourteen years old was arrested or placed under suspicion.

Of the two hundred or so officers assigned to the raid, only six were bitten by cottonmouth snakes and taken to the hospital, with only one officer going missing, never to be found. By the end of the day, those possessing marijuana, either for personal or business purposes, were arrested. The total taken into custody amounted to around fifty. Half the fishing boats were seized, and folks with newly fitted air-conditioning, brand new pickup trucks, and newly constructed swimming pools along with porches and driveways were taken to Miami to be interviewed by the Internal Revenue Service. Their recent wealth and their tax returns somehow didn't add up.

By the end of the week, the FBI Chief had summarised the situation. Standing at a rostrum outside Sheriff Bill Walker's empty office, the head of the investigation spoke to local and national TV stations, the press, and senior Collier County officials.

He stated, "From what we have discovered, almost all the people living in these Ten Thousand Islands have been either dope smugglers, friends of dope smugglers, related to dope smugglers, or knew what was going on. Even the mayor of this city found himself under arrest, having been unable to explain how he had fifty thousand dollars in cash in his safe at home. That is a lot of unexplained personal cash for a mayor to have in a small wilderness town. I think you'll agree. We now have uncovered a huge drug-smuggling community. In doing so, we have seized about one hundred thousand pounds of Colombian marijuana and closed a newly started cocaine supply route. We have also taken possession of many thousands of illegitimate or illegal assets. Our objective in this operation has been to identify and penetrate every illegal drug group in Southwest Florida. We intend to find connections between Miami, Everglades City, Chokoloskee and the area south of Naples. Over the next period, we also intend to disrupt all the smuggling routes from South America and the Caribbean into the US."

He paused for photographs but moved swiftly away before reporters could ask revealing questions. His boss held Jack's sleeve tightly.

"Jack, leave it. I know you want to say something, but it won't help. No one wants to hear hard-luck stories about people who live in a swamp. Save it for a better time."

Jack was furious that his boss, as usual, was right. When the TV and press had all gone, the FBI bedded down in the Rifle and Gun Club or the old Bank of Everglades building just along from City Hall in the middle of the city. The statue of Elizabeth Root stood watching the town slowly drain of strangers.

As Undersheriff Jack Root and his boss drove out of the city and towards their homes in Naples, they noticed how quiet it was.

There was no one to be seen or heard except a single dog. The dog howled into the night sky because it was hungry, and nobody was around to feed it.

Chapter Forty-Seven
A Fugitive Dies Twice

The police found the bodies of three men; one had papers identifying him as the escaped prisoner Kimbo Hopper. He looked very similar, and nobody could tell if it was or wasn't him, as fists and lead pipes had severely beaten his face. The FBI brought in a hooded Bill Walker to identify the body. He took one look. "Are you sure?" the officer asked. "Yes, I am sure," he replied. Bill was sure it wasn't Kimbo Hopper, but that's not what the FBI officer took as his answer.

The next day, the Miami Herald had a dramatic headline, "Fugitive Dies Twice", and explained that it had been assumed this fugitive had died in the Everglades some time ago. But somehow, he had miraculously reappeared as part of a Miami drug gang. Now, the police, but more importantly, the FBI, had found his body with some credible identification by a law officer. It was a great story that caught attention for about two days.

The Naples Daily reported it slightly differently... "Coordinated by our local hero, Jack Root, the raid on the Ten Thousand Islands was highly successful. It eventually led to the death of a hunted and dangerous native Bahamian killer, Rimbo Popper. This gangster, who had faked his death when escaping prison, was found dead with other drug gang members on Friday night..." The story continued with more misspellings and inaccuracies. Still, it was read widely in Naples. It was repeated word-for-word later that week by the oldest, most credible and most respected newspaper in Tallahassee, the state capital of Florida. Credibility indeed.

A few days after evading Purvis's men, Juan Rodriguez had jumped on an outboard with Jim-Bob Smith. They headed to Liquor Still Bay, deep into the Everglades. It was somewhere safe from the authorities, and, according to Jim-Bob, no one knew about it except him. The thought didn't occur to him that if this area in the Ten Thousand Islands had a name, someone knew about it, possibly more than one. Jim-Bob wasn't the brightest star in the night sky.

One more thing
"Well, Kimbo, there is one more thing you gotta do to tidy up this mess. You know who it is, but where he is?" Purvis wanted everything tidied up. He said his new ideas were worthless if the last piece wasn't dealt with.

Purvis had developed the stone crab business via Myron and the Seminoles to the point where it was his best income. He had learnt a lot from how the Colombians ran their pot hauling and understood all the business elements of production, shipping, and distribution to eager restaurants and happy customers in Miami. He developed his business further up the coast, from Fort Lauderdale to Palm Beach. It brought good, honest and profitable work for people in Overtown and Little Haiti, the poorest parts of Greater Miami and the Seminoles. When there were problems, people always knew where to find Purvis. The same place, the same bar stool, but always in the morning. As the population along the west coastline of Florida grew and developed, he gradually expanded his deliveries to include the population along the west coast between Naples and Tampa. He was to become a relatively wealthy man but always spent his money in the old, segregated parts of Miami.

"Kimbo, I ask again, do you know where he can be found?"

Purvis looked at Kimbo, who knew exactly what he was being asked. He hoped it would be the last severe and life-threatening act in his life. He was tired.

Chapter Forty-Eight
The Same Kind face

About two miles along the Huston River and about three miles north of Mosquito Key lies the huge alligator hole, known only to Kimbo. He found it one day by accident, and it had served him well. Several mother alligators were using it, staying with their young and protecting them with their natural ferocity. During cold weather, the mothers and the mainly young gators lay dormant. But it was now a hot, humid time as Juan Rodriguez and Jim-Bob Smith pitched camp just one mile from the hole. Not only were the mother alligators incredibly aggressive, but the male bull alligators were restless.

Juan was grateful to Jim-Bob for helping him escape. Still, he was beginning to understand why Waco, a thug and killer, got so spooked by the natural wilderness he was now hiding in – something he had previously dismissed. The first night, he didn't sleep at all while Jim-Bob snored. The bull alligators constantly puffed themselves with air, raised their heads and tails, and let out a low and deep bellow, like thunder on a silent night. To Juan, this was bone-chilling. He could handle the dangerous places he'd been in Colombia and Miami, but he'd not faced natural dangers. This was different.

What scared him most was his fear. He hadn't felt fear since he was a boy in the streets of Colombia. He didn't know what to do or where to go. Even if he had known, he didn't know how to get there or anywhere else. He was at the mercy of this mosquito-infested swamp full of loud, strange noises and threatening wildlife, but worst of all, he was being led by a dumb gringo. Jim-Bob was a mistake he already regretted.

When he heard a voice calling, Juan tried to think ahead. At first, he thought he was hallucinating. A man's face appeared and disappeared. The voice called his name. Juan began to shake with fear. He shook Jim-Bob awake.

"We gotta get the fuck outta here. I can't stay here. I'd rather fight the police than these animals. Show me the way back. Let's go to Naples and hide out. Let's go!"

Jim-Bob calmly smiled. "Ah, come on, man. If you know what you doin', these critters ain't coming to get you. This is the breeding season. They just wanna play with the ladies. You know what I mean, eh?"

"But I saw a man. He was calling out my name!"

"The fuck you talkin' about. Ain't nobody knows this place."

Then, Kimbo walked into full view. He stood with his favourite alligator club in his right hand. Immediately, Juan flicked open his knife. Jim-Bob reached for his rifle, but Kimbo kicked it out of his grasp, sending it flying and landing on a tiny mud hammock. From the corner of his eye, Juan watched Jim-Bob wade thigh-high to retrieve it, accidentally toe-poking two alligator nests. One with closely-guarded alligator babies, the other with a clutch of eggs. Both mothers went for Jim-Bob, fearlessly crunching into his legs and torso. One dragged him under four feet of water until he stopped struggling. Kimbo stared at Juan, who could barely watch.

"Want a way out, Juan? Want me to take your hand and show you around first? You are in my land now. You don't like it, do you? I see you scared as those two, Waco and Paco. They ended up disappearing down a fat and vicious gator's mouth. You want that, Juan? Do you?"

At that moment, Juan Rodriguez saw his opportunity. Much quicker and more agile than Kimbo, Juan slashed the arm holding the club and kicked Kimbo behind the knees. Kimbo went down with a thud, and the assassin kicked him hard and into the water where the alligator mothers had tackled Jim-Bob just a few moments before. But it wasn't the mothers who went for Kimbo; it was a massive twelve-foot-long bull alligator. Tasting blood from Kimbo's arm, the beast sank his long line of teeth into his flesh and started to drag him under. The assassin watched, grinned, and carefully walked away.

A big hug for Eddie
Juan Rodriguez felt good about the outcome of his plan for taking over the business and cleaning out people who could have caused him trouble or been competitive. He strode purposely as the rising sun of the new day lit the scene. *If that is east, I'll pick my way north and eventually find my way out of this stinking hole,* Juan thought. No one was there. No one left to hear him or see his final triumph. He set off as full daylight showed him firm ground or shallow, safe-looking, ankle-deep, clear water. He had knee-high leather boots, giving him confidence that snakes would not be able to bite through to his legs. He was the most careful he had ever been when taking each step. It was a new day for Juan, and he thought he would enjoy it.

Juan Rodriguez found the Tamiami Trail and took the westerly direction. It wasn't until he'd got to "Fast Eddie's Airboat Rides" that he saw another person. He walked into the chickee-style ticket sales hut alongside the road and met a Seminole woman cleaning the area and brewing coffee. He grabbed a cup and showed her his blood-stained knife. He demanded she fill the cup. Shima Billie poured boiling coffee into the cup and threw it in Juan's face. He screamed, and she ran out the door. He rushed after her.

Juan Rodriguez, blinded temporarily by the sizzling hot coffee, didn't see the pickup truck coming as he stood in the middle of the trail, arms flailing about, eyes stinging, trying to see where Shima had run. He didn't see it, but he did hear it a split second before it smashed his head and body across the shiny chrome grill and black hood. The truck stopped, and the driver got out. Shima ran to her husband and hugged him. A shocked Eddie needed the hug more than even she did.

Shima and Fast Eddie Billie pulled the body from the front of the vehicle and dragged it around the back of the airboat ride ticket hut. Luckily, it was early, but the traffic would pick up soon, and Fast Eddie was due to take visitors out on his airboat. They washed the pickup and parked it with the front pointing away from the road, shielding it from sight and the dent caused by Juan Rodriguez's head. They put the lifeless body in the airboat, and Eddie sped away into the swamp. Shima put up a 'closed' sign, waited in the shade of the chickee hut, and put on a fresh pot of coffee. Later, Fast Eddie apologised to the first airboat passengers for the blood on the ground.

"I rescued a hurt racoon this morning first thing. A gator had bitten the poor thing." The tourists liked Fast Eddie's evident care for wildlife. It was a pleasant surprise that the Indians knew all about the swampland. Who would have thought that these natives would care for wildlife?

Eaten by his own
Kimbo fought for his life, and he and the alligator knew it. He'd been holding his breath underwater for nearly a minute, struggling with the largest, strongest gator he had ever tackled with his bare hands. Although he'd been hitting the bull gator hard on the snout, it wouldn't be enough for the reptile to let Kimbo go, so he switched to eye-gouging and constantly hitting the beast hard on the top of its head. The bull gator was

enormously powerful, and all Kimbo's usual methods failed. Man and beast surged upwards and broke the surface. Kimbo took an enormous breath of fresh air before trying the only thing he had left; thrusting his arm into the gaping mouth, he grabbed the flap of tissue at the back of the tongue. When submerged in water, the flap acted like a valve covering the alligator's throat. It prevented gators from drowning. Pushing his blood-soaked arm up to the shoulder, he grabbed the valve and yanked it hard, making it useless. Water started gushing into the gator's throat and pouring inside its body. He released Kimbo immediately, and as he swam away, jerking and shaking his head, his tail swiped across Kimbo's head, hitting his eyes and temple. It was the last attempt to kill Kimbo and his last action. The reptile drowned and sank to the bottom of the narrow river, eaten by his own kind over the next several days. Kimbo lay on the bank, away from the water's edge, with blood oozing out of his arm, his head pounding in time with his heart. What he didn't know and didn't realise until a few hours later was that the blow from the tail caused blood vessels to leak, and fluids began building up at the back of his eyes, which caused irreparable damage. He ripped his shirt off and made a tourniquet for his arm. He knew he needed help to clean the deep wound and keep it from getting infected. He set off for the nearest place he thought could help him. Unfortunately, that was Chokoloskee, where he was very well known.

Except the scars
Mary Brookland heard her front door open and then the heavy sound of a large man collapsing on the floor. She was shocked and scared at first. Was it Kimbo Hopper, the man who had died twice? She had known Kimbo when he lived in Chokoloskee, but she was more familiar with Jack and Elizabeth when they ran the church and school. She had made great friends with Elizabeth

and missed her badly when she was taken ill and moved to Naples. Here, in front of her, lay a fugitive, a man sought by the police, FBI and goodness knows who else.

Kimbo was supposed to be dead but wasn't. He was there, collapsed and unconscious on her kitchen floor, with severe wounds to his arm and face. His face and eyes had the same kind, but now frightened, look. She had heard he'd suffered tragedy and yet was also caught up in crimes with a cohort of devious and deadly people. She cleaned his wounds with stinging dressing compounds she had locked away in the emergency medical wall cupboard. She knew the most important thing was to stop the bleeding and close the wound after cleaning. She did all this in an hour, using crude stitching and life-saving dressings. An exhausted Kimbo wasn't moving. She marvelled at how this man could withstand this pain and still be unconscious. Anyone who knew what had happened to him would marvel that he was still alive, let alone understand how his body could stand this pain level.

Nobody knew what this man had been through.

Mary could never adequately explain it to Kimbo, Myron or any of the few people who later learnt what she had done. Why had she treated Kimbo so compassionately? She told them all that it was because she had done it instinctively. She could tell it was the right thing to do.

"Just look at the poor man. He has that same kind face he always had... except for those scars."

Chapter Forty-Nine
Respected and Elected

Kimbo realised that you live your life forward but understand it backwards. He sat listening to his son and grandchildren. His blurred eyes saw things more clearly than ever before. He thought about the other two survivors of the 1935 hurricane: the train driver Jack Root and his fireman Bill Walker. Jack was now Collier County police chief, and Elizabeth had become a well-respected and much-loved part of the Seminole and Naples communities. Bill Walker had disappeared as though he had never existed.

The voice in Kimbo's head was still there. She told him how to look out for himself, Myron, and his wonderful family. He sat smiling, his eyesight made worse by tears. As always, as Zella talked to him, he continued to listen.

Kimbo opened his eyes. He looked out across the sawgrass without seeing it. Although his sight was affected, he could walk without aid and would always find his way. Clear-sighted or not, he didn't ever turn away the tiny hand of a grandchild who wanted to guide him along paths, help him tread carefully, or stop him from falling. He sought their hands.

Sitting still, he could hear Myron talking firmly to the eldest son of his four beautiful children: one boy, twins and one girl. Kimbo's tears were trickling down his ribbed cheeks, ribbed from knife scars healed many years before. But he was the happiest he had ever been in his life. No more struggling or fist fighting. No more strife with criminals and killers; no running or hiding. He was at peace, knowing that Myron had the best life anyone could ever have. Myron had provided practical knowledge and business insight to their wider family, the Seminoles. The tribe had grown in wealth and prosperity, unimaginable without Myron's inspired thinking and Elizabeth's dedication to teaching. The bingo halls had turned into casinos, which couldn't yet compete on size but were outstripping the growth of Las Vegas and Atlantic City. But Myron's courageous and ground-breaking achievements had not changed him.

The Seminole and Miccosukee tribes continued to develop, grow and adapt to living with and alongside the new booming Floridian population and inevitable mass tourism. The tribes grew in confidence and experience and could afford to build much-needed schools to deliver the education plan Elizabeth had laid out for them. She had grown adept at designing programmes for the different age levels and needs of the tribe. She created methods to educate the growing number of migrants from the north on how to preserve the wilderness of southern Florida; she shared the Seminole thinking with the Park authorities and centres. It wasn't much, but she thought it would help to build a better understanding between them.

Chief Bowlegs and Bad Hand died from a sickness poorly understood by the expensive doctors brought to Big Cypress to heal them. "Poisoned by something they had drunk" was the diagnosis, their livers blamed. The Naples-based doctors shrugged at the need for a thorough diagnosis. They assumed that it was alcohol-related. Neither man had drunk alcohol in their lives. The newly qualified Seminole doctors had little experience and were frustrated with their failure to help save these historic leaders.

Kimbo was confused and devastated that these two great men, huge influencers in everyone's life, had suddenly passed away. He had missed them and the many days they had spent talking, listening, and silently sitting. Each had been content to have the burden lifted by a younger, more energetic tribe. Myron Hopper, now Chief, had grown to be a strong and well-respected man, and at the age of thirty, he had been elected to the tribal council, the youngest member ever to join it.

Chapter Fifty
Kimbo Walks

A few weeks following Myron's election, Kimbo went on a walk. He liked to walk every day and find different paths to memorise; however, he rarely remembered them. He had no memory of distinct days, only moments. He knew he could close his eyes to reality but not to moments. Some nights, Zella's terrified face appeared and faded into darkness again.

He woke early to darkness and felt a compelling urge to take a long walk; he always trusted his instincts. Some moments plagued his life; others continued to terrorise his sleep; a few he treasured. He knew he couldn't relive any; he didn't want to, good or bad.

On this day, Kimbo set off for Homestead. He wanted to thank people and tell them how lucky he had been. He wanted to tell those wonderful women who looked after his son, little Myron, that he had grown to be a giant of a man, a natural leader, and a protector of people, and now a member of the tribal council.

Since his victory against Juan Rodriguez and the giant alligator, he had hidden from police, authorities, and criminals. He wanted to share his joy and happiness with those wonderful people of Homestead, tell them stories of his family, and say thank you – a simple gesture. For him, it had become a growing fixation.

He told Tehya, Myron's wife, that he wanted to walk to Homestead. She was used to Kimbo going off somewhere for "a walk", as he called it, and sometimes he was gone for a whole day, returning just before sundown. Myron Hopper and Tehya Billie didn't like it. They knew he was not as vital as he used to be and certainly not as strong as he thought, but they knew his eyesight was his biggest problem. Tehya Billie didn't know where Homestead was or how far, but she had heard of it vaguely. That evening, Tehya Billie told Myron what his father had said.

"Homestead is eighty miles away; he must be thinking about somewhere else."

Myron assumed he would wander to his favourite places nearby during his daytime walks.

It had taken Kimbo more than a day to reach the outskirts of Homestead; he'd had one or two short rides with friendly pickups but walked a good deal, too. When he reached the outskirts, he was surprised not to see anyone. He headed for the centre, where he saw the Homestead Baptist Church's hall standing strong and proudly against the sky. It was the same church and hall where he'd met Jack Root, Bill Walker and father and son Watson. It was in the same place but had been rebuilt, with two large pillars and a monumental entrance; it all seemed smaller but grander than he remembered. Kimbo couldn't understand why Homestead was like a ghost town. There were plenty of fine-looking properties, but with nobody in them. Apart from a few occupied shacks on the edges, the place seemed abandoned.

He decided this hall would be the best place to wait for those women who had helped Myron. Will they remember him? Sitting in the church, he found it very peaceful, anticipating what would come next. He was exhausted from his long walk and strangely relaxed; he lay on a long oak pew and fell gently asleep.

That morning, Elizabeth Root was on her way to the village, driven by Tommy Triggerman. Chief Myron Hopper had carefully selected Tommy to bring Elizabeth to and from the Seminole village. A vital job. She was in good health for her age; her expensive healthcare had restored her to full fitness. It was late August. Tommy turned the truck radio on Elizabeth's favourite programmes broadcast on a local National Public Radio channel. Abruptly, the programme host interrupted the discussion of the day.

"We have just been alerted that a new hurricane, named Hurricane Baron, has reached the Bahamas and is thought to be heading towards south Florida. The path is unknown, but weather forecasters predict it will probably turn north and land in Georgia or the Carolinas. Please keep tuned for further updates. Although he doesn't expect it to make landfall in Florida, the governor has recommended that households at the bottom of the peninsula stock fresh water and canned food. This was just a precaution, and not to worry. It was just in case, he said. Thank you for your attention."

Bad news travels fast. Although the folk of Homestead were constantly being told by a governor or government not to worry or, conversely, to evacuate whenever a storm was on its way, people usually made up their own minds. On this occasion, most agreed it would be best to head in the northwest direction, along the west coast towards Tampa, until the storm had blown through and away. The storm was, at worst, going to pass through the very tip of the mainland; at best, it would turn northwards up the east coast and away from them. If it did carry on its current course towards Homestead, they could always restore homelands; they have done it before. Anyone with transport or offered it left the area.

"Better safe than sorry" was another platitude used that day.

Elizabeth accelerated

Before starting her lessons for the day, Elizabeth visited Tehya Billie and learnt of Kimbo's walk. She told her that a hurricane warning was being given for the whole area, and Tehya suddenly looked anxious.

"Miss Elizabeth, it was only late yesterday that Myron noticed his father was not in his chickee hut. He was missing all night and had not returned by first light today. We argued. Myron insisted his father was the most capable man to deal with the wilderness and probably had decided to spend the night at a favourite place, probably somewhere along the Turner River. It was, he said, one of Kimbo's special places he would go with Bad Hand."

"But Tehya, did Myron send a search party for him?"

"Well, that is what we argued about. Myron said he would only do that if he hadn't returned after three days. His father would be insulted, he said. I could not persuade him. Today, Myron has taken a small group of four to the Cape Coral area to meet some businesspeople. He seems obsessed with growing the influence of our Seminole Tribe, and these days, it takes a lot to divert his attention from what he wants to achieve next."

Elizabeth shook her head

"Youth and ambition. Myron has found his purpose in serving his community, but he should be old enough to see that it isn't a whole and complete life. I hope this doesn't become a hard lesson in balancing his life."

Tehya was puzzled by Elizabeth's words. She didn't understand. Elizabeth continued.

"Tehya, I want you to assure me that if the sky darkens and a storm is likely, you must make sure you, your children, and the village have everyone in the shelters. I will look for Kimbo myself. I will go to Turner River."

"Miss Elizabeth, I don't think he will be there. Kimbo talked about walking to a place called Homestead. He seemed very stuck on that idea." Elizabeth thought she knew why.

Elizabeth went to find Tommy Triggerman so he would drive her immediately to Homestead. He could not be found. He didn't expect her to require him until later that afternoon. He was busy somewhere else. She climbed into the waiting pick-up truck and drove to the Tamiami Trail. She accelerated in the direction of Homestead.

Kimbo hadn't noticed that the sun hadn't come up that morning. He was in a deep and satisfying sleep. Sunlight barely seeped through tiny patches in the leaden sky, which, in turn, went from grey to black boiling clouds. The wind started whistling through tree limbs. A storm's orchestra was tuning up. Gusts began to send doors of houses and barns banging back against their sides until the wind ripped them off their hinges.

Suddenly, Kimbo woke and sat bolt upright. He immediately knew what was coming but instinctively didn't fear it; he wanted to embrace it. He tried to stand up and stare it in the face defiantly. He needed to take it on. His only anxiety came from the fear of dying alone. Fear released adrenaline, his heart raced, and he felt his loneliness. He then became inexplicably petrified.

Myron was terrified. The four men in the open bed at the back of his giant truck were thrown about as Myron drove down the Tamiami Trail back towards Naples and the Ten Thousand Islands as fast as he could.

The man he'd met in Cape Coral told him a storm might be approaching. He'd heard it on the radio earlier that morning, but an update was due. He'd said it wasn't yet known in which direction they expected it to go, but it had been "hammering" the Bahamas. Those words sent the bile in Myron's stomach up into his throat. The radio had promised an update in ten minutes. They all gathered around as the National Public Radio gave its latest news on the storm.

We are advised that the eye of the storm, Hurricane Baron, has left the Bahama Islands and is heading due west. It may turn north but could continue its current path and hit Elliott Key at the tip of the Florida Keys. If it continues its current track and speed, it will pass over Biscayne Bay and hit Homestead sometime at night. If this happens, it will most likely pass through the southern tip of Florida, south of Everglades City, and into the Gulf of Mexico. It is feared that it will reach wind speeds of one hundred and seventy-five miles per hour, possibly more. It is pointed out in the weather advisory that winds of this strength could lift a car, truck, or boat. This may be classified as a Category Five hurricane. If it turns out to be a category five, the governor says, it will be a relief if it follows that currently predicted path, as only a limited amount of people will be affected.

Myron was driven out of his mind with worry. His first thoughts were Tehya, the children, and his tribe. He then remembered that Elizabeth would be there today and needed protection. He thought he should visit Sheriff Root's office to ensure she was safely home, but he didn't have time.

Then he remembered. His father hadn't been seen for more than a day.

Jack Root jumped into his police car and lit his roof strobe lights and those on his dashboard and rear window. He took off as fast as the big, sluggish vehicle could take him. It was about five miles south of Naples, going west, when Jack saw Myron's truck veering wildly as it sped along the trail; four men were being drenched by the rain and thrown about on the truck bed. Looking in his rear-view mirror, Myron saw the sheriff's lights flashing behind him and realised Jack had heard the news. Elizabeth was in danger.

Both vehicles arrived at the village together. Myron rushed at Tommy Triggerman, who stood with his arms wide and showing empty hands. He shrugged.

"Chief Hopper, Elizabeth took the truck, and Tehya thinks she is driving to Homestead. She thinks your father is in Homestead. Can I help?"

"Yes, drive these men to their homes and take shelter. Check that everyone is safely in the shelters."

Tehya Billie and her children climbed into a safe, flood-protected space, made some time ago by Kimbo on the higher ground, as their refuge against storms and floods. She was going to be safe with her family beside her. Tehya had ensured that many of the tribe were shielded in their purpose-built shelters. Over many years, Kimbo and his son had designed these shelters and organised their construction for this eventuality. Every spring, they had arranged drills so the whole village would know what to do when the time came. Food, fresh water, and other supplies would be enough for several days. The village was disciplined and ready. Tommy drove into the village with the four men in the back, and they all scattered to safety.

Sheriff Root and Chief Hopper sped as fast as the police cars could take them, heading directly into the hurricane's path. Usually, it would take up to two hours. But this day, with a pounding headwind and torrential downpours veiling the windscreen, it would take double that.

By mid-morning, it could have been midnight. The wind changed to a steady howl and then a roar. Sheets of pelting rain pinged Elizabeth's face and stung her like a swarm of hornets as she walked. Now standing soaked and swaying, she knew this situation could end her life. She was not worried about herself or her children should she die. They were grown and had the most wonderful and caring father in Jack Root. Her mission was different.

Having abandoned the truck as trees and bushes blocked the road, she was just a few yards from the sign welcoming visitors to Homestead. Water was rising from the wetlands. It went from her ankles to her knees in a very short time. The howling wind was relentless. Then, it instantly stopped as if someone had flicked a switch. She had an opportunity to move more quickly. From Jack's stories, Elizabeth knew this was before the most dangerous time. She was in the eye of a hurricane, and vital questions needed answering.

Where was Kimbo? Was this a hopeless journey, which would take my life? Elizabeth was instantly focused on survival. Before her stood the only building not stripped of its roof or walls. Shutters were put up in front of the precious stained-glass windows. This could be a place of safety.

She suddenly witnessed a ferocious gust, which ripped a man from a tree. He had been escaping the floods, and the wind flipped him in the air repeatedly as if he were a leaf. He was sucked up, trapped inside a swirling mass like an inverted cone.

Elizabeth felt massive forces beginning to batter her body. She strode hard, head down, to get to the church. She had just reached the church porch when a hand shot out the door. Something flying through the black space hit her on the side of her head as the hand pulled her inside into the relative safety of the dark, screaming expanse of the empty church. Immediately, the eye wall came for the city. The deafening roar boomed, and the church seemed to shake and lurch to one side.

"Hold on to me, Zella. Don't let go!"

Elizabeth stared at Kimbo as he held her in his arms. She saw this man was somewhere else, suspended outside this world. She passed out, as he called, "Zella!" But there was no one there. He thought he was shouting, but his voice was barely a whisper, and his head was filled with a screeching noise. There she was, holding her arms out for him to protect her. Again, he kissed Zella's sweet face, wiped her terrified eyes with his thumbs, and held her face in his large, strong hands. As everything surrounding the church rode upwards into the storm, he smiled at the woman he held tightly. He didn't see it was Elizabeth. He wanted to open the door and go through it with her into the dark, baying night. Kimbo wanted to vanish forever with Zella, up skywards. But, he stared, shocked, it wasn't Zella.

He stopped immediately at the unopened door; its rapid machine gun rattling brought him back to reality. He placed Elizabeth in the safest part of the building. He found a blanket and put soft cushions under her head. Just as he made sure she was protected, a crashing sound came from the roof, and a large piece of timber swung down and struck Kimbo in the head, knocking him down and out. He lay as still as he had ever had at any time in his life.

Driving nearer than a mile from Homestead was becoming hazardous and impossible. The flooding forced Jack and Myron to abandon the car. The stronger man, Myron, took the lead, with Collier County Sheriff Root hugging him tightly from behind. They walked with their legs synchronised, trudging in short steps, head down, but bent in a single motion like two soldiers marching. From a distance, they would look like one person. The younger man in front took the brunt of the wind gusts, and the older man behind benefitted from his strength and motivating force.

Jack searched his memory for how the city was laid out. Where would be the best place to shelter in a hurricane? Where would Kimbo go? Of course, the church hall! The two men were bombarded with debris about four hundred yards from the Baptist Church. The safest way to move was for each to crawl.

Myron arrived at the door first but lost the battle and surrendered to the storm. A woman's hand shot out, grabbed his arm, and pulled him inside. Jack was struggling, still fifty yards away. Elizabeth risked everything and ran to her husband. He saw her, and unknown strength surged through his body. Together, they burst through the door to see Myron nursing his limp father in his arms, cupping his face with one hand. He was crying helplessly.

The hurricane passed through Homestead and, during the night, it emerged over the Gulf of Mexico and eventually turned north-westward. After losing strength, it ultimately came ashore once more, this time in Louisiana, downgraded, but enough to kill and drown many more people.

All South Florida's wildlife had taken shelter instinctively; all survived except birds and tree inhabitants. Alligators and crocodiles went into low-lying lakes or water holes and streams. They were safe in their natural and everyday places. In Homestead, houses were stripped of all but their concrete foundations. Still standing, but not in one piece, was the defiant Baptist Church. Part of the roof was torn off, and parts of all four walls had wooden rafters and panels ripped away. But it was upright and defiant.

Some miles south of Homestead, the Everglades National Park ranger station was wiped away – no trace left.

"She has gone, Myron; she has left me. The hurricane took her voice away from me. She vanished. She has gone." Kimbo was now conscious.

Myron didn't know, but he did guess. They hadn't ever discussed the details of that night when the beast came and took away Zella and Zakari – neither had wanted to talk about it. That night, long ago, made an indelible stain on their memories for entirely different reasons. One lost a wife and daughter, the other a mother and a twin sister – the same but a different type of loss. For both men, it was permanently painful.

The rafter had badly hurt Kimbo, but he survived. He had a huge lump growing on his forehead. He turned to Jack. Face to face for the first time since the Everglades City demise.

"Jack, will you have to arrest me?"

"How can I arrest a three-time dead man? Eaten by an alligator, killed by Miami gangs and taken away by a hurricane. Most people don't get arrested when they're dead. When you are as dead as you are, it would be best to stay dead...and out of sight!"

Kimbo looked nervously at his long-time friend. He needed more.

"Jack, Elizabeth saved me last night. I wanted the storm to take me. Without Elizabeth coming here to find me, I would be dead."

"Yes, Kimbo, I know. Would that be the fourth time you would have been dead? I'm losing count. How many hurricanes does it take to kill a Kimbo? And I'm not even counting that it was so lucky that the rafter hit you in the head." Kimbo frowned. "Otherwise, it could have hurt you real bad." They both chuckled.

"And you should know, we knew you must have left us the ten thousand dollars. It could only have been you. We knew it was you. Thank you. You should know that it made a dramatic difference to our lives."

As usual, Kimbo stood like a giant, but this time, he was reduced to a shy, embarrassed, and speechless man. As they all stood there in bewilderment, three pickup trucks set off from the Seminole village miles away, heading for Homestead.

By early afternoon, the wind was a whisper, and the sun burnt through the dirty grey sky. By mid-afternoon, the four friends found the abandoned police car. They were astonished to see it lodged high in the thick crown spread of a single bald cypress tree, which still stood miraculously eighty feet tall. It was the only tree left standing inside the city limits.

Kimbo was physically and emotionally exhausted. His sight was now lost, and his head was in pain. He called for Myron to hold his hand. He was about to return to the Seminole village, where his son lived the best life. Elizabeth was teaching children in the way she had always thought right. And Jack? He was a genuinely respected authority throughout Collier County.

Sitting holding Myron's hand in the back of one of the pickup trucks, Kimbo felt a swirling force drawing him upwards into the heavens. When he arrived, he walked with the stars, and his ancestors held his hands.

He touched all those he loved and had lost. His mother and father, Zella and Zakari, Hachi and Yuchi, Bad Hand, Billie Bowlegs, Jim Tigertail and Sengo – wagging his tail, happy to see his master.

Later, Myron would sit each night, staring at the dark canopy and disappearing sky, knowing that Kimbo had finally found his quiet place.

**"We are all travellers in the wilderness of this world,
and the best we can find in our travels is an honest friend."**

Robert Louis Stevenson

Authors Notes

Thank you to Angela.

Also, many thanks to Cathy Verghese, Norman Gaslowitz, Patrick Hosey, and William Tulskie for their patience, support, and ideas.

The Florida Keys, USA

The term "Keys" is a corruption of the Spanish word "Cayo", meaning small island. From Homestead (the last southern town on the mainland of Florida) to Key Largo – the first "island" – is about twenty-two miles. Today, from Jewfish Creek at North Key Largo, the start of the road along The Keys, to Key West is one hundred seven miles. The drive will take about two and a half hours. There are over 800 Keys, but only forty-two bridges carry the traffic over those one hundred seven miles. The highest point above sea level along those one hundred seven miles is eighteen feet on Windley Key.

The Railroad – Miami to Key West

After a few notable business failures, Henry Morrison Flagler made a fortune. Flagler and John D Rockefeller formed and built the *Standard Oil Company,* one of the US's first and largest multinational businesses. The Supreme Court broke it up in 1911. Monopolies were seen as anti-competitive and, therefore, anti-American.

Flagler, however, was much more than a money maker. He became a visionary. Owing to his first wife's poor health, he moved to warm and sunny Florida and immediately saw the potential of linking New York to Miami. He then proceeded to build a railroad infrastructure for freight and passengers. He also saw the exciting possibility of connecting Miami with Havana, Cuba, via Key West by train and ferry boats. At the beginning of the 20th century, Key West was a minor, strategic military island. In 1906, Flagler began to build a single-track railroad stretching from Miami to Homestead and then to Jewfish Creek, but still on the mainland. The first of the necklace of bridges was built here and connected to Key Largo, the largest of the Florida Keys. The railroad cost several hundred lives to build over six years and hastened the death of all the most important people connected with it. In 1912, Flagler was still living and had taken the inaugural journey. Officially, it was named the Florida East Coast (FEC) Key West Extension but was nicknamed the "Overseas Railroad." On 22nd January that year, Flagler stepped off the first train to arrive in Key West. He was eighty-three years old and blind. A large crowd greeted him, and he said to his escort, "I can hear the children, but I cannot see them."

Henry Flagler died the following year, 1913, but the railroad lasted another twenty-two years. In 1935, America was struggling to recover from the Great Depression. It was also the year the overseas railroad died in the middle of the mother of all storms.

Ernest Hemingway in The Keys

Ernest Hemingway lived in Key West from 1928 to 1939, after which he moved to Cuba. He participated in the immediate help provided to those most affected by the 1935 Labour Day Hurricane.

Hurricanes

A five-scale category of hurricanes was only developed in the 1970s by Miami engineer Herbert Saffir and Robert Simpson, a meteorologist and the National Hurricane Centre director. Even today, most information about hurricanes is only assessed after the event, like an inquest.

Most people would typically think winds of 20mph make the

weather "rather windy" or make them suggest "that's a strong breeze."

Hurricanes gain strength and power over water and lose strength and weaken as they pass over land. This was a highly relevant factor for people living in the Florida Keys (see the 'Florida Keys Prologue' above).

1970s Hurricane Classifications

Category 1 Hurricane:

Very dangerous winds, ranging from 74 to 95 mph, will produce some damage. Falling debris could strike people, livestock and pets, and older homes could be destroyed. Poorly built shacks and tents will be destroyed.

Category 2 Hurricane:

Extremely dangerous winds range between 96 and 110 mph. It will cause extensive damage, with a high risk of injury or death to people, livestock and pets from flying debris. Trees uprooted, and power out for weeks.

Category 3 Hurricane:

Devastating damage will occur with winds ranging from 111 to 129 mph. Extreme risk of injury or death to people, livestock and pets from flying and falling debris, buildings and trees. Power and natural freshwater unavailable for weeks.

Category 4 Hurricane:

Catastrophic damage will occur with winds ranging from 130 to 156 mph. It will blow out windows, uproot most trees, wreck most buildings, threaten all life (including marine life), and make the affected area uninhabitable for weeks or possibly months.

Category 5 Hurricane:

Catastrophic damage will occur with winds of 157 mph or

higher. The movement of a hurricane, at this level, will destroy everything in its path. As the hurricane gets closer to land, waves will hit the shore rapidly and increase to between sixteen and twenty feet in height. Hurricanes blowing above 125 mph will cause a tidal wave (tsunami), an unstoppable wall of water speeding across the top of the ocean.

SOURCE: Saffir-Simpson hurricane wind scale (SSHWS) US National Oceanic and Atmospheric Administration

Seminole Business Success

One of the six remaining Seminole Reservations, set on five hundred acres in Hollywood, Florida, opened a hotel and casino in 2004. It thrived.

On December 7, 2006, Rank sold its Hard Rock business to the Seminole Tribe of Florida for $965 million. Included in the deal were one hundred twenty-four Hard Rock Cafés, four Hard Rock Hotels, two Hard Rock Hotel and Casino Hotels, and two Hard Rock Live! Entertainment Centres. As of July 2018, Hard Rock International had venues in seventy-four countries, including one hundred eighty-five cafés, twenty-five hotels and twelve casinos, all owned by Seminole Hard Rock Digital, LLC. It was rumoured that the purchase was made in cash.

The Homestead Hurricane Andrew

The 1992 *Hurricane Andrew* is one of only four hurricanes to make landfall in the United States as a Category 5, alongside the 1935 *Labour Day* (no naming convention at that time), the 1969 *Camille*, and the 2018 *Michael*. *Hurricane Andrew* caused significant damage in the Bahamas and Louisiana. Still, the most significant impact was felt in South Florida, where the storm made landfall as a Category 5, with 1-minute sustained wind speeds as high as 165 mph (280 km/h) and a gust as high as 174 mph (280 km/h). It passed directly through the city of

Homestead in Dade County, now known as Miami-Dade County. *Hurricane Ian* made landfall on 28th September 2022 along the western side of the Florida peninsular. It was just short of category 5, at 155 mph winds.

A New Terror

An old terror, *Hurricane Andrew*, brought a new one to the Everglades. Many Miami residents had favoured exotic pets, including the imported Burmese python. The pythons grow to be huge, and pet owners occasionally dumped them into the Everglades when they outgrew their homes. Most experts believe the pythons established a reproducing population in the Everglades sometime after *Hurricane Andrew*, following the destruction of exotic pet shops in Homestead. The pets moved into a highly suitable wilderness for their species, right on their doorstep. The Everglades offered ideal conditions for these pythons to thrive and multiply. These massive snakes, which can grow to twenty feet long or more with telephone-pole-sized girths, have decimated the region's small and medium-sized mammal population, wreaking havoc with the area's ecosystem. *All* wildlife in the Everglades area is under threat from these snakes. Hunters killing Burmese pythons do not need a hunting permit or licence, and specific hunts are organised throughout the year, where rewards can be as much as $10,000 for the winner. Anyone can go hunting for Burmese pythons at any time.

It should be noted that in a fight between an alligator and a Burmese python, the python usually wins if it first attacks the gator's head. Up until *Hurricane Andrew* in 1992, the alligator had been at the head of the wildlife food chain in the Everglades

Laws Change

At the time of writing, nineteen states have legalised recreational marijuana use in the United States. Another twelve decriminalised its use, and commercial distribution of cannabis has been legalised in all jurisdictions where possession has been legalised, except for D.C. The current US President – Biden – has talked about granting pardons for federal marijuana possession convictions.

Sources, Acknowledgements and Inspiration
• **Totch** by Loren G. "Totch" Brown
• **A Land Remembered** by Patrick D. Smith
• **Everglades, The Story Behind the Scenery** by Jack de Golia
• **Florida, A Short History** by Michael Gannon
• **Gladesmen, Gator Hunters, Moonshiners and Skiffers** by Glen Simmons and Laura Ogden
• **Last Train to Paradise** by Les Standiford
• **Storm of the Century** by Willie Drye
• **The Creek** by J.T. Glisson
• **The Everglades, River of Grass** by Marjory Stoneman Douglas
• **The Florida Keys** by Joy Williams
• **The Story of the Chokoloskee Bay County** by Charlton W. Tebeau
• **The Railroad That Died At Sea** by Pat Parks
• **The Underground Railroad** by Colson Whitehead
• **Voice of the River** by Marjory Stoneman Douglas
• **The History of the Bahamas** by Michael Craton
• **Educating the Seminole Indians of Florida 1879-1970** by Harry A. Kersey, Jr
• **nationalgeographic.com**
• **fcit.usf.edu**
• **seminolewars.org**
• **reason.org**

- **semtribe.com**
- **Who murdered the Vets? By Ernest Hemingway** A first-hand report on Florida's "Labour Day Hurricane", published by the "New Masses" magazine.
- **Inspiration** was taken from a speech, probably made in 1854, by Chief Seattle, Chief of the Suquamish and Duwamish people. He was a leading figure among his people. The city of Seattle, in Washington state, was named after him. His exact words and who was present at the time are disputed. Still, it is commonly held that the speech was directed at Isaac Stevens, the Governor of Washington Territories at the time, and consequently, the then President of the United States (The Great Chief in Washington DC), Franklin Pierce.
- **Big Cypress National Preserve** – National Park Service, US Department of the Interior.
- **Marjory Stoneman Douglas (1890 – 1998)** for bringing the world's attention to the need to preserve the Everglades as the unique, beautiful and spectacular place that it is.
- **The Underground Railroad Records (book)** by William Still
- **The University Press of Florida**
- **Pineapple Press**